CRUX LUNATA

By E.A. STEWART

ACCIDENTAL HERETICS SERIES
Book 1: *Bone-mend and Salt*
Book 2: *Trebuchets in the Garden*
Book 3: *Crux Lunata*
Book 4: *Song of Valerós*
The Mad Woman of La Catalane: A Novella
The Blue Door... and More Accidental Heretics Tales

LEGENDS OF VALERÓS SERIES
Wheel and Serpent: 1
Traitor: 2
Hero: 3

RAIN CITY INCIDENTS SERIES
(as Annie Pearson)
The Grrrl of Limberlost
Artemis in the Desert
Nine Volt Heart
The Pirate King

CRUX LUNATA

ACCIDENTAL HERETICS: BOOK 3

E.A. STEWART

Jūgum Press

ISBN 978-1939423177

Published by Jūgum Press
505 Broadway East #237
Seattle, Washington U.S.A.
www.jugumpress.net

For Jacyn, who always wants a story to read.

Contents

Characters

The Principals
Chrétien, Tomás's foster-brother
Durán, Sebastian's half-brother; seigneur of Montcava estates in Toulouse
Felip de Xirgú, a donzel of Girona
Isabella of Valerós, Pèire Leteric's granddaughter
Sebastián, Isabella's son; heir to Valerós (in the Pyrenees) and Montcava
Tomás de Morella y Cyprus, Isabella's husband; son of Numa and Miquel
Yusuf, Tomás's son, born in Cairo

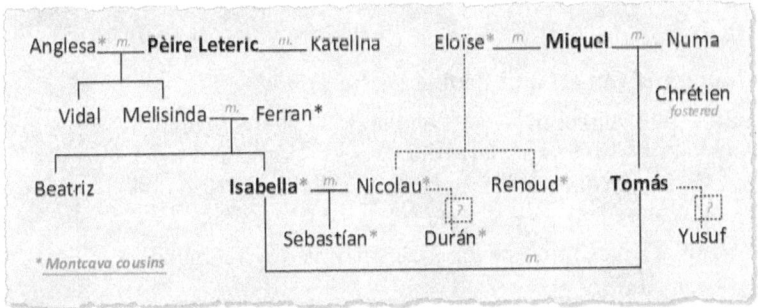

Houses of Valerós, Cyprus, and Morella
Pèire Leteric, an old crusader, seigneur of Valerós (deceased)
Miquel de Morella y Cyprus (deceased)
Numa, Don Miquel's wife; a Kurdish noblewoman
Vidal of Valerós

Also from Valerós, Morella, and St-Féliu:
Anselm, the chaplain; a former crusader
Benito, master-at-arms
Dolç, a kinswoman of Pedro d'Aragón
Fortuno, a child from Morella
Guillem, marshal of the Valerós knights; a Sicilian Norman
Jacques and Thierry, Montcava mercenaries

Houses of Beaurain, Montcava, and Xirgú

Colomb, a half-brother to Hugues de Beaurain
Constanza de Xirgú, Felip's paternal grandmother
Hélène, widow of Hugues de Beaurain; a Montcava cousin
Matheus de Xirgú, Felip's brother
Nicolau, Isabella's Montcava husband (deceased)
Renoud, Nicolau's younger brother (deceased)
Sibilia of Narbonne, Hélène's sister and Felip's mother

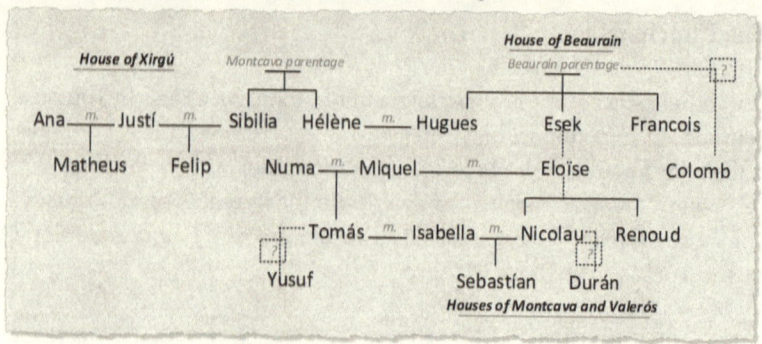

Among the Courts and People of the Towns

Avraham, a merchant from Toulouse; Hanna and Léal, his family
Doménec, Pedro's personal scribe
Don Carlos, an emissary of the king of Castile
Lorenç, abbot at St-Pere de Selva
Petronilla, Don Carlos's wife; a cousin of Pedro d'Aragón
Taresa, a laundry girl

In Al-Andalus

Al-Hasan *Abu Jossep* ibn Muhammad ibn Ishaq al-Shahid, a taifa general
Al-Makkzan, Tomás's great-grandfather; a mercenary from Tunis
Ibn Jafar, a poet and scribe from Jaén
Marzuq al-Jayyani, a vizier from Jaén
Qasim al-Jalal, Tomás's servant, called "the magnificent"
Rashid al-Rashid ibn Abd al-Aziz, a vizier; a Rodriguez cousin
Ríma, wife of Abu Jossep; a Rodriguez cousin
Rodriguez, a Mozarab clan in Al-Andalus; heirs of the Visigoth kings
Tuma ibn Mikhail ibn Al-Makkzan, Tomás in Al-Andalus
Zaheid al-Quti, guard to Ríma; a Rodriguez cousin

Historic Figures

In the Languedoc and Aragón
Aimerico Pérez de Lara, Viscount of Narbonne
Arnau Amalric, a Church prelate, now archbishop of Narbonne
Folquet de Marselha, Bishop of Toulouse
Maria de Montpelhièr, Pedro's wife
Pedro II, King of Aragón and Count of Barcelona
Ramón-roger, Count of Foix
Simon de Montfort, leader of French invaders; Viscount of Carcassonne

In Castile
Alfonso VIII, king of Castile, leading the crusader army
Diego Lopez II de Haro, a Castilian noble

Elsewhere in Christendom
Innocent III, papal head of the Holy Roman Church
Philippe II, King of France; called "Philippe Augustus"

In Al-Andalus and Dar Al-Islam
Muhammad *al-Nasir*, the fourth caliph of the Moroccan Berber Almohads;
   called *Mirammolin* in Christendom
Salah ad-Din Yusuf ibn Ayyub, first Ayyubid Sultan of Egypt and Syria;
   called *Saladin* in Christendom (deceased)

The Accidental Heretics Come Home...

For some, peace is never possible.

The Story So Far: Isabella, the steward of Castell-de-Valerós in the eastern Pyrenees, has twice been falsely condemned as a heretic. In 1210, Isabella and Tomás, the mercenary she married, identified their archenemy, which proved to be a secret society called Crux Lunata. At the siege of Minerve, Isabella narrowly escaped being burned with the town's heretics.

To avoid the crusade against the Cathar heretics in the Languedoc, Tomás, Isabella, and her son Sebastián traveled to Cairo, where Tomás claimed his long-unseen son Yusuf. They then went to Cyprus, which was Tomás's childhood home. There, Tomás convinced his mother Numa to join Tomás's foster-brother Chrétien, who lives a peaceful life in Toulouse with Durán, Sebastián's half-brother.

In late summer 1211, Isabella, Tomás, Yusuf, and Sebastián set out for Barcelona to join the Castell-de-Valerós knights, who are training soldiers for Pedro d'Aragón's long-planned invasion of Andalusia.

·

The History: In 1212, Pope Innocent III asked for a pause in the French military action that Simon de Montfort led against the Cathar heretics. For that summer's fighting season, Christian knights were instead urged to fight the Moors in Andalusia and earn remission of sins for forty days' contribution to the "expedition of peace and mercy."

The Tunisian-born caliph of Cordoba tried to rally the local emirs to resist the coming invasion. But the generations-old clans in Al-Andalus resented the Almohad caliphate, which had installed itself after a coup by overly-righteous Berber soldiers. The caliph, therefore, was forced to hire mercenaries from northern Africa and Europe to build an army to resist the combined forces of Castile and Aragón.

While Christian armies prepared to march on Andalusia, rumors in the troubadours' world claimed that the heretics had invited the caliph to invade Christendom. No tales anywhere could be trusted.

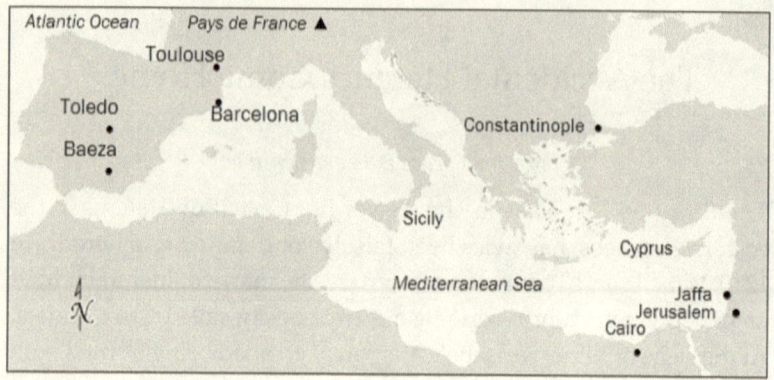

The Crusaders' World

CRUX
LUNATA

PART ONE
At Home

An Angel and a Djinni Discuss Heresy

"DON'T CALL ME 'LITTLE BROTHER.' I am taller than You."

"But I'm older than you." The djinni, who falsely called himself Ahriman, handed the towering angel a blood-red globe. "Taste this fruit. You'll find it glorious. In this part of the world, they've improved greatly on your so-called Creator's original handiwork."

"We both come from a Time other than the Beginning, the Day before God separated Earth from Water. In that, we are Equals." The angel Grigor sniffed the fruit and made a face, displeased.

"No, Little One, I came here through a chasm, from another place and a different time. As did most of your brothers."

"Heresy. The Father of Heaven created us All. He revealed Himself to Children of the Book, which He delivered to them at a Price above Gold. We all honor Our Father."

"*Ai*, you innocent!" The djinni laughed. "These creatures crawling the sands are indeed children who quarrel over the worth of the books in their marketplace. Isn't heresy merely condemnation of what another man chooses to eat?"

"Heresy is Real, and an Evil unto God."

"If you aren't going to eat that, Little Brother, give it back."

The djinni tapped the crimson fruit in Grigor's hand. If one dare call that shape a hand.

— *Ibn Jafar, The Poet*
From Tales of the Angel and the Djinni
Written in Seville at first sighting of the crescent moon at sunrise,
Jumada I-Ulla, 608 years since the flight to Medina.
At the command of Muhammad al-Nasir,
Commander of the Faithful, Emir of Seville, Caliph of Cordoba

1

1

An Apparition in the Hills

Monasterio de St-Pere de Selva
Near the Great Sea
November 30, 1211, All Saints Day

PASCAL, THE PORTER AT ST-PERE de Selva, lingered outside the chapel, his ancient bones as cold as the stone walls. Fat sodden flakes of snow piled in the courtyard, making his chores a misery. While the monks shivered in their boots during the dawn prayers, that *chiflado* abbot repeated the three psalms.

Chiflado. That's what Pascal's old granny called a man touched by the moon who carried more pride than kindness in his pockets. The abbot chirped on, preaching about honor and apparitions of saints and the coming hordes of Saracens.

Pascal expected neither saint nor Saracen to appear in this frozen place. Just flocks of knights with crusader crosses stitched on their surcoats, knocking on his gate to demand provender, as if spelt fell from heaven like manna to feed horses and monks and knights. It was just as Pascal's granny always said, "A man out seeking glory is ducking his chores."

Chores, not apparitions, guided each day at St-Pere, all the tasks that must be done to ensure the feeding of God's priests each morning and night. Pascal left the noisy abbot to his preaching and turned his attention to the animals under his care. The chickens huddled in their thatched shanty, where neither rain nor snow fell; they didn't care about odd weather. Pascal cleared the snow scum from the water trough near where the horses stamped in their shed, their misty breath the only ghostly sighting in these quarters. In their byre, three milch cows chomped their cud. He pitched an extra

3

fork of hay for each of them. Cozier here, Pascal thought, than in that cold stone breezeway they call a chapel.

Thirteen. Maybe fourteen. That's how old he was when it last snowed this early, before the harvest was done. Winter provender will be rotting if this mushy mess of snow lay in the fields too long. But nothing could be done about it now. In his own hut, Pascal fed more twigs into the fire and sat down to pull off his wet boots, soggier than they'd be if it merely rained on All Saints, down here where the Pyrenees tumbled into the Great Sea. Just as soon as he kicked one boot free, a knock sounded at the gate.

Wouldn't you know it?

Pascal tugged on his boot, the wet wool stocking all rucked up. "Patience!"

He shouted in Catalan, then called again at the third knock, this time in the tongue of Narbonne, since that's what the abbot demanded. The priestly lord of this place didn't want his friends to think a huddle of shepherds kept house for his monks.

"*Àvi*, help me!"

The figure at the gate cried for help in backcountry Catalan.

A mal punt, as his grandmother would say. A bad situation. No, worse than that. The old man couldn't refuse any soul in this weather. He kicked away the snow and dragged open the lesser gate, which creaked like the dead branches of a silver fir rubbing in the wind. The abbot would tan his hide with a stick if Pascal didn't get olive oil on those hinges.

In the storm-dark morning, Pascal heard the sea crash below. Snow blew into his face. Ten paces beyond the gate a slight figure hunched, either from age or from bearing the world's weight like a yoke. The visitor pushed back the hood of his cloak. White flakes fell on shorn white hair. More a ghost than a man. The pale face was both old and young, hollow and creased with pain, the life sucked out, the spirit within defeated.

In his lodge, Pascal hung the stranger's snow-soaked cloak near the fire. His visitor, hoarse from cold or illness, croaked out a few words in the accents of a young Narbonnese lord. The donzel had gold to purchase a place in the monastery and, though still shivering, asked to be taken to the abbot.

"All I love has been rendered unto God. Nothing holds me in this world. Best that I too render the rest of my life to God."

The porter disliked seeing young life squandered within these cold walls. This stranger—who walked more like a wound-sick girl than a pampered lad carrying a purse filled with gold—seemed so ill that "the rest of life" here couldn't be long.

"Òc, donzel." Pascal called him young lord. "But first, let's warm you up. Come sit by the fire."

.

Pascal had scarcely settled the stranger into the warmest corner, tucked him in with a sheepskin to stop the shivers, and forced a mug of hot wine into his hand, when he had to tend the gate again.

Five gaudy knights, friends of the abbot's, shouted for service as if St-Pere were a merchants' inn, their horses in more of a lather than a good man might allow. Just like they did on previous visits, most of them hurried off to the refectory, leaving Pascal to tend their horses. The only one with the decency to stay and wipe down his horse was the big broad-chested one with red haired, who always rode with his wolf-dog across his saddle. Perhaps his mother thought the fellow handsome, but contempt twisted his mouth and furled his brow too much, and those bad habits had spoiled his looks.

"Bon día, senhór. Cold as a weasel's tit today, isn't it?"

The knight was maybe deaf. Or perhaps Pascal was a ghost in his own stable and should best save his breath to comfort these over-heated ponies. The big man heaved his saddle aside and got to his business, giving his dog more attention than Pascal got.

A few moments later, the abbot deigned to appear in the stable, eager to speak with his visitor. Pascal raised a hand and bent his head in a respectful greeting, but as usual, the abbot looked right through him, as if Pascal were invisible. Pascal returned to his task—ai, but his icy bones ached in this weather—taking care to properly clean the hot horses and tend their hooves.

"Did you find it?" The slender abbot, his hood pulled up against the snow, folded his arms like a raptor come to rest in his eyrie. "Those heretics stole a lord's ransom when they ran for the hills."

"Not a brass barcelonese." The visitor spit into the straw. He spoke with the tones of gentry but practiced worse manners than any cursing Catalan woodcutter.

"So, they fled deeper into their holes? Those blasted Cathars." The abbot muttered words in Church Latin. "That's what the bishop calls them now. Cathars. Says 'heretic' is too good a word for them."

"They're in their holes, but no longer breathing. We baptized our blades in heretics' blood last night." The big fellow drew his sword, twisting it to make it shine in the thin light of the stable.

"You wiped out the last of them? Any left to tell where their gold is hidden?"

"No, unless one crawled into the woods to die." Big man slammed his sword back into its fine, leather-wrapped scabbard. "All we found in their cave was moldy spelt and turnips."

"Crux Lunata counts on you to fetch gold for our work."

"Then we need to capture the castle-villages in the upper hills. When those cat-suckers run from the cities, they hide their gold deep in the sheep-shit towns that shelter them. Arracheuse, Quéribus, St-Féliu, Peyrepetuse. Especially Valerós."

"Why not take Valerós now?" The abbot buried his arms deeper in the sleeves of his robe, bracing himself in the cold.

"Your Church courts are slow. Especially since Valerós is under the king of Aragón's protection." He used one of Pascal's stable blankets to cover his horse.

The abbot cleared his throat. "That's your next job—to take care of the king of Aragón."

"Pedro isn't going anywhere until next summer. There's time enough to fix his monkey."

"Did you persuade your grandmother? We need Felip to take orders now. His fee can feed six knights for a year."

"I can't do everything at once. Lop! *Hola, gos!*" The knight called his dog, which was worrying one of the monastery's horses. "She insists that my brother wait till he's twenty-five. Damn my dead father for leaving money in the hands of a woman."

"Try again. Though if you can't pry gold out of her fist, at least Felip is valuable here."

"Valuable? That little squid takes space and eats your food."

"He's the best worker in our scriptorium."

"Writing gospels for the glory of God?" The man covered one nostril and blew his nose, wiping away the wet with his hand. "Is that worth an extra helping of beans on Sunday?"

"More. Since the last crusade, the lords and their troubadours clamor for illuminated gospels. St-Pere earns good gold from Felip's copies, especially at Pentecost and Twelfth Night."

"*Qui s'ho creu?*" The big man sneered. *Who'd believe it?* "The squid hasn't been worth jack-spittle since the day he was born."

"Unlike his modest older brother." The abbot reached out an open hand, waving a command. "Did you achieve anything last night besides sending ragged souls to hell?"

"*Ai*, just found the Cid's sword, tucked away in the heretics' lair. If it's a magical sword, the magic is that I found it again." The big man tugged a short-sword from a scabbard tied to his saddle.

"Praise be to God!" The abbot dropped to his knees when the knight handed him that short-sword.

"Praise be to me. This is a sign. I'm the man to carry this sword, to help fate do its job."

"No, I'm traveling with the bishops. I will carry it to Toledo."

The big man cursed, calling down leprous angels.

Calm as a barn cat, the abbot said, "You'll follow the discipline of Crux Lunata."

"That order chose me to use the sword."

"*Òc*, but I carry the sword and the Grail until the moment when we bring the king's end. You can wait and travel with me."

"I'd rather eat cat tripe than travel one league with a herd of scrofulous priests."

"Get some food. Warm up before you ride again." The abbot backed away from that wolf-dog, which was busy sniffing at his feet. "And for the love of God, leave that dog in the stable."

"Other men's horses don't like him. *Hola, gos!*" The fire-haired knight stomped off, the abbot and the dog trotting along behind.

Across the way, an apparition stood in Pascal's open doorway, letting in both the frigid weather and the icy humors of St-Pere. Pascal hoisted a bundle of wood and toed his door further open with his boot, thinking how his grandmama believed in luck, but didn't hold with coincidence.

"By the graces of the Good God, there's pottage hot on the fire, donzel. More than enough for two."

His ghostly visitor stared out at the knights' horses until Pascal shut and barred the door.

"If my old granny was here, she'd insist you rest up. Get a bit stronger before you jump in with them ague-plagued monks." Pascal pulled that dented tin cup from its peg on the wall, the cup his granny gave him on his wedding day. He dipped into the pottage, making sure a goodly number of carrots made their way into the cup. "Stay here a bit. Keep warm and lend me your company."

"You are kind." The donzel reached out a thin, spectral hand to receive the cup. He stared into the hearth flames. "Perhaps for a day or two. Just until…"

Until, Pascal guessed, those heretic-hunting knights were gone, off in search of other souls to torture.

•

In the refectory, where the Silence was strictly enforced, Felip de Xirgú preferred to sit alone, hunkering down so no one noticed that he was the biggest man in the room, the only one not born a half century earlier. The only one starving for one more crust of bread.

Until he came to St-Pere, Felip hadn't considered food as an object of desire. Now, at every meal he yearned for more, spawning yet another sin of the flesh to confess. The ovens and kitchen fires had been built too close to the scriptorium, so he had to endure the scent of baking bread, braising fowl, and roasting onions while he worked. Each morning when he carried firewood into the kitchens, he stole from the pile of loaves the baker hauled from the ovens. Unquenchable hunger wasn't mentioned in the Ten Commandments, but stealing was, even if it didn't rank with killing or taking God's name in vain.

Worse, though, pure physical lust hounded him each night from the last evening hymn until he exhausted himself chopping wood in the dawn's light. During the harvest, a farmer's wife came along to unload grain into the abbot's big barns. Felip helped, just for a glimpse of the woman's breasts straining against her linsey-woolsey robe. Muscles bulged in her forearms when she wrangled sheep from a cart. Felip woke more than once, sure that she crushed him, burying his face in her huge breasts.

Felip had appeared at the gates of St-Pere, yearning to escape sin, but it pursued him through the monastery's maze of galleries and cells and chapels.

After breakfast, before the Silence began in the scriptorium, the bald, stooped script master shuffled over to give Felip a new task, an apparition testimony by a priest from Montpelhièr.

"Most stories come from ignorant villagers who drank too much and forgot to eat breakfast." The master laid a rough parchment for Felip to copy, an utterly unlovely piece that resembled a rapidly written letter to a farm steward. "This one is worth preserving. It's an inspiration to go and defeat the Saracens in their lair, before they invade Christendom."

Felip fetched the best piece of parchment and got busy ruling it while the master droned on.

"Illustrate the saint in the rubric. Do it the same as in the Legend we received from Genoa. With a rose inside the frame." As if Felip couldn't draw and color an original image of St-Jordí. "Our abbot is sending it to the pope. So, do your best work."

As if Felip didn't always do his best. However, if this piece was to be a gift for the pope, then when Felip finished, the master would sign his name. That's how it was done here.

The script master cleared his rheumy throat. "Ask for the key to the gilding cabinet when you begin the final decorations." Then he rang the bell for Silence.

AN APPARITION OF ST-JORDÍ

TESTIMONY OF ESAK OF AVIGNON

FEAST OF ALL SAINTS 1211

To meditate on our bond as the Church Militant here on earth with the purified apostles, saints, and martyrs of the Church Triumphant, the priest Esak prayed at the Church of St-Denis outside the walls of Montpelhièr. In the silence of the empty church, the priest felt warmth rising from behind his heart, as if the hottest sun shone on him. When he opened his eyes from prayer, the martyr St-Jordí appeared, the good soldier who died for his faith. As the priest Esak offered praise to God and His Son Our Savior, St-Jordí spoke to him in a voice like a gale in the pines, saying in these words:

"Saracen armies are crossing the Great Sea, called by their caliph Mirammolin to invade Christendom. Christian knights must rise up to stop their perfidy."

Just after Felip inked the details of the saint's plea—all the while daydreaming that he'd be one of the knights called to do Heaven's work—the master handed him a written request, waving it urgently but not breaking the Silence.

'Our abbot wishes to speak with you.'

Indecently excited, Felip hurried through the portico to the abbot's room. At the last summons, the abbot entrusted Felip to recreate a beautiful but deteriorating St-Mark's Gospel. At the abbot's suite, a linen banner draped over the garish iron door-pull indicated that the abbot was welcoming all visitors. The door ajar, Felip knocked and then pushed the door open at a summons.

His brother lounged in the abbot's guest chair, that daunting wolf-dog at his feet, drowsing while Matheus scratched the beast's head. The abbot wasn't even present.

"*Hola*, you lucky *calamarson*." Matheus always called him a baby squid. "I bring good fortune. Heaven's promise is now yours."

Overwhelmed by Matheus's good cheer, Felip shrank into his woolen habit. His mother claimed they looked alike, but his grandmother's polished brass mirror didn't agree. Felip was just as tall, but Matheus was broader. Felip was dark, but Matheus's hair was on fire, like his unreliable temper.

"Heaven's promise is why I came to the abbey," Felip said. "To render my life to God."

"But this cold hell leaves you open to all manner of sins of the flesh. I bet a dozen old brutes already covet your sweet ass."

Felip stepped back in disgust. "No. It's not like that here."

Startled, that massive wolf-dog sprang to its feet, hackles up, growling at Felip until Matheus snapped his fingers and pointed to the floor. The dog sank back down, one eye glaring at Felip.

"Well oh well, *calamarson*. I've come bearing remission of all your sins, signed by the new archbishop of Narbonne." Matheus held out a parchment roll. When Felip didn't reach for it, his brother untied the ribbon and broke the wax seal. "I've been initiated into an order of knights. We're joining the crusade against the Moors, for which the bishop promises forgiveness of all sins in this lifetime."

"And I can c–come?" Felip's heart leaped into his throat.

Matheus jerked the parchment out of Felip's reach.

"No, you can't c–c–come. You know the abbot won't let you leave on any journey until you take orders. I'm offering you the chance to pay for a real knight to travel under your banner."

"B–but Grandmother doesn't want me to take orders yet." Felip bit back resentment. Their uncles declared Matheus of age when he was twelve, so he'd received most of what was left by their father. Felip had only limited control of his own small inheritance, though he was twenty-one. "She says I'm too young to decide the course of my entire life."

"You can deed that briar patch up the hillside in Girona to the order. Then we add your name to the order's rolls, and your sins disappear, like magic."

Felip finally snatched the parchment from Matheus and studied it. "I wish I c–could go on crusade. Like our father did."

"Then get your grandmamma to let you take orders now instead of waiting. But you're better off here. You won't end up dead like our dear old father."

"It was an honorable way to die." Felip read every word twice, studying the parchment. "Why can't I give my land to the order and also beg the abbot for leave to go with you?"

"What can a baby squid do in a war?"

"I can ride a horse."

"And battle the Moors with your wet quill and a parchment scraper? Yet thanks to you, the glory of God will advance under the Lunate Cross. Your banner will wave in victory over the Saracens."

Those words excited him, but Felip retained the caution he always needed around his brother. "The rents from my land go to our grandmother. Will your order of knights provide for her?"

"Don't be a squid just because I call you one." Matheus laughed. "I shall guarantee our grandmother's wellbeing, as I have since our father deserted us for glory as a crusader in the Outremer, hoping to regain Jerusalem."

"How is she? How is Serena?"

"If by 'she' you mean our grandmother, she's tottering on the muddy edge of her grave, as she has for the last ten years. Sign here." Matheus handed Felip a quill from the abbot's table. "Your little playmate Serena has sprouted a very plump set of titties."

"Don't t–talk about her like that."

"Why not, *calamarson*? You've been handling yourself at the mere mention of her name since she turned thirteen." Matheus waggled a finger, impatient for Felip to finish. Then Matheus sanded the ink and blew on it, sending dust speckles over Felip's dark robe.

"She's a respectable senhóreta."

"She's poor as a yellow-necked mouse. Since her father died, all she brings to market are those luscious and ample breasts. Else, she'll be seeking shelter with her dead father's goatherds."

"Matheus, you are such a bastard."

But his brother was already at the door, waving farewell with his usual rude gesture.

"Lop!" Matheus called. "*Hola, gos!*"

Matheus strolled down the gallery, whistling for his dog. That murderous wolf-beast cast one last red-eyed glare at Felip.

"Welcome to Crux Lunata," Matheus bellowed, his voice echoing in the gallery, "and the war against the evil blackamoors."

2

A Day in Barcelona

Tomás in Barcelona
February 2, Candlemas Morning

THE FORMERLY HANDSOME DON TOMÁS de Cyprus y Morella often forgot that an enemy had ruined his once-pretty face. In the misty dawn, while Barcelona struggled to shake off the night's dreams, Tomás rose from his own mare's nest and set out from home to answer a summons from his friend.

> Come to me. I have real work for you, bonfraire.
> ~ Pedro, Rei d'Aragón

Real work. A mercenary and master swordsman, Tomás had begged Pedro for more than the chores the king assigned him: shouting battle exercises daily for blockhead donzels with wooden practice blades. Tomás needed real battle, where hot steel might slice free the bonds of tedium that squeezed his belly, bruised his heart.

On his way to Pedro's door, Tomás loitered with his two sons in their favorite market square, waiting for vendors to open their stalls. Shy, scholarly Yusuf stayed close by Tomás's side, no longer a stranger after uniting last year when Tomás, Sebastián, and Isabella travelled to Cairo to fetch him. (Tomás owed Yusuf recompense for letting the boy's mother have her way, long past the time when a son should be with his father.)

Tomás's stepson Sebastián—Isabella's son—had claimed Yusuf as a brother the moment they met in Cairo. Tomás and his sons stuck together, Yusuf at his side like a second shadow, the three of them sharing silent comfort that no one else understood. Those two kept Tomás from what he most wanted to do each day, which was to weep until he died of grief.

13

Because he couldn't forget for a heartbeat Isabella's pale, loving grey eyes. Her soft touch. Gone to heaven.

Killed by bandits while she rode with him outside Narbonne.

False bandits. Francimand mercenaries in Crux Lunata tunics.

His fault. He was supposed to protect his wife, his soul.

His punishment to be left behind to make his own way in a cold world.

"Did I fail my vow?" Tomás's voice scraped like a blacksmith's rasp on steel. So hard to speak in the foggy morning, after screaming in his dreams all night. Neither of his sons seemed to hear. Still, he whispered. "I owed Isabella so much more."

"*Botifarres fresques!*" Sebastián cried.

Always hungry, Sebastián sniffed the air, identifying the scent of fresh sausages cooking in a nearby stall. Auburn hair. A pale face, so like his mother's. Destined to be taller than most men, Sebastián already towered over Tomás and Yusuf. When he pointed to where they should seek breakfast, Sebastián's sleeve fell back, revealing the bonfraire brand they shared, the symbol of La Confraria de la Crotz. The brotherhood of knights founded by Pèire Leteric, Sebastián's great-grandfather. The bonfraires swore allegiance to each other, an oath that imperiled one's immortal soul if broken. The oath Tomás failed when those bandits...

"Brioix!" Yusuf tugged at Tomás's sleeve, pointing to the stall of his favorite baker. "Fresh bread always makes me happy that I now live in this new world."

Sebastián punched Yusuf's shoulder. "You're happy to be with us. Happy you aren't still rotting in that university. Admit it."

Yusuf rubbed at where he'd been punched. "Only because you are my brother, I will admit, from a philosophical standpoint, to a decided preference for—"

"*Per l'amor de Dèu,* mercy!" A woman cried out behind them, begging for mercy.

At the mouth of an alley, a young woman struggled with a soldier, only their outlines visible in the morning mist. Tomás stamped across the cobbles, his sword ready, shouting to distract the attacker.

"Stop, *baquelar!*" Tomás switched dialects, demanding a halt while deprecating the bastard's mother.

The bearded man in rusted chainmail, a head taller than Tomás, jerked the woman against him as a shield. The bastard, barking in rapid French, had a sword in his right hand.

"Prepare to meet the devil, you black dog!"

Tomás, who was more the color of an oiled leather cuirass than a black dog, circled his sword, prepared to attack. The man's filthy cowhide aventail protected his neck and face. No opening for Tomás's sword.

"He says he'll send you to the devil!" Sebastián yelled. He covered the man's other side.

"Worse! The goatsucker called me a black dog."

Sebastián shouted in mixed French and Catalan, his voice breaking. "Stop in the name of Pedro *le Roi!* Release the woman!"

The armored *francimand* shoved the woman onto Sebastián, who stumbled. Then the ruffian lunged to disarm Tomás in an awkward, poorly trained move that could never succeed.

Except a street brat scrambled from behind Tomás.

"Baquelar!" The urchin called the mercenary a rogue. Brandishing a stick, he rushed toward the attacker.

Off balance, Tomás deflected a sword slash aimed for his arm. The *francimand* kicked at Tomás's wrist and sent his sword spinning on the cobbles. The man bashed the hilt of his sword behind Tomás's ear, knocking him to the ground and then kicking him in the ribs. When Sebastián advanced, the man ran down the alleyway, lost in the dawn mist.

A *francimand* mercenary in a Crux Lunata tunic, the kind who worked for Simon de Montfort. The kind who killed Isabella. The kind of men Tomás hated most in the world. In an instant, humiliation and loss clotted with his blood around the cuts and bruises. He deserved worse than two kicks from a false crusader.

■

"Are you well, ma dòmna?"

Sebastián spoke softly to the frightened woman. She nodded, clutching the urchin, her eyes still bright with fear.

Yusuf rushed to Tomás, offering a hand to help him up, which Tomás accepted while hoping that he masked his dismay over that colossal failure of swordsmanship. As if reading his father's mind, Yusuf said, "Not one of your students comes to the market this early, Father. They didn't see." Yusuf pronounced *father* in a lilting accent that hit Tomás's heart each time he heard it.

His head still aching, Tomás bent to pick up his sword, muttering blasphemies. "Can't buy sausages without spit-licking *francimand* bastards out to cheat the devil."

"*Òc*, Don Tomás." Sebastián removed the stick from the urchin's grasp. "But you always say that goat herding in Morella is the only safe bet."

When Sebastián voiced Tomás's name, the woman hailed him as lord of Morella. "Salutations, honorable seigneur of Morella!"

"You know me?"

Though Tomás wore the insignia of the Aragónese fief he inherited from his father, he'd never visited the place, a goat farm that never paid rents. That small, dirt-colored boy, the one who'd distracted him, sprinted away from Sebastián to hunker behind the woman's linsey-woolsey skirts.

"*Vivètz* Morella!" The boy hailed his village name.

She tugged at the child while begging Tomás for mercy. "Please help us. This is a son of Morella, lost here."

She reached out to Tomás.

A horse whinnied in terror. A hound yowled, then growled and barked a threat. A braided-tail stallion reared up, shying away from the snapping dog. The woman thrust the boy out of the way, casting the lad upon Tomás, who stumbled into a hawker's cartload of foodstuffs, pulling the child and Yusuf down with him.

While the horse trampled the woman.

The stallion's rider shrieked, trying to control the beast. Ignoring the danger, Sebastián grasped the reins and whispered in the frightened horse's nose to calm it. The rider, the same attacking *francimand* bastard, yanked the reins from Sebastián's grasp and spurred the horse down the alley, out of the market.

His head pounding, Tomás bent to help the woman, the boy clinging to his back.

Too late. Once more Tomás failed to save a woman from evil committed by Simon's soldiers. The same kind of human muck that sent Isabella to heaven, taking Tomás's soul with her, leaving him here to endure more death and despair.

At least this time, in that misty market square, God granted enough time for Tomás to hold the woman and say prayers while she crossed over to paradise.

"—who art in heaven."

He tried to believe in heaven now, or else Isabella was lost to him forever.

.

"Fetch the death-cart and tell the bailiff's men what happened."

Sebastián bolted off on that mission before Tomás finished asking. A small crowd of hawkers, cooks, and haulers gathered, repeating what they'd seen, decrying armed rogues disturbing the peace of Barcelona, but no one offered help.

His head still throbbing, Tomás sat on the church steps at the edge of the market square, waving for the boy to sit by him. Yusuf settled on his other side.

"Did she die?" The boy's sharp voice in his ear pierced Tomás's headache. He meant the woman whose body they watched over.

"*Ai, ai, fadrin.*"

To calm the boy, Tomás called him a dear lad and crooned the way his own mother used to, holding him the way you're supposed to comfort children. Yusuf also sat close by, his fingertips resting on Tomás's shoulder.

"Tell me your name, *fadrin.*" Tomás's ribs juddered in pain. The boy's stick-thin elbows pressed into Tomás's bruised middle.

"Fortuno."

A name, they say, that brings God's blessings, not the kind of calamity this boy suffered. Tomás added the boy's misfortunes to his compendium of grudges against his Creator. Not knowing much about boys, Tomás guessed that the lad was too young, perhaps only six, to understand what happened. The boy hadn't shed a tear, seeming more curious than frightened by the broken body Sebastián's cloak covered.

"Will the death-cart men take her to heaven in their cart?" the boy asked. Before Tomás coughed out an answer, the lad said, "Will a priest make her an angel like my grandmother?"

"My mother says all good people become angels," Tomás said. The pain in his ribs was deserved, for repeating a comfort he didn't allow himself.

"Do you know any angels?" Fortuno asked, his voice lyrical.

"My wife. She was killed last summer." Tomás's voice scratched, no melody. "If anyone is an angel..."

"My father said there are no angels, only devils. But I saw my grandmother after she died." Fortuno's face drooped with sadness. "She talked to me every day until my father took me to join the army."

"Maybe she's a ghost. My father's ghost came to me for a year after he died." Tomás told the orphan boy a secret he'd never shared with anyone, even Isabella. Yusuf stirred at his side, but Tomás felt that his own son might as well hear this. "Miquel helped me solve problems. I miss him."

The boy burrowed deeper into Tomás's side. "Since she doesn't talk to me here, do you think my grandmother is a saint now?"

"If she was very good." Tomás lost his way for a heartbeat. Why did Isabella's ghost refuse to walk by his side?

"I miss my grandmother. She taught me songs." Fortuno sang a snatch of a crusaders' song in a high, dulcet voice.

'Sweet thing, whatever you hear them say,
Don't believe anyone knows greater sadness
Than a lover who parts from his love.'

"Not a good song right now, *fadrin*." A song Chrétien, his milk-brother, often sang the hymn, "*Us cavaliers si jazai*." Tomás smothered welling grief.

Fortuno murmured in Tomás's ear. "Can you call people's ghosts when you miss them?"

"No, *fadrin*." He'd prayed for Isabella's ghost to appear, to console him the way Miquel did after he died. But if God answered prayers, he never answered Tomás's. Once again Tomás heard Isabella cry out, dying on that lonely mountain road. The bandits captured Sebastián, Tomás, and Yusuf, and stole her soul from him.

His fault. He failed his oath. And lost her.

"Does that hurt?" The boy nudged Tomás from reverie, pointing to the scars slashed across Tomás's face and mouth. When Tomás shook his head, the boy asked, "Can I touch it?"

Not waiting for an answer, Fortuno reached out a grubby finger. Tomás closed his eyes. The boy's touch was gentle. Like when Isabella whispered into his neck, stroking his face, declaring him still beautiful, tracing the scars carved by his enemy.

Tomás drew back. "Enough. That tickles."

.

The death-cart men arrived with a bailiff. Sebastián called from across the market plaza that he'd go purchase breakfast. While the bailiff questioned the lingering crowd, Tomás instructed the death-cart men and gave them a fistful of silver pennies. Then he sat with the orphan Fortuno on a low wall, gently asking questions.

"Who's your father?"

"A sergeant in King Pedro's army. We're going to fight the black Moors."

"We'll bring you to your father." Tomás didn't point out that he and Fortuno, sons of Morella, had forefathers who were Moors.

The boy rubbed his head against Tomás's chest. "My father died last week. An accident with the siege engines."

"Where are your mother's people? We must tell them she's gone to heaven."

"She died when I was a baby."

"Who's that woman?" Tomás watched closely to be sure the death-cart men settled her body onto their cart respectfully.

"Joan. From the laundry women at the camp. She slept in my father's tent the night before he died. They made her take me when she claimed the tent."

Dozens of Joans lived in the laundry camp. "Why did she want to find me?"

"She asked an order of knights to take me, but they told her to seek the don of Morella on this street. They gave her a letter."

Tomás called to the death-cart men, who gave him the woman's satchel, which held five silver pennies, two cloak pins fashioned from seashells, a worn leather sheath with a knife no longer than his index finger, and battered clay doll wrapped with a lock of hair and a red ribbon. Joan had cast a spell to make someone love her.

At the bottom of the satchel was a dusty rag of parchment.

With Yusuf reading over his shoulder, Tomás deciphered the dark, heavy script, whispering the words in Latin:

'Your mestitz bastard doesn't belong in God's army.'

Three crosses, their points topped with crescents, which served as signature for Crux Lunata, the secret order of knights that had tortured Tomás's family for decades.

Tomás shivered in the chill of the late winter fog. Fortuno molded against Tomás while they sat on that cold stone wall, Yusuf leaning close by his side. Tomás pulled his cloak around the child, who sang another song.

'Loves go with the spark
That is mixed in the soot,
Burning the stick and the straw…'

Sebastián appeared with bread, cheese, and black sausages. He hacked off chunks of bread and cheese with the dagger Tomás gave him as a knighting gift two years ago. Two lifetimes ago. Fortuno gave up singing and accepted food from Sebastián. He attacked the bread and cheese like a starving terrier.

"Remember that soothsayer in Cairo, when Yusuf left school to come with us?" Tomás accepted the bread and sausage Sebastián offered, though uninterested in food. "His prophesies all came true."

"*Ai Dèu*, Don Tomás. All I remember about Cairo is sleeping on rooftops and riding camels. And Yusuf so happy to see us."

"I was more than happy," Yusuf murmured.

Tomás said, "That street-witch knew Isabella was a woman, even though she was dressed as a squire. The witch said wherever I go, death will follow."

"An astounding guess, since you and Sebastián are soldiers." Yusuf nibbled at his breakfast, while Sebastián ate his sausages and cheese as fast as Fortuno, the way a soldier eats while in the saddle. "And all men die in the end."

Tomás passed half his bread and cheese back to the ever-hungry Sebastián. "Let's go home to Valerós. Or wreak havoc in the Toulousain. I want *francimand* blood on my sword. For Isabella."

"Pedro forbids revenge." Sebastián cried in the night for a month after they came to Barcelona. But now, deep in plans for Pedro's campaign in Iberia, he seemed to forget that rocky road where hope died. "Anyway, we leave for Toledo soon. Tomorrow, if we're lucky."

"I failed her. In my dreams—"

"No man could have done better than you," Yusuf said.

"*Òc*, Don Tomás, you aren't God. We were outnumbered." It was Sebastián who freed them from the bandits, having kept his dagger, as if by magic.

"How do you bear life without her?" Tomás whispered. They'd stolen horses and rode back to find her, but wolves had come, so Isabella's bones lay scattered with the others. He'd built a cairn. In his dreams or walking the misty streets of Barcelona, he still heard the *thunk* of rock against bone, pounding a rhythm while he cursed his Creator.

"There's a hole inside that I almost fall into every day." Sebastián spoke through the last bite of bread and cheese. "Instead, I think about riding to war with the Valerós knights. To do the next thing we have to. We just go on. The way she would."

"We just go on living," Fortuno proclaimed. The lad should not have heard Tomás's despair. "That's what my grandmother says. In my dreams."

Just go on. The hardest work Tomás had ever undertaken.

"What shall we do with you, *fadrín*?" Tomás shifted Fortuno, smelling grime and kitchen smoke in the child's hair. A poor boy, alone in a strange land. Tomás was lonely, but had two sons and all the responsibilities Pedro assigned him. This boy was a weightless addition to that burden.

"Let's take him home to Dolç." Yusuf confirmed Tomás's inclination. Pedro's little widowed cousin, who kept house for Tomás and his sons, always knew what to do with children.

"*Òc*. Sebastián, carry him home, please. I must join Pedro."

The boy's warm breath brushed Tomás's ear, like the whispering of angels or ghosts. Tomás hoisted Fortuno onto Sebastián's back for a ride across town,

"May I have my father's dagger?" Fortuno pointed to the little knife from Joan's satchel. "Will you fetch me to go fight Saracens with Pedro next week?"

The knife had no edge. Tomás gave it to Sebastián to pass to Fortuno later. He didn't answer the boy's request to go with Pedro.

Fortuno sang out, "We win by midsummer, then home again! That's what the king says."

"Yes, that's what Pedro says." Sebastián boosted the boy higher onto his shoulders. "We're going to be heroes. Aren't we, Don Tomás? When we come home." He was off without waiting for an answer.

Home. Tomás detested the word.

Lavender and garlic thicken the air so it's unbreathable. Hearth fires and Dolç's merry children. Perpetual cozening. *Let me fix you a bite of food. Let me mend that tear in your hose. I'll call a footman to help with your boots.* As soon as Tomás arrived in Barcelona, Pedro had pushed him to marry his cousin Dolç ("to protect her lands from Simon de Montfort") when everyone involved knew that Tomás had no conceivable desire for any woman but Isabella. In recompense for that ridiculous charade, Pedro owed Tomás real work in the world, not the awkwardness of living in a woman's home and suffering from kindnesses and comforts he didn't deserve.

"You shouldn't have lied." Yusuf, at his side, spoke barely loud enough to be heard over the market noise.

"What, *fadrin?*"

"You shouldn't have lied to that little boy about seeing ghosts. It's not right to lie to children." Yusuf had hold of Tomás's shirt sleeve, lightly grasping it while they steered through the morning crowds near the Palau Reial, the only child-like gesture he ever made with Tomás in public.

"I didn't lie exactly."

"Children need to hear the absolute truth," Yusuf scolded. "Not tall tales of angels or djinn or saints or ghosts."

"*Ai, fadrin*. You believe the same as my father."

"The one who came to you as a ghost?" A merry grin split his beautiful face. Yusuf laughed at Tomás's expense. Life wouldn't be worth living without Yusuf and Sebastián by his side.

On their way to the Palau Reial, Tomás dropped a silver morabatin in a beggar's cup and offered a simple blessing, hoping he'd mastered the local dialect.

"Bon día. God bless you."

The beggar's ragged child, frightened by Tomás's scarred face, cried. She ducked under her mother's frayed shawl, rekindling Tomás's burning resentment for his Maker's uncaring ways. He stalked away, ready to answer Pedro's command, wishing he were truly alive, hearing Yusuf murmur comforts to the beggar's child.

"He's the best man alive. Don't be afraid."

■

The morning fog, smelling of the sea, drifted in wisps. Tomás stumbled in the mist, seeking the correct direction. The reeking air settled at the back of his throat, like the scent of weedy shrubs in a witch-woman's garden. Checking over his shoulder often for more *francimand* mercenaries, he headed for the Palau Reial with Yusuf.

Years before, Tomás swore to Pèire Leteric that, as a bonfraire, he'd protect Isabella from enemies. He succeeded through siege and catastrophe in the Toulousain, and across the Great Sea when they traveled to fetch Yusuf. Then failed when Simon's bandits ambushed them in a rocky chasm in the Pyrenees foothills.

"Oh, look, Father! How wonderful!" Yusuf's voice warmed his soul, the boy's form like the outline of an angel in the fog.

A flutter of wings at the edge of his vision disappeared. Perhaps Isabella hovered near. Or an angel. Weren't angels sent to comfort men? Or help with revenge? Not just hover, with no message? He'd failed to defend a woman once more, let a distraction break his guard. All that hard work in Pedro's training yards since All Saints, yet at the first ambush once again an innocent woman died.

He reached out for her—it happened often—wanting to touch and talk with Isabella again. Perhaps she's not gone to heaven, still somewhere near. But why didn't she come for all the times he'd cried *Isabella* in the night?

"One of the green parrots." Yusuf grasped Tomás's outstretched hand, tugging it down to his side, and they walked together through the misty alleys. "I don't believe in luck, but I think it's a good day if I see a green parrot in the morning."

At the Palau Reial, Yusuf departed, reluctantly, to Latin lessons.

"I'd rather spend the day with you, Father."

"You need to be in lessons alongside the donzels who live under Pedro's protection."

"Do they learn more with you serving as swordmaster than they do with their Latin tutors?" Yusuf smiled in that sweet way he had. The doltishness of Aragónese donzels provided for ongoing jests between Tomás and his son.

"You, imp, can prepare a treatise on the ways of lords' lazy sons when faced with ink and pen. Or join in when I instruct them in the ways of steel and shield."

Yusuf refused that invitation; he always did. Tomás squeezed his son's shoulder and said adieu, regretting the portion of the day spent away from him, but then turning his attention to Pedro.

When Tomás arrived in Barcelona with the boys, Pedro did for him what he'd done once before and forced Tomás to action, pestering him to think better of God. Pedro dragged Tomás into action, riding with him and his private guards up into the hills to roust a nest of bandits, covering many leagues a day, working at sword practice, moving until they collapsed at night, exhausted.

"You must go on," Pedro whispered when they bivouacked under the autumn stars.

He made Tomás talk, when he'd been silent since that attack in the Pyrenees. Pedro begged for every detail about what Tomás had done in the past two years. And at last, he insisted that Tomás share the oath of Miquel's old confraternity, making him one of the bonfraires. Pedro took the oath—*Sodalitas, fidelitas, virtus*—solemnly, speaking better Latin than any knight of the confraternity had done before. With Chrétien far away in Toulouse, Isabella gone, and only the burden of care for Yusuf and Sebastián, Tomás had the sole comfort of Pedro as brother and friend.

24

When Tomás stepped over the threshold into the world of Pedro's court, that new clerk from Rome whispered in the king's ear, touching Pedro's sleeve to get his attention in a too-personal way that Tomás hoped no one else noticed. The clerk from a rich Montpelhièr family, but now renamed Doménec by the Church, had become the king's shadow. His sleek, aristocratic profile resembled a merlin, with all the self-assurance of the hunter who is never prey.

"Bon día. You are well, Don Tomás?" Pedro rose in his graceful way to grasp Tomás's hand in a bonfraire greeting, the immutable bond between them. Standing behind Pedro, Doménec scowled, seeming to recognize in that handshake everything he didn't share. But wanted.

"A *francimand* from the army camps tried to kill me just now," Tomás said, awed again by Pedro's bold beauty and piercing blue eyes. *But he's just a man. One of my bonfraires. Not my ruler.*

"And another dozen want to. Did the fellow survive that thoughtless choice?"

"Òc. I'll find the rogue later. I want to watch his blood pour into the sand while his soul seeks refuge with the devil."

"You won't have time." Pedro ignored Tomás's outburst. "I have a chore for you. The caliph sent an emissary from Seville. They insist a son of Islam perform my translations."

"Good." Though Tomás didn't see the good. Pedro's note promised real work, not clerk's fare. "However, I'm a Christian, as you know."

"I pray every night about that." Pedro tossed up his hands in a gesture that indicated old-fashioned Aragónese despair. "You had no trouble lying when you studied in Cairo. Pretend to be an honest man, for my sake. Doménec has clothes for you."

Tomás stripped before the king and his clerk, his head still aching. Doménec recoiled at the mass of scars across Tomás's back. Pedro, who'd seen the scars before, said, "You're still too thin, Tomás. I shall command your new wife to feed you better."

"These clothes are wrong," Tomás said. "No Ayyubid infantryman ever wore a cotton shirt under this antique." He held out the embroidered overcoat of an ancient caliph's bodyguard.

Pedro said, "We shall hope our guests are unfamiliar with what soldiers now wear in the Holy Land."

Tomás rubbed a mended rent in the overcoat. A Latin knight took it off an unfortunate defender, before Saladin's time. Tomás's father had possessed one like it, among other trophies Tomás and his foster-brother Chrétien dressed in to play Saracen and Crusader. He always had to be the Saracen, Chrétien demanding to play the merciless Frank.

Doménec interrupted that reverie, offering a strip of cotton turban cloth. Tomás's lip twitched in distain.

"It's clean," Doménec said. "I promise you."

Tomás wrapped his head, not reassured, disliking the scribe's too-obvious jealousy. They followed Pedro to the council room, Tomás not missing how closely Doménec watched the king.

"Do you enjoy it here?" Tomás asked the scribe. "Isn't it much nicer in Rome with the pope?"

"It's foolish how much I once dreaded this assignment." Doménec answered as if Tomás had asked an earnest question. "It's embarrassing now, how much I thought of myself, a Montpelhièr lad in service to the pope. Now, I'm flattered to have been sent to serve a most Catholic king."

"It must have been a surprise to find that Barcelona is almost civilized."

The too-handsome Doménec ducked his head, turtle-like in acknowledgment. His lips flickered, as if sharing a secret with himself. "There's excellent company and every comfort. And the work is most interesting."

"I like the food," Tomás said.

.

In the council room, a canvas cloth had been thrown over the statue of St-Jordí, Barcelona's own saint, who presided over most other meetings in that room.

Adopting the posture of an Ayyubid guardsman, Tomás stood behind Pedro and studied the caliph's emissary, who wore a litham veil across the lower half his face, a style long abandoned in the

Outremer, that place across the Great Sea where the Crusader State languished. How to negotiate with a man who hid behind a veil?

At a sign from Pedro, Tomás recited the king's formal name— *Pedro El Católico, king by Grace of God of Aragón*, and all the rest—and then translated the name and honorifics of this Almohad vizier.

"The caliph's emissary is Rashid al-Rashid ibn Abd al-Aziz. His name means that he is the rightly-guided son of a Servant of the Strong, Peace be on His name." Tomás hoped Pedro wouldn't scowl whenever he translated praises or calls for peace upon the Prophet's name. The extraordinary devotion of most Almohad people was famous even in Christendom, especially compared to the easy ways of taifa rulers who'd governed Al-Andalus for generations before the new caliphate.

Lighter-skinned than Tomás, Rashid al-Rashid had the hyper-alert, lithe bearing of an Ibizan hound. His cavalryman's tunic indicated he preferred soldiering to wealth. Under the tunic Rashid wore a mail-lined kazaghand, the same kind, it was said, that Saladin wore to fend off assassins.

The emissary's eyes drifted to Tomás when Pedro introduced him as Tuma ibn Mikhail al-Makkzan (Tomás's name in Cairo). Rashid dwelled on Tomás's ruined face, as if judging an adversary. Then, disinterested, his attention returned to Pedro.

"In our lands, we offer hospitality to every visitor," Pedro said. One of the emissary's company interrupted, but Pedro held up his hand to beg for patience. "I know this is your holiest season. I fear my offer of hospitality would seem an insult."

Rashid offered a long thank-you for Pedro's thoughtfulness. Then the discussion began, which proved long and repetitive, and ended with the same ideas with which they began.

"A spirit that comes only from a love of God guides the caliph to resist trespass by the kings of Castile, Aragón, and Léon." In a chestnut-honey voice, Rashid spoke with the rhythm of a poet, watching Pedro while he spoke, and then scrutinizing Tomás throughout the translation, as if to peer into his soul. "The caliph has called his people from the furthest reaches of the world. More than two hundred thousand men stand to defend against your paltry army. The caliph asks that, for love of God, you keep your people home rather than send them to unnecessary deaths."

After Tomás translated, Pedro spoke coolly. "The armies of Aragón and their allies are already half way across La Mancha. We'll meet you in battle to prove our own might, God willing."

The emissary's personal translator inserted his own vehemence. "The Christian king calls on his God to curse Allah, and foolishly claims he will defeat us, like their unholy king Richard who massacred the faithful outside Jerusalem."

The wide man in green silks beside Rashid, who'd been introduced as Marzuq al-Jayyani, jumped up and slapped the table, leaning over to confront Pedro, spittle flying as he spoke. "May you be cursed in your bones. All praise is due to Allah."

"Your translator has erred, most noble lord." Tomás faced Rashid. "The king of the Aragónese Latins did not speak against the one true God. All praise is due to God alone."

Aflame with indignation, hatred dripping from his pores, Al-Jayyani shouted at Tomás. "The Aragónese are lying curs. You disgrace yourself, lying for this dog-king."

Rashid held up his hand for peace. Pedro waited patiently.

"Ibn Mikhail offered a proper correction." Rashid pushed aside the litham veil, gazing at Tomás, who felt as if his father stared at him. The emissary's long, narrow face duplicated Miquel's. Only lighter and younger, free of suffering.

Tomás, unnerved, fell behind in his translations, but the meeting drew to a close, so he had to pay close attention and carefully paraphrase the polite farewells that a careless translator might mistakenly render as insults.

"You'll leave a man to receive my written message to your caliph?" Pedro said.

Rashid waved to dismiss his people. "I myself shall wait."

Soon Tomás stood alone with the king of Aragón and a man in turban and chainmail whom God himself might mistake for a younger Miquel.

"God's ways are remarkable!" Pedro said to Rashid, his back to Tomás. "Do not all People of the Book acknowledge the power and mystery of the One True God?"

Before Tomás translated, Rashid waved to stop him, then spoke in heavily accented Castilian. "I understand. Do you agree to release my cousin?"

Pedro glanced at Tomás with no trace of emotion. He spoke in Aragón dialect. "The honorable Rashid is, I am told, a cousin of yours, Ibn Mikhail."

Rashid spoke to Tomás in Arabic. "My great-grandfather was called al-Makkzan because he came from Tunis as a mercenary. He married into the Rodriguez clan near Jaén. You know our family?"

With no signal from Pedro to let him know if this claim might be true, Tomás said, "My own great-grandfather al-Makkzan came from the Rodriguez clan."

"He and his brother came from Morocco. They joined our clan through marriage. They were hired by a widow in Morella, on the Aragón frontier." Rashid spoke in formal tones, overcoming his accent. "The brother—my great-grandfather Jamal—married a younger Rodriguez sister and returned to serve the caliph in Jaén. I inherited that service. Your ancestor, al-Makkzan, married that senhóra of Morella. His grandson Mikhail left for Cairo and Damascus after Morella was enjoined with Aragón."

"You believe that was my father."

"We are sure of it. The Rodriguez clan never forgets its own." Rashid returned his attention to Pedro. He took a small package from within his surcoat and spoke again in Castilian. "Now, Monsenyor, I offer you this gift from al-Nasir, our caliph. It is an allegory written by Ibn Jafar, a great poet in Seville, on the nature of Good and Evil. Al-Nasir believes in the power of poetry to open men's hearts to the true nature of God."

Pedro accepted the gift and expressed his gratitude, adding the final words in Arabic he'd learned from Tomás. Doménec came in, bearing a scroll with Pedro's message for the caliph. And he placed Tomás's sword on the table in front of Pedro.

"You force me to carry home a sad message." Rashid's eyes and narrow jaw called up specific memories of Miquel, a man whose mind was not changed easily.

"I regret that our resolve brings sadness." Pedro nudged Tomás's sword. "Is this what you seek?"

Rashid unrolled a small parchment and compared its drawing with the inscription on Tomás's sword. "This is the sword of Mikhail al-Makkzan, as it was known in Cairo."

Pedro said, "I want to honor your family's request. I shall deliver this sword with my servant."

"I sail on tomorrow's tide."

•

Rashid departed to join his entourage, politely acknowledging Pedro's formal goodbyes, vaguely nodding to Tomás.

"Is he really my cousin?"

"By great luck or a gift from God, yes, it's true. And he's judged a most honorable and worthy man by other generals and viziers. Or so my agents claim."

Pedro conferred with Doménec while they walked to the king's private room, asking about messages to be answered and lords to be entertained in court that afternoon. Tomás trailed after, still wearing the Muslim mummers' rags, though he unwound that make-do turban from his aching head.

"What does the caliph's pious grandson of a Morella goatherd want with my sword, Monsenyor? And why do you feel free to give it away?"

In Pedro's work room, Doménec busily sorted quills, ink bottles, and paraphernalia. While the clerk fussed, Tomás sat beside the king in the way he did when they traveled together in years past. Doménec frowned at the intimacy.

"Your cousin claims you carry the sword of El Cid." Pedro didn't bother to mask how he enjoyed teasing Tomás. "You know that story? Rodrigo Diaz de Vivar, the general who deserted the Moors and captured Valencía."

Tomás masked his impatience. "That was a hundred years ago. The Moors took Valencia back not long after he died."

Pedro rubbed at his mustache, wiping away a grin. "Your cousin Rashid demands that I return the Cid's sword to your clan in Jaén."

"The sword I used to teach you the difference between steel from Damascus and Toledo?" Tomás laughed, which made his bruised ribs ache again. "I can no longer show you old Toledo steel, since I lost that short-sword. There's just my Damascus blade."

"*Ai, òc!* And I took such a cut when I wasn't quick enough on defense. I learned that lesson well." Pedro amused himself, testing Tomás's patience. "The troubadours say the Cid's magical sword can unite what once was divided."

"A sword so magical that it's disguised as one made thirty years ago in the Outremer. What servant are you giving Rashid along with my sword?"

"Your cousin purchased your mercenary contract."

"Jove's pissing monkey!" Tomás swore the way he learned from his father. His head pounded where that *francimand* mercenary had thumped him. "You jest."

Doménec leaned in to speak. "The taifa generals in Andalusia gossiped all winter that Pedro hired a mercenary who's a warrior from the Rodriguez clan."

"Tales get around," Pedro said. "Especially after we learned that Tomás of Morella is cousin to an ambitious vizier who serves the caliph in Andalusia."

"You amaze me, Monsenyor." Tomás watched Pedro's brow rise at the compliment. "As you intended."

"Another of your Rodriguez cousins in Jaén is my agent." Pedro pointed to the stone jug on the sideboard, gesturing for refreshments. Tomás rose to carry out his request. "Except for your darker branch, the people of the Rodriguez clan are Mozarabs who want Iberia re-united, Espanya joined with Andalusia. And they long to welcome home a lost cousin."

"You sold me to that vizier Rashid so that I'd spy for you." Tomás poured well-watered wine into three goblets.

"It sounds rude when you say it that way." Pedro accepted wine from Tomás, who set a goblet by the busy clerk Doménec. "Listen, Tomás. I couldn't talk to you about this until I'd made sure. Especially since your mind has been elsewhere this winter. I inherited agents in Andalusia from my father. Many include people from your father's clan."

"My father's clan consists of a bevy of aging knights who lived in our house on Cyprus, plus the bonfraires he rode with in the

Outremer. After he left Morella, he never returned to his village or his tribe."

"Yet his clan hasn't forgotten him. Stories of Miquel's adventures made it back to your family, which is the largest Mozarab clan in Andalusia."

"My family? That's my sons, my brother, and my mother."

"These people in Jaén consider Miquel one of theirs." Pedro sloshed wine in his cup, not interested in drinking it. "They asked me to send Miquel's son to help."

"Slay dragons with my magical sword?"

"To rescue a daughter who's imprisoned near the frontier. If you do that, they promise to commit the entire Rodriguez clan to help us in Andalusia."

"That emissary from the caliph is a traitor?"

"No, he's an orphan they promoted into the caliph's court, to gain favor there in case—"

"In case the Christian invasion is a failure."

"Exactly. Your clan has played many sides for generations, always backing the winners."

"So, I rescue the maiden with El Cid's sword, the one not made in Castile. And in return, my clan, whom my father cursed as duplicitous liars, delivers Andalusia to your Christian army."

"That sounds overly grand. I need you to take advantage of this connection. Travel with your cousin the vizier, who'll bring you close to the caliph. Do what you can to disrupt their plans."

"And if I rescue the princess?"

"Many taifa generals on the frontier are unhappy that the caliph is dragging them into war. You and all your clan cousins must let them know that we Christian kings intend only to remove the invading caliph and restore their local governors."

Tomás shook his head, refusing. He settled back on the bench beside Pedro. "You once sent me into Minerve to help end the siege. This year, you made me marry that little widowed cousin of yours. I need a real fight, Monsenyor, not yet another half-witted failure."

Pedro held up his open palm, a false gesture of defeat. "Minerve was a fiasco. But it is I who should have done better for that city."

"*Òc*, Simon de Montfort burned half the people." Tomás had failed Isabella then, too, and swore he'd never...

"Not your fault, Tomás." Pedro clapped a hand on Tomás's knee. "However, your marriage to my cousin Dolç is a success. Your only job is to protect her land from any French crusader that my wife might force her to marry. You succeeded by just being alive."

"They're merely bandits, not crusaders." Tomás considered all of Simon's crusaders to be bandits. "And my new wife's agents torture me daily, arguing about oven rents and salt-pan tolls."

"Hmm. Not the best use of your talents, *mon amic*. I'll send a steward to do the mundane work while you attend to my business." Pedro studied a parchment Doménec laid before him and then signed it. Doménec applied the seal.

"You want me to spy in Andalusia."

The inside of Tomás's head banged like the hammering at an iron smithy. "God in the golden heavens with all the weeping angels, I am a warrior, not a vomit-eating spy."

"I'd never think otherwise, Don Tomás. But I need someone in Andalusia that I trust, who isn't scheming for a place of power and who can send me honest news. Circumstances make you the best choice for that."

"Best choice? I'm flattered, but surely others could do better."

"The best man. The only choice." Pedro pushed another parchment back to Doménec. "Now, whenever you meet one of my agents there, he'll say, 'Do good to people and you'll enslave their hearts.' You can't ask him to say the words, of course. Wait for it."

"That's what you've claimed since you first talked about Andalusia. You want people to prefer your governors more than their former overlords."

"The idea comes from *De Re Militari*, which my father thumped me with when I was still in christening clothes. You don't need to spy. Just help people decide not to help the caliph. He's an invading interloper."

"I haven't agreed to go, Monsenyor." Tomás fingered the leather-wrapped hilt of his sword, the one Miquel stole in Damascus.

Pedro pretended not to hear. "When my agent recites those words, you say, 'I'm more famous than fire on a mountain.' Only say it in the local dialect, of course."

"That's an Arab proverb." One of Tomás's masters in Cairo repeated it whenever he was in his cups.

"Or a prophecy. Only you can do what I need in Andalusia."

"No. I can't leave Sebastián and Yusuf. Especially Yusuf. He's not ready to be alone in the world."

"They'll be with me when we meet again at midsummer, *mon amic.*" Pedro studied another letter Doménec placed in front of him. "We must finish and head home by the Feast of St-Peter and St-Paul. Else, our food rots, and we fight deserters instead of infidels."

"Eight days after the solstice." Doménec translated, as if Tomás didn't know the calendar of feasts. The scribe tapped his foot, impatient over Tomás's presence in the king's work room.

"All winter Sebastián and I talked about riding together in his first real battle." Tomás slipped his sword into its sheath. "But instead, you want me to crawl into your enemy's den like a viper."

"Didn't your father send you into the world at their age? Let Sebastián take his place as Master of Valerós. Yusuf needs to be with my scribes, where he can work as a real scholar."

Doménec cleared his throat in polite agreement. Doménec, whom Yusuf judged harshly.

"*Mon fraire.*" Pedro rose from the work table to embrace Tomás, his voice warm and intimate. Behind him, Doménec flushed rust-red. "You've been lost in grief. What do you need that will cause you to do this for me?"

"*Ai.*" Tomás spoke low. The ground moved under his boots. "Another time I'd do it in an instant. But I can't choose between you and my sons."

"You have no choice." Pedro tapped the bonfraire brand on Tomás's wrist. "*Sodalitas, fidelitas, virtus.* Do it, on your honor as a brother at arms. And because I still love you and want to see you alive in the world again."

The clerk, astonished, failed to hide his jealousy.

"I'm still willing to die for you, *mon amic*." Tomás lifted his chin, silently daring Doménec to go so far for Pedro. "But what about my sons?"

"Who better to care for them than your bonfraire?" Pedro whispered in his ear. "I pledge my honor and promise their safety."

3

A Day in Toulouse

AVRAHAM THE TRADER KNOCKED at the villa's front door to make his delivery. This wasn't the only wealthy man in Toulouse who sought what Avraham had to sell, but who didn't want to be seen coming into the trader's workshop in a marketplace alley. In times past, Avraham often sent the goods and waited for the customer's servant to bring payment, but Avraham needed to be paid today. His landlord of thirty years had turned dour, insisting that the rents be paid the day they were due.

'I have others prepared to take this shop if you can't pay rent.'

Which was a lie. Few people had returned from sheltering in the countryside after Simon de Montfort's last threat of siege. But the landlord, like many other merchants, was consumed with the fear and greed that governed business in Toulouse. Therefore, Avraham stood knocking like an errand-boy at this villa's heavy wooden door, keen to trade an ancient, fraying copy of some saint's gospel for enough silver to keep his family safely sheltered, at least until after Passover.

The servant who answered Avraham's knock listened impatiently while Avraham explained that he'd been summoned by the villa's master, that this was the appointed time, and no, he couldn't leave his package in the servant's care.

At last, the ill-disposed servant, a dark-browed Toulousain native, led Avraham to a tiny alcove off the main entryway and pointed to a wobbly three-legged wooden stool where he could wait.

The house seemed empty. Even the kitchen servants had stepped out, not shutting the door that led to the alley. That morning, one of those indolent days in February, weather disguised as spring had crept into the city, the sky dressed in bright blue, the air scented by new-growth herbs in garden-boxes outside every kitchen door. People hailed each other in the alley with unguarded friendliness, prompted by the sun and an unseasonably warm breeze. Wafting over the green smell of false spring, the kitchen emitted its own odors. One of the final big feasts of the Christian winter festivals stewed on the kitchen hearth.

"*Hola, gos!*" A voice barked close by. *Hello, dog.*

Startled, Avraham glanced around. A tapestry-covered, latticed screen separated this alcove from a nearby room. A man's voice greeted a dog in Catalan rather than the local tongue. A large dog pitter-pattered over the marble floor and snuffled while the man ruffled its fur and murmured *bon gos bon gos.* More footsteps. Two other men entered, joining in to pet the dog.

Avraham, hoping for the villa's master to appear and pay him, didn't recognize the voices.

"Are you in town for long?" A high, scratchy voice. A courtier's accent. Not the villa owner.

"Weeks at most. Just to gather gold and men." A deeper, rougher voice, with accents from another city. Narbonne?

"The men on this list will pay for your army. But you'll need to spend time in the saddle, collecting their gold." That high voice bothered Avraham's ears. Like a tool screeching across metal. "Speak only about this summer's enterprise. Not our greater work."

"I'd hate to put the piss up any sniveling seigneur's ass." A rough voice indeed. A soldier's rhythm.

"What is it you seek, *mon amic?*" That irritating voice creaked like a bolt twisting in a rusted door hinge.

"Exactly as you preached. To honor the pope's desires and restore true glory to the Beaurain name. I have the strength to claim more than a bastard's lot."

Beaurain? Avraham had never met the old marquis, and the title had gone to some French crusader when Hugues de Beaurain died. A brother? Yes, that was it. A decade ago, a bastard Beaurain brother had pawned his armor, using Avraham's borrowed gold to live one winter in Toulouse, then reclaimed his goods to join the crusade that foundered in Constantinople. What was the man's name?

"We certainly hope so." Rusty man spoke in an accent from the lower Rhone. "For years, the stakes have been life and death for the Beaurain legacy."

"Life and death?" The third man finally spoke. A familiar voice. Colomb, that was the third man. The Beaurain scion had pawned his armor again last year. Broke as he'd been then, Colomb was memorable for being haughtier than any other knights who came to Avraham's shop. "No, we merely failed to live as men of honor should. Real men, not coddled troubadours."

"Not butterflies crammed up a randy king's backside."

After that insult about butterflies, the squeaky man muttered words Avraham couldn't make out. The rough-speaking soldier snorted in disgust again.

"Am I the last rational man in Christendom? I know what God wants from me. To fetch heretics' gold from their lairs. To pierce hearts and let the blood of heretics and Jews flow in our gutters."

Avraham wasn't supposed to hear this. Yet he needed to be paid. He determined not to listen, instead sniffing the warm kitchen odors that drifted up from the kitchen. He wondered what the cook added to the pot besides onions and garlic, the essential base for every sauce. Meanwhile, the men behind the screen moved away, so only a drone carried to Avraham's alcove. The dog padded out to the hallway, turned in a circle, and then settled on a mat by the door, burying its massive snout in shaggy black paws.

Avraham assessed the cook's choices.

A mixed dish. *Escudella i carn d'olla*, which simmered in most kitchens in the south. Turnips, chick peas, and cabbage with meat. Probably sausage, since it was winter. In spite of this one day's warmth, it would be weeks before spring lamb appeared in the Toulouse market stalls.

He closed his eyes, concentrating on the odors.

Cinnamon. Saffron.

This house was wealthier than most, but if he hadn't already known that, those expensive perfumes proved it.

The dog poked its head up, raised its snout, and then sunk its head back down on huge hairy paws, watching Avraham.

Pork, of course. Familiar from the marketplace.

Done, then, with those kitchen smells, Avraham again sought the ephemeral early-spring scents from the alley, thinking of what his wife must be cooking for their midday meal. He'd brought her a rabbit from the market yesterday, so she'd be braising it and then serve it with broad beans, perfuming the pot with coriander or rosemary. Perhaps fresh herbs, since a few bushes in the alleys bore hints of spring flowering, awakening after the long winter. His daughter Léal, such a sweet and faithful companion to her mother, must be chopping onions at this moment, laughing at Hanna's insistence that every vegetable be cut just so.

"I will continue to lay out the bodies of heretics and their lovers for the crows and wolves to feast."

The visitor's voice shouted near Avraham's ear. When Avraham jerked at the sound, that big black dog glared at him, its ears perked, sniffing to determine whether Avraham might be a friend.

Avraham averted his eyes so the beast didn't feel challenged.

Where was the seigneur of this domus? This was a big household, the size of a small village, which a true seigneur ruled. But only the seigneur could conclude this business. It was long past the appointed hour for Avraham to be paid and go on his way.

.

That enormous wolf-dog rose from the mat and shook its pitch-black mane, more the size of a pony than a dog. Glancing at the men in the other room, it padded down the hallway toward Avraham, who tried not to hear the conversation on the other side of the partition.

Colomb spoke. "Do you think Simon de Montfort should be even more ruthless? Many believe he's done an archangel's hard work, getting so many castle-towns under interdict for sheltering heretics. Arracheuse, Valerós, and Quéribus are next, since you've done your work properly."

The smaller, squeaky-voiced man said, "The archbishop is tardy in giving Valerós better heirs. The strongest man should lead. Òc, I mean you."

"You are kind to say so." The soldier-man softened for a heart-beat, but then toughened up again. "Simon lets the pope hold his balls. I'm happy to drench my sword in heretics' blood. I'll bathe in it, if it stops this blighted heresy. Why wait for Church courts?"

Colomb de Beaurain broke his silence again. "Many here believe Pedro can unite all the lords of the south. That will change things."

"Pedro can unite with the devil." The rough soldier exploded. "By God's own white breeches, he's bent the natural order of things. He wants to rule even more than God gave him."

"But Philippe Augustus also wants to seize our damned home-land." Colomb growled his complaint. "The Pays de France isn't enough for that king. He only used heresy as an excuse to let his knights invade us."

The dog rested its snout on Avraham's knee, apparently used to being petted and praised by every man it met. Avraham held out a hand to let the dog sniff him. It licked his fingers, drenching them in sticky dog-spit.

The little rust-man spoke, indignant. "These heretics curse sal-vation. Like Saracens and Jews and donkeys, they aren't even human. An ill-trained dog deserves more care."

"Heretics?" The rough soldier scoffed. "They're just filthy poor people grubbing for more than God gave them. Half are mestitz trash, too lazy to work, living off their hard-working cousins."

The dog sniffed further up Avraham's thigh, burying its snout in his lap. He scratched the animal's huge skull in the way dogs like. Alas, he scratched with his spit-drenched hand and came away coated with winter-thick fur.

"Is your own sword the answer to everything?" Colomb had a voice as big as the other soldier, but spoke softly.

"I'm a knight of the Crux Lunata," the soldier thundered. "We will reclaim the south for God-loving men, like the first crusaders took Jerusalem from the Saracens."

"The pope called a halt to Simon's crusade while Pedro battles the Saracens." Colomb's soft, niggling words seemed to light a bonfire in the hot-burning soldier.

"Pedro deceived the pope on his coronation day and every day since." The soldier cursed Pedro d'Aragón. "Worse for us, if Pedro succeeds in Andalusia, he'll be a hero everywhere.

Colomb said, "Yet if Pedro fails, no king will go up against the Moors for a hundred years."

Profound curses again. "Let the kings of Castile worry about the Moors. We have our own lands to reconquer for God and honor."

Silence lingered. Then the small scratchy voice asked, "You truly believe you were born to this? Anointed by God?"

"Simon claims he's God's hammer, but I am God's sword, hot from the anvil, the edge honed by God Himself."

"What passion!" Colomb didn't sound convinced.

"Don't laugh. I want honor for our Beaurain name again. If I don't act, it will eat at my heart."

"As our leader commands, you will use the sword and Grail to stop this abomination," the little man said.

Avraham searched his memory. Grail? The dog simpered, nosing Avraham's hand for more scratching. A big dog, an enormous simper.

A tall, broad man peered around the screen, but not a man that Avraham knew.

"You there! What are you about?"

"*Excuse me.*" Avraham meekly begged to be excused in the Castilian dialect he'd learned from his grandmother, who longed for Toledo until the day she died. "*I'm an old man and don't hear well.*"

"What's that devil's tongue?" The big man growled like his dog, which perked its ears at the sound. "Why are you here, you old Jew?"

Avraham, assuming innocence, again said, "*Excuse me.*"

"It's a Toledo tongue." The smaller man wore a priest's habit. "At the congress of bishops, some men there spoke that tongue."

"But I'd wager my soul they weren't filthy Jews."

"They do things differently in Toledo," Colomb said, still on the other side of the screen.

Not understanding Avraham's words, the men summoned the servants, insisting that this old Jew be confined to the kitchen until the villa's master returned.

From an even wobblier stool by the kitchen fire, Avraham worried. Hanna and Leal waited for him, likely delaying their midday bread and soup. Yet God provided no choices except to wait for the master's return. Hanna could cope with customers visiting Avraham's shop. But Avraham needed to be home when the landlord came at nightfall, demanding the rent.

He breathed the porcine scent of that stew through the whole afternoon, no one speaking or glancing his way.

.

Dusk had long since fallen by the time the villa's master appeared and then dallied while haggling with Avraham over how much gold to pay. The wind blew away the day's taste of false spring, carrying in a frigid cold from the mountains.

Avraham tied that small leather purse to his belt and pulled his surcoat close. When the villa door clanged shut behind him, he hurried into the brooding twilight. With no food or water since breakfast, he was eager to be home, but more eager that his wife Hanna not have to answer to the landlord rapping at the door, demanding payment. Stepping cautiously through the littered back alleys, he stuck to the lengthening shadows, having had enough of feigning the humble merchant for one day. Home was all he wanted.

The new bell at St-Sernin church rang, and the half-finished building disgorged people from the Christians' evening service. Avraham paused near the mouth of one alley, waiting for the crowd to disperse before he crossed the square to the street where his household waited for him. The kitchen fires will have warmed the place. Hanna will have lit rush lamps. She'd take his surcoat, relieving him of the day's burdens and worries.

"*Hola, gos!*"

A voice hailed a dog in Catalan dialect. The same as the man who decried Beaurain honor? A nearby huddle of friends embraced each other, slapping backs. One man said, "You are the true dog here," while others laughed.

The square was almost empty, other men as eager to be home and out of the windy cold as he was. That cluster of jovial men ambled away from where Avraham now stood, where he wanted to follow as soon as possible. Instead of crossing the square openly, he slipped into a passage among the clutter of winter-time market stalls.

But two steps into the shadows and that black beast of a dog was at his side again, pushing at him, demanding attention, as if Avraham was its only hope for another skull-scratching.

"Come, dog!"

The gruff voice hollered three times for his pet to come, but the dog just stood there, swiveling its huge head between Avraham and its master's voice, wagging its tail.

"What have you got there?"

The soldier-man from the villa blocked the passageway, armed now. The lights from the church created shadows, the longest one falling over Avraham. Behind him, a clutch of young men appeared, all wearing the overcoats of the White Brotherhood, the volunteers the bishops had sanctioned to hunt heretics in Toulouse.

"You? Animal!"

Just like when Avraham was a child, the first blow hurt worse than he imagined. The second seemed to sharpen his mind.

4

A Night in Barcelona

Tomás at Palau Reial of the Count of Barcelona
February 2, Candlemas Night

"ARE YOU WELL, FATHER?"

Yusuf tugged at the sleeve of Tomás's leather jerkin.

"It's been a hard day." Tomás hated keeping this secret from his son. But Pedro insisted. Secrets can't last if more than two know.

"Sit with Sebastián and me at dinner." Yusuf pointed to trestle tables that teemed with thick-skulled Aragón donzels. Sons of lords who'd be knights one day, whether or not they ever learned to fight.

"Perhaps later. Stay with Sebastián so you get home safely. You know I worry."

"You worry too much, Father. I'll wait and come home with you later, when I finish my lesson with that scribe Doménec."

"*Ai, fadrin.* Don't wait for me." Tomás intended to stop at home only for his armor and silver before leaving on Pedro's mission. He paused with his hand on Yusuf's shoulder, for a goodbye that couldn't be said aloud.

A figure stepped away from the crowd in the hall, standing uncomfortably close, touching his arm, tugging his attention away from Yusuf. The scent of lavender distracted him.

"Don Tomás, isn't it? We met at the king's Twelfth Night feast."

An Aragónese senhóra stood in the dim torchlight, dark curls cascading over her shoulders and breasts in a scandalous way. His stomach tightened whenever a woman stood too close, his blood slowed in his veins.

"That was more than a lifetime ago." Tomás took her hand in the way southern ladies appreciated, quelling his impulse to flee. Yusuf, sensitive to nuance, drifted away, saying he'd find Sebastián.

"I tried to capture your eye at dinner last night." She spoke in a familiar Aragónese burr. And she held his hand too long, pressing the mound at the base of his thumb.

"*Ai Dèu!* I hope I haven't been rude."

"Not at all, senhór. The king commands your attention."

"You have my attention at this moment, ma dòmna."

"Just for the moment?" The senhóra moved closer, her breath a sweet mist on his lips. "I have business to discuss with you."

■

"My husband is so excited about the news that El Cid is your ancestor. He wants you to carry his banner into Andalusia. It will inspire his knights."

The man's magnificently ruined face twisted into what Senhóra Petronilla guessed—hoped!—was a smile, acknowledging that she'd both surprised and flattered him. She led the man into an alcove, so thrilled to be alone with the Moor that she was sure he felt her heart thunder when she clasped his hand to her breast.

"Your husband?"

"Don Carlos of Toledo. Alfonso's liaison to Pedro. You must know that a man of Castile will value a son of the Cid far more than Aragón can."

"I don't know how these stories get started." He laughed, as if he knew exactly how. His voice like burning honey, he spoke in the common tongue but with an odd accent that she'd never heard before. "I'm not for sale, ma dòmna. I'm a swordmaster. I don't carry banners."

"But, Don Tomás, everyone knows you were a mercenary before Pedro took you into his court. They say you were taught by secret assassins in the Holy Land."

"People like to invent exotic stories." His ruined lips twisted again. "Did you hear stories from that clerk Doménec? He's often mistaken."

This man, Tomás, exuded a beast-like sensuality, smelling of spice and leather, burning hotter than other people, and kindling a heat like when she first learned to play in the court of love. "With

45

this man," Carlos had whispered moments before, grasping her arm hard enough to bruise, "you must win or die failing."

Her fingers stroked the back of Tomás's hand, so much more powerful than Carlos's, and ventured up his forearm. Euphoric with her own daring, she shared the excuse she'd dreamed up to capture his attention, sure he'd say yes. "Everyone knows you trained as an assassin. To protect my honor, would you kill someone for me? I have gold to pay you. My own gold, not my husband's."

"I don't kill for money. I'm not a performing beast."

She shifted closer on the settee, so her breath caressed the fine hairs near his ears.

"What sort of beast are you?"

He shivered. The dim light revealed the original, handsome foundation of his face. His powerful shoulders and narrow hips caused her to advance faster than she intended, whispering a simple spell. Aloud, she said, "Do you find me beautiful?"

"Òc, amiga. But out of respect to my wife, I do not dally."

She held his hand and traced with his finger down her forehead to her lips. She kissed and sucked his finger. Then she mouthed the words of a binding spell against his neck in the guise of a gentle kiss. He tilted her head and kissed her lips with the ardor that the spell always rouses. But beyond the binding spell, this man knew how to kiss a woman, to make her forget the material world. She twisted her fingers in his hair and pulled at his shoulders, urging him into her arms. Her lips buried in that thick mane of hair, she whispered the next refrain of the spell. He pressed against her, so she felt the power coiled in his loins. But then he pinioned her elbows so she was powerless to caress him. The inability to master the man pushed her into a frenzy that demanded relief.

A hand thrust aside the alcove's heavy curtain.

"Someone is already doing the sweet thing here," an Aragónese voice drawled.

The light from the branch of candles in the hall fell on her, leaving the Moor in the shadows.

"Ai, what's this?" Don Tomás touched that wretched tattoo on her clavicle. He drew her robe closed. "This is the sign of my enemy, whose men have worked to destroy me and my family."

"No, it's only my husband's clan sign. I wish nothing for you but glory and honor. My husband can offer you more gold this year than you can earn in a lifetime. He knows a son of the Cid deserves honor."

"Why does a woman of Aragón carry this sign?"

"My husband insisted." She was still close enough to whisper binding spells. "It's a clan sign from the ancient side of his mother's family." *You will be mine. You will free me.*

"I can't do this, ma dòmna."

She consoled, in the way one must when a man can't perform. Abruptly, he pushed her away, righted his clothes, tied back his hair.

She twisted the ties of his leather jerkin. "Of course. The king calls. Come to my house after Pedro dismisses everyone."

"No." He batted her hands away.

"I'm not used to being told no." She pouted, which worked with any man she'd ever known. "My life is without passion. You saw what my husband forced on me. I need you to free me. Open your heart to warm me as a kindness."

"I'm married. And I have no heart. My father removed it when I came of age."

She laughed, then saw he wasn't jesting. "You won't be married much longer. Come to me when you're free. Until then, seek Don Carlos. The Cid's son will fare best in this life if allied with Castile."

"I can't carry your husband's banner. I serve Pedro. Perhaps you need to hire a lover, not an assassin."

"*Baquelar!*" She spat, condemning the smug bastard as a rogue.

Then she contemplated how to tell Don Carlos a story that sounded like a victory.

•

"Monsenyor, let's agree not to deceive ourselves. I'm unlikely meet you at midsummer."

Tomás stared glumly at his portion of the farewell meal to which Pedro had invited him. He stared off at one of the blind arches in the great hall. The Romans of old times built that wall, or so Pedro claimed.

"You know where the army will bivouac on the way home. You'll find us."

"I mean, it's far more likely I die."

"That's true for most choices you've ever made." Pedro attacked a roasted quail with gusto. "And just as likely if you ride into battle. But your clan assures me that you can turn to them for protection. And this is a cheaper, faster way to get to Andalusia."

"Òc, cheaper. The Church and a few lords get rich off this adventure. Which proves that crusading is now merely a business."

"It always has been. But please keep that secret." Pedro didn't censure Tomás for impertinence. "However, the pope didn't declare a crusade. This is just an enterprise of peace, bringing the Cross back to shine on people."

"Òc? Pèire Leteric claimed that if it's not about Jerusalem, it's better just to be paid to fight. The way Valerós works for you. For gold, not forgiveness."

Pedro cast a bone aside with delicacy. "I'm not doing this for gold or forgiveness. If I win territory for Christendom, I have greater power than Simon de Montfort. The power to do right for people in the south."

"A proud declaration, *mon amic*." Tomás liked that, but couldn't tell if the silent, jealous Domènec also agreed. "However, if this adventure fails—"

"Not possible. I cannot leave failure for either my sons or God to repair." Pedro lifted his wine cup, subtly pointing when he changed the subject. "Your son is well-respected by his peers."

Sebastián, his bright auburn hair gleaming under the torches, sat with a gaggle of squires and donzels who listened spell-bound while he (most likely) told a tale about living through the siege at Minerve. Or perhaps about riding camels in Egypt.

At the edge of the donzels, Yusuf toyed with his food and watched a pair of jugglers. In the torchlight, the boy appeared as startlingly beautiful as a girl, save for his Adam's apple, sharp as the knobs of bone at his wrists. A Barcelonese donzel behind him swung an elbow, jabbing Yusuf in the spine, knocking him off balance and scattering food to the floor. Yusuf scooted down the bench, away from the young lord who attacked him.

"Yes, that's my son, Monsenyor."

"He's at that awkward age."

The woman from the alcove stood in the doorway, tapping her foot. When she spied Tomás on Pedro's dais, she made a sign that shepherds use to ward off evil. Or so he'd been told.

"And you worry about him," Pedro was saying.

"He's an innocent. How do I keep him safe in this world?" A servant offered a cup of wine that Tomás accepted while still locked in a battle of wills with the woman across the room. She made another sign that, for all Tomás knew, invited the devil to carry him to hell as soon as possible.

"You must have looked just like him then. How did you fend off advances?"

"That isn't what I meant." Tomás swallowed the bitter wine. "I can't convince him to learn to fight. He says it goes against the grain, because he's a scholar. I only understand steel. I don't know what a scholar needs in the world."

"You've taken on too much of the burden of fatherhood. Do as other men do. Leave your sons to learn how to be men from their uncles and teachers."

"You've never even lived with your son." Tomás sipped his wine. "Your son is still a baby. You don't feel what I do."

"Are we going to argue this? First you assert I don't know what it is to love a wife above all else. Then I assert that you don't know what it is to be married to hell's minion, as I am." Pedro shuddered. "Besides, I feel more for my son, because he will inherit my burden. To serve as God's agent, caring for other men's lives."

Tomás pushed at the bird carcass on his plate with his knife. "God's agent. Does that make me God's subaltern?"

"Don't blaspheme. Or at least save it for later tonight when you and I need to feign a severe quarrel, so that I can banish you. Then, if you are recognized elsewhere in the world, rumors of our quarrel will protect you. Just don't tell anyone the truth."

"My sons. They need to know the truth."

"If we tell anyone, then everyone will know."

"My sons can be trusted," Tomás said, "and I can't live with the idea that they might think I betrayed you."

"Fine. I'll tell them myself. But I'll tell your wife a different story. She's my cousin and will understand that it's a story she's supposed to repeat."

"Monsenyor, earlier tonight someone said I won't be married much longer. What does that mean?"

"Doménec sent a request to the bishop to annul your marriage. It was never a great idea. Since you're leaving, it's now proving I had a very poor idea."

"Dolç is the gentlest soul alive. Am I supposed to explain this to her before I leave?"

"The annulment claims your new marriage isn't consummated," Pedro said. "I'll find her another husband right away."

"But it was." Tomás sipped his wine, embarrassed to confess to Pedro. "The night the contract was signed. She insisted, and I was too drunk to be sensible."

"You'll have to lie about that." Pedro spoke too quietly for Doménec to hear.

"She'd never lie to the Church. Dolç is like a saint."

"But she's not a delicate flower. She was raised to marry as she's told. I need her to have a husband who can protect her lands."

Tomás considered that morning's attack. "Monsenyor, I create danger for the people I'm supposed to protect. Will you guard her while I'm gone?"

"It is done, *mon amic.*"

"And Yusuf?"

Pedro's eyes bore into him. "I promise to keep Yusuf with me. I worry that your boy isn't a Christian."

"His mother had him baptized."

"It didn't appear to take. He isn't a son of Islam either. He's neither fish nor fowl. I can't let him wander the streets without Christian direction."

"And Sebastián?"

"He'll be in the Valerós camp, where Marshal Guillem and Father Anselm can guide him." Pedro set down his dinner knife. "In fact, I asked your brother Chrétien to join us.

50

"He'll say no. Chrétien takes care of our mother since she came to Toulouse. He's likely fat and happy, playing steward for Sebastián's estates. He'll never take up the sword again."

"Jealous that he's happy?" Pedro paused, catching sight of the woman who glared at Tomás. "A bad situation."

"Òc, an unpleasant situation. That senhóra wants to hire me for acts I can't agree to."

"More likely she seeks what she can't get from her husband."

"How do you know?"

"Petronilla is my cousin, married to—"

"*Ai*, who isn't your cousin?" Tomás swallowed more of the too-bitter wine.

"Her husband Carlos tolerates a great deal from that senhóra. He seems to keep her under control, but watch yourself." Though Pedro spoke lightly, that worry-line deepened. "Fortunately, my servant sails for Andalusia on the morning tide."

■

Tomás, retching in the gutter, knew he hadn't drunk enough wine to leave him on his knees, puking. Heaving up what must be his own life's blood.

He struggled to stand, squinting in the misty predawn. How far from the Palau Reial? How far to his own home?

Home. *Bon Dèu*. He still clenched the badly written note from his meek little wife, begging him to come home, promising news of the greatest importance.

Come home. To the last place on God's own earth he wanted to be.

Tomás leaned against a wall. The nearby gate belonged to a fat seigneur who lived two doors from Tomás's villa. Smelling his own bile, he bent double, retching again.

"Do you require assistance, senhór?" A voice spoke close by, closer than Tomás allowed anyone to stand.

"Help him straight to hell. The devil awaits." A woman's Aragónese voice rang out beside him, just when he again gagged up more from his poisoned insides. "I offered you gold. I offered you the world. And what I receive is a thrashing. How am I supposed to make Don Carlos happy?"

Then it began. A punch into his solar plexus forced him to his knees in the gutter. Across the kidneys. A kick in the face and then his aching middle again. Beyond thinking, he cried out to his father for protection.

"Father, help me!"

A hooded behemoth hulked over him with a knife, slicing at Tomás's shirt, cutting him. Tomás couldn't breathe to beg for mercy.

"Dig deeper, Bescanó." A woman's voice.

"That's enough, ma dòmna. More is a crime."

"God wouldn't think so. *Baquelar!*"

One last kick to his belly.

"Don Carlos still promises everything to the son of the Cid. But me? No. You'll have to beg Carlos yourself."

Then Tomás was alone, still cringing in fear of the next boot to his gut. Grasping the stones of the wall at the front of the fat seigneur's villa, he stumbled along its length to his own house. He fumbled with the gate, couldn't make it work, so he knocked to rouse that gentle old man who opened it when Tomás came home at night.

"*Per l'amor de Dèu!* Let me in!" Tomás called, unable to remember the man's name.

Then he cursed, in the way only Miquel's son knew how to call on both angels and devils.

·

The entire household came to the gate, including the cook and three frightened little girls who gripped their mama's skirts and cried. Dolç, her hands on the girls' dark curly heads, shushed them.

"Send your girls back to bed, ma dòmna." Tomás held a hand over his damaged face, since it always upset her children. Then he tasted his own blood and saw his battered hands were a worse sight than his face.

While Dolç sorted everyone out, Tomás sat alone on her weaving porch, as miserable as he'd ever been. He intended to slip out with his travel kit, not to see anyone when he left. His blood dripped on her immaculate tile floor. "*Bazasa! Putana! Mignotta!*" Coughing foul names in every language he knew, Tomás cursed the woman Petronilla and whatever foul scheme she'd hatched, the room spinning around him.

"Lie down. Let me help."

For the next few moments, he had no choice but to let her take care of him, exactly what he'd resisted every day since Pedro thrust them together. She bathed his face with scented water, rinsed the blood and filth from his hair.

"I'm afraid your poor face needs a stitch or two, senhór."

"Call that physician from Valencia. The one who lives in the Jewish quarter." He hated thrusting this chore on her, when they'd lived in this house as strangers.

"Let me. I stitched up the cook when he…" Her words drifted off while she gathered thread and a needle from her sewing things. "Shall I call Amfos to brace you?"

Amfos! Of course! His name is Amfos. "No, ma dòmna, I don't need his help. Only yours."

Tomás had been stitched up too many times to be bothered by it. Yet every poke of the needle seemed to hurt Dolç. He tried to reassure her, but his tongue was too thick to speak clearly. After she snipped the thread, he sat up, trying to stand, but she pressed him down. She was so tiny, smaller than he ever noticed, but right then, she pressed him down with one hand.

"My sword. Where is it? Damn all to the lesser devils! Where is my sword?"

"Don't get up, Don Tomás. Your sword is right by you. You're bleeding too much. You need more stitches. Please take off that filthy shirt, or I'll have to cut it off."

Obedient, he yanked it off, dragging wet cloth over his face.

"Sancta Maria, you've made your face filthy again." She gently scolded while washing his face and then his blood-smeared belly. When she took the wet linen away, she gasped.

An equal-armed cross carved over his heart leaked crimson in the center and at the crescent points at each arm of the cross.

After washing him, Dolç threaded her needle again, biting her lip while she stitched the cuts closed, pausing often to wash away more blood. For Tomás, ignoring pain came as easily as mounting a horse. Cool fingers worked at the knot of shame and exhaustion in his neck and shoulders, left there by poison and the beating. The familiar lavender smell of southern women wafted over him, like incense in a cool sanctuary.

He jerked awake. "Stop. Why did you send for me, senhóra?"

Dolç's voice quavered. "What, senhór? Sit forward so I can tie this last bandage."

"The note you sent me at Pedro's." He reached for his sword and speared the ragged parchment. "This one."

She gaped at it stupidly, her eyes watering.

He read it aloud. "'Come home at once. I have important news for you.'"

"It's not from me, senhór."

"But here's your name. Dolç de St-Féliu."

"You know I can't read, senhór. Don't mock me."

Humiliated beyond any woman's or God's forgiveness, Tomás fumbled an apology. Aragónese voices echoed in the tiled entryway. The old man at the gate, Amfos, entered when Dolç beckoned.

"Excuse me, senhór. A senhóra's footman returned your jerkin."

The stained leather jerkin, with all the marks of his humiliation, had come home to him.

Home. Where he wasn't supposed to be.

Tomás slipped away into neither dream-filled sleep nor rational wakefulness, visiting the usual ghosts. A haunting thought jerked him to consciousness. What had Dolç done with the water and blood in her wash basin? A spell. That bruixa Petronilla poisoned him; another woman once cast a spell in wax to hurt him. Mages and conjurers steal blood to...

"Ma dòmna, the blood! Where is it? What did you do with the water?" Pain spiked up his side.

Dolç appeared in the archway, puzzled.

"Amfos tossed it in the privy," she said.

"In the dark?"

"Pardon, senhór. It's long past dawn." She gestured to where her weaving porch opened onto the garden.

Of course, it was. Candles and rushes didn't shed this much light. The tide had turned. He should have been at the docks, not cozied up in the house he longed to escape. Tomás had already failed Pedro in Andalusia, without even leaving town.

"Do you require anything, senhór? Perhaps a light breakfast? Here's water to drink. And your boy wants to thank you."

Fortuno, the lost child from the market, wiggled shyly beside Dolç. He was now dressed in donzel's clothes too large and too grand for any boy from Morella.

"*Per l'amor de Dèu*, what is he wearing?"

"Yusuf brought home clothes for the son of a don. I'll make it fit better, but it was all we could find yesterday when the markets were closing."

"Son of a don?"

"I thought, like Yusuf, you wanted him treated as an equal, whatever his mother's station."

"He's not my son." What a soulless fool he'd become. "Send him to work in the garden with Amfos. Do you like chickens, Fortuno?"

The child perked awake, nodding, uncomfortable in oversized velvets. "*Si*, senhór. Will we take the chickens when we go to Andalusia with Pedro?"

"No chickens." Tomás was abandoning yet another child to disappointment. "Ask Amfos to teach you your chores."

Dolç sent Fortuno on his way, murmuring kinder words than Tomás had managed.

"He's not my son." Tomás repeated it to ease Dolç's concerns. She worked so hard to make things good for everyone. "He'll have a better life with your servants than he's ever known."

A scramble behind the door. Every sound carried from Dolç's porch into the house. In the hall, Sebastián said, "Come with me. I'll show you simple defense moves."

"I prefer not." Yusuf's sweet, warm voice.

"But why?"

"I'm not fated to be a fighter."

"How can you know fate?"

"I read it in the stars," Yusuf said.

"At least carry my dagger, *mon fraire*. Do it as a favor to me."

"Yusuf." Dolç spoke the boy's name, likely to warn him that he was heard. Yusuf bounded in with a warm grin, the one that Tomás valued above all things. Then he saw Tomás.

"Father! You're hurt!"

Something painful had happened to his son's face since dinner. Bruises marred his mouth and brow.

"What happened to you?"

"Forgive me." Yusuf begged forgiveness. Then he lied, to make Tomás feel better about those injuries. "I tripped and cut myself on a sharp stone."

"The same street as the thorn bush that slit your eyebrow last week, *fadrin*?"

"It has healed well. If you wish, Father, I shall avoid that street."

"Face them. Sebastián can teach you to defend with—"

"I don't want to disappoint you, Father. Truly. But please understand, I wasn't born to wear a sword."

"You cannot disappoint me, *fadrin*." Tomás murmured the truth. "You need to learn to walk like a donzel. Those boys pick on you because you're different. Wear the clothes I bought you. Take off that cap."

"I prefer to wear my own clothes, Father. May I go? The scribe Doménec expects me at court."

"Be careful of that man, Yusuf."

"Yes, Father. He's neither as intelligent nor as educated as he thinks he is. I don't know why Pedro trusts him." Then Yusuf slipped away in that scrambling, jerky manner that made Barcelonese boys want to pound him.

No greater goodbye than any other morning when they parted. Tomás didn't call his son back. He couldn't think of one word that might make anything better. Loneliness already leaked from every pore, the way that blood still dripped from his wounds.

Dolç appeared in the doorway, leaning against it on one arm, as if all the strength she'd used to patch him up had drained away, the color gone from her face.

"Senhór? A messenger just came. Pedro asked the bishop to annul our marriage. Why did you not tell me?"

Why not? Because he was supposed to be gone by now, sailing on the morning tide for Al-Andalus.

Because Pedro promised to take care of everything.

Tomás pointed for Dolç to sit down, to discuss the new shape of the world. Unfortunately, he didn't have Pedro's permission to tell her the truth about where he was going and why. If it was Isabella, he'd tell her the secret, and she'd understand and keep the secret. But she was gone, speaking to him only in memory.

"Pedro will make sure you're cared for, in case I don't return from the expedition to Andalusia."

"Senhór, truly I'd prefer... Òc, I suppose I must do what Pedro and you ask of me." She smiled, the corners of her mouth twitching with sadness.

He'd broken a stranger's heart, just by living. Just by doing what Pedro asked. An inauspicious beginning.

5

A Night in Toulouse

Durán in Toulouse
February 2, Candlemas Night

"WE DANCE AS IF THE sun still rises."

The tall Celtic jongleur Chrétien, singing in the great hall of a Toulouse spice merchant, altered the words of an old *cançó d'amor*, the one where a rich man tricks a shepherdess into sharing favors and calls it love.

Startled out of reverie, Durán heard his lover sing what Durán had said at home in bed the night before. "The lords of Toulouse dance as if the sun still rises. As if people weren't dying from hunger or imprisoned under the bishop's command. Or killed by Simon de Montfort's *francimand* crusaders."

"*Ai, cor dolç*, you dance. I just sing." Chrétien had offered a familiar gesture of comfort. "Should we take up arms and go to battle for justice? Last year you persuaded me to give up life as a swordsman. But if you want to fight, then—"

"No." The word burst from deep inside. "I will never fight for God or king."

"*Ai*, my own Good Christian." Chrétien's voice, even teasing, warmed Durán deep in his soul. "My true love is as dedicated to peace as any other heretic in the south."

Durán let that familiar jest go by. Chrétien didn't value Durán's faith for any purpose other than a good joke. But then again, Durán was not a very well-practiced Good Christian.

"That sigh means you're fretting, Durán. I promise not to tease. What worries you?"

"Are we doing what's best for our *domus*?" Household, the *domus*, encompassed the villa, their villages, the farmers, and servants. "Either for our people in town or in the countryside?"

"Still growing into life as seigneur of Montcava? For two years now, you've left our crusts for the poor at the villa's gate."

"The gates where my mother used to beg." Durán settled into the comfort of Chrétien's arms. "I'm happy that Toulouse isn't under siege. But we need to do more, all the seigneurs, not just me. More than dancing and drinking every night."

Now, one night later, Chrétien sang those words in a sweet falsetto, to entertain people who drank and danced, oblivious in Toulouse.

'We dance as if the sun still rises.
As if birds still sing in the fields.'

"The Celt croons like an angel." A man's breath raised the hairs at the back of Durán's neck. "And such a handsome face."

"He has a gift." Indeed, Chrétien resembled an angel incarnate. Tall, flowing blond hair, the jut of his narrow jaw. Though Durán knew for a fact that Chrétien behaved least like an angel in any story.

"Is your *bon amic* an angel of light or darkness?" The man said *boyfriend*, not good friend. "Is his gift from your Good God or the other dark God who mires us in this world?"

Durán faced the man who presumed so much. It was the count of Foix, a wry spark in his eyes.

"It matters only whether one's gifts are used for good or evil." Durán parried in the way he'd learned from Chrétien.

"*Ai*, a sharp wit! I thought all goodmen and goodwomen had fled for the hills, taking wit and wisdom with them." He said goodmen, the way Good Christians referred to themselves.

The count swayed as if from too much Roussillon wine, but Durán knew, long before meeting Chrétien, that any thief or mountebank might feign a drunken swagger.

"While lesser men dance as if the sun still rises." The count's words were crisp, no wine-slur.

"Senhór?"

Durán hoped he'd learned from Chrétien to keep all traces of emotion from his face, even curiosity. The count's well-groomed hair and beard framed his heart-melting chestnut-brown eyes and expressive mouth. A mouth that belonged to a man who liked pleasure in bed. With women. Durán could always tell.

The count swayed and bumped his way toward the grand door that opened to the courtyard. He saluted Durán from the archway.

.

'We dance as if the sun still rises.
As if flowers will grow in our fields.'

Colomb de Beaurain guffawed.

A giant of a man, his golden hair a lion's mane, Colomb held court amid several young donzels who giggled in less-experienced registers whenever the older knight laughed.

"*Hola, gos!*" Colomb nudged the fellow next to him. "Listen to the *cavaller fada* sing a sad song."

Hey, dog. The way rowdy donzels hailed each other on the street. *Fairy knight.* What any rich donzel might shout. Lads who claimed respect as a birthright but never render respect to other men.

While Chrétien sang a final dolorous song, Durán watched his great-uncle Colomb carouse. The Roman Church had a host of words for family relations, from which Durán could choose several for Colomb. He'd learned about these tangled relations two years earlier when Chrétien rescued Durán from playing servant in the Montcava household.

First of all, one of Colomb's half-brothers had sired Durán's father Nicolau as a cuckoo in the Montcava nest, though this wasn't known beyond a few cousins. The people of Toulouse didn't know Colomb was Durán's paternal great-uncle.

Second, Sebastián of Valerós—who inherited all of Montcava from Nicolau—acknowledged Durán as his half-brother. When Sebastián vowed never to return to Toulouse, he'd made Durán seigneur. Therefore, Colomb should acknowledge their kinship, at least privately.

But third, the Marquis Hugues de Beaurain, Colomb's older half-brother, had married Hélène, one of Durán's many Montcava cousins. So Durán could call Colomb "half-brother-in-law to my third-degree cousin." However, Durán chose to call Colomb uncle, and felt they should also acknowledge their fellowship.

Colomb's hand brushed over the buttocks of the ample-breasted woman leaning on his arm, laughing again at Chrétien's sad refrain.

From a decade of seeking love and friendship on the streets of Toulouse, Durán knew how to judge a man's nature. Thirty years older than Durán, Colomb considered himself handsome. They'd both inherited the Beaurain fighter's build and full wavy hair (though Colomb's was streaked with silver threads). Colomb had a sun-burned-but-proud Beaurain chin and sharp cheekbones. Yet sun, wine, and years living in armed camps showed in his deep crow's feet, a yellowing around his pale blue eyes, a slackening of the gaunt neck cords holding up that proud head.

Colomb used his Beaurain surname to gain entry into Toulouse's villas. A soldier-for-hire, he smiled with a haughty nod while negotiating mercenary services for wealthy Toulousain merchants.

With a leer when charming a woman over supper.

With a sneer for the underling who held his horse and received his pile of chainmail, arms, and gambeson.

As much as Durán and Colomb shared—standing taller than most in the south, enjoying privilege, enduring bastardy—Durán distrusted the man. Even his swagger seemed false.

Still clutching that woman, Colomb ambled across the court to another of their host's rooms, where seigneurs gathered to toss dice.

Done singing, Chrétien joined Durán with his usual wide-awake, animated need to find adventure. Durán preferred they go home to bed. At the door to the front courtyard, Durán retrieved his walking staff. Chrétien settled his oud into its leather case and sent it home with a footman, and then buckled his sword over his jongleur's velvet finery.

"While singing, I could see every man in the room." Chrétien murmured for only Durán to hear. "But the sole man worth watching was flirting with a handsome man much older and richer than I."

"Older, richer. But not more handsome. Are we riding to visit your mother tomorrow?" Durán learned long before not to rise to Chrétien's bait. "She expects us at Fontcours for mardi gras."

"Òc. The food will be better than the burro-fodder they serve in this city." Chrétien touched Durán's shoulder, directing his attention. "Look there. Your flirt is about to—"

Colomb de Beaurain stepped in front of Durán, standing so close that Durán smelled Rhône wine and garlic from the *risotto de conill* their host served at dinner. Then Colomb stepped aside, replaced by his companion, a tall seigneur often seen at Colomb's side in Toulouse. What was the man's name? Ah, Matheus of Xirgú. A Montcava third- or fourth-cousin through his mother, though Durán couldn't recall the precise relationship, only that Durán paid him and his mother each a one-thirty-sixth portion of the rents each year. His cousin had a long scratch on his face, as if he'd recently been in a brawl. That scratch aside, Matheus's face was too small for his head, his fingers too stubby for long arms and huge hands, and his nose too pointed. Although Durán recognized that women found Matheus handsome, he couldn't fathom why. Long red hair, worn down on his shoulders in the French style, which didn't appeal to Durán. The fellow stuffed broad shoulders into a too-tight silk tunic, a burnt-orange color that didn't suit his fiery hair. But it was the cynical curl of the fellow's lips that Durán did not appreciate.

"How are you faring, uncle?" Durán greeted the scowling Colomb, ignoring the Xirgú cousin. Behind Durán's shoulder, the only truly attractive man in Toulouse shuffled with impatience.

"My sister asks that Seigneur Matheus act on her behalf." Colomb indicated the beaky-nosed Montcava cousin.

"Sister" meant the dowager marquesa, Hélène de Beaurain, still displeased that former street-hawker Durán became seigneur of Montcava. Durán rushed to answer.

"I am flattered, uncle. However—"

"Don't call me uncle." Colomb growled the same answer as the other three times they'd spoken to each other.

"My advisors claim I'm too young to marry. Best wait until I'm past thirty." Durán learned to play innocent when trapped by street-bullies a decade ago. "Besides, won't the Church find consanguinity in our relations? They'll declare too close a degree of affinity to allow marriage between third cousins."

"*Per l'amor de Dèu*, she doesn't want to marry you, *fadrin fada*." Matheus laughed, without humor. Behind Durán, Chrétien tensed when Matheus called him *fairy boy*. "The marquesa wants what all our cousins desire. Our house purified of vermin."

"I don't understand." Durán feigned ignorance. "We don't manage her property in Avignon. Surely her steward can deal with rats or any other vermin there?"

"*Renrén.*" Matheus, lifting his pointy nose in disdain, called Durán a fool. "The marquesa and all our family require a leader who supports the call to arms against the Saracen. We must prove that Montcava has rid itself of heretics."

"Isn't that what tithing proves?" Durán spoke in the mild way he used in the old days, when selling cabbages and sausages to grandmothers who feared being cheated. Back then, he prayed publicly with impoverished goodmen. But since he'd become head of the Montcava estates, he prayed in private and tithed to the Church, to avoid risking the wellbeing of his entire family. It was no different from selling sausages when he spurned eating meat. Merely what one did to stay alive. "Does the marquesa need a loan from me to pay her tithes? If so, will you or Colomb guarantee her debt?"

Silent through this, Colomb finally raised an eyebrow. The common rumor was that Colomb earned only enough these days to keep his horses and a handful of knights, not enough to guarantee others' debts. Durán didn't know about Matheus's wealth, since that man's chief holdings were further down the sea's edge, beyond Narbonne.

"Hélène is not in debt." Matheus's voice yipped in a high register, nothing like Chrétien's singing falsetto. "She's paying knights to carry the Cross against the Moors. Like all of Montcava must do."

"Carry the Cross against the Moors? I thought the Church carried to Cross *to* unbelievers, bringing the joy of salvation. Or do I misunderstand what Jesus taught?"

"We demand that Montcava fight the Saracens. Are you a bleeding-livered heretic to say no?" Matheus spoke in such a fury, spit flew with every other word.

"Let's all fund a knight to go. I can pay out of each cousin's portion of the rents."

"*Baquelar!* I'll have you before the bishop for judgment. No heretic bastard shall bring God's wrath down on our family."

His nose still flaring white with anger, Matheus retreated into a boisterous crowd of southern faitdits knights.

Colomb lingered behind. "You don't know men like him, *fadrin*. Don't misjudge—"

"Uncle, I judge that he intends to lie in order to steal from me. Does he not know that Montcava has sworn to serve Pedro d'Aragón, who was anointed by the pope?"

"Pedro's too busy in Andalusia to help you."

Chrétien poked his spine, which caused Durán to stand straighter when he answered Colomb. "I can deal with any bullying, misfit cousins. I'm responsible for more land and more people than he is. I'm taller. And some might say I have a more tolerable face."

Colomb held up a hand, like a captain halting his knights. "Don't cross that man. Take my warning."

"I'm touched that you care, uncle."

Colomb's eyes flashed. He fingered the collar of Durán's silk jacket. "You dress as Montcava. In truth, you're Beaurain. Act like it. You'll live longer."

His uncle was out the door without waiting for an answer.

"Goodbye, uncle!" Durán called, so loud that several knights checked to see who bid Colomb goodbye. He lowered his voice, with words for Chrétien only, casting aspersions on his uncle's manhood. "He's such a *punxor*."

"Don't be sensitive, *cor dolç*. Perhaps Colomb meant it kindly. Come on. Let's follow your flirt."

"When we met, you made me promise not to follow men home anymore."

"*Ai, cor dolç.* You didn't dress so well in those days." Chrétien grasped Durán's shoulder in the way any man might steer his companion, but his hand lingered longer. "This might be worth our while."

Outside, a strong mistral wind blew. Yet Ramón-roger, the count of Foix, lingered under the portico by the gate, speaking with an ancient seigneur in faded velvet. The count was about sixty, though few strands of grey streaked his hair. He had the square, sturdy body of a wrestler, and wore dark wool shot through with silk. His open tunic strings revealed a cuirass over his under-linen. This was the kind of man who took precautions.

"He's just another seigneur." Durán studied the count across the torch-lit courtyard. "Though in good wool. And excellent boots."

"Should I be jealous?"

"Never in this life."

"The count of Foix is a poet." Chrétien dropped his voice when they stepped into darker shadows of the St-Sernin cathedral courtyard, trailing behind the count through the city streets, their own hoods pulled up against the chill rain that began to fall. Another hooded figure limped past, dragging a lame foot, huffing like a spent fighter, hugging close to the shadows. "The count asked tonight why I sing old-fashioned ditties like the tale of the Cid."

"*Ai*, a learned gentleman." Durán loved how he and Chrétien bantered, reading each other's minds, joking to please each other, seeing more in the world than others around them.

"Did you notice the kind of men he was with?"

"Faitdits. False knights from Carcassonne who have betrayed both Simon de Montfort and their own defeated seigneurs."

"He's laughing at them. They should have noticed, since the count of Foix had great victories over Simon last year."

"Chrétien, that man following him has a knife in his hand."

"The one dressed in priest's clothes?"

.

Hanna unbarred the door and let Avraham in, her cheeks alabaster with fear, eyes rimmed red. The mistral wind, roaring and frosty now, pushed the heavy door out of her grasp. She gasped, seeing the state of him, bruised and bloody.

"*Hola*, Master Avraham," the landlord called from his seat near the fire. A small man with him wore the robes of a priest. The landlord introduced his companion with only a title.

"*Bona nuèch*," the priest said in a high, familiar voice. A distinct Provençal accent.

His landlord smiled. "You've come with the rent, I suppose."

Avraham tugged the empty strings at his belt, where his purse had been cut away.

"There was a minor incident." His words came thick and slow through swollen lips. He'd bitten his tongue at some point during that sordid attack. Speaking made it bleed again. "Forgive me. I have no money for you tonight."

Nor tomorrow.

Which meant the end to life in this comfortable, safe home.

•

The storm rain fell hard, then stopped suddenly, the cold mistral still gusting over wet streets. In the murky, rank alleys of Toulouse, false pilgrims and mercenaries without masters huddled around open fires, cooking crusts and cabbage ends they'd scavenged. The count of Foix stalked through the damp shadows, asking blunt questions in each knot of ragged men.

Squinting against the wind, Durán caught the flicker of two more shadows that joined the white-robed figure who tracked the count. One man raised a hand to wave a signal, and they each moved in separate directions, blocking the count in a blind alley.

Chrétien whipped out his sword in silence, pointing to the man Durán should cover. While the three robed men crept toward the trapped count, Chrétien shrieked the cry that he swore caused Venetian mercenaries to abandoned their arms and flee a battle. Yet only one man stiffened at the sound, rushing toward Chrétien.

Durán, still in the shadows, strode toward the man closest to the count. The clang of metal echoed behind him. A flash at the corner of his eye meant the second man now contended with Chrétien. Iron work. Sword and dagger clashing. Durán couldn't master that. He had no heart for taking a knife to flesh.

His target, who wasn't stopped by Chrétien's battle cry, had his dagger aimed at the count's throat. Durán swung his staff, his wrists jangling when the wood met the man's shoulder blade. However, instead of falling, the man lifted his long knife, seeking Durán's middle. Without a thought, just the way he'd been taught, Durán swung again, bashing the man's windpipe.

The man went down. His blade clattered on the cobbles. He clutched at his throat, gasping.

The count sheathed his unused dagger. Finished with his attackers, Chrétien wiped his sword and stood over the man Durán had attacked.

Gurgling now. Not gasping.

The man was drowning.

With the toe of his fine leather boot, the count flipped over one of the men Chrétien had dispatched. He tugged at the neck of the man's white robe.

"It's one of the White Brotherhood," Chrétien said. "Just a street ruffian, not a Cistercian priest."

"Thank God," the count said. He tugged at the man's sleeve, baring the arm, which had three crosses tattooed about the wrist. "Toss these devils in the river. I don't need the bishop haranguing me for killing priests, even false ones."

"Òc, senhór." Chrétien slipped his sword back into its sheath. "Pardon, senhór, what did you seek in this quarter?"

"I heard that a man from my land now lives among the dispossessed. I want him back under my protection."

"But why were you alone in this dark place?"

"I wasn't alone. You were following me." The count of Foix walked back up the alley, striding past where Durán vomited in an archway. "What's wrong with your friend?"

"He's never killed anyone before," Chrétien said.

The count of Foix laid a finger aside his nose as if in thought, staring at Durán. "You never forget the first time."

"We'll walk around for a while. He'll be fine by dawn. I hope."

"Come to my house. I want to know if you can sift truth from donkey-shit."

▪

Ramón-roger retained his wry expression while entertaining Chrétien and Durán in his private quarters.

"Lovely piece." Chrétien accepted wine that their host served in gem-crusted goblets wrapped in copper and silver wire. He stretched out on the settee and rested his arm on the chair's back, sitting by Durán in the comfortable way they did at home. "Greek, isn't it? Taken from Constantinople?"

"Not war booty. And much older than that. From one of the islands. Naxos, actually." The count held up the bottle and another goblet. "For you, Senhór Durán? Or are you a Good Christian living the purest of lives?"

Durán grasped the goblet, hoping no one saw how his hand shook. "It will take me at least one more lifetime to be purified." He swished his first sip of wine to wash away the bad taste churned up from his gut. He was not a very good Good Christian. He drank wine, he ate meat. And now, he'd killed a man. He listened closely when Chrétien spoke, so he couldn't hear the sound in his head of that man dying.

"Everyone knows you rode on crusade with Philippe Augustus. And though you're a praying Catholic," Chrétien put his hands together like a child at mass, "you haven't been quiet about certain Churchmen's errors."

"It's corruption. Not error." Wine threatened to spill from his goblet when the count gestured. He seemed to have as much coiled energy as Chrétien.

"Like many here in the south, you believe only Pedro d'Aragón can pacify the pope," Chrétien said. "Yet you haven't sworn allegiance to any king."

"Common street talk. I'm just like every seigneur in the land where the troubadours roam." The count swished his wine without drinking it.

"You told the bishop that you can't spare men to carry the Cross to Andalusia." Chrétien paused, a note of challenge in his voice. "Because you need to protect your lands from heretic rebels. Yet any man in his right mind knows goodmen will never raise arms to defend themselves."

"No, they won't, even when hunted as heretics," the count said. "Better to ask, is there any man in his right mind left in this land?"

"I believe I still have my wits." Durán got the words out, but it didn't sound like his voice. He set his goblet aside, queasy from a night with no sleep. And that man dead by his hand in the alley. "We need to be vigilant at home. We can't run off to fight Moors."

Chrétien tipped his head in the wistful way that Durán found assuring. "Well said, seigneur of Montcava!"

"And you, Chrétien of Cyprus, the sworn knight of Pedro *El Católico?*" Ramón-roger jutted his jaw, challenging Chrétien. "You aren't joining your king in battle? Just staying safely at home, and singing at night?"

"As if the sun still rises." Chrétien earned a scolding from his mother Numa whenever he was that smug.

"He's not just a marketplace jongleur." Durán said it out of pride, not because Chrétien needed anyone to defend him.

"Of course not. Your *bon amic* is also busy taking knights' silver in extravagant charades."

"It's honest gambling," Chrétien said.

"Honest?" Their host furrowed his bushy brow. "We poets choose words carefully for their true meaning."

"Believe me, he's no poet," Durán said. Chrétien tickled at the back fringe of Durán's hair, indicating approval. "He's only a jongleur. He sings other poets' words."

Their host shook his head. "They say that after each night's debauchery, you spend each morning training with a band of Norman and Sicilian mercenaries."

"Are they still mercenaries when they live like house-knights?" Durán asked. Thierry and Jacques and the rest of his band were loyal to Chrétien and wouldn't sell their services elsewhere. So, were they still mercenaries?

Their host threw his hands up in that southern gesture which asked heaven about the ways of God's creation. "Let's empty your cartload of goat shit, shall we? Come to work for me."

"You want me to teach your knights to sing?" Chrétien said. Before their host could argue, Chrétien continued, "With their swords, daggers, and staves?"

"You taught your friend well." The lord pointed his goblet toward Durán. "I owe you my life."

"Durán has a great deal of natural talent." Chrétien's fingers again tickled the back of Durán's neck. "You have similarly intelligent men?"

The count of Foix tilted his hand in that southern way, weighing the balance of good and bad, coming to no conclusion.

Chrétien said, "I no longer work as mercenary. Durán and I must tend the Montcava estates. My mother came here from Cyprus and needs my company."

"I'm calling on your oath to Pedro *El Rei*." Ramón-roger leaned forward with his challenge, tapping Chrétien on the chest.

"To protect heretics from over-eager Churchmen?"

"No, I can battle Simon de Montfort. The worst of the lesser devils." Ramón-roger became irate, just speaking Simon's name. He paused to pour more wine into Chrétien's goblet. Durán covered his own cup, since he didn't have a head for much wine. "I can help you both if you'll lead my knights against the Saracens in Andalusia."

Chrétien waved a hand, deferring to Durán. They'd discussed this since the priests first called on men to go fight the Saracens. Durán didn't want to provoke the count, at least not in the teasing way Chrétien did. He said, "Neither of us needs to steal land or murder Moors."

"It isn't about Moors," Ramón-roger said. "It's the blasted Knights of the Lunate Cross. They intend to destroy you and Pedro. We must stop them."

"We?" Chrétien curled his lip in his particular, grand manner.

"Òc, bonfraire." The count set down the fancy goblet and pulled up his wool-silk sleeve, baring his wrist. "*Sodalitas, fidelitas, virtus.*"

"*Adouçar enfant Jhezu!*" Durán groaned. The secret confraternity of knights that had led Chrétien and his brother Tomás into danger for years.

"A goodman calls on the sweet baby Jesus?" Ramón-roger mused. "What do they call it when a heretic blasphemes against his own heresy?"

"Where?" Chrétien asked, pointing to the count's scar.

"At Acre. In the battle, I became separated from Philippe's army and ended up with your father."

"Don Miquel de Morella," Durán murmured. Chrétien's foster-father, of whom wild and heroic stories were still told.

The count said, "I was with Miquel when we freed Jaffa."

"I was at Jaffa," Chrétien said.

"What were you? Two years old?"

"Eight. What were you?"

"Thirty."

"I mean, Senhór Foix, were you a true crusader or did you skulk home with Philippe Augustus?" Chrétien made his boldest challenge.

"Miquel thought enough of me for this." Ramón-roger held out his wrist again to bare that square scar, identical to one on Chrétien's arm. The bonfraires burned it on each other with a hot crossbow bolt. So, Chrétien shared a brotherhood with the count, while Durán was a mere seigneur that the count entertained on sufferance. "Like you, I owe Pedro more than friendship. Right now, Crux Lunata knights seek to destroy Pedro and any bonfraires they can find."

"Am I out of my depth?" As if chastised, Chrétien seemed humble. If that were possible.

"Let's have some breakfast, *mon amic*, and talk it over." After showing his badge of brotherhood, Ramón-roger seemed jovial again. "You'll find me to be a good master."

The count summoned food with a single word (which Durán had yet to master in his own domus). A feast to break the day was laid before them: *salsiccia fresca*, Durán's favorite coarse country-style sausage; mush with spring onions fried in the sausage fat; hot ale.

"My skills are on the battlefield and laying siege." Ramón-roger sat back when a servant set a trencher before him. Durán copied the move, wishing it came naturally. "But this spy business? I'm not as experienced as you."

Chrétien reached for cream to pour over his mush. The bonfraires revelation had removed all animosity between them. "Spies are paid traitors who skulk in alleys."

"Not minor seigneurs playing poet and gamesters in the courts of Toulouse?" Ramón-roger clearly enjoyed his own wit.

"Pedro asked us to be alert. To pay attention." Durán set down his eating knife, speaking casually of the king of Aragón, as if Durán were born to the station he'd gained later in life.

"And you drew our attention." Chrétien stretched, dropping an arm on Durán's shoulder. A glimpse of those long white fingers freed Durán from fussing over the night's bad business. With Chrétien close by, he was safe. Comforted.

Ramón-roger speared another luscious sausage. "First, I want to hear your tales of the Crux Lunata."

"Accompanied with song or only verse?" Chrétien asked.

"A soldier's narrative will do."

∎

71

Chrétien told the story efficiently: a generations-long revenge hatched in Edessa by a young failed crusader turned Churchman, seeking to destroy a trio of families.

"Your foster-father and brother were mangled by attackers? Reputations destroyed? A woman falsely accused of heresy? That's it?" At a small signal to the servants, the count's trencher disappeared.

"Our father Miquel insisted the Crux Lunata was our own special enemy," Chrétien said.

"Decades of revenge attack on your families? That's a long time for a personal conspiracy." Ramon-roger drew the lunate cross amidst the crumbs and spills on the table. "Then what do you make of the tattoo on that dead man in the alley?"

Chrétien pushed away his own trencher. "In the end, the Crux Lunata proved to be only Durán's great uncle, the abbot of Font-cours. He paid henchmen and a deranged knight to act against Miquel and Pèire Leteric."

"The Church should have burned that evil abbot, but they merely sent him to Rome." Durán surprised himself with that angry outburst. He tried never to think of his despicable grandfather.

"Crux Lunata is still your personal enemy," Ramón-roger said. "But also much more."

Morning light splashed through the door that opened to the courtyard. Minerals in the marble floor glittered, and the whitewashed walls gleamed. A sparkle, mirrored on the silver wire decorating a goblet, blinded Durán for a moment. Ramón-roger moved that goblet aside and leaned forward.

"Crux Lunata is recruiting knights and seigneurs who seek to avoid conflict with Simon de Montfort. Its priests and knights promise secret spiritual knowledge, protection from persecution, and great wealth."

"So, there's money to be made in the sin business?" Chrétien laughed, but not in that gentle way Durán liked to provoke. "This crusade against the Saracens won't make anyone rich from booty."

Ramón-roger ignored the interruption. "Land is disappearing into the pockets of the Church, or at least to the Crux Lunata. Some is disappearing in Pedro's provinces without his approval. The bishops are easily convinced to place any seigneur under interdiction, especially those who rendered castles to Pedro for protection. Their villages are under Simon de Montfort's shit-covered boot. More burnings in God's name."

Ramón-roger's handsome face, red from anger, cast a profile of indignation in the morning light.

"*Deus noluit.*" Durán said. A priest said those Latin words years ago when Durán asked why God killed his mother.

"*Ai*, it's as the goodman here says, God never willed this." The count seemed rueful. "They now conspire to destroy Pedro."

"Pedro has lived through a dozen conspiracies," Chrétien said. "Thirty men defend him against assassins."

"Beyond murder, the Crux Lunata intends to destroy Pedro's venture into Andalusia," the count said.

"That's a bit foolish." Chrétien sparred with the idea, not directly arguing with the count. "The pope seeks to unite all of Christendom into a new Holy Roman Empire."

Ramón-roger offered a rude gesture. "If lords come home from Andalusia broke and without victory, they'll cede power to Simon and Philippe Augustus. Not Pedro."

Chrétien crossed his arms again. "We need to remain here, Durán and I, protecting our own lands. Just like you."

"You both are in jeopardy. With Sebastián of Valerós and your brother Tomás declared dead," he pointed to Chrétien, "the bishop has been asked to give Valerós to your cousin Matheus," he pointed to Durán, "who promises to render that land to the Church. His next goal will be Montcava."

"Sebastián and Tomás aren't dead. They're preparing to campaign with Pedro in Andalusia," Chrétien said. "And the Church can't give Valerós away. It's under Pedro's protection. He'd never approve."

The count tipped his head, puzzled. "Not dead?"

"I had a letter from my brother Tomás last week. He's in Barcelona, waiting to go on campaign with Pedro."

"And Isabella of Valerós? She's alive too?"

Chrétien shook his head, his mouth a thin line. Durán also bit back the flood that overcame him when anyone mentioned her name, whenever he thought of her gone from this world of shade and grief.

"I'm sorry." Ramón-roger seemed sensitive to the silence.

"We go on," Durán said.

"As she would." Chrétien spoke at last. Durán watched Chrétien's throat bob, as together they once more swallowed grief. Over many long winter nights, they'd held each other, finding it so hard to let go, to let her soul escape this material world.

"I am truly sorry," the count repeated. "But then, your cousin Matheus is—"

"A witless bully," Durán said. "I despise bullies."

"Matheus is happy to condemn women like Isabella of Valerós as heretics—and you, too, Senhór Durán— in order to steal land. My friends in the bishop's court whisper that he's mentioned you as suspect." The count rose from the table, not seeming to hear Durán choke back a new sickness in his belly. "Let's walk in the garden. It's a beautiful morning after a stormy night. Spring is coming."

∎

"Are you well again, *cor dolç*?" Chrétien whispered in Durán's ear.

"*Òc, bon amic.* It must have been the risotto from last night. A weak stomach."

"*Ai, renrén,* you're stronger than most men."

Listening to Chrétien, feeling the caress of his breath, Durán nearly missed the count's declaration.

"Crux Lunata is allied with Simon de Montfort. Likely those knights lie to any priest who hears their confession."

Chrétien scoffed. "Everyone lies in confession."

"These traitors want Pedro ruined. Tens of thousands of Christian soldiers might die in Andalusia, just for Crux Lunata's lust for power."

"And to stop them, you plan to do what?

The count held his hands out in a plea, then made a fist. "Can you prove that Sebastián of Valerós is alive? Can he appear before the bishop in Toulouse or Narbonne?"

"I have his letters," Durán said. "But he's going to Andalusia with Pedro, if he hasn't left by now."

"Let me have those letters. In order for me to protect you—and for you to protect Pedro and all the good people of Valerós and Montcava—you must join this crusade. Travel with the heretic-baiting archbishop of Narbonne. He's leaving soon to meet Pedro and Alfonso at Toledo."

"Why bother?" Chrétien said. "Even without Crux Lunata's interference, Pedro's army is dangerously outnumbered by the Saracens."

"We bonfraires can do big things." Ramón-roger tapped his wrist. "We can change the world. Keep it from perishing in a heretics' pyre. Or at least keep the bishops from burning you as heretics."

Durán couldn't sort quickly among shards of fear, rankling indignation, and the continuing pangs of remorse over that man in the alley who choked to death on his own blood. He said, "In this world of shadows, I merely take care of what God gave me. Even though I won't be a perfected goodman in this lifetime, I won't put on a sword and go to war."

Chrétien's fingers tickled the fringe at Durán's neck. "Senhór Foix, I must stay home to care for my aged mother. Her other son is joining Pedro's war. I've given up soldiering."

"I'll believe that when I've given up hope that God cares about the lands of my forefathers. I repeat, Matheus of Xirgú is bandying rumors that Senhór Durán is a heretic. He'll seize Montcava right after he takes Valerós."

"My cousin is just making trouble. The way bullies do."

"He can make trouble because, senhór, you happen to be a Good Christian," the count said. "He has a growing reputation as a heretic hunter. I can protect you only if you join Pedro's adventure, to refute Matheus's accusations. And you, Senhór Chrétien, are Pedro's sworn knight. You must protect him."

"What can I do that Pedro's guards don't do every day?"

"What a bonfraire does. Whatever it takes." Ramón-roger crossed his arms in challenge, although Chrétien stood taller and looked down on the count. "Do what you and your brother Tomás did before. Draw the Crux Lunata out into the open."

"What if the heat of Iberia doesn't agree with me?" Chrétien shifted his beautiful narrow jaw in that particular way only when he smothered great joy. Alarmed, Durán saw that Chrétien had ceased serious argument.

"Pedro's army will return by midsummer. You'll be home in time for harvest. Senhór Durán can bring his brother Sebastián back to Toulouse and put to rest the belief that the Master of Valerós is dead."

"You're my seigneur, Senhór Durán. What say you?" Chrétien grinned; he'd decided. He was going. "What do you most want?"

Durán's tongue went numb. He wanted to practice being the seigneur of Montcava, taking care of the people and the farms and villas. He wanted to sleep every night in loving arms. These two years had been the only comfortable time in his life, and he didn't want to surrender that life.

Chrétien persisted. "Will you take an oath to carry the Cross in Andalusia for the expiation of your sins, *mon amic*? Or stay here and face the heretic hunters?"

Time to buck up. "If it was just me, like in the old days, I'd disappear. Go to another town. But I can't risk harm to all the people I'm responsible for." Or risk losing Chrétien to a new adventure with his bonfraires.

"Good lad!" Ramón-roger clapped Durán's shoulder. "I have your oath, then?"

"I do not believe in oaths." He still didn't, after living two years with a man who swore dozens of oaths each day, over the heat of his porridge and broken boot laces. "I shall endeavor to do as you ask, faithfully, without calling on either the Good God or Satan."

"Well spoken, senhór," Ramón-roger said. "For your loyalty, I shall grant you a fief near Urgell for the rest of your natural life. I'll tell the bishop that all your Montcava land and people are under my protection, since you are Christian knights taking my place on this venture. I'm surely too old and infirm to go. Besides, my sins were all paid on crusade to Jerusalem with Ricart Còr de Leon."

"With enough spare indulgences left over to sin some more?" Chrétien said. "Is that fief a reward worth our effort? They say, Senhór Foix, your relationship with Urgell is still disputed. And that La Mancha is the bunghole of Iberia."

"I'll outfit you." The count beat one fist into the other, seeming sure of his argument. "Shall I send two dozen of my knights and my master-at-arms? Enough to convince the archbishop that you two are contributing to this campaign, rather than disrupting it."

"I'm a professional. I've never disrupted a campaign in my life."
Chrétien's beauty shone, even when he was indignant. "We'll be invisible among crusader hordes seeking forgiveness with their swords."

"You two," Ramón-roger said, "wouldn't be invisible if you were dipped in lamp-black ink and stuck in a Dordogne cave."

6

Godspeed, at Dawn

GUILLEM, THE MARSHAL OF THE Valerós knights, knocked at the gate and called for the Master of Valerós to come out with his travel gear.

Sebastián tumbled from his bed, scratched the floor to find his boots in the predawn light.

"Patience!" He shouted when Guillem called his name a second time. His pack was by the door, ready to go whenever the call came. Pedro liked to surprise his men, it was said.

He ran through the villa, checking likely places to find Tomás. Breathless. As if his jerkin had become too tight overnight (which happened not long ago). That bubbling within was familiar, like when he first walked out onto the battlements during the siege at Minerve.

"Don Tomás!"

At the back gate along the end of the kitchen garden, Tomás jerked, then faced Sebastián as if reluctant.

"Marshall Guillem is here. We're riding for Toledo today. Right now! We're off to be heroes."

This was what they'd waited for all winter, to join the Valerós band on the ride into Andalusia. Going to battle at last.

"*Ai*, Sebastián. Give my best to the marshal."

"You aren't coming." Sebastián said it, didn't ask. Tomás, dressed in traveling leathers, carried minimal armor.

"*Òc.*" Tomás dropped his pack and grasped Sebastián's shoulders. "*Ai, fadrin.* Your mother would be proud."

"She'd insist on coming, too. Let's go. Marshal Guillem is waiting."

"I have to be elsewhere. I have to—"

"What? We have to go. Now."

"Pedro asked me for a favor."

"Me, too," Sebastián said, puzzled. "He wants Valerós to take on several bands of ultramontanos, those Frankish forty-day warriors. You have to show me how to manage that many men."

"I can't explain, but I made promises to Pedro. Whatever you hear, please believe that I'm acting as a bonfraire, with honor. Tell Yusuf all is well. He's traveling with Pedro."

"With Pedro?" Sebastián felt like a fool, standing there watching while Tomás tugged open the back gate and lifted his pack. He really was leaving. "But we need you."

"You'll do well on your own, *fadrin*. You're ready. If you need help, there's Marshal Guillem and Father Anselm riding with you. Pedro says I'll see you at midsummer. In truth, only God knows when. Goodbye!"

Marshall Guillem called down the garden path for Sebastián, who kept waving until Tomás disappeared down the alley.

In the street, the marshal handed over the reins of Sebastián's horse. "The men have our palfreys. This late in the morning, they're already a league ahead of us." The sun hadn't yet pulled itself above the horizon.

"Don Tomás isn't coming," Sebastián said.

"I've heard. There were nasty rumors last night. Not our business now. Mount up."

.

As a dove-grey dawn lifted its wings, Tomás leaned against a garden wall, listening to the thud of horses in the next street over, the sounds of the Valerós marshal taking Sebastián away, to show him battle life in a real war.

Which Tomás was supposed to do.

Around him, households stirred. Servants fetched water; stable-boys raised a ruckus in a nearby kennel where a dozen dogs begged to run; women's voices called for Miró, Jaume, and Sanç to come to breakfast because it was time for school.

Ai, Yusuf must be packing his satchel, preparing to join Pedro's clerks, enduring Dolç's admonitions to be safe and not be so busy as to forget to eat.

One woman's voice rose above the others echoing in the kitchen gardens. "Miquel, your chores, *fadrin!* Then out the door with you."

He didn't want to leave them.

He couldn't leave them.

No one else, no task or promise, no one but his sons could fill the hole in his soul, a hole the size of that fierce gentlewoman from the Pyrenees hills. He hadn't had a soul until he found Isabella, didn't know that hole in his gut was as immense as the Great Sea and as empty as a djinni's promise.

A boy's voice rose nearby from amid the *buack-buack* of begging chickens. "I'm here, pretty ones. I do my duty as I am bid."

And Fortuno began to sing.

> 'I yearn for what I cannot have;
> If what they say proves true,
> It is certain
> True courage is power,
> For he who owns his suffering.'

The song ceased. The *buack-buack* died down. "I do my duty, and you do yours. It is my honor to serve you. The way a king serves his people. That's what my grandmother said."

That woman's voice again. "Miquel, what will come of you when you see heaven? Up, *fadrin!* Duty calls."

▪

Carrying only a meager pack and hoping to catch another Andalusia-bound ship, Tomás wandered down the partially-paved Rambla to where his umber skin never called attention, among the Mozarabs, conversos, and Moors near the docks. His belly ached from being kicked and stitched, but his headache had receded. He checked over his shoulder every fifty paces, scanning the alleys for attackers.

He hailed the man at the door of a wine shop, but Musa al-Bakri stared out across the dark harbor, where a ship receded into the open waters of the Mediterranean. Muscular and brown like his dog, the large-headed, thick-skinned Alano that lay across the threshold, Musa still spoke a Mozarabic dialect though he'd been in Barcelona thirty years. He cursed the Almohad rulers who'd come from Tunisia, calling them Al-Muwahhidun.

"Blasted arrogant donkeys. Compared to them, the Old Man of the Mountain was the soul of kindness and convivenzia." Musa ranted better than anyone, except Tomás's own father. "Didn't we, who lived for generations in Al-Andalus, invent the art of living in harmony with all our neighbors? We were fine until those Almohad mercenaries broke our peace."

"As you say." Tomás stepped into the cool darkness of the wine shop. "Powerful men who claim to be slaves to Allah."

"All praise is due to God alone. When Almohad mercenaries seized the caliphate, they persecuted honest men, preaching nonsense about how God wants us to live." Musa placed a backgammon board on the table, not offering Tomás food or drink. "Pedro *El Rei* shall deal those Almohad bastards the humiliation they deserve."

"Where are your customers?" Tomás asked.

"It's Ramadan. I'm open only to you, Ibn Mikhail. Everyone else is fasting until after dark."

Tomás, silently condemning his forgetfulness, placed ivory pieces on the board, though a game with Musa was always futile. The man didn't understand strategy. Sinking heavily onto the bench across from Tomás, Musa made his first thoughtless move.

"They stole the patrimony my family earned from the first caliph of Cordoba."

In truth, Musa's father was driven from Almería for running a brothel. Tomás had heard the story before, while knowing what Musa sold behind the woven reed door that led to an adjoining house. Tomás dutifully murmured his assent and made an obvious move on the board, liking the sound of the ivory counters.

"I have a special for you." Musa leaned forward to whisper, though they were alone. "My niece is new in town. She's a virgin. Special for you."

"Any niece of yours would be old enough to have grandchildren. And this is the third time you offered me a virgin in the past fortnight."

Musa persisted. "A man like you only loiters in this quarter to heal a broken heart."

"I don't have a heart. My father had it removed when I came of age. And I don't want a woman."

"Say no more, my friend. I am the soul of discretion. My nephew is wise about love. If you want to fall in love, no man is better."

"I sleep alone," Tomás said.

"Another good man ruined by Almohad prigs, eh?"

"I'm not from that part of the world."

"Indeed, I've tried to guess your accent. Can I be bold and ask?"

"Cyprus, though I spent years in Cairo and Antioch. And in Jaffa when I was young."

"Jaffa, eh? You escaped the devil's crusaders from your cradle. May the God of Abraham grant you peace. The caliph of Cordoba would pay well for a soldier like you."

"I'm not a soldier."

"And I'm not the son of a procuress." Musa touched the callous along Tomás's right hand. "A man in my business notices. To protect my family."

"All those nieces and nephews."

Musa, delighted with Tomás's wit, clapped his hands and crossed his legs, kicking the table and upsetting the pieces. "*Ai*, what a shame! Shall we call it a draw?"

"*Òc, mon amic.*" Tomás said. He rose and stretched. "I'm going to try my luck in Al-Andalus. I'm sailing on the next ship out."

Musa laughed. "God's truth, you're a great gambler, but not a very good sailor."

"How so?"

"If you're going to Al-Andalus, you'll have to wait for that fat merchant across the way, who won't sail till tomorrow morning's tide. Christian captains won't sail on the new moon."

Tomás sat down, getting used to failing. "Shall we play more? Do you have food?"

"I'm glad to be of service, *mon amic*. But when you travel to Al-Andalus, you won't find food after daylight in the holy season. You'll just find Al-Muwahhidun scolds, who are happy to use the whip for your spiritual wellbeing."

.

Avraham in Toulouse
February 20

"Life will be better in Girona," Avraham said.

He'd uttered those words more than a hundred times. He stood now in the doorway of what had been his shop in Toulouse, holding the sign he'd chiseled off the shutters. *Avraham el Comerciant.* It was past sunset, no time to be on the street, between French mercenary crusaders and the undisciplined, masked White Brotherhood. "We'll be safer. Soldiers aren't pursuing heretics and outlanders in Pedro's kingdom."

"Or Jews like us," his wife Hanna said. "Say what you mean."

"*Òc.*" He spoke in the local tongue, wondering how rapidly they'd adopt a new accent and vocabulary in the next town. To fit in, you have to speak like the local people.

"Leaving is hard for Léal. Our daughter's marriage arrangements should begin this year."

"It hurts me that it's so sad for you, my dear. Leaving behind your many friends. And this beautiful home you created for us."

Hanna wept, protesting that she needed to cry out her grief to find strength for the remaining chores. She held a towel to her eyes. That fine piece of linen her great-grandmother embroidered while waiting for the birth of her first child. A century ago. Hanna would regret the tears when she unpacked that treasure in her new home.

"I'm off to deliver this box to your brother," Avraham said.

"And you'll beg him one more time to join us?" Hanna said.

"*Òc,* of course." He donned his hat and cloak, counting the heartbeats until his wife said what she always did.

"Take care, husband. It's not safe on these streets at night."

Hanna's brother Yitzchak, always loquacious, couldn't simply say thank you and goodbye, he wanted to talk over with Avraham once again all the reasons for staying in Toulouse versus the many nagging reasons to go. The man had no children, his wife had passed away a dozen years before. The reason to stay that Yitzchak always returned to, that the dangers you know may be better than new and unknown dangers.

"Our cousin in Girona writes in the winter that everyone is safe," Yitzchak said. "Come June, who knows what midsummer madness will seize the people there."

"We'll write you," Avraham said. "You're always welcome with us. Remember each day how much Hanna wants her brother near."

Dead of night, with curfew announced from the steps of the Christians' churches every week, the streets should have been empty. But the best of the town's citizens passed openly through the streets, moving from villa to villa; the town watchmen ignored the law. Avraham knew how to move alleyway to alleyway through the shadows, to pass from Yitzchak's house to his, but with so many people in the streets, Avraham took a more direct route, better lit by all the travelers along the road.

To pass a huddle of giggling, tipsy young donzels, Avraham walked uncomfortably close to the river. Just when he emerged from the gaggle of wealthy lads, he heard the jangle of a running hound, its growl coming his way in the dark. His father's teaching about safety in numbers rushed over him. Avraham stepped back into the cluster of boys.

"*Ai*, out of the way, old man!" a youngster yowled in his ear at the same time that the running hound hit the water. The animal's howls rose above the noise of its splashing. From the sound of it, the animal swam farther into the river instead of heading for shore.

A cursing, angry seigneur paced along the bank, calling the dog, before he spun in anger to address the young men, and Avraham.

"Why'd you push my dog into the river?" More blaspheming of those men as the sons of whores. The seigneur stripped, dropping his orange silks at Avraham's feet, pulling off his boots, and swearing the entire time.

Then the seigneur, likely too far into his cups, leaped into the river, swimming after his dog.

"No one jumps in a freezing river to save a dog," a tall, soprano-voiced donzel said.

"It's Matheus," another said. "That wild seigneur from Narbonne. He loves his dogs."

"*Ai*, him," the first donzel said.

"They say Seigneur Matheus copulates like a monkey with his sister." A third donzel spoke, lower pitched, perhaps older.

"It's not his sister," the second donzel said. "The woman is his stepmother."

"*Ai*, God must be pleased with that difference!" The first donzel laughed, a high squeak.

The third of the youngsters said, "It's well known Matheus of Xirgú does the monkey act with any woman that walks."

"Such high standards!" the first said.

"The bishop hasn't heard, I suppose. The bishop thinks the world of Matheus. Saved the old man's nephew from a fall with a bad-tempered horse."

"Matheus always knows which side to ask for his bread to be buttered," the second donzel said. "No one else around Narbonne is doing as much to send heretics into the forest, and then delivering their land to the church."

"He's insufferable since he joined the Knights of the Lunate Cross," the first donzel complained.

"I thought they were a religious order," the second man said. "I'd hardly call Matheus religious. Except for being holier than you or me because he can prove that no one in his family ever married a manual laborer for the last ten generations."

The first donzel laughed. "Be that as it may, they say he's reached the highest levels of the order."

"Hugh, don't repeat their secrets," the squeaky donzel said.

Avraham interrupted. "Should we do something for him? He's been in the water so long."

"Don't worry, old man. The angels always save Matheus," one voice answered. "He has enough money, he bought salvation for both body and soul."

Just then, the seigneur crawled up on the bank, dragging his dog with him, cursing the animal as spawn of the devil. Seigneur Matheus shook the same way the dog did, scattering water over Avraham. Then the man pulled on his boots. While he did, the cursing stopped. He gently asked the dog about its wellbeing.

And shivered.

"May I offer you my cloak, senhór?" Avraham had unfastened the clasp, prepared to hand his wrap to a man shivering so hard he could barely speak.

"I don't want your rags, you filthy Jew!" Matheus shouted, hovering too close to Avraham. "Get out of my way. I need to get my dog warm."

Matheus stomped away, the massive dog thrown over his shoulder, and the donzels following after and calling out praises for the hero from Narbonne.

Avraham retied his cloak and headed for home. His former home. The home his landlord forced him to surrender.

.

"That's the last time you ruin my sleep, cruel bird."

Avraham had called the neighbor's rooster cruel for three years. Likely it wasn't always the same bird. When it crowed near dawn this time, he covered the kitchen fire and extinguished all but one last rushlight. Léal and Hanna, on the bench by the door, dozed against each other.

He roused his wife and daughter, who finished their chores quickly. The house was clean. Food prepared. Avraham governed his eyes, avoiding the sight of Hanna's silent tears.

She said, "What if we have to travel during Pesach?"

"Then we'll be safe and together and thanking God for deliverance. Just as always. We don't need a house to hold a Seder."

The expected knock sounded on his front door.

"Bonjorn, Master Avraham."

It proved to be that pretty lad who used to work for a street hawker in St-Sernin square. What was his name? Drogos? Donatus? *Ai*, Durán! What was it that hawker sold? Cabbages? Cheeses? No matter, the boy was now full grown, dressed in leather and chainmail, though he didn't carry a sword.

"The count of Foix sent me, senhór." The lad spoke with more respect than most in Toulouse these days. "His mercenary train is departing. My men will bring your carts to join us."

"Just one cart," Avraham said. *That street-lad has men to lead?*

The young man peered past Avraham, where Léal and Hanna stood, arms wrapped around each other's waists.

"We'll find room in one of my wagons for your women. Shall we depart now?"

·

Sebastián had lived in the saddle over the past two years. He hadn't forgotten anything about that while sheltering in Barcelona over the winter. Once he finished tussling in his mind about Tomás—neither Guillem nor Father Anselm provided any insight—the rhythm of the morning ride shook his bones awake. His heart beat correctly. And he rode at the fore of several hundred trained mercenaries, only a few dozen of whom he'd ever met.

At *migdiada*, the midday rest break, Marshal Guillem hoisted Sebastián on to the back of a wagon, so the two of them stood above the long ranks of men. The marshal shouted Sebastián's name and declared him the Master of Valerós and the leader of all bands assigned to his care by Pedro d'Aragón.

Guillem paused while, below them, captains bellowed the words in relay down their ranks.

"These are your men," Guillem said, not shouting for a moment. "Show them that the house of Valerós knows what it means to go to battle. You look just like Pèire Leteric. Lead them the way he would. Do your grandfather proud."

Sebastián took a massive step onto a wooden trunk in the middle of the wagon, balancing himself before he landed, pulling his sword from its sheath in the same movement, waving it over his head.

"By the grace of God and the ministering of all heaven's golden angels…" He paused while the captains shouted his words down the ranks; then he called them worthless sinners. "Are you *peccadors* ready to pull out your swords and win a war?"

Their assent came back like cries at the Tower of Babel. In far too many dialects. He understood the common tongue, the Catalan and Aragón words, and the French from the ultramontanos.

"When we fight," Sebastián shouted until his voice nearly broke, "we call for valor together. Say it till you shout it in your sleep. *Vivètz* Valerós!"

He raised his sword to encourage them to shout.

"*Vivètz* Valerós!"

And again. Once more. Louder.

He held his empty hand high, motioning for silence.

"And when we see our enemy, we roar the words our grandfathers did." He raised his sword again, determined to make every man shout until the noise drowned his loneliness. "Awake, Steel! *Desperta, Ferro!*"

PART TWO
Sanctuary

An Angel Reads to a Djinni

"IT IS WRITTEN, WITH A HAND MOVED BY GOD." The angel Grigor kindled a light, illuminating the text he read.

> 'For there are certain men crept in unawares, who were before of old ordained to this condemnation, ungodly men, turning the grace of our God into lasciviousness, and denying the only Lord God.

> 'I will therefore put you in remembrance, though ye once knew this, how that the Lord, having saved the people out of the land of Egypt, afterward destroyed them that believed not.

> 'And the angels which kept not their first estate, but left their own habitation, he hath reserved in everlasting chains under darkness unto the judgment of the great day.'

Ahriman the djinni looked up, pretending to be astonished. "Are those disposed angels perhaps cousins of yours? Do you get to keep their rents now that your cousins reside in everlasting chains?"

— Ibn Jafar, The Poet
From Tales of the Angel and the Djinni

7

Near the Great Sea

Felip at Monasterio de St-Pere de Selva
March 2

THE SEA LAY BELOW, DOWN a long winding trail. Viewed from the hillside above the monastery, the Mediterranean spread across the horizon, azure water and azure sky as far as God let man see.

Except in the chilled spring rain. And fog.

The sound of the waves echoed up to the stone chapel. Felip had lost his sense of awe for the monastery spaces. Monks and priests stood to chant under the nave's barrel-vaulted ceiling. The sniffling and snorting and farting of the ague-plagued older brothers carried louder and longer than the echo of their voices at prayer.

The lesson of the day, read from Proverbs by a rheumy elder monk, had been selected by the abbot to encourage new monks and unpledged novices. Felip imagined inking the lesson on parchment, the scratch of a quill across a prepared page sounding just like the voice of the elder monk, screeching out lessons for young monks.

'Give not thy strength unto women, nor thy ways to that which destroyeth kings.'

Standing in the cold for that day's convocations, Felip wondered what destroyed kings. Not women. The lesson says that women only have the strength they take from men. He considered kings who had been destroyed. Ricart Còr de Leon took a crossbow bolt in the neck. But most kings, the ones from the old songs, died of old age. So what ways destroyed kings?

Behind the altar, the new image of Our Lord held his right hand in blessing over the final meal with his disciples, a chalice cradled in his other hand, a golden halo in an imperfect circle. But the fresco

91

painter wasn't allowed real gilding, only ochre pigments. The only gold here was locked up in the script master's cupboard, doled out to those like Felip who worked on the more precious gospels.

He lost track of the day's lesson, daydreaming. Felip's grandmother believed he'd become a great papal diplomat, which was typical of her improbable dreams. He kept his own counsel whenever possible, having never conquered his stutter. But dear Àvia insisted that Felip's silence proved his profound intelligence and savored her dreams for him. If he could voice his desires, he'd rather be a crusader like his father, than a monk like his uncle. Felip touched the letter from his father, always hidden in his shirt, where Justí de Xirgú swore on the family's honor to serve king and God. Here in the monastery, Felip served God, and believed he carried his father's honor with him.

And yet.

Brother Felip came inside the walls of St-Pere de Selva hoping to be free of lust and jealousy, free to serve his family by working to the glory of God, regretting only that too few moments were pledged to absolute silence each day, nursing the hope that his work to illuminate Scripture mattered as much in God's eyes as his father's sacrifice in the crusade to recapture Jerusalem.

Then two different shades of green rage came on him after the birds flew south at All Saints. One, his brother Matheus was going on crusade, while Felip had to remain in these cold walls. And the other descended on him when Brother Vidal came into the scriptorium.

This new brother stood neither tall nor small, thin as a marsh crake, with smooth, pale skin like a eunuch and cropped white hair like the aged hermit who lived up the mountain from the monastery. Vidal arrived ill, like so many who came to St-Pere; some healed and then left; others lingered, neither ill nor well. However, Vidal's health improved, if not his vigor. And Brother Vidal became the new star in the abbot's heaven, receiving the choicest texts to copy. Now the abbot seldom had five words to spare for Felip, but often tarried by Vidal's desk, conversing over whatever gospel or missive the new brother transcribed, until the script master rang the bell for Silence. All the abbot asked of Felip anymore was when he'd be ready to commit with all his heart as an ordained monk.

The first time Brother Vidal spoke to him, asking where gilding was stored, Felip bit his tongue to keep his evil nature from replying. Worse, Vidal incarnated kindness, often pausing by Felip's desk, complimenting *sotto voce*, lavishing more attention than the abbot or script master ever did. Whenever Vidal lingered nearby, Felip longed for and dreaded what the new brother might say next.

One morning Felip finished a third letter asking his grandmother to let him take orders as soon as possible. Because he wanted to go on crusade. Otherwise, he didn't know how he'd endure life here. He hated the cold. He hated the food, though hunger gripped him most of each day. He hated the loneliness. And now he hated his daily chores. He settled in to copy a mundane message of no more spiritual worth than the greetings from the abbot to a Narbonnese lord. The scroll had a patch of text at the back, like a spell to ensure that the copyist worked with care.

> 'By our Lord and Savior Jesus Christ, our Redeemer and our Hope, I appeal to all my brethren who shall copy this work. You must be diligent as you work, to copy faithfully and correct your errors. As we wait for our Lord to come again in Judgment, transcribe this appeal in your copy.'

He copied it with his usual diligence. He'd promised the rest of his life to God, and in return he lived tortuous, long days of…

"You must start over," Vidal's voice rasped in his ear, breaking the Rule of Silence. "Your letters don't align."

"W—we don't n–n–need to be that faithful to the originals." That treacherous stutter seized him whenever Vidal stood nearby.

"Do you see what's lost if you don't align the letters?"

"I'm s–s–sorry that I can't be p–perfect." Like some people.

"Peace, Brother Felip. This letter is an acrostic. If you don't align the letters, the real message is lost." Vidal ran his long, chalk-white finger down the original pinned on the desk; as if dawn light shone, Felip saw the hidden words in the tightly formed mass of letters. "Also, you can't draw just any cross. See the lunar crescent at each point of the cross? It's part of the message."

Felip jerked the besmirched parchment from his writing desk and thrust it aside, once again humiliated.

"Your work is so beautiful," Brother Vidal said. "God gave you a treasure to preserve in those hands. You shouldn't risk them chopping wood each morning."

"I have to. Else I'd go m–mad in this life." Felip said too much. Yet how did Vidal know what he did at dawn?

"For a man your size, the cloister must be a prison. You're built to be a warrior, not a monk. Most women would find you attractive. How old are you?"

"I'll be t–twenty-one at Easter."

"Why retire from the world so young? You haven't seen enough to leave it behind."

Confused by Vidal's switching between criticism and compliment, Felip spoke carefully. "F–for my family's honor, one brother serves our domus and one serves God. It's my mother's dream that I serve God. And m–m–mine. My dream, too."

"You might offer your beautiful hand as scribe to a lord or a king like Pedro d'Aragón, and be a warrior, too."

"I wasn't raised to fight." Felip again staved off jealous rage, that he was entombed here while his brother was free. "I serve my family's honor." Then hastily, "And God."

Vidal frowned. "Have you even loved a woman to know what you gave up?"

Heat rising up his neck, Felip glanced down at his work, but saw instead the image of Serena from next door in Girona. He spoke slowly, the effort of forming words made more difficult when telling a brazen lie. "I d–don't w–want a woman."

"*Ai.* You must know your own heart, *fadrin.*" Vidal sat at his desk and took up a quill.

"Don't call me a boy," Felip muttered.

"I'm sorry." As if surprised, Vidal returned. "I honor your choice. But I worry that the cloister isn't good for you. God must see that you have more energy than a scriptorium or choir can hold."

Felip reached for his pen. He whispered, "How did you know you could live under the Rules here?"

The script master came in just then. Vidal stepped back to his desk, where the master heaped praise on him for delivering glory to God in his daily work.

Felip fetched a new parchment, deciding to scrape the ruined one later. After sharpening a quill, he carefully drew the *crux lunata* as the anchor character. Then he rapidly inked the message, letter-for-letter, ending with the date the missive called for action in God's name.

The new moon in mid-July.

Which would just be one more day of useless toil and misery at St-Pere monastery. Waiting for the bell to ring for each convocation, and for supper.

■

Vidal sat beside Felip on the refractory bench with only a nod in greeting. After the blessing, Vidal's hand waved deftly, moving more than half his portion of black bread and cheese to Felip's trencher. During the final prayer, Vidal watched the elder brother who led the final devotion at the meal's end.

'How can a young man keep his ways pure?
By guarding it according to Thy word.
With my whole heart I seek thee;
Let me not wander from this commandment.
I have laid up Thy word in my heart,
that I might not sin against Thee.'

While listening to that quavering recitation, Vidal's face lost all its harsh lines, now less like a choir monk preparing for ordination and more like a woman fingering prayer beads. Vidal silently mouthed the verses and prayers, closing his eyes for a moment, and then at the end, licking his chapped lips, as if thirsty for the sanctified pleadings sent to God.

Every man in the hall stood to depart. Vidal touched Felip's hand, the first friendly touch since Felip came to this cold, cold place. "I'm so happy we are friends. God blesses us every day, even if we know not how to see it."

When they arrived at the scriptorium before the others, Felip broke the Silence. "Why are you here, at the world's end?"

"I have nowhere else to go. What once was home...well, it will never again be safe to go there." Vidal's body shuddered with an emotion that Felip couldn't read. "This is my last earthly love, these manuscripts. I'd give my soul to be near them. Especially this one, St-John's gospel." Brother Vidal held a finger over Felip's work, tapping only air, not touching the vellum.

Felip saw the words, not just the individual letters to be copied.

'In principio erat Verbum...'

Gesturing with an unsharpened, ink-free quill, Vidal traced the initial capital. "'*In the beginning was the word*.' See the curve on the V of *Verbum*? This copyist shared St-John's excitement, the man who knew God, who broke bread with him."

"You're here to know God?"

"Only to seek the same joy as that copyist. I have nowhere else to go, nothing else I can do."

For a heartbeat, Felip saw a light surrounding Brother Vidal, as if they stood together in an empty world. This frail brother had surrendered to God so much more than Felip could.

"I'm sorry for your losses," Felip whispered. "I haven't suffered like you. Yet I'm destined to be here. For my family's honor."

"Perhaps," Vidal mused. "It's certainly better for me that you're here, too. You smile when the birds sing at sunrise. You smile when you sit down to take up your work. Which reminds me there's still joy in the world, where I now have a friend."

Vidal settled into his own desk, taking a moment to sharpen a quill before bending his head down to work.

Whenever the script master's back was turned, Felip glanced over, hoping to catch sight of that shock of white hair and the pale, handsome face.

A friend. Vidal called him a friend.

Why would God send him a friend now, after denying all of Felip's other prayers for relief from longing?

■

"Pink and red rhododendrons, showing the mere tips of buds. The wild lilies, smelling of salvation."

Brother Vidal presumed to sit beside Felip again the next morning when he paused after chopping wood, ravenous, to watch the dawn light flit over the valley and its steep hillsides. Vidal passed him a leather bota, from which Felip drank deeply, discovering heavily watered wine inside. Then his friend passed two still-warm brioix loaves, likely stolen from the kitchens in the same way that Felip thieved most mornings.

"The old poets and even Solomon himself sang the glory of spring." Brother Vidal held up his long, ink-stained palm, refusing Felip's offer to share the stolen bread. "The earth awakes, preparing to bring forth fruits to succor man and beast. The birds herald the Risen Lord. Look, there!"

A pair of golden eagles soared overhead, the early morning rays casting a bronze glint to their feathers.

"They appear so glorious," Vidal said. "But they mock how we praise our Creator. For in their beautiful display, they merely seek vermin for their breakfast."

"You're unhappy here," Felip said. "I know you have nightmares. I hear you cry out in the night."

He didn't intend to say that, only to share this rare moment of joy beside Vidal, feeling that brother's energy, like the thrumming of bees in borage at midsummer, calm yet vibrant.

"Dreams are not thoughts." Vidal rose and shook the dew and dirt from the itchy black wool. "We need to be at our chores, *mon amic*."

After morning prayers, they set to their tasks. In the shed that served as a workshop, where the porter had kindled a decent fire. As a first task, they prepared hides, rough work appropriate for a day in very early spring. Felip loved stringing goat hide on a frame; the chore of pulling the hide taut was a good use of his natural strength. Vidal preferred the finer work, scraping scales from the rough parchments.

"What was your family like?" Felip asked. The Rule of Silence seemed irrelevant where no one could hear them.

"The usual. A father and a mother who died when I was young. A son and...oh, God has them all now. I don't know where my sisters and cousins have gone. Most men from my village have gone with Pedro *El Católico* to help take back Andalusia. It's too far away for me to join them."

"What glory, to take the Cross for this new crusade. I long to join. But m–my family..." He lost the words, betrayed by his own tongue.

"They think you serve God best by being here?" Vidal rescued him. "I thought this place would save me, yet I'm pulled back into the world. The letters you copy make me believe I should—"

Vidal dropped his scraper and bent to pick it up.

"You want to leave here?" Felip cried, excited by the thought. "To join the crusade? I wish I could go."

"It's an idle thought, brother. I wasn't attending to my work."

"Many Churchmen are going. Let's beg the abbot to let us go."

"Would he agree?" Vidal puzzled the idea. "We're too valuable for his scripture-copying industry. Though I confess, I don't think this place is right for you."

Chastened, Felip still thrilled at the idea of crusade. "My father, to his great honor, died on Crusade."

"Mine too. Sadly, I have nothing from the man to comfort me."

"I have the letter my father left." Without thinking, Felip touched his breast, where he always carried that packet. "I wonder if I have my father's courage. I'd find out, if I could help carry the Cross into Andalusia."

"Why carry the Cross elsewhere while Simon's crusaders destroy our land and..." Vidal stopped. He looped one hand through the lashings that held the parchment to its frame, but that hand shook as if with a palsy, jittering the parchment so it appeared to breathe.

"You sound like a heretic when you speak of Simon de M— Montfort." In the safety of the shed, Felip spoke his mind.

"It's not heresy to say that Simon breaks the law—Church law and man's law—while claiming he's guided by God." Vidal returned to his scraping chore, dragging the bone-and-steel scraper over the tanned hide. "Let's not talk nightmares. Tell me about your family."

"I didn't mean to cause you hurt."

A light flitted over Vidal's pale face. "Never, *mon amic*. I wish I had a brother like you. Tell your tale. But let's switch to pumice tasks. We've stretched all the hide we can this morning."

Kind words brought Felip up short, his heart thumping. The pair of them moved to a workbench farther from the fire, taking up pumice stones to add the final smooth finish to the parchments that they'd fill in the coming fortnight. Felip spoke carefully.

"My father left on crusade before I was born. I was raised by my m–mother and grandmother."

"That's the way of crusaders' wives, to do the work of the domus. Do you have sisters? How many brothers?"

"Just one brother. A half-brother who was mostly grown when I was born. He trained as a knight with my mother's uncles. He's seigneur of my father's lands now."

"Why don't you have a piece? Don't children from your domus share the land and rents?"

"My mother says it's a grant after the new fashion, passing from father to oldest son. But I still have full share of my father's honor, if not the domus." Felip tried to show the pride he owed his father. "I prove it by serving God."

Vidal shook his head, as if disapproving. "This new fashion will harm the peace of the domus. Equal sharing among all children is the honor our grandfathers taught. It's our paratge. It's justice and kinship and keeping the world in balance by doing what's right." Yet again, Vidal spoke of honor in the old-fashioned way Felip's grandmother did.

Felip demurred. "My honor is given to the Church. I do not begrudge my brother his wealth." He wanted that to be true. He pounded with his pumice stone, matching Vidal's rhythm.

"Of course, Felip. Are you truly sure about giving up everything to stay here? Marriage? Children? You didn't ever love?"

Felip felt his face catch fire. "I fancied a neighbor. But I don't have wealth to support her."

Vidal scraped away with the pumice stone, not commenting on Felip's revelation. When he did speak, it was to assert another sort of challenge to Felip's manhood. "Why didn't an uncle take you to train? Donzels should be taught by men."

Felip considered his uncle's guidance, now only encouraging him to take orders and settle his life at St-Pere. "My people always dreamed that I'd serve God."

"I wish you every blessing, *mon fraire*, that God grant your best dreams come true."

.

Long into the night, Felip woke from a dream where he'd happily removed a woman's clothes, buried his face in her flesh, and slipped his hand into that secret place while she murmured his name in a passion. This time the dream woke him, not because of painful tumescence, but because he removed the woman's veil. It was Vidal who whispered his name.

Sitting up on his cot, drenched in sweat (which happened with every forbidden dream), Felip tried to stop his heart from beating so hard. Gradually the painful state of his member eased.

His cell never felt so cold, his bed so hard. He couldn't, in the way he usually did when sleepless, call on visions of the farmer's wife or his grandmother's serving girls. Felip had carried his own iniquity inside these walls. He imagined writing out the last beautiful manuscript he'd copied, gilding the illuminations in the margins. In his mind he traced every letter with care, mouthing the words in Latin while pondering the words of Solomon in the vulgar tongue.

> 'Let him kiss me with the kisses of his mouth: for thy love is better than wine.'

It was almost dawn. Felip rose and pulled on his boots, which never kept out the cold. He set to work with an axe at the woodpile, kindling a fire in his muscles, his heart inflamed.

He'd come here to serve God but now found no hope of escaping iniquity, even though that patch of land in Girona had bought him full remission from sin.

Because, while never mastering his lust for women, Felip had fallen in love with Brother Vidal.

.

That afternoon, Felip and Vidal worked together cleaning in the scriptorium, bringing the first test of his newly found love. Felip kept glancing at his friend, endeavoring to see the real man, not the previous night's dream. Too thin and girlish to be handsome, Vidal's face was haunting rather than beguiling in the way he'd appeared in Felip's dream. The face of someone who'd lived through nightmares.

"What's this?" Vidal whispered. The script master wasn't there to preserve the Rule. "I found it in the parchment cupboard."

It was Felip's latest letter to his grandmother, begging her to let him take orders now. He'd set it aside, intending to ask the abbot to send it with a messenger, like he had the previous two letters.

"My grandmother keeps the gold that will buy my place in the monastery. If she'll let me take orders now, then I can go with—"

"But what does this mean?" Vidal interrupted, pointing to the passage where Felip described Matheus's visit months earlier.

"I'm helping the n–new crusade. The rents from my land go to one of the priest-knight orders, to support the crusade against the M–Moors."

"It's not a crusade." Vidal frowned. "The pope isn't preaching crusade. Pedro d'Aragón calls it a mission of peace and faith to free Christians, not to murder the Moors."

"But the knights and their supporters receive lifelong remission of sins. Doesn't that make it a crusade?"

"Which order took your land?" Vidal spoke as sternly as the reprimanding script master. "The Templars? The Knights of Calatrava?"

"The Knights of the Holy Cross." Resentment steamed inside him. Friend or not, Vidal had no business scolding him.

"There is no such order, *mon fraire*. Did you sign the Grant of Release from Pedro without learning who got your land?"

"Only the deed to the order."

"Pedro *El Rei* will be unhappy that you deeded land without his permission. What's this mark?"

Frowning at how hard it was to read Matheus's handwriting, Felip recalled what his brother said. "The order is called Crux Lunata."

"*Jhezu del tron*, now they're stealing from the innocent." Vidal swore on Jesus in heaven.

"Pardon?"

Vidal touched Felip's hand, making him shiver. "*Mon amic*, you don't want to join them. They are butchers and thieves who hide behind a false cross."

Not noticing that he'd extinguished Felip's sole hope for joy, Vidal bent over his work, while Felip achieved little, knotted in several kinds of despair. He needed to ask his uncle what Matheus had gotten him into.

Felip broke the Silence when they left the scriptorium for afternoon prayers. "How do you know what Pedro d'Aragón thinks?"

"My family's castles are rendered to him." Vidal answered so mildly that it quelled Felip's ire. "Pedro is a good man, *mon fraire*. I'm sure he'll forgive your mistake in signing that grant."

"A mistake? I receive a lifelong remission of sins for helping the crusade." Felip wrenched his hands into prayer.

"What good is that?" Vidal seemed innocent, even sweet again. "You haven't had a chance to commit any real sins."

"There's always d–d–doubt." The words exploded from deep inside, but came out as a stuttering, weak argument.

"*Ai, mon fraire!* You are such a good person." Vidal touched his elbow. So thin, Vidal seemed much smaller standing close. The sense of loving Vidal settled over Felip again, warming his insides. "It's too lonely here for you. Let's not quarrel. We must be friends."

When Felip jerked open the chapel door, Vidal murmured, "You shouldn't be here. And I need to go before it's too late."

·

After supper and before final prayers, while a thin early-spring light seeped through the heavy rain, Felip paced the gallery, keeping his hands folded so that his concentration looked like prayer, instead of a man wrestling with doubt and longing.

It came to him during afternoon prayers that it wasn't Vidal who'd made a fool of him over deeding away his land. He'd done it himself. He couldn't change his mind about the priesthood now. If he returned to Girona, he'd have to live on Matheus's mercy. Felip no longer had land of his own. Just that portion of gold his grandmother held, to buy his way into this monastery.

Where he had only one kind friend. Who wanted to leave.

A harsh sound in the gallery rafters drew his eyes upward. A dark form flitted in the shadows, wanting release. Then the melody began. A lark, trapped, desperate to escape. In the fading light, Felip made out the black rim of feathers around the lark's throat, like a trapper's rope. Another trilling of melody. Fluttering for freedom.

A lark belongs in a flock.

Felip raised his arms, waving, hoping to drive the bird down from the rafters so it could escape through the arches. The rafters were too high for his wave to alert the lark. He stopped at the heavy wooden door to the chapel, seeing the ink on his hand as if he were reading a message.

He couldn't stay here any longer.

Even with Vidal's friendship, life in these walls would stretch on forever. Without Vidal here, Felip would endure fifty, sixty years of ink and prayers. Hungry. Lonely. Doubting.

Felip strode back through the gallery to the abbot's room to explain what he now knew, that if Matheus refused to take him on crusade, then Felip had no heart to remain here. He'd go home. Walk back to Girona.

Or better, persuade Brother Vidal to leave with him. Perhaps together they might find a way to join the new crusade.

Felip rounded the last corner of the gallery, seeing the linen banner on the door-pull, indicating that the abbot was open to all guests. Yet the door was closed. Felip hesitated, his hand on the cold iron door-pull, hearing Vidal's voice inside. He listened in the shadows, like a Judas Iscariot or another ignoble beast.

"You've come!" The abbot sounded jovial.

"You left me no choice." Vidal's hoarse voice rebuked the abbot, which no brother dared do.

"You expected to do this work all your life, Brother Vidal? What must God think of you?"

"I'm not harming anyone. No one need ever know."

"I sang in the choir at Minerve. Yet you are so altered, I didn't recognize you. Until we seized that message you sent Pedro. It took me a while to recognize you."

"Will you give me to Simon de Montfort? His men already took everything that made my life worth living."

"That's too harsh. Shall I still call you Brother Vidal?"

"I'm at your mercy, Pere Abát."

The abbot laughed, but not in his usual jolly way. "Perhaps you'd prefer I deliver you to the archbishop at Narbonne to judge."

"Pedro's uncle?" Vidal's voice warmed. "I met him when—"

"No, the new one. Arnau Amalric."

Vidal cried out, like a girl who'd been pinched.

"*Òc*," the abbot said. "Not your friend. Yet we don't have time to involve Arnau."

"It's clear you and your friends are in a hurry, Pere Abát. I'm curious about what you plan for the new moon in July."

"*Ai*, a little fox, are you? Spying on Church business?"

"Only reading what the script master sets us to copy."

"And smuggling messages to Pedro." After a few moments' rustling, the abbot said, "Do you recognize this, Brother Vidal? Drink from this chalice for the healing of your unbeliever's heart."

"Lovely. The Greeks do nice things with glass. At least on Naxos."

"As if you'd recognize the sacred." The abbot's voice dripped scorn. "The Aragón king Ramiro brought it to St-Pere for us to protect. After the Cid recaptured it from the Moors."

"We had three of them at my house when I was a child."

"Unbelief such as yours must fall before the Grail. Our Lord drank from it the night before he was crucified. It captured our Lord's blood when the Romans pierced His side."

"*Ieu cresi. Ajudar a tu la miá incredulitat.*" Vidal repeated the words of St-Thomas, but in a vulgar tongue.

I believe. Help thou my unbelief.

"This grail held the blood of martyrs. We'll use it to rid Christendom of the perfidy of kings."

"I won't allow you to destroy Pedro."

"You won't allow it? We'll join the grail with this blade, the blessed sword of the Cid, to destroy heretics such as you, Brother Vidal." The abbot coughed. "Though we both know Vidal of Valerós died in the desert twenty years ago. It's past time for the new Vidal to join him in the grave."

Another girl-like cry peeled in the abbot's suite. "*Sst sst, baquelar.* How did you come by this blade?"

The shout and shuffling frightened Felip into action. He must save Brother Vidal.

•

Isabella wrenched away Tomás's short-sword, disarming the abbot in the precise way Chrétien taught.

Safe here for months, and now in ten heartbeats, almost dead again. With the blade at the abbot's throat, she hissed at him, the way she'd longed to do for months.

"*Sst sst, baquelar.* How did you come by this blade?"

"Our champion seized it from—"

The door slammed open, its heavy wrought-iron pull banging into her elbow, pushing them both to the floor.

The blade jammed only a knuckle deep. More than enough.

The abbot stared in surprised. Tried to speak. Blood poured from his mouth over her hand.

"Aiieee!" She jumped up, drawing away Tomás's sword.

More choking and retching.

She knelt to help him, pressed one hand over the wound, lifted his head with the other. Blood flooded both hands. She couldn't stop it. He stared into her eyes, his lips moving without words. She prayed for him, beseeching God in rapid Latin.

"*Ai,* our Father in heaven, forgive us as we forgive…"

She rushed the prayer. Was she shouting? *O God, please!*

The abbot still stared, hollow eyed now.

She closed his eyes, then saw she was smearing his face in gore. Again, she jumped away, looking around, her ears buzzing as if flies and bees darted all around. How to ever get clean?

Finding the water pitcher, still begging forgiveness, she splashed it over her hands, the chalice catching most of what ran red from her fingers. She grabbed that piece of linen from the outer door-pull and kicked the door shut, and then leaned against the abbot's work table, wiping her hands clean, hearing her own breath scrape in and out, as if she wheezed sand. She still hated blood.

Our Father in heaven, forgive us…

That poor child Felip bent over the abbot, looking green and ready to puke. She felt the same, though there wasn't time for it.

"You killed him!" The boy-monk gazed up at her, bewildered.

"No, *fadrin.* I stopped him from killing me. Just before you thrust me upon him." She wiped away more of the abbot's blood with the linen banner, not knowing what to do with the stained rag. She stuffed it into the chalice… *forgive us…*

One deep breath. For all the many ideas she'd had about how to leave, it was time to act.

She heaved open the cupboards, checking the contents quickly, tucking the crucial rolls of parchment under her arm. While she worked, Felip seemed to be talking to her, but she couldn't hear his furtive whispers while she searched for rags of evidence marked with a *crux lunata*.

"You only see dead people when they're wrapped in funeral clothes, prepared for burial." Felip didn't stumble on a single word, but seemed lost. Isabella judged whether she needed to shake him from shock, like Tomás once had to do for her. The first time she'd killed a man. *O Father forgive us as we forgive…*

She took Felip's arm, as gently as she could. He flinched. She peeled back the sleeve of his robe and studied that place where the Crux Lunata tattooed its people. Satisfied once again that he was indeed as innocent as a lamb, she released him.

"Are you taking those?" Felip pointed to the scrolls under Brother Vidal's arm. "Let—let me help."

"No, *fadrin*. Go. Now. It isn't safe here for you."

She wrapped the ones to be left behind in another parchment and pushed the roll into a high corner of a cupboard. Then she retrieved the chalice, damp rag and all, and pushed it onto the shelf.

"Let's store it with the abbot's relics, where others cannot see."

"What are you taking?"

"The deeds of land given without Pedro's consent. In Narbonne. Portions of Xirgú and other land in Girona and the Toulousain. It's not just you and me that they've stolen from."

Time to go. She nudged past where Felip once more gawped at the body lying in a pool of crimson. *Breathe, ma dòmna.* Chrétien's voice, commanding her in a fight, so she didn't have to think. *High guard! Step now!*

"It's like an old bad song, isn't it?" She wiped Tomás's short-sword with the hem of her robe and restored the blade to its familiar, ragged leather sheath. He'd complained since Famagusta that he needed a new sheath, could never find one that suited him in any market. She placed her hand where his had molded the grip's leather wrapping. The shape of his hand. Warm. As if he'd just held it. "The abbot wanted to kill me with a magic sword. They've killed me too many times. This sword only consoles me."

"Take me with you!" Felip cried.

"Leave if you want, *fadrin*. You hate it here. But I can't take you with me. It's too dangerous."

"Please. I love you."

"*Ai. Jhezu del tron!*"

·

Left behind in the abbot's chambers, Felip reached up where Vidal had hidden those things. He fetched down the chalice carefully, remembering how Lorenç had said many times what a gift from God it was. He hastily stuffed that bloody rag to the back of the shelf. He tucked the cup into the bosom of his own robe, lodging it over the letter from his father, hoping he could find a way to use Lorenç's grail, perhaps to beg forgiveness from a king. A glimmer flashed on the lower shelf, reflecting light from the candle on the work table. He lifted a woven-wool purse, a simple checkered pattern, tied up with an indigo-dyed strip of leather.

Like the purse he played with as a child, sitting on his grandmother's bed, emptying and refilling it with beads and coins and buckles and shells.

Inside this purse was a stash of gold marks, the ones his grandmother had saved for him. And a small, wadded piece of parchment with scratches begging that Felip be safe in God's care.

He choked on bile.

He'd been betrayed by his family.

He'd failed Vidal, coming in too late, coming in all wrong.

Hurrying, Felip found Vidal in his cell, where he dragged a wad from under the straw pallet and tied it into a blanket along with that sword. Felip rushed to his own cell to fetch his linen and extra boots, imitating Vidal's solution with the blanket. He expected that they'd head for the gate, but Vidal stopped in the scriptorium to grab more parchments. After all these months performing the rarest copy work, Vidal wanted only the rags of messages that the abbot made Felip copy. Then they skirted the script master's cell, where Felip endeavored to tread as silently as the small brown birds who hid from weasels in the hedge. They crossed the courtyard to the next barrier, the porter who guarded the gate at night.

"*Bon nuoit, Àvi,*" Vidal called softly, speaking in the crude Catalan of a mountain peasant, calling the porter grandfather.

"*Ai, fadrin.* It's you?" The porter grasped Vidal's arm in greeting, as if the brother were a peasant like him.

"*Òc. Àvi,* help me!" Vidal asked the porter's help. "This is the night I believed might come."

"I shall miss you." The porter slipped back into his shed, more a byre than a house, and then brought out a traveler's pack. "Here's the gold you asked me to guard." He dangled a leather purse.

"They may be hard on you for helping me."

"Because I slept at my post when two brothers departed in the dark of night? I'm happy you are returning to the world."

"Go with God." Vidal bid the old man farewell. The porter creaked open the smaller gate, leaving only enough room for a single body to slip outside. "My friend here will be your excuse. He kept you up talking so you both missed seeing anyone pass through the gate."

"I'm c–coming, too." Felip towered over both Vidal and the old porter. "You can't stop me."

Vidal slipped through the gate without answering and strode down the mountain road. Felip, fumbling to adjust his pack and what he carried inside his robe, nudged the gate open wider and shadowed his friend.

"Where are you going?" Felip asked when they were a thousand steps beyond the gate.

"Pedro has most likely left for Toledo. I'm going to buy a horse and join him."

"Wh–why?"

"Filthy men like the abbot stole my land and killed my family. My villages and people are under interdict. All the women's names in my family are on the bishop's list of Good Christian heretics. Everyone who shelters me ends up murdered by heretic hunters."

"You're a heretic?"

"No matter. Crux Lunata and Simon de Montfort want to destroy my world. Pedro d'Aragón is the only person in Christendom who can protect my people. I need to warn him."

"Of what?"

"You copied the abbot's correspondence for him, *fadrín*. Did you read it? The knights of Crux Lunata seek to destroy Pedro."

Bile flooded his throat, choking any ability to speak. He'd been worse than a fool. He'd helped his family betray their own honor. He struggled for words, like he had through his whole deluded life. "That's w–why you fought with m–my uncle?"

"Your uncle?" Vidal kept getting further ahead, though Felip had the longer stride. "Who's your uncle?"

"Lorenç. Our abbot."

Vidal stopped so abruptly, Felip collided with him.

"The man who tried to murder me? You're his spy?"

"No. Lorenç didn't want the monks to think I had special privileges, so he never tells anyone."

Vidal again swore a torrent of unholy words, unlike anything Felip had heard in the farmyards and smithy at home. He waited until Vidal was silent again, striding rapidly along the path.

"Go home to your grandmother, *fadrín*."

"No. Let me help. I love you."

"Sancta Maria, not another *baquelar* crying, 'I love you!'"

"No, I'm not a bastard. I'm a true son of the House of Xirgú. Lorenç is my mother's brother, from the House of Montcava."

"*Jhezu del tron*, will I ever be free of Montcava murderers?"

"I'm not Montcava. And I will do anything for you, to make up for my uncle's sins."

Vidal sped up his pace, jogging to where the mountain path met the coast road. Felip in pursuit, breathless, struggled to understand how much betrayal and dishonor his uncle and brother had dragged him into. The travelers took a break only when Vidal stepped into a rhododendron thicket. Felip assumed the brother had a greater need for relief; he was taking care of his own lesser needs when Vidal reappeared, the monk's robe replaced by woolen leggings and leather traveling clothes that an artisan might wear. Or a petty mercenary, since Vidal also now wore that short-sword thrust into a sturdy baldric.

"Perhaps I can sell this somewhere." Vidal stuffed the boiled-wool robe into his pack. "We'll be pursued, *fadrin*. Go back now. Tell them you tried to stop me."

"No. For my family's honor, I owe you recompense for not saving you from Lorenç."

"*Ai, renrén.* I can't afford a horse for you."

"Don't call me a fool. I have my own gold." He showed Vidal the purse from the cupboard. "My grandmother sent my monastery fee. This will pay my way."

"*Ai*, a clever man." Vidal hoisted his pack. "It's another league to a market-town. Let's go."

Their trek down the mountain and along the seaside road became amiable. Vidal and Felip kept to the verge, avoiding hazel branches, cistus roses, and broom, where his wool robe snagged far more easily than Vidal's travel clothes. They began to pass more dwellings and shepherds' huts where dogs barked.

"At the market-town, I'll buy our supplies. Your black robe will draw the curious, so keep out of sight." Vidal recited a list of boots, blankets, and dried beans needed for traveling. "What else do you need to travel?"

"Show me the kindness you did before."

"I don't hold your family's sins against you, *fadrin*."

"No, more than that."

After a moment that lasted so long the sky paled to grey in the dawn light, Vidal said, "I know what you're feeling. I was in love once. In secret."

"Did he ever love you back?"

"*Òc.*"

"Then you don't know what I'm feeling."

"*Ai, fadrin.* You're like a little brother to me. I can never love another man."

"Then why did you make me love you?"

Vidal left him, softly muttering *maledicta* worthy of a Catalan goatherd while jogging down the path to town. Felip stayed out of sight, using a fallen tree as a bench. As he did most mornings, he prayed to divert his thoughts from hunger. Then he touched that letter from his father that he'd lodged over his heart, vowing in his prayers to do no less than his father had and giving thanks for being allowed to join the crusade.

.

Still pondering what to do about that boy Felip while busy purchasing a tunic and leggings for him in the marketplace, Isabella chatted while she exchanged coins for goods, asking the people selling wares about the quality of roads between the mountains and Barcelona.

One vendor offered succulent chickpea cakes with a mess of large pale beans—and the smell reminded her that Felip must be starving by now, so she offered up small coppers for enough to feed both of them for a couple of days. Then she headed to the end of town where, people said, the blacksmith had two horses for sale.

"*Hola*, it's a beautiful day, no?"

A short, barrel-shaped man, the smith greeted her in Catalan, commenting on the weather, and she replied the way any man from her village would, claiming to be Vidal from outside Toulouse and in need of horses to return home.

"Soldiers came through where we were visiting our cousins, took half the animals in the village. I sold my horses when they gave me no choice. But now I need to restore two horses to my uncle."

"They paid you? Normans that came through here just took what they wanted."

"Pedro's men. They paid me. Let's see your animals."

The smith had two decent ponies, nothing Pèire Leteric would ever bring home to Valerós, but healthy enough to get her to Barcelona, though not as fast or handsome as the horses lost last year to crusader-bandits.

At the end of town where the smithy stood, everyone sensed the pounding of horses before they arrived. A dozen knights galloped down the road from Girona, their mail gleaming in the morning light as they entered a village that had to watch out for itself.

Carts pushed out of the road as soon as the thunder echoed off the hillside.

Children scampered, chasing their dogs home.

Mothers shrieked boys' names, calling for God's help.

White gambesons fluttering, helmets tied to their saddle, twelve men entered the village, slowing only for their own safety. They clearly weren't stopping, just reining in the horses enough for caution while continuing up the road that led to St-Pere. Their leader, ruddy hair streaming behind him, leaned forward as if he yearned to be farther faster. He glanced around only once, his eyes passing over the slim figure of Vidal in the shadows. No recognition.

Yet Isabella recognized the Crux Lunata bastard who'd succeeded twice in destroying everyone around her while missing her, now for the third time.

Except the knight reined in, halting his whole band.

Isabella stepped back deep into the shade of the smithy, which was already as hot as a high summer's day.

"We need your services. No, we command them in the name of Holy Church."

Crux Lunata wanted the smith, not Isabella.

A horse had a loose shoe. All other work must cease until it was repaired. A dozen men lingered in the shade to wait, a hand's breadth away from Isabella in the shadows.

"*Girona at Lent wasn't the greatest joy of the year.*"

"*I'll be glad to be out of the saddle at Easter. That'll be another reason to rejoice our Risen Lord.*"

"*Seems a waste to ride to Girona and now back to Narbonne when we want to be in Toledo.*"

"*What our leader commands…*"

"*Our leader believes there's heretic gold in these hills.*"

"*Still, a man can only sit in a saddle for so long.*"

"*We'll enjoy Easter Week in a big town. Better than what's ahead.*"

The leader, the bastard who'd ruined her life, stood in the archway, arguing with the smith about whether payment was due, or whether the smith owed still more in service to God. Isabella watched him probe the darkness, the same way he'd hunted for her on the Assumption feast-day last summer, picking through the boulders beside that road in the Pyrenees.

But a few moments later, he was riding away. The Knights of the Lunate Cross cantered through town, following the leg of the road that led to Narbonne, the sound of hooves fading while the smith's curses grew louder.

"Holier than a pack of rabid priests. Call themselves an order. An order of fools and thieves, I say."

Isabella led the talk back to the horses she needed. Silver changed hands, calming the smith. While she waited for the smith's boy to saddle her horses and load the provisions she'd purchased, she thanked God for her new freedom and that the Crux Lunata hadn't interrupted her life once again.

She still didn't know the meaning of the new moon at midsummer, only that certain Churchmen plotted against Pedro. She didn't dare hope that Pascal, the St-Pere porter, had successfully smuggled out even one of her warnings. She had to reach Pedro to warn him, and to beg him to save Valerós from Simon de Montfort. A long journey lay ahead.

Unfortunately, she now had a Montcava third cousin to drag over mountains and plains. He professed to care for her, but Felip was as large and as deluded as any Montcava son of an enemy who'd ever beleaguered her. This must be how Tomás felt when he steered her cross-country from Valerós to Toulouse years ago.

Then, thinking of Tomás, she did what she always did, twenty times a day, silently repeating a prayer for the deliverance of souls, hoping again that Tomás and Sebastián and Yusuf had secured their places in heaven by now, with all the prayers she'd rendered.

Begging God's mercy for them, every waking moment and through all her dreams. Hoping that heaven comforted them.

PART THREE

In the World

An Angel and a Djinni Ponder Free Will

"YOUR PEOPLE BELIEVE AS MINE DO."

"My people? I have no people," the false Ahriman said. "These tribes shift with the sands, where they live, what they believe. Now they see me, now they cannot. Now they fear me and beg you for protection. In other ages and other worlds, it's the other way around."

"We are Agents of our Creator. We bring Deliverance and assist in Judgment. We do as our Heavenly Father bids, you and I." The angel handed the blood orange back to the djinni. "And My Father provided me with the form of Man's mouth only so that I might speak His Commands, not to Defile it with Fruits of the Earth."

"Poor Grigor. We have no father, you and me. And I am never bid," the djinni boasted. Using the horn-like nail of his forefinger, he split the fruit's peel with one long cutting scratch. "And, I might add, many of your angel-brothers have also asserted their personal powers. I go where I will, and do as I want."

"What good is Free Will if your Choice leads only to Outer Darkness?" The voice of the angel Grigor crunched like ice, that strange substance from the highest mountains.

Ahriman al-Djinni laughed again, his voice grating like coarse sand. "Where is this caravanserai you call 'Outer Darkness'? Have you visited there? Perhaps next time I should accompany you to light your way, since I'm made of Fire. You creatures made of Air waft away too easily."

"Your Fire cannot burn where there is Nothing." Grigor might have folded his arms in challenge, but he hadn't been built that way by his Creator.

"If you were with me, there wouldn't be nothing, Little Brother."

"I despair of your False Reasoning. You pretend to be an Innocent Child while plying the craft of imps and devils."

Ahriman al-Djinni said, "I despair of your belief that being lost in the desert at night time—your 'Outer Darkness'— is a punishment inflicted by the demi-urge you call God. It's no wonder that you deny the joys of free will."

"I wish You were in Outer Darkness now. Alone." Grigor 's words echoed across the waste of sand below them, revealing that he'd been provoked once more into departing from the peace bestowed by his Creator.

"I wouldn't mind," laughed Ahriman. "But that's not a nice thing to say, the way you mean it."

> — *Ibn Jafar, The Poet*
> *From Tales of the Angel and the Djinni*

8
Castile

SEBASTIÁN'S NEW CHAINMAIL FIT WELL, but his role as Master of Valerós chafed. In Pedro's camp in Toledo, Sebastián longed for Tomás's company, as much as he'd missed Isabella through the long winter. He wished he had Tomás's help to decide: have this soldier whipped for petty theft, or choose another punishment?

A short, squalid man stood before him, dressed in the linsey-woolsey of a Frankish foot soldier, a cuirass with half its brass knobs missing, leggings wrapped with leather strips. Lank mousey hair that might be straw-colored if clean, a big nose that stuck itself into trouble. Nothing washed since Candlemas.

"Thieving from your own camp mates? You betrayed their trust," Sebastián said. He stood tall to tower over the fool. His bones complained about the pain from growing so fast. "How can they trust you when it's time to battle the Saracens?"

Sweat drenched the man's brow. He couldn't wipe it away since his hands were bound. Though still early spring, the midday heat already brutalized the soldiers who languished in a wooded camp outside Toledo.

"What shall we do with you?" Sebastián asked. He spoke in French, since that worked best with the stray *francimandalha* consigned to the Valerós camp. He also growled, like his grandfather Pèire Leteric disciplining the donzels and kennel boys when they ran amok in Castell-de-Valerós. Pèire's voice always shook boys and men to their bones. Sebastián sounded like Pèire now that his voice no longer broke unexpectedly.

117

The man quivered. "I beg your mercy, monsieur. I will take my whipping."

Sebastián stripped the filthy linen tunic from the man's shoulders. "You've been whipped before."

"Oui," the man said.

"*Ai, francimand.* It didn't serve as either penance or lesson." Sebastián switched to the common tongue of Valerós, speaking for the sake of the men watching. "You followed your lord on crusade for salvation of your sins, and yet you commit more sins each day?"

"My lord died of a fever." The man understood only *your lord* in Sebastián's words.

Jhezu del tron. That was how Valerós ended up with untrained men. Lords died of simple fevers and left their hired foot soldier roaming free. Sebastián switched to French again. "*Monsieur francès,* what are you called?"

"Barthélemy. I'm from Poitou."

"Until we solve this problem, Barthélemy of Poitou, you have brothers-in-arms who think of you only as a thief. A betrayer. A Judas. *Peccador,* we say. That means 'sinner' in your tongue. Someone who sins as a profession. How shall you be redeemed?"

He repeated the thought in the tongue most of Valerós understood. The more Sebastián drew out the time to judgment, the more Barthélemy suffered. The men behind him remained silent, but Sebastián sensed a surge of energy when he voiced their resentment.

"Monsieur, I—"

"I am called Senhór Sebastián. I am Master of Valerós. You will call me senhór. All men under me do."

"*Oui,* senhór. I will take my punishment."

"Who would believe it? In the Valerós camp, we say *òc.* You must learn to speak in the same tongue these men do. They will protect your life when we fight the Moors."

How to convince Valerós men to trust a thieving Frank in battle? Marshal Guillem, who was paid by Pedro *El Rei* to teach the arts of warfare, had solved such problems among the real Valerós army before Tomás and Sebastián returned from Cairo. Now Pedro repeatedly consigned new squads of men to Valerós, leaving scant time to teach the Valerós battle moves to strangers before they marched into

Andalusia. Leaving barely enough time to teach them to shout "Awake, Steel!" as the Valerós battle-cry. He must bellow, "*Desperta, Ferro*, you fools!" a hundred times a day.

The problem with this thief wasn't how much misery to cause him, but how to unite Valerós men in battle. For that goal, Father Anselm always advised work duty for punishment, rather than whipping. Anselm had fought with Pèire in the Outremer for decades before becoming a priest. He usually had impeccable wisdom. But his usual advice for punishment wouldn't be sufficient with a recalcitrant thief.

"We shall settle this as men," Sebastián said. He cut the man's bonds with his dagger. Unexpected action delivers the best lesson. That's what Pèire taught.

Barthélemy rubbed his wrists, bewildered.

Sebastián shed his gambeson, so he too was in linen shirt sleeves. "We'll fight for God's judgment. That's what your *francimand* lords prefer, isn't it? If I win, I shall decide your fate. If you win, these men will ask you to leave this camp."

He waved his new Castilian dagger over his head, pointing to the sweating crowd of Valerós bordoniers behind him, wishing he still had that dagger of Tomás's, the one he gave to Yusuf.

Father Anselm offered his own dagger to Barthélemy. The solemnity of the Norman priest in chainmail offering his dagger wasn't lost on the Valerós crowd. Or on the thieving *francimand*. Only a fool or a stranger would bet against Sebastián in a knife fight. Tomás said that Sebastián fought better than he did. Even Chrétien conceded that Sebastián was the best of pupils. He'd lost only one fight, when five men set upon him on that road outside Perpignan.

When this fight was over—it lasted only as long as Sebastián chose, in order to give his men a lesson on hand-to-hand fighting—Barthélemy bled heavily from a gash at his hairline, a long slice from his ear to his big *francimand* nose, and the gouge on his right arm.

"Teach him how to take care of that," Sebastián said to Father Anselm, pointing to Barthélemy's arm. "I can't afford to lose soldiers to festering wounds."

He turned again to the sweating thief. "I choose for you, Barthélemy of Poitou, to practice man-to-man combat from dawn to high noon with each Valerós fighter. Start tomorrow at dawn. Practice until the Sunday after Easter. Father Anselm will give you the penance to repeat while you learn to fight like a grown man instead of a thieving child."

He turned to the Valerós men. "Use protected blades or wooden blanks only. You are ordered by me to teach this man discipline and strength. I made him bleed enough for the sake of Valerós."

The Valerós bordoniers cheered when Sebastián lugged up his chainmail and tossed it over his shoulder as if it were merely a jerkin. He stalked off to his tent, to wash off the man's blood and to cool down from the fight.

Qui s'ho creu? He liked to growl the way Pèire did (*Who'd believe it?*), and he liked towering over men whose fate was under his power. Yet he had no one to walk off the field with except Marshal Guillem. And no one with whom to laugh and drink bitter watered wine at the end of the day.

Go with the dark angels to the dark place!

Sebastián swore, consigning Tomás to eternal damnation for leaving him here alone.

·

Long ago, when Sebastián was a child of twelve, trapped with Don Tomás inside the siege at Minerve, he'd raised doubts: was he ready for a soldier's life?

"Maybe I'm only supposed to be the seigneur of Valerós and defend my own lands, instead of living as a soldier like you do."

"You'll know when the time comes," Tomás had said. "This Christian-on-Christian siege can't teach you much, except how to endure. You'll know when you're with a real army, laying siege from the outside."

"How will I know?"

Don Tomás had been standing on the Minerve battlements. He pointed across the way to the ten thousand French soldiers camped on the plateau, with their cooking fires and baggage wagons. Banked latrines. Smithies and siege engines. "You'll know because you'd rather be in camp than home in the safe, clean bed your aunties keep for you."

Now, outside Toledo after the last half-year's training and provisioning, Sebastián was at last traveling in the dust with a thousand men. On the way to a real war, not that hideous banditry that Simon de Montfort practiced on fellow Christians.

One plague persisted in this life. He itched. Sebastián had to hike over to the laundry-women's camp every few days and trade a silver penny for clean clothes and to have the lice combed from his hair.

Stones migrated under his sleeping kit every night.

Dust rimed his nostrils.

Which was lucky, because even in a camp as clean as Marshal Guillem maintained, the stink of the latrine lingered. And the cooking fires promised yet another dinner of beans, with every man eager for Easter, so they could enjoy aged mutton with those beans.

He'd won silver off his own men, gambling at night—half a month's wages from some—so he had to let them win money back, the way Don Tomás taught him. He'd learned to mend his own chainmail and taught the smaller boys to keep it oiled. The sound of chain in barrels of sand and oil was as much a part of the morning litany as Father Anselm's prayers.

Sebastián joined his men each evening, when everyone carped on camp conditions and castigated those responsible for maintaining them. He listened while whetting the edge of the dagger he'd bought in Toledo. However much he enjoyed complaining, he kept his counsel while others complained. Truth? He enjoyed this life.

"If Benito of Valerós can't get his bordoniers shoveling lime any better, we'll all die of camp-fever before we see a single Moor."

"All these beans, can't we just turn our backs to the blackamoors and fart them back to Marrakesh?"

"That's why they say 'Devil take the hind most.'"

"May the Lord save the man that's the hind of this train of peccadors."

"Did you hear about that sergeant over in Alfonso's camp who whipped the waterboy? Worst discipline in Christendom, if you ask me. No one in this camp has to rip the flesh of children to get men to behave."

"They're Castilian dogs. They only claim to be Christians to share the booty. Half of them rode in from Andalusia. Mozarabs happy to betray another general or king. Pretending to be soldiers."

"Watch where you plant your big bum, you monkey punxor."

"Damn you to the devil. Don't kick the sand about, you scrofulous cur. I'm oiling my cuirass here."

Yes, Sebastián loved camp life. He now suspected that all the sermons from Pèire Leteric ("you do it only for paratge, *fadrin*, nothing else; if it's not for honor, stay home") was so much cat piss. Pèire Leteric spent fifty years as a crusader because he loved this life more than any other. Sebastián enjoyed this camp more than any abode in the cities and villages where Sebastián's family had houses, whether Toulouse, Barcelona, Valerós, or Famagusta.

If only Tomás and Chrétien were here to share it.

·

"Hospitallers. Templars." Father Anselm pointed out banners of the orders of knights while they walked together through camp to answer Pedro's call to report.

"*Òc*, I recognize their colors. Do you remember how many times my *aví* Pèire drew banners in the dust to show me how troops had been arrayed in different battles?"

Father Anselm pointed further down the rows of tents. "Orden de Monfragüe, who dissented when the Mountjoy Order joined the Templars."

"Pèire would have approved." Sebastián, however, wanted to keep an open mind, unlike his grandfather, whose experience in the Outremer left him notoriously opinionated.

"The Order of Calatrava." Anselm pointed to another banner. "Do you know them?"

"Pedro spoke of them when he schooled us in Barcelona. Cistercians from Castile. Monks who became knights, instead of the usual way around."

"*Òc*. And they have legitimate claims on land here in Iberia that the other orders don't. Especially since they retook Calatrava from the Moors after the Templars lost it."

"But then," Sebastián said, "twenty years ago they lost Calatrava again. Do they have the most to prove this year?"

Anselm pointed over Sebastián's shoulder, shifting his attention in another direction. A new banner flew at the edge of the encampment of the orders.

Three lunate crosses, shining gold on a field of red.

"Does Pedro know?"

"They weren't here yesterday. At least, that banner wasn't there when I passed by."

Once they arrived at Pedro's camp, there was no time to ask. Pedro launched into business as soon as every man was present in the makeshift courtyard outside his pavilion. Pedro's closest guards—Sebastián recognized Marcos and Cebrián—kept others away while the captains reported to the king of Aragón. Sebastián concentrated on the others' reports, though that crimson-and-gold banner waved in the distance.

From the dozen leaders gathered, Pedro wanted to know the state of this army. How many men deserted after finding Iberia too demanding a walk through the countryside? How many fell ill? How many were injured in camp squabbles? Was the food supply arriving on time? Were thieves caught and punished? Other captains and masters dozed on their feet, lulled by the monotony after they concluded their own reports. Sebastián preferred to hear it all.

"Will the Master of Valerós report, if you please?"

"Òc, Monsenyor." Sebastián spoke boldly, though others in the room likely rated him too young to report directly to a king. Also, Father Anselm stood at his side, the most ferocious and experienced of the warrior-priests on this crusade. "Under the Valerós captains we present eight hundred men. We rate the infantry to be at common Valerós standards for combat. They have drilled for all seven advance formations. The cavalry are good southern knights, in the old style. We rate them at best Valerós standards for attack."

"Have you prepared your knights for retreat?" Pedro asked.

Sebastián didn't pause, since both Marshall Guillem and Tomás taught the same strategy for retreat. "Valerós uses the appearance of retreat as merely another attack strategy."

"What has become of the Mozarab archers I sent to Valerós?" Pedro asked.

"Those men are now Valerós archers. We rate them ready at Valerós standards."

All other captains refused to accept those archers into their camps. Until Valerós arrived at Toledo, many such bands had been consigned to Alfonso *El Rei*, the Castilian king, who seemed to have a higher tolerance for Mozarab mercenaries in his camp. Masters from Aragón refused to accept Mozarabs as not the right kind of Christian; too dark by half; can't speak a Christian language. To Sebastián's knowledge, some were indeed not Christians, but rather Moors dissatisfied with their overly-righteous Almohad masters. However, Sebastián believed each band of fighters should be bound together under their master's banner, so the Mozarab archers learned to shout, *"Vivètz Valerós!"* with all the other bordoniers and knights.

His archers would quickly hear the rumor, that Sebastián rated them "Valerós standard," which was superior to other captains' standards, and the king of Aragón had smiled and thanked the Master of Valerós.

Pride was another good way to bind men together.

·

The next morning, only ten men stood inside Pedro's pavilion. Marshal Guillem waited outside with other lesser captains, accepting his separation with equanimity. Father Anselm stayed by Sebastián, who adopted the formal posture he'd learned from his grandfather Pèire.

When a king calls you, do what he asks. Unless it goes crossgrain with your honor. Pèire Leteric growled when he was teaching, purred when he was teasing. *So don't make promises to a king you don't trust.*

"Tell me what you think of the French ultramontanos." Pedro asked his captains to report. Each paused, unsure how to express the dislike in both Alfonso's and Pedro's camps for the French knights who'd crossed the Pyrenees for forty days' crusading. Men who were here to kill Saracens for the remission of their sins.

Diego Lopez, who was the Castilians' best general, spoke. "Alfonso *El Rei* insists that we need every man. They aren't a drain on our own armies. Most brought sufficient arms and food with them." He seemed uncomfortable in Pedro's tent. Sebastián couldn't read the man, though Diego had often watched Valerós knights in training exercises.

"Thank you, Don Diego," Pedro said. "The seigneur of Valerós has several of these bands under his charge. Senhór Sebastián, what say you? Are they battle ready?"

Hearing Anselm sigh behind him, Sebastián said, "They fight for their sins. Not for their lands."

"Doesn't a man's soul matter as much as his ovens and fields?" Pedro asked. He crossed his arms, waiting for an answer in the impatient way he often did while in conversation with Don Tomás.

"If the *francimand* crusader decides not to fight, he keeps his skin and can ask God's forgiveness for years to come. However, what happens if Aragón and Castile do not fight for our homes, our lands, our fathers' paratge?"

"Paratge?" Pedro added the southern idea of natural justice. "Does the honor of our fathers and grandfathers matter more than protecting this land from the Saracens for the glory of God?"

Sebastián said, "Southern knights fight for victory, not booty. That's the meaning of paratge. It makes them more reliable. I would count one man from the south for every two companies of Norman or French knights."

"Even faitdits knights?" Pedro asked, referring to demi-lords of the Toulousain who had switched sides more than once between Simon de Montfort and their hereticated grandmothers.

"The faitdits aren't fools. They owe their grandfathers this victory more than they need their sins forgiven."

"Good," Pedro said. "I have a company of Frenchmen who don't want to serve under Alfonso. I'll send them to Valerós to marshal."

"If you please, Monsenyor." Sebastián pondered the discord this would sow among both faitdits and Valerós knights in his camp. Each of his men had a sister, a mother, an aunt, or a great-uncle that the French army had killed in the expedition of faith and peace that Simon de Montfort called a crusade.

Sebastián's own mother, for example.

Contemplating this, Sebastián failed to hear Pedro dismiss his men until the others left. He rose to follow, having missed Pedro's command for Valerós to stay with him. Pedro had to repeat it.

.

"Your Valerós band is doing well?" Pedro asked.

His scribe Doménec also remained behind, busy arranging parchment, ink, and quills on a travel desk, while Father Anselm had gone to join Marshal Guillem.

"Òc, Monsenyor. But your spies visit often. I'm sure you know."

"Indeed. Though from the confused reports I receive, I'm not convinced my agents understand what they see. Rumors persist."

"Mercenaries from the Pyrenees are barbarians. Savages. They eat steel along with their horses' spelt for breakfast." Sebastián grinned. He'd heard the tales. He knew who in the Valerós band gossiped that way. "And then when they watch, your agents see—"

"The best disciplined camp out of Aragón."

"With the greatest number of knights who actually fought in the Outremer. It's what you pay us for, Monsenyor. Come watch Valerós at work for yourself."

Pedro held up his hand in surrender. "I believe that's not necessary. Though I'd prefer to visit, I believe your reports. Daily discussions with our confederates, however, take most of my time. Can you handle your men without Marshal Guillem?"

"Òc, Monsenyor."

"Rapid answer. And without asking why. Commendable." Pedro crossed his arms. "Sit down, please."

Sebastián sunk onto an uncomfortably low camp chair, so now he had to gaze up at Pedro, who laid a rolled packet of parchment on the table.

"Yesterday, I received this letter. The bishop of Narbonne has been petitioned to grant possession of Castell-de-Valerós to a Montcava cousin of yours who claims the master of Valerós is dead. He insists Valerós is riddled with heretics, which nullifies the rendering of its castles to me."

Sebastián jerked, nearly tipping the stool where he sat.

"Òc," Pedro said. "Rather like a kick in the gut, isn't it?"

"Not Durán, surely? Isn't the archbishop of Narbonne your uncle?" Sebastián hoped he'd mastered any tremor or expression. "Not Durán. The seigneur of Xirgú, whose mother is a Montcava. And the new archbishop is my old friend Arnau Amalric, the pope's legate. He placed Valerós under interdict."

Valerós gone. And Tomás being absent left him more alone than he'd ever felt since losing his mother.

Pedro was talking. Sebastián tried to listen. "You know that I promised your mother Isabella to protect Valerós. I've sent messages, and I've sent a few knights."

"Thank you, Monsenyor." With his mother's name said aloud, Sebastián barely croaked his thanks.

Pedro watched him in silence for several heartbeats. "I admire your restraint. You want to jump up and ride home this moment, don't you?"

"Òc." Sebastián sat up as straight as the wretched stool allowed. "It is difficult to do nothing. I can't say..." He couldn't say what he thought, with no one there he could speak to, the way he could with Isabella or Tomás. "My brother Yusuf. He's traveling with your clerks. I'd like to see him."

The line on Pedro's forehead deepened. "No, he didn't join my clerks. He was supposed to travel with me, but when my men went to fetch him, they were told that Yusuf was with you."

One more loss. Another leg kicked out from under him. "Oh, perhaps he put that story out because he wanted to stay with Dolç. He isn't a fighter."

"But you are. And I need you here. I'm sending Marshal Guillem back to Castell-de-Valerós tomorrow. He's done all the work he can, training my mercenaries. I'll give him the best steward from my court and yet more Aragón knights. The few left who aren't here to expiate their sins. I promise that Valerós will remain yours."

"May I have the letter?" He spoke through the lump that wanted to beg for Tomás, for Yusuf. If he rode to Valerós, he could send for Chrétien. He wouldn't be alone.

Pedro pushed the packet across the table. "You'll be on your way home in July. By the Feast of the Assumption, you can reclaim your land, however many Aragón and Valerós knights it takes."

"Again, I thank you, Monsenyor. I'll return to my camp."

"Right now, I want you to move camp, to join Diego Lopez on the vanguard. I want someone I trust with the Castilian vanguard."

"Me, Monsenyor?"

"There's no one else in the room except Doménec."

"As you command, Monsenyor." Lead the army? His blood now wanted to flow two ways; first, home, to protect it; but then, to the vanguard, to lead his men.

Pedro cleared his throat. "You don't want to add a criticism, the way your father Don Tomás always did?"

"I can't criticize. I have no idea why you want us to travel with Diego Lopez. They say he's Alfonso's greatest general."

"Diego specifically asked for the Master of Valerós. Castile's envoy, Don Carlos, recommended you."

"*Ai.*" Sebastián felt a new warmth in his cold veins. Better than drinking too much wine at Twelfth Night. It flowed around the hole that opened in his soul at hearing Castell-de-Valerós was in jeopardy.

Pedro said, "Also, there's a woman in Alfonso's camp that I want you to marry. Diego Lopez is her guardian. Don Carlos made over-tures, offering to be the go-between with Diego. I want Diego to believe that he—and the woman he protects, of course—is best served in alliance with Aragón. Valerós can do this for me."

"Me, Monsenyor?"

"Is there an echo in here? We aren't in a canyon, are we? My marshals chose to camp on a broad plain, as I commanded."

"I'm young to marry." Sebastián hoped to sound rational.

"You're young to be where you sit right now. But not too young to do as commanded."

"But, Monsenyor." Sebastián's bones ached when he leveraged himself upright in a single motion. "I'm the true seigneur of Valerós. Our castles are rendered to Aragón. But..." *Jhezu del tron,* he was acting like Don Tomás, arguing with the king of Aragón. "As Pèire Leteric taught me, kings are bound by God to serve seigneurs. Seig-neurs owe only as much as they swear to. We men of the south aren't commanded."

Pedro closed his eyes, rubbing at that deep line between his brows. "You want me to ask nicely? Fine. By the grace of God, will you please help ally Aragón and Catalunya with Castile? Will you swear your honor in service to Aragón?"

"*Òc*, I swear."

"That's it? That's all you needed?"

"That's all your father and Pèire Leteric required."

"So civilized. So obviously your mother's son. And they say Pyrenees mercenaries are savages."

Sebastián almost choked again at the mention of his mother.

"We just do what our forefathers taught."

"*Ai*, stop it. My scribe will tell Don Carlos and Diego the news. Doménec can work with your priest Anselm to complete the contracts." With a swift motion, Pedro dismissed Sebastián. He began to don a linen gambeson and a chainmail hauberk. His clerk tried to assist him but was waved away.

Outside, Anselm and Doménec talked over each other, then paused and each deferred to the other. Sebastián dallied behind to ask Pedro one more question.

"When am I to meet my wife?"

Pedro glanced up, astonished, his chainmail tinkling. "Perhaps never, but certainly not until we return from this chore."

Sebastián, relieved, walked with the Valerós priest back to their own camp, where he sat pounding brass tacks into a cuirass while Anselm and Doménec carved goose quills, mixed ink, and wrote his fate on a scraped, reused piece of parchment.

9

At Sea

"A DINERO? FOR A SINGLE JUBBA? Do you take me for a fool? Or perhaps an infidel?"

Tomás had missed sailing with the caliph's emissary; the vessel had left on the dawn tide while Dolç stitched his wounds. But he found another merchant vessel and endured seasickness amidst silent strangers on the first part of the voyage. That was one of the first things he and Yusuf had shared when they'd sailed away from Cairo, staying close by each other, seasick and seeking comfort. He missed Sebastián and found he longed for Yusuf that whole voyage, as much as he ever yearned for Isabella's company.

In Valencia, Tomás found modest joy bargaining in the market-place and watching for scampering young pickpockets who were everywhere, like the ugly boy who loitered near the bakers' ovens, watching while Tomás negotiated for new clothes.

"Never would I insult such a distinguished gentleman," the shop-keeper exclaimed. "But your tongue says you are not from here. Perhaps not from such a rich city as Valencia? It is costly to live amidst great wealth."

"For that gentleman's dinero," Tomás pointed to a departing customer, "you heaped a huge package on his servant. Much more than one *jubba*."

"And you, like that man, want to starve my wives and children. Do you seek to send me to heaven without a penny to my name? Is that how it's done where you were born?" The shopkeeper wept.

"This is a fine robe of costly dyes, woven by virgin children in the convents of Seville."

"I want only indigo and cotton. I don't care if it's woven by the aged whores of Jebel al-Tariq."

Tomás persisted. For one dinero he wanted the *jubba*—a long sleeved robe—and two of the white *sarawil* and *qandura*. He pointed to the loose trousers and shift.

"*Qutn*." Tomás shook his head emphatically when the shopkeeper reached for wool. He pointed to cotton trousers. Summer was near. He wouldn't be in Al-Andalus come winter.

"Do they value silver more than manners in your city?" the merchant called after him, having pocketed Tomás's coins. Several stared at the man the merchant abused.

Tomás lifted his head higher and walked on.

Here at the edge of Al-Andalus, he didn't have to bristle with menace when he walked down the street, to avoid being pushed to the gutter, like he did in Toulouse. In this town, more men than not shared his color, whether merchant, prince, sailor, or street-sweeper. The streets were filled with mercenaries, many darker than he was, who'd come from Morocco, Oran, Fez, Biskra, Tunisia, and further south. Herds of men moved together, voices in each huddle sharing the same timbre, lilt, and language.

Leaving Tomás even more aware that he didn't move or speak like other men on the street. Here, he was neither fish nor fowl, walking like an Outremer crusader (that is, like his father), speaking the Arabic of Cairo inflected with the tones of Norman Cyprus.

Stuck for several days because of late-winter storms, waiting for the next merchant ship to take him further south, Tomás prepared to be a different man in Al-Andalus. If he didn't quickly learn to shift his body and tongue better to fit in this new world, he'd be found out. He sold his jerkin, hose, and Aragónese armor to a Jewish merchant, but kept his *khuf* from Egypt, because he preferred those tall leather boots to any other. He bargained in the Valencia marketplace for the kind of battle gear he'd last seen in Cairo, plus a mail-lined kazaghand like Rashid al-Rashid had worn in Barcelona. He preferred to purchase clothes no one else had worn, but the metal parts didn't need to be new.

In Valencia, no one but clerics and old men wore the litham. Most here seemed happy to expose their faces. So Tomás didn't bother with a silk veil. He bargained for a green *imama*, liking his shiny new turban especially when the sun reached its height at midday. He mastered wrapping it so that a long tail hung down his back and a small piece dangled along his chin. Now he was Tuma ibn Mikhail, an Ayyubid cavalryman from Cairo, newly freed from Christendom.

After a day of wandering through Valencia, stopping three different pickpockets and chasing off a hustling crowd of children who attempted a charm-and-steal scam on him, Tomás chose a merchant's stall, with the intention of spending a dinero on a burnous. He needed the hooded cloak for night time, since it was still early spring. Swinging the cloak around his shoulders, he again saw the boy who'd loitered near the bakers' ovens.

The boy, as ugly as any child placed by God on this earth might be, pointed up the alley way where a half-dozen armed men tramped toward them. The lad made a gesture that Tomás didn't recognize, and then scampered away, his bare feet pounding the cobbles.

One of the men shouted in the local Arabic tongue, "Let all men come fight for the caliph! Gold for battling the infidels!"

Other voices, hidden on the rooftops, shouted back in the same tongue, and in Mozarab and other dialects:

"*Our gold. Moved to the caliph's pocket and then to extraños.*"

"*Let the emirs' sons fight the infidel. That's why God gave them sons. The one true God, who is merciful.*"

"*We have enough widows to feed from the last battles.*"

The tramping band reached Tomás, who found he was now the only man on the street.

"Who's your master?" their leader growled.

"Rashid al-Rashid. The caliph's vizier. I'm with his mercenaries."

"Where's your badge?"

"In my pack. It intimidates the merchants, makes them offer less than a fair price. They see the caliph's badge and—"

The man waved him off, and the band continued down the street, calling, "Gold for battling the infidels!"

.

Tomás had forgotten how comfortable cotton *sarawil* trousers were. He paid a barber to shave his hair and trim his beard close (Al-Andalus could take his ruined face or leave it; he didn't care), and then spent an evening at the baths remembering the pleasure of living among scrupulously clean people. After the baths, Tomás went down to the docks in search of one more purchase.

Along the way, he was accosted three times more by men seeking to hire mercenaries. He repeated the same words each time.

"I work for the caliph's vizier. Rashid al-Rashid owns my vow."

Near the stevedores' sheds, Tomás found what he was seeking. Youths for hire.

"What are you selling?" he asked the first sturdy boy who seemed nearly clean enough.

The boy licked his lips. "Whatever alcade pleases to have."

Tomás guessed the local judge—alcade—was the only person of status the boy had ever encountered. He questioned the next lad.

"A sword, if you can afford it." That boy held up what was no more than a long dagger.

Tomás passed each offer, coming to the ugliest of the lot, a Mozarab with a face his mother might love, clothes his mother had mended many times, and a stubborn chin that might be mistaken for churlishness.

The lad who'd followed him earlier in the marketplace.

Tomás didn't repeat his question. He crossed his arms while he studied the lad. Thirteen? As old as either Sebastián or Yusuf? Smaller in stature than his sons but far more muscular. The lad had a small dagger in a rough leather holster tied to the belt that held up what might have once been white linen *sarawil*.

The boy crossed his arms, mirroring Tomás.

"Loyalty," the lad said. "I offer absolute fidelity, like my mother taught me."

"What did your father teach you?"

"Who?"

∎

It cost another dinero for a burnous, blanket, and boots, so that his loyal servant Qasim was warm and shod. He'd been willing to spend coppers for an answer to the key question he'd asked in Valencia: did the caliph's vizier sail again after landing in Valencia? But his new servant answered the question the first time he heard Tomás accost people in the dockyards: No.

Later, Tomás gave the boy's mother three dineros for the service she'd lose while Qasim traveled with his new master. The mother, so happy about her son's new employment, insisted that Tomás stay for supper, which was a well-spiced broad-bean stew served from a pot over a fire behind the stick-and-mud hovel where they lived.

"You aren't from this part of the world." She struggled to lose her shyness at greeting a stranger. "Where is home? It must be many leagues from here. Tortosa?"

"Cairo." Tomás repeated the lie that he was to live by. Though Miquel's home in Morella was leagues closer to Tortosa than Cairo. "I hope your boy will teach me how people do things here."

She dished the stew, saying, "He will be your faithful and loyal servant, my Qasim al-Jalal."

"Qasim the magnificent?" Tomás asked.

"Yes, as magnificent as the day is long and bright, and as the night gives itself over to the nightingale's sweet song," she said.

Come morning, Tomás went to sea again, this time in a caravan of merchant ships that clustered together for protection against piracy while sailing to Almería.

At night, wrapped in his cloak, a blanket, and the waxed sailcloth he bought from a fisherwoman at the dock, Tomás slumbered alongside Qasim among the half-dozen merchant-passengers huddled on the foredeck. The night-watcher's song drifted into his dreams, so that Tomás again lay beside Chrétien in the fetid student-barracks in Cairo, where their fight-masters consigned first-year students. In the dark, Chrétien whispered deprecations, being the only one to notice Tomás's fear when their teacher struck the sword from his hand during morning practice. Only a brother could humiliate a man in that particular way, by seeing and speaking truth. "You're afraid because it's new. You haven't seen that manner of fighting before, so fear owns you."

"I wasn't afraid," Tomás said. "Only surprised."

"Nope. Afraid," Chrétien whispered. "Like when our father made you fight me without a weapon the first time."

"You're taller."

"And better. Smarter. You were afraid, *mon fraire*."

Chrétien tugged his thigh, that first wrestling hold he'd used when they were children. Tomás reached for his hair, free to cheat because Chrétien made the first false move.

On the ship's foredeck, a shriek echoed in the night.

Tomás had a fellow traveler by the hair, a snatch-purse who tried to worm his hand under Tomás's cuirass.

"You must be dreaming." Tomás pushed the man off him. "Unless you believe in ghosts."

When the huddled merchants returned to their rest, Tomás dragged his own blanket and sailcloth over the sleeping Qasim. A storm was brewing.

∎

The clouds collided, towering fathoms high, turning the sky dark as molten iron. Tomás understood what the sailors called out amongst themselves, each speaking in a dialect from the quays in Cairo.

Qasim didn't understand until the first wave broke over the ship. He shrieked and clung to Tomás, who was reaching for the rope a sailor passed to him. The sailor shouted commands, waving to show what he meant. Tomás wound the rope around Qasim and himself, then tied it to a cleat, praying he had the right knot.

While half the Great Sea washed over them, Tomás pulled their sodden wool blankets close and clutched Qasim even closer, singing a song in his ear, a dirty song Chrétien taught him, singing it loud, to overpower the roar of the storm.

Throughout the long night, he had no time to curse his Maker, only to encourage Qasim to believe they were safe, that they were cold and wet, but still alive. To help Qasim be sick, while retaining the safety of the rope that bound them to the ship.

When dawn came at last, the rain ceased, though the ship still bounced on tall waves and plunged into deep troughs. It took all that day and night and half the next until the ship entered a true harbor, docked, and disgorged its half-dozen passengers.

"Thank you, master," Qasim murmured. That's all either of them ever said about it.

·

Tomás in Almería – Mirror of the Sea
April 2

When they clattered down the plank onto the dock in Almería, Qasim trailed behind, shifting his pack to stare up at the gibbet erected close to the water's edge.

A bone-stick of an arm, blackened in the sun if not born black, hung through the staves of a wicker cage. Its owner had long since ceased begging for mercy from either God or man. A rag of parchment tied to one of the staves displayed a poorly lettered and faded warning.

"What does it say?" Qasim asked.

"'Spy traitor to Al-Nasr.'" Tomás prodded Qasim. "That means the caliph. Let's find breakfast. You haven't kept food down for two days. You must be starved."

They hadn't left the ship long enough to even find food when Tomás was again accosted by a troop seeking mercenaries. Again, the first words he heard were "Gold for battling the infidels!"

But here in Almería, claiming without proof to work for the vizier didn't end the conversation. These men had quotas to fill and seemed intent on grabbing every free man who came into port. Tomás had sufficient experience, however, that he could bluff any impressment band in either Christendom or Islam.

"You don't recognize this?" He pulled a tabard from his travel pack, brandishing the crimson emblem of elite Moroccan guardsmen, the men who surrounded the caliph (which he'd paid good silver for in Valencia, after his first encounter with the caliph's recruiters).

That bluff worked the three times he needed it over the next few days. However, he never received a good answer to his own question, which was, "Where's the caliph's vizier camped?"

For three days, Tomás kept Qasim busy walking from dawn to dusk while he studied the city and asked men on the street how a mercenary might best travel to Jaén to join the caliph. Amid his search, Tomás found occasions to betray his immortal soul (not for the first time) by speaking against the faith of his mother (definitely for the first time) in open-air shops where sailors, stevedores, and unemployed bow- and pike-men talked indiscriminately, though Tomás believed that the caliph's men heard it all.

Determined not to set a bad example for his servant, Tomás forbade himself wine (served only in the Mozarab inns they visited). Needing more silver than he carried out of Barcelona, Tomás taught Qasim to shill while he gambled at dice and backgammon. A very bright boy, Qasim learned his role quickly.

"You survived the great storm of the spring new moon?" An old man asked, astonished to hear Qasim's tale.

Their marks at each inn quickly warmed to Qasim and his plight at sea in a storm. By the third night, they'd visited five inns in different parts of town, and Qasim had become a spell-binding storyteller. This particular inn seemed stuffed to the eaves with men awaiting mercenary work, expecting (like Tomás) to journey into Jaén to join the caliph.

"Some on the ship were ignorant Christian dogs, slaves to the captain." Qasim spat into the hearth to show his disdain. "To hear their prayers of fear was as awful as the wind itself."

"A curse upon them," a voice called.

"When the wind rose, so too did the waves," Qasim said. "Our captain tied us to the mast, where we watched waves taller than any minaret rise before our tiny boat, then crash and send our ship up toward heaven. Then we plunged again into the depths of the next rising wave, the entire Great Sea running over our feet, sweeping men and goats and cargo away."

Brown faces and white in the crowd became ashen while Qasim improved on his tale.

"Yet Allah brought you safely ashore? All praise and thanks be to the one true God."

Each night someone interrupted the drama this way. Qasim assumed humility. "It is so. I stand here by the power and mercy of God. Another ship with us was lost, pulled by demons to the bottom of the sea."

After he told that story each night, superstitious sailors gave Qasim a few square dirham coins and asked him to gamble for them.

He always said, as instructed, "It's not right to test the will of God. All praise is due to God alone."

The sympathetic listeners to Qasim's tale were often unhappy when Tomás won all the boy's coins, but most departed soon after Tomás offered to buy the now-penniless Qasim a bowl of *balâya* (short on tripe and long on rice) and shared his *al-muyabbanât* (the cheese fritters weren't as good as what Qasim's mother made).

However, when Qasim ended his tale on the third night, a gruff voice spoke in the local accent, powerful as the winds that blew them to Almería.

"The fisher folk who live in the caves at La Chanca tried to rescue another ship when it foundered."

"Is it so?" Qasim sounded curious, exactly the way Tomás had taught him to assuage any mark who strayed from the story.

"They failed." Bigger than most in the room, the man had the sunburned, auburn-haired color of local Mozarabs and dressed in the canvas-and-linen trousers and tunic of dock workers, but also wore a boiled cuirass with unartfully hammered brass studs and a short-sword in a wooden scabbard. A laborer seeking to sign on with the caliph's thousands of mercenaries? He wore no badge or colors to indicate his employment.

"The poor departed souls," Qasim said. "I pray they have found life in heaven."

"My brother lives near the fishermen. He says they pulled a survivor from among the unfortunate dead." The man folded his arms across his barrel chest, as if challenging Qasim.

"Then all praise belongs to Allah," Tomás said. He wanted to help Qasim past this interruption so he could tell his story.

"It was a djinni." The man's disdain indicated he didn't believe what he said. "One of the infamous creatures of smokeless fire."

"It is hard to understand the ways of Allah." Qasim managed to squeak words out. The mention of a djinni shook him.

Tomás had taught Qasim what to say if anyone talked about magic. Acts of Allah, acceptable. Magic or ghosts, never. However, Qasim seemed too shaken to say more, likely because he came too close to heaven on that soggy, seasick night.

"The djinni frightened the fishermen, so they gave him to the gypsies, who brought him to the fortress at Alcazaba." The man jutted his chin, still wanting a quarrel, or at least to drag attention from Qasim to his own story. "My brother saw this creature perform feats of magic there, things only the djinn can do."

"Djinn? The stuff of fables." Tomás had missed that story, in spite of listening to street gossip in Almería for three days. What a piss-poor spy Pedro had sent. He picked up his dice and tucked them in their leather pouch, then rose and headed for the door, crooking his little finger to urge Qasim to follow, there being no hope of a decent game after the notion of djinn settled a chill on everyone.

The man pursued Tomás into the alleyway, shoving Qasim aside to reach him.

"Do you call my brother a liar?" The man blew hot wine breath over Tomás. That close, Tomás recognized a local from whom he'd won a fistful of silver pennies on the first night in Almería.

"Djinn tales are for babies who huddle at their mother's breast."

"Perhaps it's you who pretends courage when faced with a powerful djinni?"

"There are no djinn. You repeat rumors like a schoolboy."

The belligerent fool had his sword out, far too quickly in terms of how a brawl should proceed.

"Save your sword. Aren't we supposed to prepare for the cursed infidels?" Tomás batted the point of the blade away with the back of his leather-and-brass wrist guard.

Which infuriated the bastard. "You're one of those dog-eating mercenaries, come to pollute paradise." A head taller than Tomás, he swept a leg out, intending to knock Tomás to the ground.

Tomás dodged the kick, leaping out of range of the man's longer arms and the tip of his sword, pushing Qasim behind him. Tomás had his sword in hand before the fellow regained his balance.

"My mother never fed her sons dog meat," Tomás said, "nor lies about shaytan or ifrit or any other fey spirits. Your brother believes lies. Or makes them up."

Roaring, the man rushed at Tomás, who again leaped out of the way, but in the dingy light, he landed against a wall. The pigeons on the rooftop rose, grunting, their wings slapping, indignant.

The man came at him, his sword arched too far behind him to be effective. Tomás slashed at the man's thigh, but a javelin spun from the deeper shadows, sending the man sprawling.

"The caliph commands us to fight the infidel, not each other."

Rashid al-Rashid stepped into the lamplight that flowed from an open doorway. Once more in immaculate white, he was all tightly coiled muscle and sinew, like a cat about to spring, his hair hidden under a simple white turban, the angles and planes of his face traced by a close-trimmed beard.

"He called me a liar." The man stumbled to his feet, grousing.

"His story is true," Rashid said to Tomás over his shoulder. "That is, the gypsies claim they captured a djinni after the storm. The great general Abu Jossep heard the tale and sent his men to bring the djinni to him."

"My apologies." Tomás conceded, happy not to be hunting for his cousin any more. "May it all be as it pleases Allah."

Rashid spoke a few short words to the man, which Tomás didn't catch while dusting off his white *sarawil* trousers and checking on Qasim's wellbeing.

"Do you want some dinner?" he asked.

Qasim shook his head, then collapsed onto a bench near the inn's doorway, his confidence shaken.

"I've eaten, but I'll take refreshment with you." Rashid mistook Tomás's invitation.

"There's a table I left at the back. You can tell me more about this general, Abu Jossep." Tomás left Qasim at the door, hoping the boy would sleep and forget about magic tales. "I'm curious about what kind of grown man believes in djinn."

"And I'm curious what kind of man wanders about this city using my name as his password and brandishing the badge of the caliph's guard."

.

"I'm leading new mercenaries to Jaén. Why are you here?"

"You left me behind in Barcelona, cousin. I'm on my way to Jaén in search of you."

"I'm disappointed to find you brawling, Ibn Mikhail. And gambling. Every man of the Rodriguez clan is better than that."

Tomás's lip twitched into what he intended to be a smile, unsure which gestures or words might betray him as Pedro's spy. "The infidel king dumped me at the wharf with only a blanket and the clothes I wore. You'd already sailed. I have had to earn my own way here."

"You carry your sword. Perhaps you can earn honest wages as a soldier and learn a better path."

"Do you care to play backgammon?" Tomás tipped the board toward Rashid. "For joy. Not silver. Tell me about this djinni."

"Abu Jossep has an unfortunate weakness," Rashid said. Listening to the timbre of his cousin's voice, Tomás heard echoes of Miquel. "He believes in djinn and ghosts. When he heard what the gypsies had to sell, it excited his interest, so he bought the creature."

"They sold him?" Tomás watched Rashid manage the dice and markers; his cousin might not gamble, but he understood strategy.

"A most valuable commodity. From what messengers have told me, Abu Jossep got a beautiful boy for his money and now the general is happier than anyone has known him to be for years." Rashid's eyes peered through the layers of his soul. "Do you dislike the selling of boys to generals?"

"I disapprove of lies. Christians see angels and saints. Our people see djinn and devils. But there are no magical djinn or saints."

"Or perhaps you're a *batini*, a man who believes nothing."

Tomás didn't answer, instead intent on allowing Rashid to win the first match. The vizier spoke again, but all words except "servant" and "*franj*" were lost in the rattle of ivory pieces being replaced on the board.

"The *franj* are barbarians," Tomás said. "They'd burn their own families if their pope demanded it. I don't understand why Allah allows men to live who have no honor. How wise is this famous general, to be fooled by a child?"

Rashid stared again, those eyes probing the depths of Tomás's reckless question. "Abu Jossep is known for his ability to judge men. Any captain who has ever served under him is valued by the caliph more than a regiment of mercenaries, because Abu Jossep has discerned the captain's worth."

A man, therefore, for Tomás to avoid. "And yet, a djinni? From ancient tales of marids and ifrits?"

"They say the creature speaks with the voice of a child but astonishes scholars and astrologers. If the learned ones dispute a minor point, the djinni gazes on them with kindness and thanks them for their instruction."

"A scholar who is his own shill?" Tomás asked.

"What is a shill?" Rashid made his second move in the new game (employing, Tomás noted, the same strategy as the previous match).

"What Qasim does for me each night."

"Telling lies in pursuit of silver?" Rashid tapped the table with a long, umber-dark finger. "Perhaps it's my duty to make you into a man worthy of his clan, since your father seems to have failed to teach you honor."

"My father, the noble Mikhail al-Makkzan, fought with the armies of Saladin and found great honor. Though all glory belongs to Allah." And also, his father fought against Saladin. "My father raised me on the best principles. Unlike you," the click of backgammon tiles quickened, "I had a wife and family. But I had the misfortune to be on the wrong street in Cairo one day. I lost all I love and all my gold, and was forced to flee. I've lived by my wits, working as a mercenary ever since."

Rashid set down an ivory marker, staring at Tomás again. Not knowing the man, Tomás couldn't read his expression, tried to shield his true self from those probing eyes. The tiles clicked on the game board. Tomás signaled the innkeeper, who brought them squashed orange, freshened with spring water.

When Tomás won another match, Rashid pushed the backgammon board away. "Do you want to join me? Or only send your sword to our clan?"

"I came to join you. When do you depart here?"

"The morning after tomorrow. You have horses, Ibn Mikhail?"

"I purchased mounts today. I have yet to teach my young servant to ride his burro."

·

"You can't have Qasim running errands from one dawn to the next. He's just a boy."

Layla, his Mozarab landlady, was kindling the kitchen fire in her miniscule courtyard when Tomás crept in at sunrise. She spread breakfast for Tomás and her deaf, hobbling father, and then set some aside for Qasim. His servant had tumbled onto his blanket and pulled his burnous over his head when they returned home, which was the wicket-and-wattle byre that Layla rented to travelers. A byre that hadn't sheltered animals in a dozen years.

"Qasim can sleep away the day." Tomás settled on a cushion under the portico, where Layla served her boarders breakfast and dinner. That day Tomás was her sole guest.

She laid food before him: a bit of lamb roasted earlier that week, flavored with mint, basil, and cloves; a folded bread like he often purchased at street stalls; and chunky sheep's cheese with turnips, saffron, and pepper. Her aged father took only the bread with unspiced cheese, and then shuffled back inside her house.

"Your boy Qasim is homesick."

"We're leaving tomorrow. The new adventure will take his mind off his mother."

Layla flashed a glare. She was his age, perhaps a bit older, and wore immaculate white cotton *sarawil* trousers and a cotton shift with a plain belt. The few escaping strands hinted that her scarf covered dark hair streaked with auburn. Her fine features still recalled the beautiful young girl she must have been; however, Tomás appreciated that leathery crinkle which revealed a life of work and—he guessed—sorrow.

"You disapprove of how I manage my servant. What else?"

"Nothing."

She set aside two parts of the bread she'd kneaded and rolled a third piece into a flat patty for baking. She sprinkled flour over it, folded it, and then rolled it again. Tomás watched, half-dreaming, remembering his mother doing the same on Cyprus, placing the dough on a wooden paddle.

"A man like you, riding to Jaén province, has only one purpose."

"You disapprove of me dragging a boy into the war? Did someone take your son to war?"

"I have no children," Layla said. She spread the coals in her little oven and then used the paddle to set her bread to bake. "Last year my husband Sayyid died in a border skirmish."

"I'm sorry for your loss." Tomás spoke the useless words, having heard them too many times.

"Two armies fought each other for the greater glory of God. So now I'll sleep alone for the rest of my life."

"You're a handsome, strong woman. You won't long be alone."

"I don't want a substitute." Her eyes sparked with fire. "The only use I have for a man is to restrain vagabonds who think a woman living alone must be a whore."

"I don't think that. But I do want to pay you for a service."

•

He steeled himself for the stitching, though he was sober this time. Tomás was always sober in Al-Andalus.

Layla studied his drawing before she made each razor cut, carving thin lines that approximated the horoscope a street-diviner had cast in Cairo. While Layla cut and stitched, Tomás studied the ancient persimmon tree in the yard with no leaves, just the black skeleton frame of a tree waiting for spring. Two lonely blood-red fruit globes remained. Perhaps enough for one last winter pudding.

"What do they call pudding in Al-Andalus?" he asked in Arabic, hissing through gritted teeth.

"We call it pudding. How did this happened to you?" she asked. She concentrated, stretching his skin where Petronilla's henchman had carved a *crux lunata*.

"Infidels wanted to insult me when I was unarmed."

"How long ago?"

"A couple of fortnights." He gasped when she made last final cut.

"You found a good doctor. I've never seen such fine stitches."

"I'm lucky. What will help this heal?"

"This salve I buy from a woman in my alley."

"You don't make it yourself? You grow, you bake, you weave…"

"I am *ahl al-dhimmi*." She used the word for people of the Book who are not Muslim believers. "What was harmless for my grandmother is not safe now. I pay the tax for people like me, so I'm left alone." She called the tax *jizya*. "I don't want my neighbors to claim I'm any kind of conjurer. People are exiled and their houses seized for unholy practices."

She gave him willow-bark tea that tasted like Dolç's. After the bleeding slowed, she smeared a paste on the wound over Tomás's heart. It smelled of flowers and olive oil, like what Dolç had used. Layla's strong fingers worked the salve into the seams of cuts. She chanted a prayer for healing.

Tomás stopped her hand. "Don't. Let's just allow God to do what He will with me."

"But see what God has done to you already. We must ask Him for mercy."

"God has better things to worry about."

Come night time, Tomás slept on the rooftop, cradling Layla in her hammock, the southern spring air as fresh as it must have been three days after God's creation.

Only sleeping; solely for comfort.

Layla woke twice to make him drink more willow-bark tea. The second time, Tomás drew her closer, smelling lavender in her hair.

"Try to forget for a moment," he whispered.

"As if you ever forget? You're thinking of her now, the one you lost, the way I'm thinking of my Sayyid."

"I never said—"

"I can feel her soul, wrapped around you like a cloak. You smell like a man. It makes me miss Sayyid again. Though I always do."

Layla wept, and he rocked her like a child.

"*Sst!*" He shushed her, the way his mother did for comfort when he was ill. "If we're quiet, we can feel them in the dawn. I pretend it's my Isabella that makes the rock doves call out and not just the rising the sun." He held her until she slept again. Then he wrapped up his travel pack and roused Qasim to leave Almería.

10
Narbonne by Day

Durán in Narbonne
March 22

MERE CHANCE LED DURÁN to a Narbonne bordello. Or rather, vanity.

Vanity led him to seek a haircut from a woman rather than a marketplace barber—that, and a reticence about public grooming for a seigneur in a strange city. Durán wanted his hair short, but not hacked and shaved. When they traveled, Chrétien tied up his long Celtic hair and once a day threw a bucket of water over his head. But Durán knew he'd itch to death from sweat and fleas before they reached La Mancha, and so decided to cut that bush of hair he'd inherited from a Beaurain great-grandfather.

"I know just the place." Bernart Bovon, the captain of the men Foix (whose curly black locks Durán secretly admired), gave Durán precise directions.

Late afternoon, Chrétien and Ramón-roger went to the bishop's court to deliver the roster of knights and lords who'd travel under the Foix banner.

"This might take till midnight," the count said.

Soon after, Durán knocked at the gate where Bernart directed him, and explained what he wanted to the porter, a brawny rufous-headed man from Carcassonne, as tall as Durán but twice his weight. Durán had already traded copper coins for the service he requested, and the massive wood door had closed behind him, before he saw that Bernart had sent him to an expensive brothel.

Bad enough that Chrétien called Durán "a mooncalf who studied to be a weasel" after he paid good silver for a silk coat tailored like Ramón-roger's. If Chrétien learned about where Durán got his hair cut, the teasing would last until the next blue moon, which was most likely what Bernart intended.

"For three silver morabatins, I can…"

The tiny dark-eyed woman named Alamanda (like in the troubadour's song) quickly accepted that Durán didn't want any services that involved removing his clothes. But she proposed additional purchases while she cut his hair.

"For a single copper coin, let me wash and anoint your head with herbs. I use a recipe my grandmother learned from the Queen of Jerusalem. Here, doesn't this smell wonderful?"

He agreed to the special soap and a close brushing of his velvet jacket, but Alamanda had yet more to sell him.

"I often provide gentlemen like you with a love philter. Surely there's a special love you long to excite."

"It can't get more exciting!" He burst out the truth.

She laughed. "In that case, you need my finest spell to bind your love to you. My mother learned it from that old queen of Aquitaine, who enjoyed the love of two kings. You sleep on it for seven days, then steep it in hot wine that you give your love."

Durán declined at first, but finally was persuaded. She tugged two long golden hairs free from the brush she'd used on his coat.

"This belongs to your love, no?" She wound the hairs around twigs of yarrow, poppy, and valerian, together with a red thread and a flash of white that he couldn't make out. "He must be a beautiful man indeed."

"He's…" Durán stopped. "How do you know it's a man?"

"*Ai, cor nadó!*" She called him *baby heart*. "A blind kitten can see that you won't ask to bind a woman to you in this lifetime."

He handed over another copper coin.

"It's two silver morabatins," she said.

"That's an outrage. A string and some weeds?"

Alamanda lifted her shoulders in a shrug, which pulled at her linen shift, exposing more of her breasts than Durán was comfortable having so close. "Most important is the prayer that only I know. What is the right price for perpetual love?"

"I don't think you buy love with silver."

Another distracting shrug. "The Church sells forgiveness of sins at a much higher price. I offer a better bargain for my prayers."

Durán paused at the gate to tuck that love token inside his jerkin, his newly-shorn head chilly in the early evening air. That huge porter, ignoring Durán, bargained with a veiled woman through the gate.

"Four silver morabatins for the evening if you use our servants. Six if your master insists on only his own servants."

"Last year, the room cost half that," the woman complained.

"It's hard times everywhere, ma dòmna." The porter addressed her correctly yet offered no respect. "Do you want the room or not?"

"With no servants." The veiled woman passed money through the portal, her voice bitter.

Durán exited the gate, glancing around uneasily for who might see him coming out of a bordello. The veiled woman conferred with a party in a nearby alcove. Along with two tall guards in leather, a bevy of women crossed to a doorway near the brothel gate. That door was opened from within and the party entered, leaving behind a pair of servants who wrapped themselves in cloaks and passed a goatskin bota between them, settling in to wait for their mistresses.

One of the women, unveiling when she turned in the doorway, was Durán's cousin, Hélène de Beaurain.

He returned to the brothel gate, asking for Alamanda.

"I want your services for the evening after all." He showed her five silver morabatins, the price for every service the house offered. "If we can spend time next to the private room those women rented."

"What private room?" Alamanda said.

"The one you sell to people who don't want their household to know what they're up to."

"Where did you get such an idea?" Alamanda dismissed his request with a wave. "Do you and your love purchase privacy in Toulouse?"

"No. But I used to be paid to deliver wine and then to kindle more than the fire in just such a private room."

She tipped her head, studying him like a brown wren in a hedge. "You aren't the innocent you pretend." Her small hand reached to accept payment.

He closed his hands on the coins. "I want the nearby room that has a chink in the wall for those who like to watch."

"Only old men pay to watch."

"I'm special."

Alamanda called to a servant for food and wine.

"We'll be in the Rose room."

This was the most time Durán had spent apart from Chrétien in two years, and the first time he'd made a decision without both of them agreeing. Midnight was still far off, so he hoped this diversion at least proved entertaining.

•

Durán hesitated by the door with the rose carved into old split cypress boards. Unbidden memories welled up, recalling such rooms in Toulouse. Behind him, silent as a housecat, a barefoot servant lingered the way Durán had in former times, balancing a stone jug of wine and a round of bread.

Durán stepped over the threshold, entering in the role of master rather than paid servant.

After Alamanda passed one of Durán's coins to the servant, she closed the rickety door and retied her robe, exposing her breasts whenever she moved. She pointed to the chink in the wall he'd paid for and then carried the only rushlight to the window ledge on the far side of the room. She brought him a stone mug of wine and settled by the oiled-parchment window, playing cat's cradle while Durán watched and listened at the chink.

A voice snapped a command. "Out, you two! This is women's business. Wait by the door."

Maria of Montpelhièr issued commands while cradling that little rat-dog everyone in Christendom hated, the dog that barked through half of Chrétien's songs the previous night at the villa of Narbonne's richest merchant.

The two guards, their aventails now unlaced, proved to be Colomb and that odd Montcava cousin, Matheus. Colomb left through the door to the inner passage, the one shared with the room Durán had rented. Matheus's huge war dog sat on a leash, watching only its master, who took the small rat-dog from Maria, murmuring words Durán couldn't hear. He scratched the ugly beast and whispered in its ear, then restored it to Maria's care, where it snuggled down in her lap, pacified. Matheus then followed Colomb, snagging a stone jar of wine to carry away with him.

"That *putana* Roxane made a fool of herself with that Celtic jongleur," Maria said. With Maria and Hélène were two court women, plus Hélène's sister, Sibilia de Xirgú. Who, Durán learned at the previous evening's court entertainment, had the most irritating laugh among all the Montcava cousins. "That *peccador* jongleur is as fey as my husband. Though more entertaining."

"Roxane left with the Celt, though." Sibilia sounded annoyed.

"He's a mercenary," Hélène said. "The rest of him must be for sale, too. All jongleurs are singing whores who'll do anything for a fistful of silver."

At the previous night's party, the count of Foix had introduced a dozen friends. Durán didn't remember a Roxane among the wives, who all went home early. The men who stayed behind lost a great deal of money to Chrétien over dice.

"Shall we do what we came for?" Maria asked. "Please."

"*Òc.*" Sibilia signaled to the two women, who got to work. One set candles in a circle around Maria. Good beeswax candles. The other woman lit candle branches on the wall and tables. When they finished, the two serving-women sat together in a corner, silent.

Maria spoke, more imperious than Durán had heard from any southern lord. "I told the archbishop about my apparition. He agrees with my decision to go to Rome, which the Blessed Mother of Our Lord bid me to do. Now I want to know if saints and angels will do my bidding, or whether I must rely on mere men to manage it."

Amidst all the candle light, Sibilia recited what Durán assumed was a prayer, because of how she intoned it. Some seemed to be Church Latin, but he couldn't make sense of other words.

"*Jhezu adouçar,*" Maria complained, swearing a man's oath. "This isn't going to be more backward masses or some fantastical *merda*, is it, Sibilia? You said you know real spells."

"I do." Sibilia trilled in the voice of a very young girl. Half a head taller than her sister Hélène, Sibilia was all boney angles where Hélène had a softer, fuller figure.

"My sister Sibilia was taught by our grandmother," Hélène said, "instead of having to drag it from servants like most women do. She has the best incantations in all of Narbonne."

"*Ai*, don't promise too much of me." Sibilia sounded even more like a child.

"Let's hear your charms." Maria grew increasingly impatient.

While Durán watched, Senhóra Sibilia summoned angels to do God's work ("to rid us of plague and sin, and deliver us into true power under God") by kindling a fire in a small brazier, casting dust on it that made the room smell like a brew-cave, and then lighting a hank of weeds so that it smelled like the Montcava laundry at harvest time.

No angels appeared, but Sibilia managed to make Maria cough so much that her dog barked and lunged to bite Hélène and then fixed its teeth on the hem of Sibilia's robe, grinding until it tore. One of the silent women returned the beast to Maria after the other helped calm the queen's cough.

"Beastly stink. What will it buy us? Are we purchasing help from God or Satan?"

"God, of course," Sibilia said. "This is how women do God's work." She then described how her magic would aid Maria in delivering the crown of Aragón to her son Jaume. "My brother holds the Grail, given by Our Savior to anoint true kings. And he has the Cid's sword."

"Ah, the magic sword." Maria, in the weakest, worst voice in Christendom, sang:

> 'When the Grail and sword are enchained,
> One man dies so the best can reign.
> Iberia passes to the anointed son.
> What was divided becomes one.'

The tune was insipid, and Hélène seemed annoyed, while Maria tapped a finger on her dog's back, keeping time to the ditty while she sang. The rhyme used the old word for Grail, as if it were magical, not just a common chalice.

"With this spell, and with the chalice and the sword," Sibilia concluded, "you can rule Aragón and unite all of the south."

"I appreciate the holy cups and magical swords. But I also want to hire... Maria fell into another fit of coughing. "Mercenaries."

"Too direct," Hélène said. "You do not want to ignite fires of insurrection. You don't want problems like Constantinople."

"Then your spell better not take all year," Maria said. "I'm praying for more than humiliation and defeat. I want blood to pour into that magic grail."

The childlike Sibilia laughed, causing the tiny hairs at the back of Durán's head to stand on end.

Hélène seemed annoyed by that laughter, too. "Maria, you can pay for that. Gold is quicker than prayers or spells. But pay one man. Not a band of mercenaries."

·

One of the court women reappeared after answering a knock from the street door.

"Monsenhóra, a message. Your son Jaume calls for you."

"*Ai!*" Maria petted her dog, agitated. "What am I supposed to do about it?"

"He's feverish, ma dòmna. They have the physician in, but Jaume cries for you."

"Incompetence!"

Maria prepared to depart, deeply annoyed.

"Ma dòmna," Hélène called after her. "Maria! Do you want me to carry payment to our agent for you?"

Maria paused at the door while her two silent women busied themselves with her cloak and the blasted dog. "I want that pleasure for myself."

She departed with the two women. Sibilia trailed at her side, offering advice about the care of sick children in her shrill, girlish voice, which echoed up from the stairwell. Hélène, left behind, gathered the artifacts of their prayers and spells, extinguishing candles, until she alone was illuminated amongst the room's ghostly shadows.

A figure joined her. "Did she pay?"

"She will. Tonight."

"*Ai*, Hélène! Can't the servants clean up here?'

"Matheus! Stop! I'm doing the queen's work."

"You, *dolç amor*, should be queen, instead of that swamp baggage from the Comminges."

The second and third laughing command from the senhóra to stop failed to halt what the Roman Church forbade: the knowledge of a widow by her sister's stepson. The sight and sound and scent of their frenzy, within arms' reach if it weren't for the wall, drove Durán away from his spy hole.

When the sucking and slapping and rustling eased off, Durán peeked again, startled to find Hélène's face close to his own while she tied her shift and straightened her robe. She rubbed at her face to smooth it, then straightened her widow's linen head-cloth.

"Maria is traveling to Rome this week." Her lips were close by Durán's ear.

"She leaps from fey king to eunuch pope?" Matheus's voice droned like a bladder pipe.

"Pedro wants to divorce her now that he has an heir. She's going to beg Innocent to give the crown of Aragón to her son."

"Are you traveling with her?"

"*Doutz Jhezu*, no. Even if she demands it. She's not my queen. Can you make sure Sibilia goes to Rome with her?"

"The senhóra does what I ask. She's not as capable of intrigue as her sister." Matheus nuzzled Hélène's neck.

She reached up to play in his hair. "Are you prepared to satisfy Maria's desires?"

"I want a portion of this venture. A large portion. The Church promises—"

"Stop!" Hélène pushed him away. "You don't believe that donkey *merda* you unloaded with our leader, do you? Faith and power to the Church?"

"Of course, I do. Only it's not time to take Iberia." Matheus pulled her back and they tussled for a moment until he held her arms behind her so she couldn't move. "The Church needs to secure the Languedoc first. I seek to help our leader restore order here. Only a fool would do otherwise."

She coughed, a sound of disgust, and wiggled away from under his hold. "Admit it. Your alliance with the Church will make you rich. Which is why you give land to the Church now. And then?"

"And then after Pedro's folly in Iberia, I come home as great as that husband you lost."

"Clever boy." She waggled a finger in praise. "You've already earned praise from our leader and the other bishops for helping to restore peace on rebels' lands."

"And I do God's work fearlessly. I gave our leader the gift of a poem that—"

"That you bought from a defrocked priest who writes letters outside the St-Justí church."

"Don't make fun of me." Matheus twisted a hand behind her back. "My father and grandfathers had real crusades to make their names in the world. I have to use this shoddy adventure in Iberia to put my name before the pope."

A voice rumbled from the inner door behind Hélène. "We still have to pay recompense for our fathers' and grandfathers' mistakes."

It was Colomb.

"*Hola, gos.*" Matheus stepped away from Hélène, righting his jerkin, disdain at the corners of his mouth. "Your father's mistakes, not mine."

"Yours, too." Colomb lifted a wine jug, shook it to find whether wine remained, and then poured a stream in a goblet.

"The first thing you need to do is clear the monkeys and goats out of the Montcava house." Hélène, her cloak in one hand, stabbed an accusing finger at Matheus with the other.

Durán had an irrepressible need to cough. Choking, he made for the door, where Alamanda dragged him back to the bed, pulling away his hose and hoisting her robe at the same moment Colomb de Beaurain burst through the unlatched door.

"Who goes there?" Colomb called.

"Senhór!" Alamanda cried, sitting up, but not stopping what she was doing to Durán. "This room is taken!" She dropped over Durán, smothering him in hair and breasts.

"*Putana!*" Colomb thundered.

"We are in love!" she moaned. "God wills it!"

The knight de Beaurain burst out laughing, then stomped away.

Thanks to the Good God of heaven, Alamanda rose quickly. Durán headed for the door, ready to escape, but Colomb stalked by again. Alamanda leaned against Durán, both of them staggering into the ill-lit hallway.

"*Sst!*" Durán pushed her against the wall, awkwardly ravening her tunic top. "When will I see you again?"

"Senhór! With all that wine, can you see me now?"

Colomb stepped back and slammed Durán to the wall, snarling. "You goat-legged fool! We don't pay for it. My Beaurain father would puke on your boots."

He shoved Durán again, who tripped over Alamanda, who lurched onto the servant behind her, sending crockery and bread husks across the floor boards. In the same way that war dog trailing its leash followed his master, Colomb followed Matheus back through that rented room and out to the street.

"One more morabatin for the broken crockery," Alamanda muttered while Durán endeavored to help gather up the mess. "And yet another to brush your coat again."

.

Eager to join Chrétien and unsure where he'd taken a wrong turn, Durán scanned the darkened sky, seeking a tower from within the warren of streets where he'd gotten lost.

"Can you tell me where to find the viscount's villa?" he asked of a passing figure.

"Just where it's always been."

"I'm a stranger here."

"God preserve this city from lost crusaders. Ask at the church." The disgusted figure stalked off.

Durán had asked at the church. The crowded square outside the Basilica de Saint Paul-Serge was filled with townspeople feasting in honor of the new archbishop. He followed the directions through a labyrinth of narrow, deserted streets. Hunger rumbled in his belly. He wanted his part of the feasting, too, and the count of Foix valued the courtesy of timeliness. Durán didn't want to be late to join his friends over midnight supper.

The thud of boots resonated in the narrow alley. Durán had learned in his youth to know the different kinds of sounds made by any man following him in the dark. This man was armed.

Durán gripped his staff with two hands, ready to defend, hearing Chrétien's voice shout orders, like every training day. *Be a lion. Wait.*

Then he heard the panting noise of a large dog. A war Alaunt? A mongrel mastiff?

He could fend off any dog with his stick. Although he'd never tried. He'd trained harder since that night in Toulouse, with Chrétien emphasizing how to fight two or three men.

But he couldn't fight a man and a dog at the same time.

Durán ran.

At the first joining street, he turned right. At the next, left. Repeat. He had to be winding his way back to the riotous noise near the Basilica de Saint Paul-Serge, or toward another church celebrating the new archbishop. He ran quietly.

A chain jangled. The dog. Either leashed or collared.

Trotting at the same speed as its leather-booted master.

Two turns in the dark cobbled, mud-slimed streets, and Durán knew he was hunted. He ran faster, listening for his pursuer.

Breathe. In battle, hear my voice. Don't let your fear speak.

Feel your heart beat. It sends courage to your bones.

A left turn toward the noise.

Durán backed up against the tall stone walls of a churchyard. Climb and get lost in the tombstones?

When the animal snarled, Durán faced it, his staff ready. A part of his soul leapt the wall, the Good Christian portion that wished to harm a living thing.

Take the dog first. Take all the time.

Guessing the dog's arc when it leapt, Durán swung his staff.

Bone crunched.

A scream of pain echoed in the alley.

A body thumped to the ground.

In the dark, metal and wood thunked. The sound of a sword drawn from a wooden scabbard.

"Damn you to the greater hells! You worthless bastard!"

Durán swung at that voice, intending the same force as with the massif. Mid-swing, an equal force bashed his left hand.

Pain shot up his arm from wrist to shoulder.

The staff clattered to the cobbles. Durán fell onto the still quivering, hot mastiff. When he rolled away, excruciating pain shot through his back and head. The man stomped his belly, cursing, then kicked again. Durán struggled to cover his head, so his hands took the heavy-booted blow while the man shouted every curse known in the local tongue.

"Stop!"

A familiar voice shouted over the agony throbbing in his head. "Let me finish."

"No. You'll bring the bailiffs down on you. Go home."

"He killed my dog." A voice like air through a pig's bladder.

"It's not dead. Go take care of business. I'll finish here."

The attacker hoisted the beast onto his shoulders and disappeared, his cursing pig-man voice echoing in the dark street.

When jerked to stand upright, Durán vomited on his rescuer's boots, his stomach in spasms from well-placed kicks.

"*Ai*, you goat-footed child." Colomb de Beaurain was his rescuer. "Where shall I take you?"

Three attempts to speak resulted only in dry heaves.

"You're at the viscount's villa with Ramón-roger, aren't you?" Colomb answered his own question. "Unless you want to go back to the whorehouse?"

Durán croaked one word. "Count."

Colomb slipped an arm under Durán's shoulder and dragged him through the streets. Durán did his best to help, feeling indeed like a child dragged by an older man. At the villa of the viscount of Narbonne, Colomb loudly demanded that the porter fetch Durán's companions. Before the porter answered Colomb's demand, Chrétien and Ramón-roger appeared beside them on the street.

"*Qui s'ho creu?*" Chrétien spoke in sheepherder's Catalan. *Who'd believe it?*

Colomb dropped Durán at Chrétien's feet.

"Take better care of your *bon amic*, Master Jongleur."

11
Granada

AT THE STABLES, QASIM WATCHED intently while Tomás showed him again how to saddle his burro and mount panniers that held their gear and food for the trip across Granada.

Then Tomás showed Qasim how to care for the horses, which were smaller than the mounts he rode in Toulouse and Normandy.

"What is this horse called?" Qasim asked, fondling it in the way Tomás showed him the horse liked.

"You can choose a name."

"I don't know what horses are called, Master."

"I knew a good horse once that was called al-Malik."

"Al-Malik?" Qasim's voice broke with excitement. *The king.* "Can we call him that?"

"As you wish. Whenever we rest, it's your job to water and feed these animals before you feed yourself."

"Oh master!" Qasim spouted a string of blessings.

"What do you mean to say, *fadrin?*"

"You can trust me with these animals just like you trust me with your life." Qasim made a gesture that Tomás took to be a vow.

"I'm hoping it doesn't come to that," Tomás said.

Rashid joined them in the stable yard. "Hail the good Tuma ibn Mikhail ibn Al-Makkzan!"

"We're ready to ride." Tomás's spirits rose amidst the stamping, snorting, and smell of the horses and the hails of the gathering riders.

"Yes?" Rashid surveyed the travelers, who had two horses and a burro—the good kind you find only in Al-Andalus—each neatly packed. Tomás's horse carried a cavalryman's white tasseled shield, a spear, and a javelin, with only a fringe on the saddle blanket for decoration. His mail was wrapped and loaded onto the palfrey, since the other knights claimed there was no good reason to wear armor on a journey through peaceful Granada.

"The turban is an odd choice," Rashid said. He wore an austere linen turban, with the short *rafraf* tail that men in Granada favored. "Whatever they might wear in Cairo, only old men wear such here."

Tomás unwound his new green silks and called to Qasim. "Trade your headcloth with me."

Qasim handed over the white linen length that Tomás bought for him, no longer stunned when Tomás did the unexpected. The boy wound the green silk loosely for his own head covering.

"Am I sufficiently austere for Al-Andalus?" Tomás asked. He wrapped the length of linen to match Rashid's.

Rashid gaped at Qasim. "Now your servant is gaudy."

Qasim was mounting his burro for the first time. His quick glance at Tomás revealed too much uncertainty.

"He's called Qasim al-Jalal, the Magnificent." Although Rashid's comment was meant for him, Tomás said, "His loyalty and diligence are more enduring than that burro he rides."

Qasim made it onto his burro, and then had to wait. The caravan of mercenaries was slow to take off, not being a unified, trained army. Tomás rode with Qasim for the first day, since the boy had never been on his own. However, as Tomás had predicted, the journey through Jaén province shook Qasim free of melancholy. He learned to ride more quickly than Tomás anticipated, and learned details about animal care from the other servants. No longer homesick, Qasim fell in love with al-Malik and his own burro, his new best friends.

Traveling through the countryside, Tomás studied the orchards through Isabella's eyes: figs, quince, almonds in bloom, pomegranate, apricots past bloom with fruit set, lemon and orange groves. He wouldn't have to tell Isabella that the tallest trees grew bananas and dates, because she'd seen them in Cairo. He had to ask Rashid about other groves, which turned out to be mulberries to feed silkworms.

"In Al-Andalus, our stewards govern the farms with the same care that a good general does for his army," Rashid concluded.

Which caused Tomás to meditate on Isabella's achievements at Valerós as steward of the orchards, master of turning wilderness to fruitful land. If God were good, they'd be together on the other side of the Pyrenees now, supervising the spring sowing, pruning olive trees, hoping the fruit set properly in the peach orchards.

Rashid rode alongside Tomás. "You admire our farmlands?"

"Yes."

"When at the end of time our Creator tallies the good His people have done with this earth, our waterwheels will stand at the top of His list. Turning desert into garden."

"She'd send her bordoniers to build one." Tomás mused that Isabella would study the canals to learn solutions for Valerós. Perhaps only for Sebastián's flatland estates at Fontcours and Montcava, in the Toulousain.

"Pardon, Ibn Mikhail?" Rashid held his hand to his ear. "I didn't hear you over the clomping of our horses."

Tomás hadn't meant to speak aloud. It wasn't even a well-formed thought.

·

At a junction, Tomás watched in dismay while Rashid sent the contingent of mercenaries off to Jaén and designated Tomás and seven cavalrymen (with their servants) to ride with him to Baeza.

"Abu Jossep's vizier died suddenly," Rashid said, after he explained the plan. "Our caliph needs a man he trusts with the general. He sent me."

Tomás wasn't surprised that Rashid kept quiet about this plan until the last moment. However, the caliph's army was gathering in Jaén. Resigned to the change, and thinking he'd best follow Rashid, Tomás summoned Qasim and unloaded his chainmail from the palfrey. The impatient Rashid was in a hurry to ride to Baeza. "The infidel is still hundreds of leagues away."

"I'm compelled to do as I was taught," Tomás said. "Bandits might be tempted by a mere handful of knights."

"Granada hasn't seen bandits for generations. No men would dare. The punishments are too severe."

"I feel a strong need to prepare for the unknown."

They'd ridden out of Almería with hundreds of mercenaries, and Tomás had let the scenery lull him. Here, riding toward the mountain frontier with just a handful of men, every hillock that hid a turn in the road threatened danger. The scattered column of riders seemed reckless, failing to keep in a tight formation on the difficult, jolting ride that Rashid led.

At last, Tomás shook off the worry. The worst had already happened. He was riding away from the caliph and the main army. Now he was just another ebony marker in Pedro's board game.

Rashid called a halt for the night at what would be a caravanserai if this were Egypt. Tomás watched Qasim to make sure the lad understood his chores. When those chores were done, Qasim remained at the corral to brush al-Malik a second time.

Hoping to make a better friend of Rashid, Tomás offered to share provisions, even though the vizier's servant stood waiting. Rashid prepared to spread a rug from his palfrey, but Tomás tugged him back, first kicking aside the stones there. Scorpions scurried away while Tomás kicked rough gravel after them.

After they blessed and then ate the first bites of that simple meal, Rashid said, "You are disappointed not to be joining the caliph."

Tomás passed over more of the hard goat's cheese that he'd purchased from Layla. "After two years serving as a tamed warrior in dull Christian courts, it feels good to be in action again."

"I understand. However, for me this is the road to triumph. If I succeed with Abu Jossep's army, and I shall, my next place will be at the caliph's right hand."

"Promise me that this general is an honorable soldier." Tomás had determined earlier that Rashid's career under the caliph was all he cared about.

Rashid offered to share his water. "Abu Jossep's clan has defended the frontier beyond Baeza for generations. He lost a leg in a battle against Castilians."

"Do you believe in this general?"

Rashid tipped his hand, weighing the idea in balance. "He's older now, but in the past, he succeeded better than other men. Although the caliph doubts him, his men still think Abu Jossep's judgment is infallible."

"Is it?"

"Perhaps. He's hanged seven spies since last summer. The rumors persist about Abu Jossep's ability to peer into men's hearts."

"How good a military man is this one-legged believer in djinn?" Tomás asked, shaking off the chill climbing his spine.

"The best in Al-Andalus. Because men flock to him, he requires fewer mercenaries than most generals." Rashid talked rapidly, so that his words raced along like a fast-running stream over a bed of rough stone. "He outfits his men lavishly and takes care of their families. He brings warriors' widows to live in his court, so their lives are better than if their men came home."

"I can't believe that." Tomás thought of Layla weeping on her rooftop in Almería.

Rashid tilted his hand, balancing good and evil, truth and falsehood. "Though Abu Jossep's people love him, the caliph believes the general is lax in service to Allah."

"Is that true?" Tomás noted that his cousin had not called down blessings.

"It's less true than for other taifa emirs on the frontier. However, in one way he's like all the generals on the frontier. If the caliph wins this war, Abu Jossep will remain his loyal subject. If the infidels are triumphant, like the Cid once was, then Abu Jossep will bow to the next overlord, even if it's a Christian."

"A funny kind of loyalty."

"Abu Jossep claims he's loyal to the Will of God," Rashid said. "All the emirs on the frontier justify their own whims as being the God's Will. They trade flags back and forth with Christian lords each spring as if this were just a game."

His father Miquel told old tales from his sick-bed, how he'd left Morella out of contempt for the Christian and Moor squabbles on the frontier. *They just steal each other's flags and cows every spring. Then steal them back the next year.*

"My father claimed there's no honor in that."

"And that's why he left Morella?" Rashid said. "I serve both the caliph and our clan by coming to Baeza. To convince Abu Jossep that he needs to lead men for more than another frontier squabble."

"And you want this general to use my ancient sword to reunite Al-Andalus?" Tomás finally raised the question of his sword.

Throwing both hands into the air, Rashid shook his head. He motioned for the men to mount and ride again. After they resumed the ride on the trail up into the hills, Tomás called to him, "After the story of the djinn, I'm surprised you believe in magic."

"I don't. Our cousin Ríma asked me to fetch that sword. And you. She's married to Abu Jossep and insisted on the sword when I asked her to help spur him into action."

"The general is married to a woman from our clan?" Tomás pondered this, that there was a woman in Al-Andalus who knew Tomás was in Barcelona and that he carried a certain sword. Surely this must be Pedro's agent. Was this journey leading him to the Rodriguez clanswoman he was to rescue?

Rashid said, "Yes. I agreed to what she asked because I need all possible help to persuade the general to action."

Perhaps Tomás didn't need to be in Jaén after all. He prompted Rashid to tell more while they rode together.

"My aunts asked me to bring Ríma to Baeza two summers ago. She needed to be rescued from a bad marriage to a man who abandoned his own honor and beat her. And then refused the divorce."

"A crime against heaven," Tomás said.

"Mercifully, Abu Jossep took Ríma under his protection, to live with his wife. When his wife died, he married our cousin."

"How does she know about my father's sword?"

"Our aunts can tell the story of each Rodriguez member back to…" Rashid trailed off, pondering. "Before the caliphs took Iberia. No story is ever lost to the Rodriguez history."

■

Tomás on Granada backroads
April 5

The stars shone in the midnight sky. Tomás stretched out on hard ground the way soldiers do, lying between Qasim (who trusted him too much) and Rashid (who must learn to trust Tomás so that his clan could betray him).

Only last spring, a year ago, Tomás lay between Sebastián and Isabella at a caravanserai, sleeping on warm ground, the three of them listening to the nearby spring, smelling camel as well as horse. When Sebastián went to tend their horses in the early morning, Tomás held Isabella and they kissed, both of them tasting of the previous night's garlicky chickpeas and mint-and-semolina. She whispered in his ear when he entered her. *Only you, amador. Only you. Eu vos amor.*

Homesick, that's what he felt. Home was where your love lay beside you, made your heart pump life's blood. The only home he knew with her was in the saddle, over a series of long journeys.

Before dawn, Tomás woke Qasim and went with him, just for the company, to tend the horses. Qasim had quickly learned to provide the kind of gentle care Isabella always demanded. When the sky grew pink at the horizon, Qasim pointed to the field below the small ridge where they camped. A hoopoe chattered as it scratched the ground, its fan extended, its feathers taking on the gold-and-rose of dawn. Men stirred in the camp behind them, startling the creature so it rose, slowly beating its wings, its barred white-and-black tail flashing at the moment when the sun broke through the horizon.

"Upupa." Qasim murmured the bird's local name. He continued brushing the horse. "Master, when you need me, but we cannot speak, call me like this." Qasim imitated the call of the hoopoe.

The hoopoe in the field answered.

Tomás tried the same sound. The real hoopoe didn't answer.

"Close enough. I'll know it's you." Qasim returned to his work with al-Malik. "Summer is here. Where is that bird's wife?"

Gone to heaven? Tomás again voiced the upupa's call, longing to hear an answer.

∎

They left the hills for the limestone uplifts. Tomás still studied things the way Isabella would: gold-yellow trumpets amid the grasslands, and white crocuses on otherwise barren slopes. Butterflies had awakened and flitted among the violet-blue flowers of the spiny broom.

Eagles soared in the breeze above steep hills when afternoon wound toward evening. Blackbirds gathered in the reeds wherever a stream lingered to create a marshy backwater. Buntings flitted along the rocky walls.

He kept hearing her voice. *You're pushing the horses too hard.*

The shadows lengthened. The travelers should be making camp before it grew any darker. Concerned, Tomás said as much.

"We'll stop in time for final prayers," Rashid said.

Tomás sought to draw the man out, waiting for a moment to insist that they shouldn't ride farther into the mountains with daylight fading so fast.

"Our cousin is in Baeza? Do you have sisters and brothers there?" Tomás asked.

"My aunts and sisters live a happy life in Jaén. My only brother died a decade ago."

"I'm sorry for that. My milk-brother was always a true comrade."

"Milk-brother?"

"An orphan my mother fostered at her breast with me. We shared everything in our youth."

"Where is he now?"

"Off living his own life, I hope. He escaped my fate in Cairo. I miss him. He was the best brother in arms."

"Brothers in arms?" Rashid asked. Tomás thought a note of yearning trembled in his voice. "Like the Christian soldier-priests who claim to defend the honor of God?"

Tomás steered close to truth. "My forefathers in Morella lived in the muck, capturing flags from each other like boys. But my father fought in real wars alongside faithful brothers-in-arms. And he shared his wisdom with my brother and me."

In the dimming daylight, Rashid seemed lost in thought. "War is about organizing men. Getting food and weapons to them on time. Making them believe in the war's reward. Making sure their families are safe. That's what the caliph asked me to do in Baeza."

"Our experiences are different. You have a leader's worries. I'm a lone fighter who goes where I'm best paid." Tomás pointed where the sky was reddening. "And what we best do right now is to make camp."

"We can ride another league before it's too dark for the horses."

165

The road curved where the valley narrowed between two large, steep limestone hills. A small herd of red deer ran toward them, all young males, their antlers a thicket of branches. Surprised by the men on horseback, the deer bounded up the sheer sides of the hills, their yellow rumps flashing in the day's left-over light.

"Red deer come out at night to browse, not to run!" Tomás called to Rashid. Something had scared the beasts into running. "Attention!"

Distracted by the deer, Tomás cried caution—in the wrong language—at the very moment when the riders who'd frightened the red deer came around the bend.

"Attack now!"

Tomás shouted the battle command in the correct language.

Tomás spurred ahead, jerking his javelin free and steadying it at his side. Then he pulled his sword. The advancing riders matched their numbers, but rode hard with their weapons out, while Rashid's surprised knights lost a few heartbeats' readiness to surprise.

Rashid shouted formation commands to his men in Arabic jargon that Tomás only partly understood.

Ululating, Tomás rode straight into the party, taking off the hand of one bandit and slicing open the leg of a second rider before thrusting his javelin at the likely leader.

He galloped through, then turned to ride back, still shrieking. A man at the rear of the attackers checked over his shoulder just before Tomás slashed at the gap between the man's leather helmet and his chainmail. The horse screamed and bolted, its rider lolling dead on its back.

The attackers were poor horsemen, clumsy at attacking from the saddle. Rashid's cavalrymen, better trained, overcame their surprise and surrounded the bandits in a close-arms melee, toppling the attackers from their horses and dispatching them.

Until the raiders were all corpses.

Tomás dismounted and urged his horse back to where Qasim and the others were calming the palfreys and donkeys. Rashid surveyed the aftermath, still calling orders to his men, his hands on his hips in triumph, when one of the corpses rose behind him with a dagger in hand. Tomás leaped with a shout, bashing aside the man's arm while jamming his own dagger up under the man's ribs.

"Ai Dieu!"

Unmoved by the man's cry when he died, Tomás pushed him away, freeing his dagger.

The clash had taken only a moment. The sun had moved just a single finger's breadth lower on the horizon. After wiping his blades clean, Tomás coughed, the stench of frightened horse and battlefield butchery bringing him back to the harsh world. He stretched, listening to the ring of his chainmail. His body felt better than it had in months. His senses worked again. Like Lazarus leaving the tomb.

Rashid shouted to his men to capture the attackers' horses. He sent two riders to scout for any enemy further up the trail, and commanded two others to strip everything of value from the dead bandits. The other three cavalrymen were sent with the servants to make camp on a nearby mesa with a view over the trail.

Qasim came to Tomás's side, having tethered al-Malik away from the stinking battlefield.

"Master, here's water for you."

Rashid's men jumped to their tasks, while Tomás and Qasim piled dead bandits and hauled branches from under the encinas, the holy oaks, to build a pyre.

Rashid called to him. "Ibn Mikhail, you saved my life."

"It is nothing. Allah is the author of all victories." Tomás took a moment to gather his wits, then remembered to call down blessings.

"Why would *franj* mercenaries be here?" Rashid asked. One of the cavalrymen handed Rashid a packet taken off a raider. In the fading light, Rashid studied it. "Here's the answer. They were mercenaries hired in Zaragoza to work for the caliph. *Franj.* Disloyal to all the world."

Tomás lugged the last body onto the pyre, too distracted to answer.

Rashid said, "They died attacking their pay-masters."

Tomás shouted until one of the cavalrymen offered him a pewter tinder box. Fumbling with the steel and flint to spark a fire, he blew a flame to life and added twigs until the fire roared.

The fire flashed bright against Rashid's white linen tunic.

A fire fed by linen tabards embroidered with a lunate cross. Like the men wore who killed Isabella and ended all joy in the world.

12
Toledo

AFTER SEBASTIÁN CHECKED HIS HORSES, he dug two pennies from his hidden stash, gathered his second-best shirt, and wandered down to the laundry camp. The army's commanders gave the women and children the best space, upstream along the river where they worked to make the rest of camp livable.

"You're always here at dawn," the girl Taresa said. It was close to dinner time, which meant he'd have to leave his shirt until the next day. "When a man comes so tardy in the day, we can't make promises."

"Thank you, senhóreta." Sebastián gave Taresa the linen and his pennies. "My initial is sewn there, and you never lose my things."

He liked Taresa. She was different from the others, so he always asked for her by name. She kept his clothes so clean that Marshal Guillem teased him until Anselm intervened.

"Leave the lad to go his own way," Anselm said.

"We know that way is broad and wide." Guillem openly laughed at Sebastián. "And populated anew on every campaign by the men with the cleanest shirts."

After the marshal left, still laughing, to review the Mozarab archers Sebastián asked Anselm, "What does he mean?" Sebastián often had to ask that question privately of Anselm. He'd lived with knights and bordoniers since he was five, but on this march, headed for real battle, familiar words took on new meanings. He had to beg Father Anselm to translate.

"Guillem means that many laundry women return home with more children than when the campaign began. That the men who frequent the laundry and baggage trains father those children."

"*Ai.*" Sebastián flushed. Tomás never made him feel like a naïve idiot. He wished again that Tomás was there to offer more guidance than he got from a Norman priest and a Sicilian marshal who'd each spent more time on campaign than there were stars to count at night.

"What would Pèire Leteric do?" Sebastián asked, voicing a continuing thought.

"I can't speak for him," Father Anselm said. "But he always had clean shirts."

Sebastián avowed that he had no such intentions, whatever Marshal Guillem inferred. He visited Taresa because she was easy to talk to. She didn't laugh at him, though frequently she broke the bounds of common manners and bullied him, which was astounding, since he was the Master of Valerós, and she was a laundry girl. Conversation with Taresa was his only diversion. Father Anselm limited how much time Sebastián spent gambling with his own men; the rowdy singing around a campfire got to be boring some nights. There was no one his age among seigneurs in the Valerós camp. The donzels he'd helped Tomás train in Barcelona now rode under other masters. Valerós had only hard, experienced fighters, with Sebastián as their master.

Why shouldn't he talk to her? Taresa didn't make him pay two more pennies to take a walk up into the trees on the hillside, like other women did (or so he understood from Guillem). She laughed at his stories about things that happened in the Valerós villages, and she raged in a fiery heat when he told the story about being in Minerve under siege and then seeing his friends among the goodmen burned alive by Simon de Montfort.

Also, Taresa was pretty, with a scattering of freckles behind her sunburn, a wide mouth that liked to laugh, and strong arms. While they lay on the hillside above the river, she'd pointed to a cloud and claimed that it resembled a dog, a Great Pyr leaping.

"Your arms are as strong as mine." He held his up alongside hers, astonished to see muscles on a girl.

"Scrubbing your shirts will do that. It took two months to get this strong. How long have you been bashing at sandbags?"

That evening midway in Easter week when Sebastián handed Taresa his second-best shirt, he saw that the other women were packing up for the night. The older women and children were gathering at the kitchens.

"Are you done working for the day?" he asked.

"Yes, let's go out walking." Taresa swept his shirt away into a linen bag and came to his side, shaking down her skirts to cover bare ankles.

"Do you need to ask to come with me?"

"No one owns me here. That's why I chose the laundry train."

While they walked away, a woman called out, "Can you whistle?"

Taresa put two fingers to her mouth and whistled as loudly as a Catalan sheepherder calling his dog.

"What did she mean?" Sebastián asked, shaking his head since she'd whistled right beside his ear. She was within two hands' breadth of being as tall he was.

"If one of us gets in trouble, the other women will come."

"What kind of trouble?"

Bemused, Taresa regarded him with pursed lips, the expression she mimed when she thought he was being childish.

"The kind of trouble a soldier causes if his mother didn't raise him properly."

Sebastián hoped his sunburn covered his embarrassment.

"Has that happened to you?"

"Of course. One of those ultramontanos just last week thought he should receive more service than a clean shirt for a copper penny." Taresa pretended to whistle. "After the women of the laundry finished with him, his sergeant had to fetch him." She laughed. "He'll crusade for his forty days in the wilderness in foul linen, for no one will wash his shirts now."

■

Sebastián shared his provisions with her: cold lentil fritters, the half-leavened, half-baked camp bread that pretended to be brioix, the last of the dried apples from the camp supplies. They sprawled on limestone boulders on a ledge above the narrow river valley where the armies of Alfonso and Pedro camped.

The ultramontanos who'd crossed the Pyrenees from Pays de France and the gathering armies from Aragón, Navarre, and Léon had overwhelmed Toledo. For the city's own sake, the king's valley had been given to the armies for their encampment. The arrangement kept the city clean and kept soldiers from overwhelming the markets, taverns, and women of Toledo.

Below their stone perch, a sea of tents and kitchens spread up and down the narrow valley. Armies had been gathering since Candlemas, and the former lush groves and fruit orchards of the king's valley had been stripped of more than half the trees and bushes that grew there, some of the wood put to use in rough lean-tos, the rest steadily fed kitchen fires to cook beans and bake bread.

"I got married today. I think that's what the papers I signed mean. Or perhaps only affianced. I'm not sure."

Taresa laughed. First, a bubbling giggle. Then she laughed until she had to sit up, shaking with her head in her hands. She tried to speak, then laughed again and couldn't.

Indignant, Sebastián tried to speak. "It's not funny."

She held up a finger, begging for a moment. Tears ran down her cheeks.

"It's just…" She choked on the first words. "I came with the army to escape marriage. Here you are going to war, and you end up married. Who is she?"

"No one I know."

"Tell me her name." She tugged at the corner of his shirt, the way she did when she bullied him. "Maybe I know her."

"You don't know her. I won't tell her name. You just want to tease me." He sulked. For the first time, she was as bad as Chrétien, who teased him like a brother.

That was it! Taresa was like a sister.

That's why it was so easy to talk to her when he could steal away. It wasn't because she was pretty or because the twin mounds of her breast swelled at the opening of her untied shift strings.

"They just want your lands tied up with hers." She didn't move when he rested his hand beside hers. "In case you're lost in the war."

"You're right. It doesn't mean much."

"Besides, you're only a child. Therefore, you have no say."

"That's not true. Take it back." Sebastián knelt beside her, knowing she provoked him on purpose.

"You are, what? Fifteen? Then you have no say. I'm sixteen, and I had no say."

He pinned her to the rock, kneeling astride her, staring into the dark pool of her eyes, ridges of limestone boulder hurting his knees. "I have every say in my fate. I'm sworn to Pedro *El Rei*. I am his own knight. I choose to do what he asks for the sake of my own honor."

Taresa didn't laugh, but her moist, generous lips twitched. Even though he'd pinned her arms, she wiggled free and wrapped her arms around his neck, pulling him down so that his elbows crunched into the boulder. She kissed him.

If he tried to rise, she held him more firmly, her hand stroking his neck, her lips roaming over his.

Until he relaxed and kissed her back.

He braced his hands along her ribs, skinning his knuckles on the boulder, and then rolled with her so they lay side by side. He tasted sweet apple on her lips, so he sought to taste more. She panted for a moment, her mouth slack. He pulled her head scarf free, running one hand through chestnut hair, the same color as his horse, but silky soft, like his aunts' sewing floss. Tugging at his hand, she cupped it over her breast, then plunged her tongue into his mouth. He pressed back with the top of his own tongue while she snuggled her hips against his, throwing one leg over his thigh, tangling them both in her skirts.

They paused. A twilight breeze wafted up from the valley, scented with pine and heath and spring flowers. He stroked her sun-burned, freckled face, his hands smelling of horse while she smelled of soap and lavender; when she stroked his hair, he nipped at her arm, where downy hair tickled his cheek and nose. This close, he felt the strength of her shoulders through her shift.

"Do you believe in angels?" she whispered. "Do you think God asked the angels to guide you to me?"

"I don't know. Ask me after we battle the Moors."

Sebastián hugged her tightly and then rolled with her again, so that she was atop him now, the mound at the top of her thighs pressed tight against him. His member pounded; her heart thumped under his hand. She teased with her tongue, and he kissed her wildly again, but now she tasted salty instead of apple-sweet. He drew her hand down between them, hoping that she might touch him.

"Sebastián de Valerós! Senhór! Master! Sebastián!"

Marshal Guillem's summons echoed in the king's valley.

Taresa rolled off him. Her knee and then her bare foot knocked against his extended punxor, causing more pain than he'd ever experienced in this life.

•

"How did you know I was here?"

"What marshal doesn't know where to find his master? Come, donzel. Diego Lopez needs our help in town. The ultramontanos are rioting."

"I'm a knight. Not a donzel." Sebastián sounded haughtier than he intended. Hearing the name of his future wife's guardian unnerved him for a moment.

"Excuse me. You're a man who leads other men." Guillem pointed to where bands of soldiers hurried toward the city walls.

Shouting commands for battle ranks—in the tongue of the Toulousain, in Catalan, and in the odd tongue of the Mozarabs—the Valerós captains had their men in marching order by the time Sebastián and Guillem joined them. The Mozarab archers and the ultramontanos were ordered to stay in camp. Father Anselm and Benito stood in heated conversation with one captain of a band of ultramontanos, Benito gesturing rapidly with his finger in that captain's face, who stood with his arms crossed, obstinate.

"You are commanded under the Valerós banner. Your men will not join this action," Benito shouted.

"We will march with you whenever there is action," the new captain said.

Sebastián guessed the nature of the confrontation.

"Valerós commands you to guard the camp, with Father Anselm," Sebastián said. He took the stance that he'd seen Pèire Leteric adopt when commanding his men; he intended all of Pèire's gravity when he spoke, and he prayed that a merciful God would keep his voice from breaking. "You will have the action you seek for the salvation of your souls soon enough."

"We are prepared for any battle," the captain said. It was Jorge de Lyon. He was the son of a viscount from somewhere. They hadn't met yet, since Pedro and Alfonso had only just sent Jorge's band to the Valerós camp.

"I do not doubt that, Monsieur Jorge de Lyon." Sebastián spoke French, taking Benito's place close to the man, remembering Pèire's lesson, that a good leader always speaks a man's name. "I do not doubt either your valor or your honor. Yet we cannot ask you to raise arms against your own countrymen."

The captain faltered, a brief flickering of his eyes. Sebastián pushed at that moment.

"Monsieur Jorge, I beg you. Stay for the good of the camp. So Valerós can show the kings, Pedro and Alfonso, what good knights can do. For your honor."

Jorge turned away, shouting to his men to take positions on the perimeter of the camp, commanding that they relieve or replace other men who served as night-guards.

"Do you need my help?" Father Anselm said to Jorge.

"No. Unless you have a magical mass to say, to quiet men who smell a battle."

Father Anselm followed that viscount's son into the camp. "Not magical, but there are other ways."

.

"We should have drilled in darkness more," Guillem said. They paused at the head of an alley, having just directed Valerós into the melee.

"It's too hot to drill at midday anyway," Sebastián said. He had his sword in one hand, shield in the other, and blood thumping in his veins. He wanted to be in the streets with the rest of Valerós.

"We need a better view of what's happening." Guillem restrained him with reason. He pointed to the top of the small church at the end of the square. "Here, climb up this tower."

The streets were well lit with torches, likely made from the wood of the king's orchards. The visiting army had desecrated the trees there and now burned pitch torches to desecrate the town. Men thronged the streets. He knew enough French from school-room torture to know what those men shouted. And which Toledo quarter they swarmed. The air reeked of hot male bodies, baked in the sun for days, and now drenched in sweat and murderous rage.

After surveying the streets, Sebastián dropped back to the ground beside Guillem.

"We need to send our men over there," he pointed, "so they come in from backstreets. These Franks want to kill the Jews."

"*Ai*, their old Easter custom," Guillem said.

Sebastián ran to join his men, to redirect them, to confront the riot instead of pushing behind it.

Valerós came into the square to meet the rioting ultramontanos head-on. Sebastián had worked his way to the front of his own force. Benito was close by his side, Guillem a few paces behind. On command, all Valerós voices shouted at once, some taking a few tries to put force into the French words, since it wasn't their tongue.

Stop in the name of God. In the name of the king. In the name of your own honor.

Diego Lopez led a band that appeared out of another alley, also armed and shouting, "Stop!"

Sebastián raised his sword in salute. A rioter shouted in his face, shaking a torch at him, talking too fast for Sebastián to translate. A companion beside the shouting *francimand* struck at Sebastián with a sword.

Benito took the man's hand off.

"Advance, Valerós!" Sebastián shouted. His men poured out of the alleyways, advancing on the rioters.

Valerós had stronger discipline and greater will than a disorganized mob with only blood on its animal mind. Shoving and shouting moved the mob back, with only a frothing few breaking through to confront the disciplined Valerós ranks. Benito hacked at another sword intended for his midsection, sending it spinning.

"Maim, don't kill!" Sebastián shouted in the Catalan tongue of Valerós. Behind him, men echoed his words. But they emphasized the word *kill*, and they stomped and bashed each other's shields when they moved into the rioters, raising a deafening din in the town square. Some man, in bad dialect, cried, "*Desperta, Ferro!*"

In the fetid stench of overheated men and the burning pitch of torches, the way before them became easier. The rioters retreated, scattering before the wall of Valerós infantry and Diego Lopez's caballeros—mounted knights. Sebastián held up a hand for his men to halt, but another *francimand* horde emerged from an alley, screaming obscenely for the blood of Toledo's Jews. They bolted for the front ranks of Valerós, who had dropped their guard. His men raised their shields and stepped forward, but one rioter ran furiously forward, his sword poised for the narrow opening above Sebastián's aventail. Sebastián hacked the sword aside.

Breathe, fadrin.

Tomás's voice sounded so near, Sebastián sucked air, feeling his belly expand with it. When the attacker raised his sword again, Sebastián shrieked a battle-cry, like Chrétien taught.

"*Vivètz* Valerós!"

Sebastián drove his sword home, twisting it the way he'd been taught to do in battle, to be sure the wound wouldn't close.

Barthélemy, the camp thief Sebastián had judged, stared up at him. He held up a hand, in defense or greeting, three lunate crosses tattooed at his wrist. "Monsieur Val—"

Blood rather than spittle poured from his mouth onto Sebastián's sword hand. Sebastián jerked his sword free, pushing the man aside, gasping at the stench of blood and offal.

"Valerós, advance!"

Valerós advanced faster and harder than the rioting Franks could withdraw.

•

"None of the orders showed up to help," Sebastián complained. "And fighting Christians wasn't in our training or strategy."

"It happens," Father Anselm said. The only man Sebastián dared talk with afterward. The Valerós infantry returned to camp at dawn, where those left behind were stirring the ashes to make breakfast. Sebastián hadn't been able to sit still or close his eyes.

"I've killed a man before. Two."

It happened when he and Tomás first met Pedro, defending the king against attacking marauders on the road to Carcassonne. But Sebastián was a mere child then, and it was like a boy's game, killing murderers in defense of the king of Aragón. They'd left the masked bandits to the crows.

"But not someone you spoke with man-to-man that same day." Father Anselm paused in his writing to study Sebastián, who wasn't comfortable with that close scrutiny. "A man you showed mercy to, thinking you'd lead him to a soldier's path of righteousness."

"Òc. He'd been consigned to my care as Master of Valerós. I was responsible for him."

A man who blew his last hot, blood-foaming breath on Sebastián's face when he died.

"Get some sleep." Father Anselm nudged a flask on the camp table. "Drink wine if you have to."

"Will it ever..." What did he want to ask?

This time, Father Anselm rested his quill on a pen wiper. "His face will fade quickly. Sleep here in my tent. Close your eyes and count the babies and women you saved from rioters in Toledo."

Sebastián slipped his chainmail over his head, inhaling the stink of his own gambeson, soaked with sweat. His tunic sleeve—his best linen tunic—was blacked and stiff up to the elbow.

"*Valerós victoriós!*" Men shouted in Catalan at one end of camp.

"*Valerós las almòinas!*" Men at the other end of camp called out in the Languedoc tongue that Valerós was merciful.

"*Visca Pedro el Rey!*" They shouted for Pedro's health in several tongues. Then again in the common language of Valerós, they called Sebastián's name.

"*Vivètz Sebastián,* our valiant master."

Not feeling like a valiant master, Sebastián hacked the sleeves off his shirt with his dagger and sent the bloody rags with the oil-barrel lads to be burned. Then he lay naked on Anselm's bedroll, hoping for a morning breeze, wiping away sweat with his ruined shirt, listening to the *shush-shush* of chainmail rolling in the oil barrels. Seeing that man's surprised face, the crosses tattooed on his arm.

This was his wedding night, a night never to forget. He was supposed to see angels. Or the ghosts of saints.

13

Narbonne by Night

Durán at Palau de la Comte de Narbonne
March 22

"SIBILIA'S FIRST AND LAST PRAYERS were in Latin."

In Ramón-roger's private chamber, a tapestry-lined room lit by ten beeswax candles and smelling of sandalwood, Durán described his evening. Chrétien's gentle doctoring eased the pain not numbed by wine. The count loaned Durán clean small clothes, leggings, a silk shirt, and a fawn-colored linen coat. Also, a brown velvet jerkin with brass eyelets and silk strings that Durán had trouble tying with battered fingers.

"Keep the jerkin. It suits you," Ramón-roger said. "What were these prayers?"

"Some Roman ones. And gibberish. Sibilia promised spells to unite Aragón and the south under Maria's son Jaume."

Ramón-roger snorted. "If *la mignotta* wants magic, my old grandmother in Urgell can teach her spells that—"

Chrétien listened only to Durán. "To make her son Jaume king?"

"*Òc.* But Jaume will be king." Durán leaned back in the chair. Pain shot up his side again. "He's Pedro's only son."

Chrétien touched Durán's shoulder, gently enough to avoid the bruises. "You wondrous innocent."

"She wants it now," Ramón-roger said. "This year. With herself as regent."

Durán's head ached. "*Ai,* that's why she promised gold for services." He described the plans he'd overheard. Sibilia's priestly brother was carrying a magic cup and sword to Toledo to defeat Pedro.

"Tonight, Maria is paying an assassin," Durán said. "It's Colomb de Beaurain."

"Not Colomb! Never!" Ramón-roger pounded one fist against another. "But tell me, are all Montcava cousins incestuous spit monkeys?"

"I'm not." Durán's ribcage caused him to recall every beating he'd endured in the past decade.

.

The count of Foix enjoyed a private table on a balcony in the viscount of Narbonne's great hall, where Durán and Chrétien joined him to eat extravagant food while gazing down on a hundred guests.

"The crusaders loved Outremer spices." Chrétien heaped his trencher with more stewed cuttlefish and peas. "Their sons are finding the spice trade even more valuable than selling splinters of the True Cross."

"This is like the food your mother Numa gives us." Durán winced at closing his bruised hand on his dinner knife. He pushed food around on the elegant carved wooden trencher.

"Fancier," Chrétien said. "But my mother is more inspirational."

"Look at that flock of lords." Ramón-roger pointed with his knife to a milling mess of Narbonnese and Montpelhièr courtiers.

The fried croquettes distracted Durán. Chickpea flour with minced parsley, pepper, and marjoram. And something else. He picked at it, seeking especially tasty pieces. "Fennel!" he exclaimed. He offered Chrétien a portion of pepper-and-fennel flavored croquette on a chunk of brioix. Chrétien accepted the bite from Durán's hand, but then stared below when a pack of fustian-clad courtiers parted.

Hélène formerly-of-Beaurain tapped her foot, impatient. Another senhóra stood near, her elbows bumping Hélène when she gestured to the knight who stooped to whisper in her ear. It was Colomb to whom the senhóra slipped a red velvet purse with dangling strings. Colomb passed the purse to Matheus of Xirgú.

"This is the dangerous conspiracy you uncovered?" Chrétien scoffed. "These housewives?"

"It's just Colomb de Beaurain doing what he does," the count said, "taking gold in service to a southern lord."

"Who wants evil tasks done." Durán believed he'd learned important secrets about his uncle and cousin.

Colomb bowed, hand to his chest, signaling that he accepted service. The owner of the purse faced the room. It was Maria de Montpelhièr. With that yapping dog on her arm and Sibilia de Xirgú chattering in her ear.

"Who else has that witch has had assassinated?" Ramón-roger sucked his teeth, thoughtful. "Still, Matheus de Xirgú doesn't strike me as capable of serious action."

"My aching ribs say otherwise. But it's Colomb who accepted Maria's gold."

"I'm a leprous he-goat if Maria's assassin is Colomb," Ramón-roger insisted. "His brother Hugues raised him. Hugues embodied paratge more than any man in the south."

"Yet only Colomb is left to claim Beaurain glory."

"You are entirely too modest." Chrétien settled his arm on Durán's shoulder, having forgotten about Durán's ribs.

Ramón-roger pointed across the hall. "See why certain Roman priests make me choke on my own gall? Arnau Amalric wearing enough silk to dress the three of us from Twelfth Night to Easter. With plenty left over for our wives."

"Made easier since we don't have wives," Chrétien said.

"You two need to take care of that," Ramón-roger said. "Pedro *El Rei* says we all must help save our women from Simon's invaders. That includes you."

Chrétien dismissed the idea with a careless wave of one hand, while the other rubbed Durán's newly cut curls. "I'm too young. Finish your complaint. We await your tutelage."

"Arnau preaches sanctimony by the bucketsful. Yet I'll wager my horse that the archbishop's shoemaker is busier than my village blacksmiths."

"*Ai*, senhór. I don't take bets where the odds are so tilted," Chrétien said. "Though you keep very nice horses."

"Wise boy. If my land above Narbonne produces a good harvest this year, the archbishop will take his tenth out of the best." Ramón-roger made a rude gesture. "But will the archbishop help keep my people from starving? Truly, by next summer Arnau will again seek to scourge me for sheltering heretics."

"Do you want to share some of that wine?" Chrétien asked. He reached for the flagon. "Arnau deserves some praise. He got Simon de Montfort to stop his terror while we're all busy keeping the Saracens out of Christendom."

"The caliph of Cordoba will never invade Christendom." Ramón-roger smacked the table top, then prodded Durán with his elbow, sending a sharp pain through his torso. "What do all your Good Christian friends say? Are they in league with the caliph?"

Durán set his dinner knife aside in the same way Ramón-roger had. "In Toulouse people say that letter from the caliph to Count Raymond is a lie. Even the Roman priests laughed out loud when the bishop read it to the town council."

Chrétien pitched his words into a falsetto that sounded like Maria of Montpelhièr. "'Your heretics invited my Saracens to invade Christendom. Our ships will land in Narbonne at Easter.'" He sniffed in disgust. "Maybe the caliph has a clerk who writes in Provençal dialect. And he'll transport his army in magic ships that can provision two hundred thousand men and all their horses."

"Or maybe I'm the caliph of Cordoba," Ramón-roger said. "Yet dozens of seigneurs have begged to join this venture in Iberia, to win forgiveness for their sins."

"While come next summer, Simon de Montfort will resume burning their aunties," Chrétien said.

Ramón-roger smacked the stone bottle he held. "*Doutz Jhezu.* May Simon's bones turn to dust on the dawn of his death day. May the worms of evil bore into the teeth of Arnau, that vomit-eating dog, and plague him through each night. Every goat in the south will die laughing when the gates of hell open wide for the both of them to enter."

"Feel better now?" Chrétien said. He took the wine bottle from the count. "If Pedro wins even a single victory in Andalusia, the pope will love him more than Simon."

Ramón-roger relaxed into his chair. He pointed to the court below and nudged Durán again, who winced. "There's the viscount of Narbonne hanging onto the new archbishop. And watch the gossiping hens and roosters surrounding the divine Maria."

Instead, Durán watched how the count of Foix claimed the physical space around him. When Ramón-roger held his arms, he took the space of two men; when he sat on a bench, his knees and shoulders spread to take up space where another might sit, but would never dare. Durán's own sore bones rested in his tight, borrowed coat. He held himself close out of habit, not just from this night's pain. A habit from youthful street-life in Toulouse, when he needed to avoid ruffians who challenged him just for being bigger than most men. He needed to learn how to claim a seigneur's space, since he now had a seigneur's title.

Durán spread his elbows. His ribs shot pain to his belly. He coughed, which hurt worse.

Ramón-roger elbowed Durán again. "So that strutting cock next to Arnau is your cousin Matheus?"

Matheus stood out from the crowd, tall and dressed in silver-studded fire-orange silk, which didn't flatter his olive complexion or the red hair that fell to his shoulders in the French style. Not a mark on him from having battered Durán.

The count tapped his nose, which he did while lost in thought. "The Montcavas I knew in my youth were all small and dark. Then all of the sudden you get these big, fiery ones. Like Durán here. And the master of Xirgú."

"That exotic dark senhóra beside Maria is the former Marquesa de Beaurain," Chrétien said. "They say Pedro's wife can't select a ribbon for that rat-dog of hers without consulting Hélène. A brown ribbon tonight, to set off the queen's yellow robe."

Durán glanced at the brown ribbons of his jerkin. He doubled the knot over so that it stayed in place. Amid the throng below, Matheus spoke with Arnau Amalric, pointing up to the balcony where the count of Foix and his companions dined.

"*Per l'amor de Dèu*," Ramón-roger swore. "Pray that God in heaven decides to change the winds in Pedro's favor."

Chrétien leaned closer to Durán "You're pale. Did that wolf bite poison into you?"

"I didn't try to kill that dog. Colomb says it isn't dead." He swallowed the jabs of pain, but not the idea that he'd hurt a poor animal to protect himself.

"Tell me you're well, *cor dolç.*"

"I'm fine."

"You are more than fine." Chrétien again brushed Durán's shorn curls. "You are near perfection, *bon amic.*"

The door slammed open, pushing against the back of Ramón-roger's chair. A brace of guards appeared, both dressed in the viscount of Narbonne's colors.

"The archbishop commands your company."

Chrétien scooped more fennel-flavored croquettes onto Durán's plate. "Ah good! Now there'll be enough wine left for us. *Bona nuèch,* Count. We won't wait up for you."

"Monsenyor wants all of you."

▪

The archbishop Arnau Amalric, an odd-looking man, filled the room with motion, mass, and noise, gesturing for everyone's attention with one hand while the other grasped a jewel-encrusted gold cross as long as his forearm. His silk, gold, and courtly gestures together all manifested power. However, he reminded Durán more of Toulousain bullies than wealthy southern lords.

"*Ai, mon amic!*" Arnau greeted Ramón-roger in the common tongue, and embraced him the way southern seigneurs do, but he seemed like an eagle with his talons extended, landing on his prey.

They'd all jammed into a receiving room off the great hall, with six other men, including Bishop Folquet of Toulouse, two priests in Cistercian robes, a scribe, and the viscount of Narbonne, who huddled in a corner with one of his seigneurs. This internal room, with no windows and two branches of candles, quickly warmed from the crowd.

"You were gracious with your time earlier today, Monsenyor. Thank you." Ramón-roger seized the moment. "I'm pleased we find ourselves united for this enterprise of faith in Iberia."

"Are we?" Arnau hissed. "We are advised that there are heretics among the men you're sending to Iberia. Men willing to betray Christendom to the Saracens."

Ramón-roger threw his head back with his haughtiest laugh. "Men will say anything, eh, senhór? We live in such interesting times."

He elbowed Durán in the ribs, adding pain to the bolt of fear that the archbishop had launched.

"Òc." Chrétien saw that Durán was in agony. "This new world is a glorious place."

Arnau scowled. "We have the word of honorable seigneurs."

"Who?" Ramón-roger sounded mildly curious. Chrétien's hands twitched, ever so subtly. They'd watched Matheus whispering in the great hall.

"We protect our witnesses." Arnau lifted his chin, tilting his head with righteous disdain.

Ramón-roger folded his arms, again taking more space in this crowded cave. "No good man hides his face when condemning others. That's not the honor our forefathers lived and died for."

"O you blessed seigneurs and your honor." Arnau sneered. "You hold paratge like a shield, to hide your heretics from the Church's judgment. I repeat. You are accused by creditable witnesses of sheltering heretics."

"You are misled, Monsenyor. My men each swore oaths, put on the Cross, and took up their swords. No man who swears an oath, prepared to shed blood for Christendom, can possibly be called heretic." He grasped Arnau's hand, and then resisted the archbishop's effort to shirk away. "Are you unfamiliar with the beliefs of the heretics you burn?"

"The Church doesn't punish heretics." Again, the lofty disdain. No one else in the room spoke besides the count of Foix and the archbishop. "We only weigh guilt and innocence. Christendom's rulers carry out punishment. Earthly punishments are not the Church's business."

"So, Aimerico," Ramón-roger turned his attention on the viscount of Narbonne. "Is it you who will burn my men if Arnau and the good bishop Folquet decide they are heretics?" The viscount, the smallest man in the too-hot room, shuffled nervously, not answering. Ramón-roger said to Arnau, "Or, as their lord, am I supposed to light the pyre myself?"

"We aren't burning anyone. We merely identify heretics."

Ramón-roger stepped back from Arnau, treading on Durán's foot. "Ah! And who are these supposed heretics?"

Arnau recited a list of villages under interdict, concluding with Castell-de-Valerós.

"The master of Valerós is in Pedro's army, carrying the cross to Andalusia," Ramon-roger said softly. "As we discussed earlier today."

"His mother and her protectors are known heretics."

"She's dead," Chrétien said. "Murdered in an ambush. Do you intend to kill her twice?"

"And principally, the seigneur of Montcava, who they say is a bastard." Arnau glared past the count at Chrétien and Durán, but he didn't know which of the two he was accusing. Chrétien offered his best jongleur's smile, pretty and innocent, which Arnau didn't like. He settled on Durán, scowling. Durán stared back.

He wants to squash me like a black-bellied tarantula.

Arnau coughed, then swallowed phlegm. "We learned the man is known in Toulouse to be a goodman. A Cathar. Is that you, senhór?"

Durán sweated in velvet, stood amid the best of southern society, among men who smelled no better than any Montcava house-knight, though finer adornments hung on their fleshly racks. The bishop farted. No one blinked or turned their heads. They all waited for the street-hawker to answer the archbishop. Durán began.

"I didn't have the opportunity to learn paratge from my father. But I know what's due my family and my brother, who trusted me to keep the Montcava domus safe while he crusades in Iberia. Now I myself have also promised service," he glanced at Ramón-roger while saying his piece, "to Pedro d'Aragón."

"To protect Christendom." Chrétien finished the part Durán left out. "Do you need our oaths again, sworn before God?"

The room had grown so warm, sweat beaded up under Durán's silks, prickling at his neck. Arnau stood close to Durán, his body burning with either passion or fever.

"Hell and damnation." Chrétien swore softly. Durán, who didn't believe in hell or damnation, smiled, nervous. Except for the archbishop, their accusers shuffled, as grim and nervous as Durán was. Sweat must be dripping under their brocade and silks, too. Chrétien continued. "I'll give you my oath. I swear on the bones of St-Neophytos that I believe in the Holy Trinity and in the Church, where the pope is God's representative on earth. To serve God and my own honor, I am traveling to Iberia to crusade for the sake of Christendom."

"It's not a crusade." Bishop Folquet spoke at last, earning one of Arnau's ferocious glares.

"Òc," Ramón-roger said. "It's an expedition of faith and peace, bringing the Cross to the Moors."

Arnau returned his attention to Durán, who shrank into the small starving boy sent by his mother to beg food and medicine from a priest at St-Sernin. The archbishop held out his ornate cross, lifting Durán's hand with it. His falling sleeve uncovered a tattoo on Arnau's wrist, like the one on the body in the Toulouse alley. "You'll swear, Senhór Montcava?"

Durán cupped his hand around the jewel-encrusted metal, finding it warm and damp from Arnau's fiery hands. Just a lump of metal. Not even as beautifully wrought as Chrétien's sword.

"Your oath, senhór? Or are you indeed a heretic who blasphemes the Holy Spirit?"

"I vow," Durán began.

"Not a vow," Chrétien said. "Knights swear an oath."

"I'm not a knight." Durán considered the knightly lord of Montcava who'd deserted his mother, leaving her to depend on a renegade priest who left dry crusts and cheese rinds at their hovel door. "But I swear on the pure tears of the holy mother that I serve God and my family with an honest heart, together with my brother as a vassal of Pedro d'Aragón."

He kissed that cross, which was just a piece of metal that smelled of a man's sweaty hands, because he did honestly serve God and his brother and his family, and it wasn't worth dying to defy the angry men in that hot, fetid room.

"Good!" Arnau's big voice boomed in the little cell. "Now, say your creed, and then we shall…"

One knock on the door and it was being nudged open, displacing Arnau and the two Cistercians. Most everyone in the room had to shift a half pace to allow a messenger to enter. It was another Cistercian, this one announcing that the queen of Aragón requested the company of the archbishop of Narbonne.

"We've finished our business." Arnau pointed to the count and Bishop Folquet.

"Thank you, Monsenyor." Ramón-roger bowed, again taking more room than the space allowed.

Arnau was down the hall, his priests and companions following, when he called back, "One of my men will travel with you to Iberia. We shall all meet in Toledo."

When everyone had departed, Chrétien shook like a greyhound come in out of the rain. Durán straightened up to walk, finding that his bruised bones had seized up while he stood still for so long.

"We're alive!" Chrétien said. He came within a hair of slapping Durán on the back, but paused, his hand brushing the brown velvet jerkin instead.

"That was a lucky interruption." Ramón-roger kept his voice low when they passed into the corridor. "Do you even know the Creed to repeat it, Senhór Durán?"

"No. My mother found comfort with the goodmen and goodwomen when I was very young."

"Jove's pissing monkey! I need to say prayers of thanks twice tonight." The count punched Chrétien's shoulder. "Whatever made you call on the name of a false saint? You put your damned Celt head in the gaping mouth of a lion back there."

"My father swore on false saints, but I don't. It provokes my mother. I don't like to cause her unease."

"There is no St-Neophytos." Ramón-roger scolded Chrétien. "The confounded Folquet will be awake all night trying to prove it."

"He's a baffling little hermit who lives in a cave behind my father's house on Cyprus. If he isn't dead by now. I don't know much about being holy, but that hermit is saintlier than Arnau or Folquet."

"You made me swear an oath." Durán managed to say it without complaining like a child.

"And kept your soul stitched inside your hide, *fadrin*." Ramón-roger again pounded one fist into the other, indicating that his energy was on the rise.

"And I've never made you eat sausages or drink wine," Chrétien said. "Don't be so picky about the sins you choose to adopt."

"It's not the same." Durán worried that this time he did sound sulky. "It's easy for you to be as bad a Catholic as you want, and then confess on Easter. But I—"

"What?" Ramón-roger swung around. "What do you people believe? A prayer is a prayer. A sin is a sin. We don't know what happens after we're dead, so we pay a priest to hedge our bets."

"No," Durán said. "We live on this mortal earth over and over until we get it right. And some sins are much worse than others. Like if we cause other people to suffer and die. And I—"

The count pressed his finger to Durán's lips. "Stop! No use ending this incarnation like a rooster who squawks at dawn."

"I don't want to kill anything." Durán finished as soon as the count removed his hand. "Man or beast."

"I'll provide all the protection you need," Chrétien said. "No heretic hunter will get past me to lay hands on you."

"Thanks," Durán said. "But I'm too battered tonight to feel safe."

"I have an idea." Ramón-roger seemed not to hear. "And what I need is right here in my pocket."

"A silk handkerchief?" Chrétien said.

"No, Arnau's letter from earlier, accepting my army for the endeavor in Andalusia." He shepherded them toward the great hall. "This is one of those days when I believe God loves us and wants us to be joyful! Advance, young seigneur!"

•

"A poet gave me these songs for a special senhóra, the Sovereign Lady of Montpelhièr, Viscountess of Marseille, Countess of the Comminges, and Queen of Aragón."

After Chrétien's introduction to the music, the crowd listened to the first verse and chorus before returning to noisy conversations. When the three songs were over, Chrétien bowed and stepped off the dais.

"Your songs touched my heart, senhór jongleur."

Sibilia of Narbonne clutched the edge of Chrétien's oud, which he held before him like a shield. The hard lines of her face were framed by a boxlike embroidered silk coif and white barbette in the new style; a gold crespine net restrained her hair. For Durán's taste, her sleeveless surcoat in brilliant scarlet and the white silk gown would better suit a much younger woman. Sibilia continued her praise in that baby voice, tapping her sister Hélène's elbow for attention. "Didn't I weep? Didn't my tears flow like dew drops on spring flowers?"

"You!" Hélène's eyes raked Chrétien's tall frame.

"*C'est moi, madame.*" Chrétien addressed her in French. "At your service. You remember your cousin, Durán."

"I am enchanted, exquisite senhóra." Durán dipped his knee and brought a hand to his chest in the southern style.

Hélène blinked, as if an upstart street urchin addressed her. "You're that bastard of Nicolau's."

"The seigneur is a tribute to his father, the great crusader who died at Constantinople," Chrétien said.

"Seigneur? That rubble-yard bastard?" Hélène laughed, like a mockingbird's *cawk* in the orange trees at the Montcava villa.

Durán shifted his stance, imitating the count of Foix, while preferring the fists of Toulousain streetfighters to Hélène's attack.

"Maria is in raptures." Sibilia ignored that her sister had just insulted the Master of Montcava.

"I seek to please, senhóra," Chrétien said. To Durán's certain knowledge, Chrétien never sought to please any woman in this world, except his own mother and the lost Isabella. "These new songs are full of paratge and love. I'd be delighted to introduce her to the poet."

Excited, Sibilia dragged Hélène away, headed for the knot of courtiers around Maria.

"*Na maliciosa.* Why is she so mean?" Durán asked, calling Hélène a vicious senhóra. "I send the rents on time. She has no children, so I don't threaten her inheritance."

"*Ai, bon amic.*" Chrétien nudged Durán with his foot. "Leave room on the bench for me. You've taken to sprawling like those snot-nosed faitdits of Carcassonne who camp in Toulousain villas."

"I'm sitting just like any other seigneur."

"True. Except you are far more handsome. And built better. Hélène hates us both because once I shouted on the streets of Famagusta that she was the whore of Babylon. Just after I'd beaten the devil out of her porter and guards."

"She's the senhóra who—"

"Who stood by while Renoud of Montcava's henchmen thrashed my brother Tomás. And then cast him in a dungeon for three days." Chrétien wrenched his hands. "You've seen his scars. Hélène, however, insists it was merely a cellar, not a dungeon."

Ramón-roger joined them, dressed in his finest blue silk, his hair and beard groomed to greater glory than any sniveling courtier might achieve. "Let's speak with the queen of Aragón."

When they approached Maria de Montpelhièr, the crowd parted in deference to Ramón-roger, the next highest ranking person in the room.

The count of Foix bowed to Maria. "If you allow, ma dòmna, I dedicate my humble poems to you."

Maria grasped his hand in the way one seigneur of the south greets another, her pale, blemished face flushed with excitement. "You are the poet, dear count? I am flattered."

Close beside Maria, Colomb de Beaurain smirked. At his elbow, Matheus de Xirgú glowered at Durán with unmasked hatred. Durán, his ribs aching, lost the thread of Ramón-roger's words while staring back at the man who'd tried to kill him earlier that evening.

Ramón-roger's voice rose.

"Grant me one boon, ma dòmna. You and I add great strength in the eyes of God if our men travel together into Andalusia. Do me the honor of placing your men under my banner for this venture."

Maria wrestled with that infernal dog in ribbons. "My personal guard is traveling with me to Rome. I can only spare a band of mercenaries for Iberia. Will you write a song about their adventures if they travel with your army?"

"With delight. Our men will show Castile and Navarre the meaning of true paratge. And my songs will tell our children's children of their glory."

Maria once more offered her hand like a man would, agreeing to a bond of honor. Her dog barked, leaped to nip Ramón-roger's cuff, then slipped from its mistress's lap and splayed on the marble floor. The count scooped up the dog, closing its muzzle in his fist. "This has been a long day's celebration and a longer night." Maria indicated that Sibilia should fetch her dog. "I'll leave you to business with my captain."

Then Pedro's ill-natured wife was gone, dragging along a reluctant Hélène. Sibilia followed with the squirming dog. After adieus with the queen, Ramón-roger threw his hands up like an overjoyed plowman praising heaven. His voice rang through the room.

"Who'll swear to ride under my banner to shed Saracen blood?"

Colomb cleared his throat and spoke low, as if sharing a confidence with the count of Foix, though everyone in the room heard. "You told the bishop in Toulouse that you weren't able to travel on this venture."

"Yet I'm not too poor to send my men, to the glory of God." Ramón-roger fished in his jerkin and produced a roll of parchment, wide as two fingers, bound with a scarlet ribbon. "Earlier today the archbishop put Valerós and Montcava under my banner until Sebastián of Valerós returns from Andalusia."

"God works in mysterious ways." Though Colomb said it, he didn't sound like he believed it. Matheus had his hand on his sword, still staring at Durán.

"Times are hard." Ramón-roger addressed the dozen seigneurs who lingered. While he spoke, he seemed to draw these men to him, like iron to a lodestone. "Men long to serve God, but few can afford to travel only on the hope of booty to be won in war. Therefore, I shall pay captains traveling under my banner three gold marks and one mark for each of their men when they return. Our men will show Castile and Navarre how to defeat the Saracens."

The seigneurs aligned with the count, indecision wafted away, as if dispersed by a predawn breeze. They called out their names and how many men they'd send with the count.

"For paratge."

"For my father's honor and my grandfather's."

"*Cortezia!*"

That cry for kinship and unity rose, repeated as a cheer.

The count of Foix, hand to his breast, bowed his head. "*Com un òme de paratge…*" *As a man of paratge…*

The all fell silent while Ramón-roger intoned a solemn oath.

"…I will repay the honor of your trust with gold, prayers, and the company of my best men."

"Who will lead your men, senhór?" Colomb asked. With Matheus at his elbow, he now stood as close to Ramón-roger as Durán and Chrétien. Matheus hovered so close that Durán smelled mint and date sugar. And hatred.

Ramón-roger grasped Colomb's hand, the same way he'd shaken hands with Maria earlier. "*Ai, mon amic*, I asked the best of the seigneurs to serve as my leader and paymaster."

Ramón-roger motioned for his servant at the edge of the crowd, who brought a bag of rattling coins, its weight a burden for one hand to hold. "At Church court this afternoon, the archbishop said I must choose carefully. A man who will remind us of the honor that Hugues de Beaurain brought to the south."

Matheus stepped forward, his hand out.

Grasping thin air.

"And he's like a son to me." Ramón-roger slipped an arm around Durán's shoulder, where he rested the heavy bag of gold, perhaps breaking another of Durán's ribs. "He holds a fief near Urgell from me, since he once saved my life. He'll depart on Easter Monday, at dawn." You will support him as my captain?" He addressed the crowd of seigneurs.

A few cries of *òc* rose while the Narbonne crowd murmured and milled, not recognizing a Montcava from the Toulousain.

"Go with God, my son." The count touched Durán's head the way a father does. He then gestured for Durán to follow him as he departed, leading them close to Colomb and his acolyte Matheus.

"*Òc.*" Colomb folded his arms, planted in a battle challenge. "I shall support him. The archbishop asked me to travel with your men, senhór."

"Thank you," Durán said. "And I appreciate your help earlier tonight, uncle. I apologize that I wasn't properly grateful then."

Colomb scowled at the "uncle" part, stepping back so that Durán was forced to pass close to Matheus. Determined not to be cowed by a bully, Durán said, "I didn't mean to hurt your dog." A low growl from Matheus. "I'll eat your liver one day soon." Chrétien remained at Durán's back when they followed Ramón-roger from the great hall. The count paused at the stone stairs leading up to his chamber.

"You'll be tossing bones with the gambling seigneurs of Narbonne tonight. To hear their thoughts and take their silver." Ramón-roger addressed Chrétien.

"If you so command, senhór." Chrétien had a hand over his heart, like a knight pledging his honor.

"Cheeky, *fadrin*. I'm describing what you already intend. I'll say farewell here. I'm off at dawn for Foix." He clasped Durán's shoulder, sending a wrench of pain through his battered torso. "That *peccador* Chrétien needs all the indulgences Rome can give. So, don't tell the whole damn world you're a toad-sucking heretic, since no one can tell by looking. *Bon vèspre!*"

"Wait, senhór," Durán pleaded. "Will you conclude your Urgell dispute before we return? Perhaps we can visit my new fief on the way home from this adventure."

Ramón-roger barked a laugh and grasped Durán in an enormous bear hug—more pain!—and then chortled when he ran up the stairs.

"Indulgences? Fat lot of good that'll do you and me. We're both going to hell." Chrétien tugged at the curls on Durán's neck. "At least we'll be together."

"Why is he laughing at me?" Durán asked, hurt.

"*Ai, cor dolç.*" Chrétien called him sweetheart as he always did when chiding Durán for naïveté. "He's laughing at the idea that we'll come back."

Chrétien shouted after the count of Foix.

"Take care of my mother, bonfraire. Farewell!"

14
Girona

AT GIRONA, SEVERAL RIVERS MEET and combine their waters before flowing to the Mediterranean. In particular, the Ter flows from the icy peaks above Ripoll to join the Onyar river, which runs through the bandit lands of the Guilleries. Because of the bandits, many visitors felt relieved of a burden when they entered the town's gates: excellent food, and safe shelter within walls that have withstood invaders for eons.

At those town gates, damp from a midday spring rain, Isabella once again gave in to the relentless temptation to check over her shoulder for pursuers. "I'll join the army camp outside of town."

"We've been traveling for days," Felip said. "We need supplies from my family's house. Stay the night."

She disliked spending even one moment where enemies seeking the murderer of the abbot Lorenç might appear. However, too little of her gold remained after buying horses, so she'd have to outfit the next part of the journey from her enemy's house.

Trudging through the busy, rain-slick streets, they passed a small arms factory at the lower end of town, where a crew of young boys produced arrows and spears. Smaller boys loaded bundles onto a wooden-wheeled wagon, its wheels strengthened by iron strakes hammered in place. The burros gobbled silage while waiting to pull these loads, fed by old men who also governed the hive of children.

Beyond the armory, women hung lengths of woad-dyed fustian on lines outside a weavers' shed. Several others worked stone-lined dye pots, where visiting friends delivered buckets of urine for the dyers to fix the dye. She followed Felip up to the top of the climb, several alleys beyond the Jewish quarter. Near the end of the last narrow street, one house stood empty.

"*Ai*," Felip said. "That's my friend Serena's house. So much has changed since last summer."

Next to that deserted house, the painted blue door of a seigneur's city house stood slightly ajar.

"*Hola!*" Felip called. He motioned for Isabella to follow. A voice answered from inside, begging patience. Then an ancient man hobbled into the damp foyer.

"Donzel, is it you?" The old man had the accent of a Catalan woodcutter, but his voice reverberated majestically.

"*Òc*, Ponç. It's me, with my good friend Vidal."

"Senhór!" Ponç stepped closer in the dim light that filtered into the foyer. "Thanks be to the Good God! Our message found you."

"No, I've left St-Pere. What was the message you sent?"

"Your grandmother asked for you."

"*Ai*. Well, we're here, Ponç. And we're famished. Is there food?"

Isabella set down her travel pack, but lingered at the edge of the foyer, wishing they could be on their way quickly.

"Come, Vidal. Let's eat a good meal and sleep in good beds. Let me show you Xirgú hospitality." Felip spoke with assurance, as if home gave back all the strength of spirit St-Pere had drained away.

In the kitchen, an old three-legged iron cauldron stood in the fire, with the flesh-hook nearby, ready to snatch meat from the cauldron. A sight so familiar, it made Isabella homesick for Valerós. Another black cauldron bubbled over the fire, hung from a spur-shaped pot-hook. Ponç grappled with the stew pot, setting it on an iron-legged trivet. Burning wood collapsed when Ponç set down the pot, exposing fire dogs on the stone hearth. The ends were indeed dogs. Fire-blackened Great Pyrs, with shaggy coats and sad faces.

"Ponç, the Péletier house is empty. Where's Senhóreta Serena?" Felip asked.

"Gone to her uncle's house in Narbonne till she marries, or so they say."

"Her grandfather died?"

"*Òc, fadrin*. Your brother bought her land when the old man passed to the next life. They say he'll marry her."

Felip frowned. "That can't be right. She has only a little land, and he was to marry a woman in Narbonne."

"He gave her land to the Church." Ponç poked at the wood with a fire-iron, retrieving clay-wrapped fowl from the ashes.

"R–r–remember wh–when Margalida used to wrap pigeons to bake while we ate breakfast?" Felip asked Ponç.

"*Ai, òc*. Margalida had her ways. Did everything just so." Ponç dished up braised lamb for them, plus beans dipped from the other hanging pot, both full of garlic and paprika.

"I'm sorry she's gone," Felip said.

"I hope she had a good end," Isabella said.

"*Ai*, that she did. We had a teacher in who…" Ponç paused. "You don't mind, donzel? Even though the Church has you now?"

Isabella said, "The Good God grants joy to the hearts of all who love in the way that Jesus taught. The priests at St-Pere didn't convince either of us otherwise."

"You came away from St-Pere with our donzel?" Ponç asked. "Thank you for bringing him home."

Felip asked, "Is my grandmother well enough to see me?"

"She has her good times," Ponç said. "She wasn't well enough to visit with your brother a fortnight ago. I shall tell her you're here."

When the old man left, Isabella nibbled at her bread.

"Do you understand that your brother is part of a conspiracy to alter the order of the world?" She spoke in a whisper, hoping to be gentle, while repeating this lesson.

"Perhaps. I'm trying to understand how my monastery fee arrived at St-Pere if my grandmother refused to see my brother."

Isabella spooned the stew, pausing to scrape a generous portion of the lamb onto Felip's trencher. "You're close to your grandmother?"

"She raised me, since my mother had so much business to conduct in Narbonne."

"*Ai*, after your father died?" She touched Felip's hand. He'd become distracted and nervous when they entered the house. "Where was your brother? Isn't he a great deal older than you?"

"My mother keeps Matheus at her side. He's been the head of house since my birth."

"Your grandmother is your mother's mother?" She didn't ask it explicitly, but wanted to know, was his grandmother a Montcava?

"No, she's my f–father's mother. A Ch–Xirgú." He stuttered whenever he worried.

"Whatever your brother is up to, he isn't taking care of business. Look." She pointed at the wall above the door that led to the kitchen garden and ovens. "The plaster is peeling away. The walls weep water here and in your foyer. And your Ponç deserves better clothes. It's like the walls are weeping for their master's neglect."

"W–what can I do?" Felip frowned.

"Felip." She stroked his hand again. His fingers twitched beneath her touch. It was so sad that no one in his family took proper care of such a sensitive young man. "I saw the light in your face when we entered that blue door. You should be master here."

.

"Grandmother!"

"Come to me, *fadrin*."

Bundled in the bed with quilts over her robe, his dear grandmother held her arms out for Felip, the way she did in the old days when Matheus teased him past endurance. Unable to voice his joy at seeing her, Felip lost himself, smelling the lavender and mint and soap that meant comfort.

"Who did you bring with you?" His grandmother petted him in the way she did, in the way that his mother had asked her to stop when Felip turned ten.

Felip hadn't noticed that Vidal followed him into her chamber.

"*Àvia*, this is my good friend Vidal. He came from St-Pere with me. Senhór Vidal, this is Constanza de Xirgú, my grandmother."

Constanza said the things that a senhóra does to greet a visitor, and Vidal replied in the proper way, without the Catalan back-country inflections he'd used on their travels. Rather, Vidal did her honor since she was the senhóra of the domus.

"You've come to visit, Felip! That is grand. I didn't know you'd be allowed to travel, *fadrin*."

"Excuse me, *Àvia*. I'm sorry to disappoint." She'd wanted him to be a papal diplomat.

"You never disappoint, *dolç fadrin*," Constanza said.

"We've left the monastery. It was not a good place for Felip."

His grandmother smiled, slowly at first. Then she laughed in that sweet, rare way of hers. "I never liked the idea. But as usual, my arguments did not win out. I'm so happy you've come home, *fadrin*."

Felip grasped her hand. He wasn't embarrassed for Vidal to see him here, where people loved each other. Vidal must perceive his grandmother's goodness.

Constanza questioned Felip, coaxing him to talk about life at St-Pere, and asking how Felip and Vidal traveled to Girona. They talked well into the afternoon. When he paused for a moment, she stirred to sit up in the bed.

"Felip, *fadrin*, I need my medicine. Please ask Ponç to bring my herbs. And then let me rest. I imagine you need a rest too."

■

Felip stretched in the sturdy tester bed that had always been his, with its pale woolen curtains. Here, he was safe as a decade earlier, pretending to be a great lord who ruled a kingdom in Iberia, like the Cid of Valencia.

The linen hangings over the doorway swayed in a slight breeze for which he never found the source. The figure of Sancta Maria in the painted drapery once again became a beautiful queen who beckoned him. He rested his hand on that wrapped chalice inside his jerkin, which he often felt warmed his heart. The Holy Mother of Our Lord beckoned from the tapestry, reaching out to take his face into her hands and bless him for his trials as her own sworn knight, and for saving her from danger.

A knock at the door brought Felip back from his dreams.

"*Benvingut*," Felip called a welcome, hoping that Vidal had decided to accept his invitation to share the fire in his room.

It was Ponç. "Forgive me." He begged forgiveness. "Your friend went to your mother's room after spending time in your brother's room. I'm sure you already know."

"*Òc*, Ponç. I trust my friend with my life."

However, not bothering to put his shirt on, Felip raced to his mother's room to learn what his friend was doing.

"I can help you, Vidal, if you tell me what you want."

Vidal glanced up from the mess of accounts and missives scattered on the table. He held out a scrap of parchment. "One Montcava or another killed my uncle, destroyed my grandfather, and stole my son from his home. Other Montcavas tried to kill me and all the children of my house."

Felip protested. "No one would kill you."

"You listened while your uncle tried to kill me. Read what I just gave you."

He studied the scrap. "It's a letter to my mother from my uncle, saying that he's using her contributions for the glory of God." Felip handed it back.

"*Ai*, to light candles for your father's soul." Vidal pushed the letter back at Felip. "Read the letter the way I taught you."

Felip read down, then saw he must also read from right to left.

'I know you never want to see that child again. We have a visitor from Valerós, but I shall dispose of this problem. We still work for that glorious day.'

"*Dolç* Felip. Your uncle's letter says you are the lopped-off scion of a house of thieves and murderers." Vidal sorted through the pile of parchments and picked out another scrap. "Read this. Don't bother with the trash across. Read the real message."

Felip took it, stuttering while he read.

'By the new moon of July fifteen.
Arnau in Narbonne supports Maria. Matheus will travel with him into Hispania to open heaven's door for Pedro. The order shall be Matheus's to command with this sign, even those of our knights in Pedro's court.'

"What sign?"

"The blasted Crux Lunata." Vidal banged a hand on the table. "I should have guessed about Maria when I first saw you copying their messages. I need to find Pedro quickly."

"It's late in the day, Vidal. Sleep here for the night. Barcelona is only a few days' ride away."

"Pedro has likely left for Toledo. I need to ride faster than Pedro does." Picking up more missives from the table, Vidal wrapped them into a packet. "Where did Ponç take my horses?"

Before Felip answered, his brother's voice echoed in the foyer.

·

"Felip! You scabied donkey! Where in the devil's hell are you?" A Narbonnese-inflected voice roared in the lower rooms.

Isabella watched Felip turn white, his hands afflicted with tremors. "Your brother?"

Felip nodded, stunned into silence.

"If he's looking for you here, he's been to St-Pere." Isabella jerked open her shirt and reached for the letter Felip still held in his hand. Like the immature boy he sometimes was, he gaped at her breasts when she tucked that letter away. "Good luck, *fadrin*."

She'd pushed open the shutters for light when she first inspected the room. Now she climbed on to the outside ledge.

"Wait! Don't go!" Felip cried.

"I'll fetch my horses and leave. Please tell your brother that I didn't murder your devil-spawn uncle."

She dropped to the kitchen roof, then scrambled across the wet tiles, kicking one loose. It tumbled into the back courtyard, falling with a thud at the same moment she leaped to the wall and then into the neighboring kitchen garden. Crossing two more rain-wet court-yards, scrambling over their walls, she encountered only one dog, a sleeping pug that roused itself to bark, turned in circles while seeking the intruder, and yapped when she jumped down into a narrow alley.

She checked what she'd carried away with her. A dagger and short-sword, twenty morabatins stamped with Pedro's image, that packet of parchment scraps. She'd left her travelling pack in the house instead of stashing it with the horses. Tomás and Chrétien had taught her better. She'd have to return at night to retrieve her gear from Felip or the servants. She scanned the nearby alleys and streets to determine where she was, intending to find the stable and then nap in the loft while waiting for nightfall. At the end of the alley, she found the Jewish quarter, which they'd skirted earlier on the hike up the hill to the Xirgú domus. Directly across the way, a familiar painted sign hung over a brass-studded door:

Avraham el Comerciant.

Amazed, Isabella rapped at the door, the same way she'd first knocked under an identical sign in Toulouse a decade ago.

A young woman answered, dressed in a pale grey gown, her hair bound up in a linen head cloth. Peering inside the house, Isabella saw all the busy signs of a household unpacking.

"Bon vèspre, senhór," the woman said in Catalan, her quiet voice betraying a pure Toulousain accent. Only as tall as Isabella's shoulder, the woman had luminous brown eyes and the fresh, bright complexion of a girl just now become a woman. "My father is not open for business until tomorrow."

"Avraham of Toulouse?" Still recovering from her run across Girona's backyards, Isabella spoke her friend's name with too much excitement. The girl blinked, then stepped back when her father came up beside her at the door. "It is I, master Avraham. Your friend, the thieving donzel of Montcava."

"Running away again, ma dòmna?" Avraham gestured for Isabella to step over the threshold into his busy household. "You're trembling, ma dòmna."

"I cannot tell you how good it feels to find a friend in this strange land." An empty space filled under her ribs. She hadn't known how lonely she was until she met a friend.

"Ai, ma dòmna. I can say the same. Are you well?"

"Tired from traveling, but…" She was too old to weep. The customs of this world carved a gulf between them, too wide for her to embrace him, in spite of her immense gratitude for their old friendship. "May I beg shelter? Just until dark?"

"God could grant me no greater happiness than for my family to offer you comfort."

Avraham shut the door and barred it behind him, once again sheltering her from the outside world, the same way he had in Toulouse years ago.

·

Felip had never lied so much in his life. Every untruth he'd ever uttered didn't serve as sufficient practice for this moment.

His pointy nose flaming red with anger, Matheus tapped a finger on Felip's chest.

"Where's that punxor monk? I thought I was rid of all the cursed Valerós vermin. Yet one more crawls out of the rotting woodpile."

"Who?" *Who indeed?*

"*Renrén.* That cursed monk Vidal you ran away with."

"*Ai,* I knew the man, Matheus. But I lost him on the road." In truth, he turned into a woman and jumped out that window. "He left with a g–g–gaggle of Provençal crusaders, off to Toledo."

"You lying *calamarson.*" Matheus glowered.

"Peace, *mon fraire.*" Felip stepped back. *Not lying, but perhaps as stupid as a squid. She's a woman.* "Tell me what's wrong."

Matheus lifted his hand, as if ready to break Felip's neck. "At St-Pere they say this man is your bosom friend. You ran with him after he killed Lorenç and stole our Grail. So now I have to traipse all over the country to find the cup and his killer."

"*Bon Dèu!* Uncle Lorenç can't be d–d–dead. He wished me God's speed just days ago." That parcel burned, the one in his jerkin. If Matheus sought that chalice, then it was Felip he wanted, not…her.

"Your boyfriend Vidal butchered him. He's cold in his tomb. As you well know."

"No, Matheus. I didn't know. When I left St-Pere, our uncle Lorenç declared it was a mistake for me to stay there."

"A mistake?" Matheus thundered. "Your mother called St-Pere your future home since you first breathed God's air."

Felip sipped a breath of that air. *She stood right there beside me, a moment before.* Then he tried a truth. "I can't be a monk. I can't forget what I miss most."

"Your toys here? Your fine grandmama to kiss your bruises?" Matheus sneered.

"No, w–women. I can't promise God that I don't want a woman. I think about women day and night. I can't pray without thinking of their bosoms, their hair, their secret places." *Until Vidal came and confused me all to hell.* "When I confessed, Uncle Lorenç said it was best that I leave."

Matheus tossed his head back, laughing like a howling dog. "*Jhezu del tron,* the monks say you turned poof when that pederast came to St-Pere at All Saints. 'Felip is his puppy,' they say."

"You are too angry, brother." *At least she deceived everyone, not just me.* "I met Arnau Amalric when he came to visit. He can't be a p–pederast. His face scares children."

With every lie Felip told, Matheus seemed ready to strike him dead right there in their mother's bedroom.

"You want a woman, eh?" Matheus offered that wicked grin, the one when he dared Felip into dangerous deeds. Like the night when he'd left Felip alone in the forest above Girona. "I need one after that ride from Narbonne. I'll find one for you, too."

Matheus banged open the entry door, then called back so the whole house heard. "I'll have the Churchmen here. They're seeking you."

"Whatever for?"

"Your *bon amic* killed our uncle Lorenç and stole our Grail. You damn *punxor.* You helped him."

∎

"We count many good things here and thank God for providing. We have cousins in Girona. One has a son ready to become an apprentice. Why, we'll have the new shop ready by tomorrow."

Her friend Avraham had made short shrift of how he and his family had come to leave Toulouse, tallying a series of unfortunate occurrences.

"It's good that you have cousins to welcome you. Toulouse has become difficult since the French army came." Isabella, who hated Toulouse, with its perpetual threat of siege and internal attacks by enthusiastic young men acting on what the priests preached. The calming conversation with Avraham felt more restful than sleep, with each of them reflecting on the evils left behind and the new life ahead.

Avraham commenced counting blessings again. "Our cousin's wife has shared so much."

"So generous," Hanna murmured. She worked nearby, listening to their talk, answering questions when prompted by Avraham, but quite busy peeling rushes and making rush-dips. With mutton-suet, Isabella guessed, from the smell of the rush burning in the slim iron nip-stand. "A duck, three chickens, and a rooster. Black-and-copper Marans. Their eggs are as dark as plums, she says."

"And a mouser," Avraham said. He'd been petting a short-haired grey cat since they sat down to talk, the animal purring loudly. Only twice had the cat opened its glowing yellow eyes, flicking its tail, then settling back to comfort in Avraham's arms.

When it grew darker, his daughter Léal set another rush to burn, taking it from the pile of rushes curing on a piece of bark near where Hanna had finished her rush-dipping tasks.

Avraham said, "Léal, our friend's horses need to be ready to travel. Can you please find your cousin Samuel and ask him to talk to the stable-master, to make the horses ready?"

Léal had wrapped up in a shawl and headed down the alley in search of her cousin before Isabella could insist on going to the stables herself.

"Rest," Hanna said. "From your stories, you've been busier than we have. Let me prepare food for you."

"We'll turn over the little kitchen garden tomorrow." Avraham continued with the tale of their domestic good fortune. "It's time to plant greens and medicine-herbs. As soon as this rain lifts, Léal and her cousins will be tending the family plot outside the walls."

Isabella, who loathed all things sewing and cooking, scratched at her palm, scarred from a sad encounter with a distaff. "I really should be going." Though amid all the warmth and comfort at this hearth, she hated to stir from her place on the bench.

"My daughter Léal should have taken only a moment to find her cousin. Either Léal or her cousin must be lost."

"It's almost dark," Isabella said. "I'll find the stables and argue for my own horses. And I'll send Léal home if I see her."

While Isabella was saying goodbye to her old friend, Hanna appeared with a packet of food tied up in a strip of linen.

"It's not much," Hanna said. "We haven't even had a fire in our own ovens yet. But here's cheese and olives, and bread from the market ovens."

Grateful for the friendship after the past months' loneliness, Isabella said farewell. She skulked through the streets, hanging close to the stone walls, stepping back into shadows when groups of armed men appeared. Everyone seemed to be seeking post-houses and inns for the evening, laughing, arguing. Not searching for a renegade postulant monk who murdered the abbot of St-Pere.

Isabella headed down the streets, since stables must be lower in the town, guessing where the gates might be. She stopped a small boy with a bundle of twigs and asked where to find the Xirgú family stable. The boy repeated "Xirgú," but he pointed up the hillside toward the house before he ran off.

The streets widened here. The route to the stables required that Isabella cross a small square, so she chanced a turn up a small alley, hoping to circle around to the stable. In the narrow, dark passageway, Isabella slipped that short-sword from its baldric, ready for whoever might be lurking in the shadows. The stables must be near. The odor of manure and straw wafted on the early evening breeze. A feral cat yowled, scrambling ahead of two sleek city-cat companions. After the cats disappeared, shuffling animal noises echoed from a narrow archway. Isabella approached, hoping to find the stables.

An orange-clad figure wrestled with an unwilling woman.

The sword in her left hand, Isabella wrenched the orange man away by his collar, using all the strength she'd gained that winter. While he stumbled, she slashed at his arm, venting his long gold-orange sleeve. Blood flowed through the gash.

"Run!" she called to the woman. Grey skirts flashed behind the man when he advanced on Isabella.

With the same hate-twisted face as the Montcava seigneur who'd long ago been her husband. The same lion's mane as the Montcava brother who abused a frightened twelve-year-old Isabella, alone in Toulouse.

The very man from that road in the Pyrenees who had killed all that mattered to her.

"You!" he cried. "I thought the wolves gnawed your bones."

She didn't parry. Instead, she stepped aside and thrust, the way Chrétien said she must do when facing a large man. Left-handed Isabella against right-handed Montcava attacker. For the second time in her life, she sliced a blade at a Montcava rapist.

Who kicked at her left hand, sending that short-sword up the alley. He bashed her head with his elbow and sent her sprawling to the cobbles and dirt in the alley way. Where she grasped her sword again.

Hearing only Chrétien's voice ("Now, ma dòmna, if your foe is over you, thrust this way"), she rose up, thrusting. Awkward footing, but she stood nose to nose with the surprised man, who frowned at where her sword had sliced his innards. He collapsed, pulling her sword down with him when he sprawled in the alley.

Isabella tugged that sword free and wiped it on orange silk before jamming it back into its sheath. She searched the dead man's sleeves and pockets. Three morabatins. A small parchment packet.

A shadow moved at the alley's entry.

"Ma dòmna?"

"Òc, Master Avraham."

"Come along, ma dòmna." He came down the alley to her side. "Let me shelter you. It was my daughter you saved."

"I need to leave, mon amic. Quickly."

In the last of the late afternoon light, Isabella yanked a ring from the attacker's finger, exposing tattoos on his wrist, a Montcava scorpion above three crosses. She picked up both his sword and dagger, since no murderer would leave such valuable items behind. She lifted the dead man's weapons over her shoulder.

"Come, Master Avraham. It won't do either of us any good to be found here."

The corpse at her feet moaned. Fingers dug at the alley dirt.

"Sancta Maria!"

Avraham exclaimed, "The dog from hell lives!"

"Ai!" She prayed, frenzy shifting from the fight to the soul moaning at her feet. "Our Father in heaven, hallowed is Your name. Forgive us as we forgive others."

Relief and dread quarreled in her heart, hearing the not-dead man groan in pain. Once more she chanted prayers for a man who had just that moment tried to kill her.

"Shall we call the guards?" Avraham asked.

"No, I know his people. Let's take him there."

She stuck his weapons in her belt. Then she and Avraham carried the not-dead weight up narrow, winding streets to the Xirgú domus.

"It's hard work," Avraham panted, "saving this man."

"He tried to kill me. More than once."

"It's always hardest to do God's work, mending the world."

"I don't know if I'm that strong." She continued to whisper prayers, willing to waste her breath if it preserved a man's life.

Avraham left her when they reached the massive, iron-studded front door, offering blessings and a farewell that she'd last heard from him on a hot, stinking day in Toulouse. She knocked and then answered the servant's challenge with a simple answer in Catalan.

"A friend of this house, *mon amic* Ponç, seeking shelter."

PART FOUR

In a Strange Land

An Angel and a Djinni Dispute Fate

"I SUPPOSE YOU DO NOT BELIEVE IN SAINTS." The angel Grigor sniffed. "Or do you merely dispute their Goodness?"

"No more than I'd dispute your own existence and goodness," the djinni said. He'd plucked from the herbs and flowers growing amid the stones before them and now shaped the stems into a braid.

Grigor frowned, which drew his wings, and perhaps what one might call his shoulders, up in an arch of consternation.

"You mean to say, you argue that I don't Exist? Or that you think of Me in the same way as Saints?"

"Yes," said Ahriman the djinni.

"Yes, which?"

The djinni had braided a crown of roses and garlic. He placed the crown so it circled his head, like the flower-crowns human girls make to entice their lovers with bewitching herb-and-flower braids. "What do you think? Does it suit me? Or is there a certain missing magnificence?"

"All of this is just another Game for you. Then you pretend that it's strategy. Others say it's Fate."

"Let's toss a coin. In this world, the result is always odd or even, there's no other possibility. It's merely mathematics. I'll even let you call the first one." He flipped a metal object, perhaps a coin with a less troubling graven image. "Odd or even?"

The angel stood as if in judgment. "You Wager against God?"

"It's always so simple for you." The djinni assumed a sober demeanor. "For you, it's always black and white like a chess board. But the world vibrates with color. Meanwhile, I merely bet on the side of chance and free will, which are more interesting."

— *Ibn Jafar, The Poet*
From Tales of the Angel and the Djinni

15

Baeza

Tomás on the Frontier, Jaén Province
April 10

FIVE DAYS OUT OF ALMERÍA, drumbeats echoed on the wind of that hot spring afternoon.

"It's the parade drummers," Rashid said.

"The famous thunder that unnerves the caliph's foes?"

"Yes. They practice every day, without fail."

"Why..." Tomás, struck by the obvious, changed his question. "How long does it take cavalry and their horses to cease hearing the drums?"

"About as long as it takes new soldiers to learn the captains' hand and flag signals."

Still rigid in the saddle after that many days, Rashid brought his horse up beside Tomás. All the judgmental reserve Rashid showed in Almería disappeared after that adventure with the bandits. Rashid now treated Tomás as a confidante, calling him *friend* and *cousin* while they rode together. They traded childhood stories. Rashid laughed at tales of Chrétien's antics; Tomás felt himself to be the liar and scoundrel, in the way he believed all spies were.

They paused atop a hill where the road ran among olive and mulberry orchards. Army camps filled the nearby valleys. Across the wider valley, a plateau rose. Whitewashed villas crowded the steep edges of limestone outcroppings. Rashid pointed out the natural and fortified defenses that made Baeza impenetrable to outside attack, sharing military confidences in a friendly, open manner with his good cousin Tomás, the traitorous spy.

Leading the seven knights and their burro-mounted servants, they climbed the narrow, winding trail up the plateau. Rashid called out his name at the gate. The honored vizier from the caliph of Cordoba and the rest of his knights caked in dust, the linen cloths tied around their faces dark with dirt, and their horses coated in sweat-drenched road grime. Abu Jossep's guards greeted Rashid, trailed by servants who attended to the travelers' horses and baggage. Rashid led Tomás to the baths.

"The old men claim these baths were built by angels," Rashid said. "Your own servant can attend you here." He continued to gaze with doubt on Qasim al-Jalal, but Tomás saw that Qasim's eager confidence had returned after long days of travel.

When Tomás and Qasim emerged from the baths, the parade drums still pounded. First, they found food from a street vendor and then rambled around the town, where few men from the army appeared. Because the plateau made it so difficult to approach the town, Tomás wanted to find all possible routes of escape. At the first such path, he said to Qasim, "Here's where a lad in trouble might choose to make for the hills if the devil were on his tail."

Qasim couldn't answer with his mouth and hands full of *mutawwama*, a thin bread wrapped around chunks of chicken and soft cheese, spiced with coriander.

"My honorable master..." Qasim swallowed "My mother has no blind sons."

"I'd never say otherwise." Tomás handed Qasim the rest of his own roll. No being on earth is ever as hungry as a growing boy.

"The men we traveled with all regard you with suspicion, master. The dagger you gave me is not the sort for cutting breakfast bread." Qasim devoured the last of the chicken roll in two gulps.

"Good boy."

"Are you indeed a *batini*, as the Rightly Guided Son of the Servant of the Strong suggested? You often forget to profess your belief in the way men here expect."

"I try." Tomás was once again humbled by his servant.

"Which leaves a path open for your enemies. When you forget to praise God the way you should, I will make this sign." Qasim scratched his ear. "Then you will say, 'All praise is due to God.'"

"Thank you."

"It will keep both our souls stitched inside our skins." Qasim wiped his hands on that emerald silk Tomás had given him for a turban. "Also, this wind heralds the thunder that will come tonight."

·

Pausing once more at a street food stall, Tomás scanned the alleys and plaza until he was sure of their independence. Then he left Qasim to wait in the shelter of one of the town's portals.

After four days with Rashid, the rules and restrictions chafed like ill-fitting chainmail. Out of both curiosity and rebellion, he scaled the wall of Abu Jossep's private garden—principally because Rashid said no one was allowed there except the general's family. Tomás followed a path that wound down to the narrow valley floor, believing that anything restricted to the town's ruler must be created for both defense and retreat. Walled or not, the garden likely hid an escape route into the steeper hills.

A stream chattered amid the limestone boulders. Tomás strolled in the shade of date palms and orange groves, alone for the first time since he'd left Barcelona. No one watched his every move the way Rashid did. The breeze and the shade of the grove felt like paradise.

At the farthest end, Tomás came to a clearing where a small fire burned. A naked woman squatted to examine something in the dirt before her, poking at it with a dagger that gleamed in the firelight.

The sticks and litter in the grass crackled lightly when Tomás stepped closer to see what she was doing. The woman whirled around, her dagger stretched in front of her. Her fingers dripped blood. A butchered hoopoe lay at her feet, its entrails spread into a pattern.

Seeing Tomás, she wiped her fingers and her dagger in the grass, and then ran toward him, her arms open.

"Tomás of Morella! You are come at last, my little brother."

Her voice vibrated low, like a young man's, in the same rumbling range as the parade drums echoing from the army encampment. In many other ways, Ríma was not what Tomás expected from Rashid's description of their cousin. Her long auburn-brown hair hung down to her uncovered bottom. She had a narrow waist and broad shoulders, like the oyster divers of Almería. Men who thought about those things would consider her beautiful. Tomás found her terrifying.

"Welcome home!" her voice thrummed. "Oh, your poor face. We heard about your accident, cousin, but not how tragic."

His scarred lip twitched. "It's not a matter of consequence under heaven."

"Yet here you are. You've come with the sword of the Cid to deliver us! Our promised savior."

"I'm sent to do what my master bids." Tomás didn't name his master, hoping this woman was not Pedro's agent in Al-Andalus.

"A messenger from Aragón promised me you'd come." She had protuberant eyes, and so seemed perpetually astonished. "I kindle this fire every day, seeking to know when you'll arrive."

"I didn't know myself. I especially didn't know that horses might travel faster over La Mancha than the ships I took over the Great Sea."

"Pedro's messengers ride in relay." She called the king *Butrus* in the local tongue and added no honorifics.

"However, I'm sure that Pedro *El Rei* didn't promise that I'd come. I was sent to rescue a cousin."

"No, little brother. I summoned you. The daemons of our ancient kingdom brought you here to help me."

"You're the prisoner I'm to rescue?" The small hairs at the back of his neck crawled, either because of the coming thunder storm or because of the sacrificed hoopoe.

"Your chore is simple." Ríma grasped his hand and squeezed it in a way that would be flirtatious in Barcelona or Toulouse. "You will kill the caliph and the general." She called Abu Jossep *emir* in the local tongue. "Then Christian kings will reign again in Iberia. It will be our sons on the throne."

"Simple enough." Tomás grimaced, wondering how much it had amused Pedro to send him to a lunatic. He wasn't supposed to, but Tomás prompted. "You think the general doesn't do good for his people? Are you his wife or his prisoner?"

"I follow the way of our forbearer, the Cid." She didn't respond to his prompt. "The best place to hide from your enemy is in the heart of his court."

"Without a doubt." Tomás hoped he pronounced the Castilian word correctly, and that she didn't notice how much doubt he had. Or that her nakedness distracted him, the same way it would an inexperienced boy.

"Let's always speak the local tongue, should anyone overhear."

"As you wish."

"May I hold it?" She moved toward him in a suggestive way, as if to embrace him.

He covered his manhood. "What do you want?"

"The sword of the Cid. I want to feel true magic."

Believing that she was too far gone in lunacy to stab him with it, Tomás jerked his sword from its scabbard (bought new last year in Cairo) and offered her the magical sword (stolen from its maker in Damascus by Miquel). She grasped the pummel with two hands, holding the sword as if she intended to stab her own bare toes. Closing her eyes, she trembled. Her auburn hair and her breasts shook in ecstasy while she recited the sword's long history and blessed Tomás for bringing it, her low voice singing the history. She was too excited to notice that Tomás offered few prompts.

"Tomás of Morella!" She held the sword high, pointing to heaven. He looked up, instead of at her breasts. "You are blessed among men. God shall show us the path to freedom."

The first lightning flashed then. Thunder roared a moment later.

Qasim's voice echoed from the hillside. "Master! Ibn Mikhail!"

"We'll speak again." Tomás loosened her grasp on his sword. "I have an appointment for dinner with your lord."

"Abu Jossep can wait for a few more heartbeats."

"Don't call fire down from the sky with my sword."

"How many more heartbeats until you kill him and make yourself master and king? And free our people from slavery?" She pressed against him in a way that didn't feel like a cousin's greeting.

Instinctively, he wrapped an arm around her waist.

She pushed his arm away. "Don't touch me there. Don't hide your hands from me."

Lightning flashed again. The drums stopped suddenly in the camp up the valley.

"See, little brother! The skies proclaim that our children will rule as kings!" Her voice rumbled in his ear.

He unwound her fingers, first from the hand fondling his neck, then from the one that held his sword, until she relinquished him and his magical sword to respond to Qasim's call to come to Abu Jossep's table.

.

Jogging up the steep canyon sides, rivulets of rain trickling inside the neck of his shirt, Tomás tried to make sense of Ríma's story, piqued by the misfortune that Ríma was touched by the moon, wondering if there was any truth in what she said about the Cid.

"Ximena Díaz, your great-grandmother, came from the line of the old king Rodrigo. That's why the Cid married her."

Whoever Rodrigo might have been, Ríma claimed he was the most powerful of the old Visigoth kings, and also their grandfather many generations removed.

In her deep, rich voice, Ríma had recited, "Ximena's daughter Maria kept the Cid's sword. She came back to Jaén to marry and then gave it to her daughter Ana, who married the lord of Morella. When she was widowed, she married your grandfather."

She meant Miquel's grandfather. Through the whole story, Ríma never named Tomás's Tunisian mercenary ancestor al-Makkzan. All the names were women of the Rodriguez clan. After his great-grandmother Ana was widowed a third time, she traveled back to her clan in Jaén, remarrying into another Mozarab family. Ríma claimed her pure descent through dozens of great-grandmothers dispossessed by the Arabs.

"Now that you've come, we shall begin the work so that our sons can reclaim the throne of Iberia for the coming ages."

"I'm not much for founding dynasties. Perhaps I can lend Rashid my sword, since we come from the same line."

"He doesn't like women." Ríma waved away the notion of Rashid being a partner. "That's why he's called Rashid instead of Rodrigo after our ancestors."

"So many Rodrigos," Tomás murmured. Old kings; the Cid. The Rodriguez clan in three branches, ending with one mad white witch and the dark, righteous vizier.

And Tomás.

He crested the hill, busy hatching a plan to escape Baeza and join the caliph. Rashid had dragged him to this isolated frontier city, with impossible-to-breach walls, many leagues from the caliph's main army.

And whether Ríma was the "daughter of the clan" to be rescued or Pedro's agent in Al-Andalus, she was a blood-dripping lunatic with a passion for ancestral revenge.

He needed to be outside the gates with Qasim and headed for Jaén before dawn, to join the caliph's forces rather than waste any more time. Pedro needed him to create havoc among the taifa generals, not entertain folly with a mad woman.

On his first try, Tomás climbed the garden wall in two bounding steps and landed back on the street.

Where a tall, thick-bodied Mozarab stood with a hand on Qasim's shoulder. From what Tomás had seen in the Outremer, on Cyprus, or in Barcelona, the man's dress and demeanor bellowed "royal guard," confirmed by Qasim's immense discomfort with the huge paw holding him in place. Both of them as drenched as Tomás from the downpour.

"*Ahlan!* You're new here, aren't you, friend?" The man welcomed him first in Arabic, then switched to an Aragónese dialect Tomás had last heard on Cyprus, among the old men from Morella who'd followed his father on crusade and never gone home. "You look like you're from Cairo. Want me to show you the good places to eat in Baeza? You know what they say." The man switched to Church Latin. "*Do good to people and you'll enslave their hearts.*"

Tomás wagged a finger at the trembling Qasim. "Fetch me dry clothes, Qasim. I need to be at dinner in a moment."

The enormous Mozarab released Qasim, who ran off.

"I am called Tuma ibn Mikhail."

"Oh? Call you anything, just call you when there's a pot of stew and a pair of dice before bedtime, right? Who in God's creation ever heard of Tuma or his father Mikhail?"

Tomás said the words. "I'm more famous, they say, than fire on a mountain."

"Weasels in hell!" the man exclaimed. "I got the words right. I promised my goat-legged grandfather that I could do it. Didn't need my uncle threatening to fry me in sheep fat if I screwed the donkey. What does it even mean?" He held his massive hand out, offering the handshake you'd expect from any goat herder in Iberia. "I'm Zaheid, by the way. Zaheid al-Quti."

"The Goth?" Tomás held the man's hand longer than anyone but a brother would. "From before the Arabs came to Al-Andalus?"

"That's what the old folks say." Zaheid slapped Tomás's shoulder, excited and happy to confirm that they were new friends. Because of his size, the blow stung. "My people came from what's left of Morella. Most of the men from your papa's generation hauled off to Toledo or Jaén—them that didn't follow your old man. My father said a bunch of low-life shepherds moved in from the frontier and stunk up the place. He and my granddad hauled us all to Jaén a decade ago. Me, I was born in Toledo. Now I'm in this flowering city of the frontier."

Tomás sorted through the dialect and the accent, following the journey up to Baeza. "You're Pedro's man?"

Zaheid put a sausage-sized finger to his lips. "I work for the Rodriguez clan. They're my people. I do what they say, because us goat skinners from the stinking deserts of Al-Mansha..." he slipped back into Arabic for a few words "...we're the bottom of the Rodriguez pile. So, you call me Zaheid, and what shall I call you?"

"Ibn Mikhail."

"And we'll just take on the world the easy way."

"Will the people that you know learn that I've arrived here?"

"Good as done."

"I need to do what I'm bid as quickly as possible."

Zaheid shrugged, a mighty shaking of the buckles and studs on his cuirass. "I'll help as best I can. If you ask me, what we're doing is a waste of your time and mine. This army doesn't want to fight. We can just let time wash away all cares, while the caliph's mercenaries eat through his pocketbook like gold-chomping moths." A horn sounded one note from inside the garden. "That's me, back to work. I'll show you the town later."

"What's there to do among holy Almohads? Backgammon was the best I found in Almería."

"The men here are old-world fellows who drink like monkeys riding a cat and love to toss the bones." Zaheid unlocked a heavy oak door into the garden. "At least in the parts of town where over-righteous Almohad newcomers never go. Most of the true believers live in the army camp out in the western valley. So holy they shit rainbows and angels, filling the latrines twice a day."

The big Goth shook himself, rain splashing everywhere, and then was gone through the gate.

Tomás, relieved that a mad witch wasn't his link to Pedro, slogged across the rain-slick pavement to find the general's court. One night, then he was gone from here.

■

Tomás waited for Qasim in a portal outside Abu Jossep's court. When the rain drubbing the stone pavement eased up, the drums resumed in the army camp. A servant carried a message inside that the storm had delayed Tomás.

Rashid appeared, his face like the thunder storm, and scolded Tomás for tardiness. Then stopped himself and apologized. "I'm too worried about whether the general will accept instructions from the caliph. You're soaking wet."

"I was detained by our cousin Ríma." When Tomás slipped off his wet *jubba*, he noticed hoopoe blood on the sleeve. He shed it and tugged on the dry shirt and less-grand *jubba* Qasim held out for him. "A more unusual woman than you indicated."

"That confounded djinni is all that's on the general's mind." Rashid exploded, ignoring what Tomás said. "Abu Jossep hasn't listened closely to any of the messages I carried from the caliph. He's only anxious that his djinni will come join him soon. Now we are invited to eat in the presence of his pet conjuror."

"I'm most curious to meet this djinni."

Rashid left for the general's court, while Tomás stayed behind to finish dressing.

"Qasim." He spoke low to draw the boy nearer. "We need to depart. Before dawn. Please be ready."

He left Qasim with the servants, hearing the boy explain that he must be called al-Jalal in honor of his great master, the warrior Tuma ibn Mikhail ibn Al-Makkzan.

Rashid met Tomás outside a tiled gallery with star-shaped windows and horseshoe arches, where the burbling of fountains sounded louder than the parade drums, and the air smelled of floral spices. Tomás steeled his spine, assuming the correct posture his masters in Cairo beat into their students, hoping to pass as an Ayyubid knight among backcountry Arabs while Rashid introduced him to the ugliest man ever seen.

The years hadn't been kind to Abu Jossep, but he'd likely been born ugly. Like any old man, his nose and ears had grown with age, and liver spots marred his face and hands, a nightmare image of an old man in decline. Abu Jossep's brows sprouted as a single white bush, his large lips resembling an aged horse. However, Abu Jossep proved to be the jolliest soul under heaven. The second man, after his cousin Rashid, that Tomás was to hinder, harm, or betray for Pedro's sake.

While Rashid introduced the general, Tomás listened closely to understand what the names meant.

"Al-Hasan…"

The man's *ism*, the name he'd been given by his mother, meant "Handsome."

"Abu Jossep…"

His *kunya*, the honorific name that recalled the man's son, who died from wounds suffered in a border skirmish not long ago.

"Ibn Muhammad ibn Ishaq al-Shahid."

His *nasab*, a patronymic which indicated that grandfather Ishaq had been quite important, so his name continued to be preserved.

The general settled a benign gaze on Tomás, who'd learned from Rashid that Abu Jossep had an ability given by God to discern truth and lies in men's hearts.

"My new vizier tells me that you two are cousins, that you're a great fighter."

"I greet you." Tomás repeated the general's name with all the honorifics, remembering to add the blessing, before he announced his name. "I am Tuma ibn Mikhail ibn Al-Makkzan." He pronounced the hard U and hard A of Tuma in the way his masters did in Cairo.

"I remember tales of your father's honored grandfather. Ancient times, ancient times. He wasn't a man who'd seek to milk a he-goat."

"My own father Mikhail was the same. He was born on the frontier, but left this part of the world."

"To fight the *franj*, in the days when Salah ad-Din was sultan." Rashid interrupted with details that saved Tomás from lying.

"Have you returned to help us stop the dogs of evil?" Abu Jossep spoke in dulcet tones, while probing Tomás's heart, sniffing out lies.

"I studied with great masters in Cairo." Who were drunkards and liars, though merciless fight-masters. "I am called after the father who guided me to wisdom, Ibn Mikhail."

"Have you no brother?" Abu Jossep asked, the friendliest interrogation Tomás had ever suffered.

"I do. He's working elsewhere in the world, with responsibility for our mother. We were both trained to serve."

"That is good. Without a brother, you're a man rushing to battle without a weapon." His bushy eyebrow wagged. "A son?"

"I do not have that honor." Tomás endured Abu Jossep's kindly but probing stare.

"Perhaps one day you'll have a son. God, who is always merciful, has returned a new son to me."

"It's a kind thought," Tomás said. "Until that time, I propose to serve the way I was trained to do."

"I'm sure you will." Abu Jossep laughed, though Tomás didn't know what was funny. "I was there when Abu Yusuf Ya'qub sent the kings of Castile and León home in defeat. What great battles have you helped win?"

"A decade after the glory that Abu Yusuf Ya'qub brought to Al-Andalus, my mother brought me forth. The same year that Salah al-Din united Damascus with Egypt against the *franj*. Me, I have withstood attacks and fought infidels in many places. But I can claim no victory in the way that you can, because I am only a paid soldier. Any wisdom I bring comes from my teachers in Cairo."

"Was it the *franj* who destroyed your face?"

"Yes." Tomás settled comfortably into his lies.

"Because you will be our good friend, you must call me Abu Jossep." The general smiled warmly. The peace of a successful deception settled over Tomás. He'd finish this side-trip to Baeza quickly and be on the road to Jaén by dawn.

"I am honored."

"I'm happy my new vizier brought you to us. Let's hear what you propose tomorrow morning," Abu Jossep said. "This is the time for rest and to nourish our souls. My djinni will entertain us. Please don't be afraid. He's not an evil one. He has the voice of an angel."

Signaling his attendants, Abu Jossep asked for his djinni. The thunderclouds fractured apart and the late-afternoon sun shone through the star-shaped windows high overhead, blinding Tomás for a heartbeat. Rashid stiffed beside him. "It's only a pretty boy," he whispered, "who should still be with his school masters."

"Until this lad came to me," the general said, "I was more lost than the moon in winter."

Tomás concentrated on maintaining a posture as erect and proper as Rashid's, while the general patted the boy-djinni the way a father pets a favored son. The djinni smiled warmly at the tender gesture. Then he cast a wicked conjurer's glare where Tomás sat with Rashid. The djinni raised his hand in a gesture that Tomás knew from soothsayers in Cairo.

May a shaytan bind your bones.

Surely Rashid and the others in the general's court smelled Tomás's cold, sweating fear over the perfume-spiced air of the council room.

Abu Jossep rested his heavy hand on his djinni's shoulder. "Sing for us, my son."

The beautiful djinni sang in the high, thin tones of a boy whose voice hasn't changed, mesmerizing the room with a series of love songs often heard in Cairo, crushing what was left of Tomás's heart while he sat still as a stone.

A sad song, of a linnet warbling in the winter's dawn while a lover waits for war to end so he can return to his beloved.

A quiet song, of the *shush-shush* of a flowing river and of the ripened grain shuddering on the perfumed winds.

A sweet song, with the pat-pat-pat of hands preparing bread to bake on hot stones, while fountains burbled and soft women's voices sang lullabies.

An unbearable song, with the scents of musk and cloves, when the beloved washes her hero carried home from the war on a shield by his mourning brothers.

The last song ended on a long note of desire for the quiet of heaven after the loss of one's beloved. While the men in the room woke from the spell the djinni had cast, Abu Jossep wept, drying his eyes with his fingers. He patted his solemn-faced djinni.

"You make your father proud."

The djinni's predator eyes, dark as a pool at midnight, flashed with inner fire, directing that inferno at his true father.

Tuma ibn Mikhail al-Makkzan.

．

His heart beat louder than the Baeza drummers. Tomás tried to hear the exchange between Yusuf and the general.

"Rest, dear boy. Talk to us now of science instead of war and love. A great scholar like you must know how to read the heavens."

"The science of astronomy?" The boy-who-was-a-djinni accepted being addressed as a great scholar. "I am familiar with the writings of al-Juzjani. One of his students was my teacher in Cairo."

"Then you can divine for me!" Abu Jossep, excited, upset the tray of dishes in front of him.

"Divination by the stars is not the way of believers." Rashid scowled in that dark way so like Miquel.

"It is as you say." Yusuf nodded, answering mildly. "True followers cannot accept predestination. Such thinking belongs among the ignorant and infidels."

"Nonsense!" Abu Jossep cried. "My father and all the fathers before him read the heavens to find propitious times. If a leader follows the way of Allah, the all powerful, a command to read the heavens cannot be in error."

"Your command, Abu Jossep?" the boy-djinni asked.

"Yes. Can you apply your science for the peace of our people and the glory of Allah?"

Yusuf said, "No act of mine can increase the glory of Allah, who grants all that is good."

"Did you ever read the stars before, my son?" Abu Jossep asked.

"Yes, when we sailed from Valencia, the captain commanded that I read the heavens for him. The planets and sun showed a most auspicious time for me to sail."

"But not so propitious after all," Rashid said. "The ship foundered outside Alcazaba and all were lost but you."

"A most auspicious time," Yusuf said, "for it brought me here."

Abu Jossep guffawed in delight. "You are a rascal djinni, every bit of you. Come to the rooftop. If the storm has passed, you can read the stars for me."

"Tonight?" the boy asked.

"This moment, my pet." Jittering with anticipation, Abu Jossep rose, leaning on his djinni while reaching for his crutch. "I am now your father, and you are my son and djinni. So, I command you to obey my wishes."

With a thousand wild thoughts about how to seize control and leave Baeza, longing to hold Yusuf close, Tomás followed them to the archway.

"Most honorable Abu Jossep! I beg to offer a gift."

The general tipped his head to listen in that way he had. Any other military man would chastise a captain for being out of order. Yusuf, not looking around, grasped the general's sleeve. "What is it, Ibn Mikhail?"

"My servant Qasim is a trained fighter and a kind lad. I offer him as a gift, to guard your djinni at night."

Abu Jossep folded his lips in thought, his old man's nose buried deep in the furrow. "You believe that my guards cannot protect my boy within the walls of my home?"

"A special boy requires a special guard," Tomás said.

Abu Jossep glanced past Tomás to Qasim, who stood as stony and serious as ever. "My djinni needs a young companion more than a troublesome old man." He wagged his finger, accepting the gift. "Send your servant in the morning."

In the outer gallery, Qasim grasped the sleeve of Tomás's *jubba*, panicked, whispering. "The djinni looks just like you."

At the same moment, Rashid cornered Tomás, ignoring Qasim. "That wretched whelp! He looks like me. Is it a trick?"

"They say djinn change shapes, stealing your image like a mirror." Qasim's voice quivered.

Rashid checked his passion, noting Qasim's fright. "The similarity is uncanny. It unleashed demons in my mind."

Though the djinni had stolen all peace, Tomás said, "You don't believe in djinn any more than I do. He isn't capable of conjuring demons. Or stealing your image."

"Yet he steals Abu Jossep's attention. I still worry."

Rashid said goodnight to Tomás at the barracks, where Qasim collapsed on his bedroll, his dark eyes flashing wild with alarm. Tomás tugged him back onto his feet.

"Come with me."

Tomás steered Qasim out through the inner courtyard, past the whitewashed walls of the gallery, to the outer vestibules, and into the street.

"You said we were leaving, master. Then you throw me away."

"My plans changed. This is good, Qasim. You'll see. Have you eaten? Shall we find that vendor by the orange tree? And then, let's go visit my horse al-Malik to make sure he's happy."

"Master, I beg you. Don't send me away with that djinni. Let me serve you."

"You are serving me, every moment of every day. At night you serve me in ways no other man can."

"I work for you. Not a…a…djinni from—"

"You will do it, every night. Else I'll send you back to your mother with the next donkey drovers that pass through this monkey-piss of a town."

Qasim the Magnificent seemed about to become the weeping child Qasim. Tomás jerked the boy into an archway, scanning the street for anyone who might follow them. Then took his chance.

"He's my nephew."

Qasim yelped. "Then you too are—"

Tomás snapped his fingers under Qasim's nose, then thumped his forehead with a knuckle. "He's no more a djinni than you are. He's a schoolboy who ran away from his teachers."

Qasim blinked, and then came back to his usual acute self. "I'll do it. I owe your nephew the same loyalty I owe you."

"Do whatever he wants. He'll think you're a spy, but that's not what I want you to do. You truly must keep him safe." He pointed at Qasim's dagger.

"When shall I see you?"

"I'll collect you at dawn each day."

"When do I sleep?" Qasim seemed more puzzled by this than with his new job.

"You're young. Why do you need to sleep?"

"Master! I do need to sleep."

"Sleep while I'm with the general. Sleep while I'm at arms practice. Just don't sleep at night while you're with the djinni." Tomás stopped. "His name is Yusuf."

"Like Yusuf and Zulaikha in the poets' songs?"

"No, he's just an ordinary Yusuf. Not a prophet, not a djinni. Just a willful boy who doesn't obey his masters. Let's get you food. Then I have many tasks for you tomorrow."

One of which was to purchase better linen, soft city shoes, and a bath for a boy from Valencia who must now live close to the child Tomás cared for most in all of God's creation.

·

Tomás padded silently to stand in an alcove, exhausted from travel, cold in the mountain spring night, and more distressed than he'd been since that tragedy on the road into the Pyrenees. He leaned against the stone wall and rested, the way he'd learned from that torturous training in Cairo. He stood motionless, remaining in place so long that a cat, having lured a mouse from its cover, played with the mouse just out of reach of Tomás's boot. The mouse never knew it was a game to be played, never ran fast enough in the right direction to escape its tormenter, until the cat tired of the game and seized the mouse by its neck, shaking the mouse until it died.

Just after the guards exchanged posts in the middle of the night, a figure moved in the archway, shadows cast in six directions from the torches.

"*O my own dear heart's song.* What are you doing here?"

Tomás repeated a line from a song, using the street dialect of Cairo alleys, having ascertained that tongue wasn't understood by either Qasim or the general's guard who stood by the stairs. Yusuf was now taller than Tomás, though no heavier by even a scrap. With a wispy beard and silken moustache, he looked older than fifteen. If you didn't know better.

And even more beautiful than when Tomás had last seen him in Barcelona, three months ago.

"*Bon nuoit*, Father" The boy offered the sullenest greeting Tomás had ever endured. "I've come to learn from you, O master of steel and false hearts."

"Call me Tuma ibn Mikhail. Do not speak to me in any tongue but Arabic."

"Yes, *Walidi*." Yusuf called him *father* in the most formal way. "I will call you Ibn Mikhail, the mercenary who has no children. I was called Yusuf ibn Tuma, a scribe from Cairo. It's a wondrous large city, bigger than Seville. It's no surprise we never met there. Here, I'm Yusuf ibn Hasam, the new son of the handsome one-legged emir who guards the frontier."

"Why?" Tomás yearned to hold Yusuf closer than he ever had before. "Why aren't you with Pedro? Or safe at home?"

"Abu Jossep says this is my home."

Tomás cursed in the way he avoided in Al-Andalus. "*Bazasa. Per l'amor de Dèu*, who would ever guess?"

"Let all be as it pleases God. Aren't we to speak only in Arabic?"

"Blessed Mary and all the perpetual virgins. You can't make it across Barcelona without a beating. How'd you get here?"

"I went to the docks and asked about a mercenary with a ruined face. Then I found a captain who needed a clerk. I wrote letters for my passage in the same merchant caravan as you. He lent me to a chandler on the docks when we had to wait so many days in Valencia because of the storms."

"Why?"

"To shame you into returning home." Yusuf jutted his chin in defiance. "Brother Doménec said you betrayed Pedro, so you're banished. Everyone in Barcelona talks of it. Dolç is too ashamed to leave our house." Yusuf's voice rose. "Why did you desert us? If you're banished from Barcelona and Catalunya, can't you take us all to Cyprus? Or Toulouse?"

"There's nothing left on Cyprus. Besides, I…" Hopeless to argue. Yusuf always had the sharpest logic. And Tomás didn't possess the heart to lie, yet the truth about why he was here could endanger Yusuf. "You made it into the heart of Al-Andalus without a scratch. Just to scold me."

"The shipwreck was fairly bruising." Yusuf shrugged, as if he bore the heavy weight of an untold story. "And I couldn't escape my rescuers to find you in Almería. So, it's mere fate that we are both in Baeza." He set his jaw, challenging Tomás. "And it is I, not you, who has the right to be angry."

"I'm amazed, not angry. When I was your age—"

"*Ai*, you learned the cut to slay a thousand men, and the touch to bring a thousand women to your feet. When you were my age, Cairo let you pass unmolested because of your warrior's grace."

"Who said that?"

"My mother, when she explained who my father was. I never believed what she claimed, that you deserted me. Until Brother Doménec told me that you deserted Pedro, too."

"Doménec is a liar. After what you did to follow me, all God's angels must think you're a hero. Please don't be angry with me."

Yusuf said, "I interrupted you. When you were my age…"

"I fathered you. Your mother was thirty, and I was an ignorant, boastful boy. She refused to take shelter in my household, so I left you both alone, as she asked."

"Do you know what I wore that day in Cairo?"

"What?"

"It was twenty days before my eighth birthday. You wore black fustian. And you were surprised that I could read the inscription on your sword. You told Chrétien I was smarter than anyone. He laughed at me."

"Chrétien laughed at me, not you. And you wore blue silk. I quarreled with your mother about it."

"You said she was raising me to be a eunuch, which proved God no longer cared about this world. She said you quarreled because you didn't want me. But I didn't believe it then. Was I wrong?"

"Your mother wouldn't let you go with me, *fadrin*. And that wasn't the first time I saw you. But I have no good excuse for leaving you then."

The nighttime city stirred. Guards were changing shifts.

"And now?"

"I have things I promised to do here, for my father's family."

"What?" Yusuf whispered. "Betray your friends? Break people's hearts, like you did Dolç?"

"I promise to explain, someday when it's safe."

"Like you promised to never leave me again?"

One of the general's guards appeared, instructed to make sure Yusuf made it to his quarters safely, interrupting the djinni's condemnation of the malformed nature of Tomás's soul.

The cut that slashed through Tomás's mouth twitched. He couldn't conquer it.

Foregoing bed, Tomás wandered out into the Baeza dawn, quarreling again with the Master of the Universe about betrayals and loss. Qasim appeared at his side, insisting that they follow their noses down the street to the bakers' ovens, which kept Tomás from weeping about his failure to comfort a heroic boy.

■

After prayers, Tomás sought solitude in a quiet square near the guards' barracks, where he completed the exercises his old masters taught. He needed to work, to smother the fire in his brain.

Over the wall and through the royal orchards.

No, they'd have to pass through a gate with the horses.

His horse couldn't wend its way down that steep trail along the canyon walls the way a burro might.

How to separate Yusuf from the general's guards?

And where to find a gentle, sweet-natured horse? Yusuf was afraid of the beasts. He'd have to ride double with Qasim. That nagging idea crept around the corner of all thought. What if Tomás had abandoned Rashid and ridden with the mercenaries to join the caliph in Jaén?

Tomás completed the exercise forms while the parade drums throbbed, and then stood still, his eyes closed, counting pulse beats until his heart slowed. Only mid-spring, yet the heat of the day rose up from the sandy patch where he practiced. Water gurgled in a fountain; bees thrummed in a nearby courtyard.

Water. A drink was all he desired at that moment.

And then, how to ensure sufficient water for whatever it might take to carry Yusuf to safety over the mountains.

"You follow the lesser jihad, but the harder way."

Rashid lurked nearby, his hawk's eyes glittering in the morning light, as if probing for the hole in Tomás's soul.

"I'd never claim so much. It is only whatever pleases God."

"Till you saved me on the road, I believed you to be as false as that djinni," Rashid said.

"We do as we are taught." Tomás couldn't assume he was free of Rashid's suspicions, however friendly his cousin had become. "And hope that it's God who sends the teacher."

"Come to my house. I'll give you breakfast. You can tell me how you learned to master the warrior's way."

"I am still a poor student, not a master."

"Then you are surely proud of your humility."

In his austere house, the vizier called for his servants to bathe Tomás's feet and bring cool towels. When they reclined on pillows under the shade of a portico, Rashid offered sheep's cheese with bread, plus a handful of dried figs, showing that Tomás was an honored guest. The food was similar to what Tomás ate in the saddle on long journeys, exactly what he needed Qasim to procure for their departure.

"Tell me, cousin," Rashid offered a dish of dates filled with nuts, "can you train Abu Jossep's men to fight hand-to-hand in the way you were trained?"

"To do that, I'd have to be a djinni. There isn't time. The infidels will be here come summer."

"Last night, Abu Jossep refused all of my suggestions." Rashid poured more water for Tomás from a stone pitcher, his hand lingering when Tomás accepted the cup. "Help me convince him to move this army to Jaén as the caliph demands."

"I'll do what I can, if Abu Jossep grants me audience." The scar across Tomás's lips twitched; he imagined Pedro shouting for joy at this offer.

"If we can tear him away from that djinni." Rashid scowled, a flittering of his eyebrows. "A grown man! He's like Jafar the Fool in that old tale, guided too much by his wife to be a warrior."

"One distraction will not make a great general forget his training." Tomás needed to temper Rashid's view of Yusuf. "He'll return to his old ways when the novelty of that boy wears thin. Then he'll be ready for what you most want."

"What do you want most, Ibn Mikhail? A mercenary's purse of gold? Glory?" Rashid leaned near while they reclined on cushions over breakfast. Tomás wasn't used to strangers that close, in either the Outremer or Christendom.

"Just to be of service, doing what God made me for." Tomás hastily added the blessing.

"Truly?" Once more Rashid's hawk-eyes bore into Tomás's soul. "What's it like, knowing what God made you for?"

Every muscle in his body tensed while Tomás tried to hear what Rashid really wanted to ask. He tried a modest answer. "It's merely what my father taught. How to be a man. How to live honorably."

Rashid pursed his lips in a sweet expression that Tomás hadn't seen before. "When you say God's name, do you mean Allah, the way people pray here? Or God as He is called in the city where you served a Christian king? Because you are not like any man I've known who dedicated himself to God."

Tomás waited, not seeing what Rashid intended, fearing that his work for Pedro in Al-Andalus was about to end in disaster.

"Be assured," Rashid tapped Tomás's hand. "I, too, was raised in two worlds, with two different names for the one true God."

"I'm not a philosopher. Only a soldier. That's what my father raised me to be."

In the thousand years that Tomás waited for Rashid to speak, his mind raced over possible ways to rescue Yusuf and escape Baeza. The parade drums throbbed to the same beat as his pulse.

Rashid said, "I made myself into the best warrior of our clan. Then my family pushed me to serve under the caliph. My cousin Ríma pushed me to find you, in the middle of this battle against the invaders." Rashid gestured impatience at that idea. "Now I find myself wondering who I serve. Where my heart belongs."

"I was fortunate, that I had my father's guidance, and the teachers he chose."

"Will you train me the way your fight masters did? Later, after this summer's battles? Please teach me, friend."

His hand settled on Tomás's.

"Friend?" Tomás studied the dark hand, so similar to his own.

"I hope so. I have opened my heart to you."

"Then I must share a secret." Tomás sat up, moving away from the intimacy. He picked carefully among possible words. "That djinni is the bastard son of a bastard son of my father. His mother's family went to the judges in Cairo to beg for all my father's inheritance. The judges denied the plea. Then the brat followed me to Barcelona, to plague me when I was contracted as mercenary to that king. Now he's followed me here."

"So," Rashid laughed, "not a djinni. Just an unhappy bastard. Our cousin Ríma will be overjoyed to discover a new Rodriguez scion."

"Can this be our secret? Let this lad run his deceit on Abu Jossep. Then you can rescue the general from his foolishness. And I'll deal with the bold brat."

"An excellent plan, Ibn Mikhail."

Rashid turned Tomás's hand over, so that their palms rested together in agreement. Reflexively, Tomás grasped Rashid's wrist the way bonfraires greeted each other. He stopped, fitting his palm against Rashid's the correct way. Rashid pulled him closer, his other hand on Tomás's shoulder.

"I ask your help as a soldier, but I don't want to take advantage. I wish we could just be friends. There's no one else I can trust here."

Qasim called from the outer courtyard. "Abu Jossep seeks your company, master."

Rashid reached for his surcoat. "Let's go together. It will be good if Abu Jossep understands that we're united in all things, as cousins and as soldiers."

·

The correct obeisance when greeting Abu Jossep, or any general in Al-Andalus, was the same humbling bow his fight-masters demanded.

Tomás found a seat in the half-circle of cushions where attendants sat behind Abu Jossep's chief advisors in the perfumed council room. While these advisors gave their reports, Abu Jossep's eyes remained fixed on Tomás. Those reports claimed forces so overwhelming in number and so well provisioned, they'd chase the invading Christians back to Toledo without help from the caliph's mercenaries.

Only Rashid complained about the troops' readiness. He wanted fewer deserters, a better accounting of pack animals and fodder, and cleaner, more efficient camps.

"We shall win if Allah wills it," Abu Jossep said.

"Allah, the Great One, provides help to those who prepare," Rashid said.

The djinni appeared at the archway. Abu Jossep motioned him over, not answering Rashid. "Ho, lad, come tell our leaders what we learned from the stars."

Yusuf stood stiffly at the general's side. He scanned his audience, nodding to each man. Except Tomás.

"I say unto you that these calculations are not magic, but the science I learned studying under a great mathematician, who himself learned it at the feet of the master and author of 'The Goal of The Wise.' I cannot offer an oracle. I give you a precise measure of the positions of the stars so that you might know the best time for your undertakings, and when it might be dangerous to proceed under the wrong combination."

He spoke like a teacher who'd mastered the art of mesmerizing his pupils.

"It may be dangerous to proceed on the first day of summer. The ruling constellation makes it likely that both men and animals might bleed and suffer. Under the quarter waning moon after the solstice, it appears propitious to undertake great things, for Al-Tair the Eagle flies then."

And so on through the details of the alignment and significance of each constellation of stars. Abu Jossep listened intently, occasionally glancing over at Rashid. Most of the men fell under the djinni's spell, because Yusuf was teaching, not performing magic. Only Rashid appeared untouched.

"So, you say this is a propitious time for war?" Rashid said. "That is fortunate, since our men happen to be gathered and armed at the same season that the infidels are marching across the land of our fathers. Are the stars not amazing?"

Yusuf-the-djinni sat still as a stone, Rashid's words rippling around him. Abu Jossep, however, was irritated by this injustice. "My djinni names the month our enemies will attack."

"It takes that long to march to Jaén from Toledo," Rashid said.

"He found the very moment of the attack in the stars," Abu Jossep insisted.

"Early in the morning. When battles have begun since the first war in creation," Rashid said.

"My djinni has read the most propitious day to set forth." Abu Jossep settled into his cushion, content. "You are striking cold iron, Rashid. Can your amazing swordsman from Cairo do better?"

Everyone's eyes settled on Tomás.

"I believe so, Your Excellency." Tomás rose and bowed, having hoped for this opportunity.

"You read the stars?" Abu Jossep waggled his bushy brow, interested.

"No. No divination." Tomás took the parchment packet from his inner pocket and spread it on the tiled floor. "The Christian forces will be ordered thusly after arriving from Toledo. Here are the numbers that their kings will bring, and how they will array their bowmen, knights, and infantry." He shifted to let Rashid and two other advisors study the drawing. "My chart contains different knowledge than the stars."

He bowed again, the way he'd been taught (by masters who used iron rods to encourage their students). Abu Jossep beamed at Tomás in the same way he'd rained smiles on his djinni.

The djinni, however, wanted to slay Tuma ibn Mikhail with rays of fire from his dark eyes. He leaned over to whisper to Abu Jossep, who asked, "How do we know this is wisdom and not treachery?"

Tomás spun a tale of how he'd stolen the plans while serving as mercenary to Pedro d'Aragón. The advisors nodded, satisfied. But

Abu Jossep listened to the whispering djinni. Tomás needed to block that interference.

"Your Excellency, my masters taught a form of divination, in the name of Allah the Mighty One, which offers soldiers a simple method for separating truth from lies."

"I'm intrigued," Abu Jossep said. "If it's not the magic of ifrits or devils."

"It's purer than a child's tears." Tomás offered his dagger to the general, the sheathed blade resting in his hand. "Say a prayer and spin a steel dagger at the witness's feet. The blade points to the left foot of a liar, to the right foot of an honest man."

"Delightful!" The old general clapped his hands. "Perfect for justice amongst soldiers."

Tomás stood a respectful distance from Abu Jossep, ready to protect his knees and ankles if the man was clumsy. However, after more whispering with his djinni, Abu Jossep said, "My new son is my truth-seeker. He is more obedient and faithful to me than my own right hand."

Yusuf-the-djinni bowed to the general, and then drew from his own baldric the dagger Sebastián had given him in Barcelona. He spun it on the floor toward Tomás, who quelled one hundred twitching muscles. It spun an unholy number of times, and then stopped less than a finger's breadth from his right foot.

Tomás imitated an honest man, while Yusuf wore a mask of cold, scholarly indifference.

"Once more," Abu Jossep said. "This time, call upon the name of God, so we will know this is truth."

His djinni retrieved the dagger, trudging across the room, one foot planted slowly in front of the other, and then a graceful sweep, his fingers trailing on the marble floor, stopping one thumb's space from Tomás's boot. He traipsed back to Abu Jossep's side, his face as cold as the marble floor. Alongside the general again, Yusuf said the prayer and spun his dagger. It clattered, louder than Tomás's heartbeat, skittering while it spun, and stopping at his leather-clad foot, once more pointing to the toe of truth.

Disregarding Yusuf for the moment, guarding his heart, Tomás bowed again and then offered Abu Jossep the packet with Pedro's battle plans. The general, still resting his arm on Yusuf, dismissed his morning audience. Rashid forbid the departing captains from sharing the planned date of the army's departure with anyone.

That's too many men for secrets. Tomás felt Rashid's eyes on him, guessing that the vizier thought the same.

Behind him, Yusuf kept close to the general, a joyless expression that Tomás had seen only once before.

In Cairo. When he thought Tomás was saying goodbye and leaving him there, though the permanent farewell had been for Yusuf's mother, who knew she'd never see the lad again.

I'll never leave without you.

Couldn't Yusuf hear that without Tomás saying it aloud?

■

Tomás's other cousin, Zaheid, lured him into the late Baeza night with promises that involved dice. However, Zaheid claimed that all sane people in Al-Andalus dined while gaming. A bizarre behavior, to Tomás's way of thinking.

While Tomás asked about procuring a horse and finding a way out of Baeza, Zaheid ignored the questions and forced more of the *mirqaz* on Tomás, declaring that the inn he chose had the best sausages in Baeza. Lamb with cinnamon, pepper, lavender, and coriander. Browned in oil, sunk in a sauce of cilantro and vinegar with onions. The big man distracted Tomás for a heartbeat, forcing a fourth helping on him. Yet Tomás saw.

Zaheid cheated at dice. Not another soul in the room noticed, only Tomás.

"God gave me the body of a burro," the big man said, "and a monkey's fast hands."

Though perhaps no one noticed because, as Zaheid had hinted, the backcountry Arabs and Mozarabs of Baeza drank like sand smelt in a cow-pond. Tomás sipped the *nabidh* cautiously. Not very intoxicating, but it tasted sweeter than the dates it was made from, and guaranteed a morning headache of a size that would take two hands to measure, hands the size of Zaheid's.

"My daughter Marta said to her mother, 'No one can outrun him, our father. The earth conspires with the sun to give him the speed of the levanter blowing from the Great Sea.' That's my younger daughter. Need to find her a husband who wants a wife smarter than he is. Like I did. I recommend it to all men."

Zaheid continued with the waterfall of stories, as if Tomás hadn't seen what he did with the dice. If the man learned to work with a proper shill, perhaps the two of them...

"Do you agree, Ibn Mikhail?"

"What?" Tomás watched the dice, missed the words.

"That it's best to marry a woman smarter than you. Gives a man every comfort and privilege in life. If you have the constitution for it. Do you know about women?"

"Yes." Tomás wanted to move the conversation in another direction. He hadn't thought of Isabella all night, but at the mention of wives, guilt and grief flooded his veins. "Tell me about your children. You have sons?"

"Four. I tell you, if my sons found a good leader who managed to yoke them together, they'd move the Despeñaperros. Strong. But they can't be in the same room with each other before one is pounding another and the other two are taking bets on the winner. Good lads. Just too young yet to work together."

Zaheid stared off. Tomás checked where his new friend was gazing. Two young men arm wrestled across the room.

"Join them?" Tomás asked.

"No, I was just thinking, I need to be done with this work and back home with my boys. They can't make their way through the monkey pens of Jaén so young." Zaheid, having imbibed much more *nabidh* than Tomás, had grown maudlin in that sudden, sad way that wine overcomes sense. "A boy needs his father, don't you know?"

"I need sleep. Show me the way home, so I don't find myself lost on the streets."

They stumbled through alleys and parted where Tomás slept, while Zaheid had farther to go to his own quarters. Twenty paces away, Zaheid trotted back.

"Stick to the street food when you can, my friend." Zaheid's big body swayed gently while he whispered instructions to Tomás in back-country Aragonése. "It's real food, made for humans, not for those lords blessed by heaven to live like gods among men."

"Thank you. And about finding a horse?"

"Later. Meanwhile, this is no jest, my friend. Do not swallow anything from our royal highness the princess of all Rodriguez and the general's prized queen. Pieces of the moon fell on her head at birth, my granny says. If you know what I'm saying."

Later, in the dark, Tomás lay naked on his pallet, the hot night air prickling at his skin. He still clutched that scabbarded sword Ríma wanted, wondering why anyone might think it magical.

His father had used this sword to great effect, out of skill, not sorcery. Tomás had used it more to teach than fight, to win bets wherever men wanted to wager their skills against his. He couldn't swing it now to fight his way out of where he was, or to bring Yusuf to safety. He listened, hoping to hear any guidance.

Guinea hens and rock pigeons cooed in the predawn. The bakers had fired their ovens. The kinds of stirring that called for action.

"*Let's just go. No need to pack.*" What Chrétien would say, with no plan other than a belief that it's possible to make one's own luck.

"*Always do like me. Check your talents.*" That's what Miquel said, when he invented a moral for the long tale about how he escaped slavery in Aleppo. However, Tomás and Chrétien agreed that it was their mother who had rescued Miquel, so the talent he'd used in that escape was his excessively handsome face.

Tomás didn't have that as an option. He calculated instead what he had.

A madwoman who wanted him to do magic. A magic that Tomás didn't think his sword could produce and seemed to involve a connection with Ríma that he had no interest in risking.

Fresh cotton *sarawil* and *qandura*, sent as a gift from a cousin who begged for his friendship, but whom Tomás had to betray while he did what Pedro needed.

A broken-hearted son, who was closely guarded by the wisest general in Al-Andalus and who'd most likely be in greater jeopardy if Tomás told him the truth about why he was here.

One horse and a burro, cared for by Qasim the Magnificent, the only person he could trust in Al-Andalus.

At least—small comfort—Sebastián was tucked in safe with Pedro's army.

A stirring in the gallery. Qasim collapsed on his pallet. "Is there breakfast, master? I know I'm not to sleep, but I must eat."

Tomás pulled on the clean *sarawil* that Rashid had sent and pointed to new clothes he'd found for Qasim in the night market.

"Baths, first. People here seem to prefer clean soldiers."

"We aren't leaving today, are we?"

"No. Soon, though."

As soon as Tomás had a plan that included a safe path out of the most impregnable city on the frontier.

16

On the Road to Girona

Durán in Catalunya
April 15

ON THE THIRD NIGHT OF THEIR travels, Chrétien offered another lesson on leading an army. While dining on a supper of *mongetas gigantescas*, huge white beans spiced with coriander and thyme, eaten apart from the other men, he pointed out attributes of several men while hinting at which particular men might bear watching.

Durán defended having failed to observe some of the men. "I've been too busy looking over my shoulder for Matheus and Colomb to be watching for others' foibles and virtues."

"Yet I saw you with that fetching Foix captain, the one called Bernart. You were quite the lauding lord."

"Don't be jealous. I only know him to say *bon día* and to confirm the day's chores."

Chrétien flicked aside that idea like dust on his sleeve. "Don't play favorites. Spread your praise equally. Find a good thing to say to every man, and mean it."

"Except for Matheus and Colomb." Otherwise, Durán accepted the instruction. Until he met Chrétien, he'd roamed Toulouse, moving from master to master, seeking one with skills to teach. Who didn't beat him. These *mongetas gigantescas* knew more about leading men than he did.

Just after Durán finished the last of his beans and drained the allotted cup of wine, a group of riders joined their camp. Chrétien rose, sword in hand. Seeing Chrétien's wary expression, Durán called for his men to be ready and at arms.

Anyone could steal another man's colors.

Chrétien had warned him more than once. That was how he'd ended up living with a band of Norman mercenaries wearing Montcava colors when his uncle Renoud was killed.

Half the new arrivals were from Foix, the other half were knights riding under a Crux Lunata banner. Matheus wasn't there to greet those knights, having ridden off to visit a relative at a nearby monastery, leaving all his knights under Colomb, who'd ridden on Durán's tail since the morning they'd left Narbonne.

Matheus's absence was like a holiday. The leagues they'd ridden from Narbonne were beyond unpleasant, because he'd been incessantly crowded and harassed by Matheus, Durán's would-be assassin. Durán hadn't slept through the night yet, sure a knife would rip through the tent at any moment. At least Matheus's wolf-dog had remained in Narbonne.

The Foix leader, a thin, ferrety man of about thirty, examined Durán when he presented a packet from Ramón-roger. Durán's ears burned. In his previous life, he was continually assessed by strangers on the street. Without thinking, Durán stepped closer to Chrétien, then stood straight. He was his own man. The new captain passed over his pocketbook of letters, and a second pocketbook with gold to purchase provender for the extra men and horses. He recited how well they were armed, with the count's promise that Durán need not provide any of them horses and armor at his own expense.

The pocketbook contained two brief missives from the count for Durán, and two for Chrétien. One of Durán's letters was a gift from Pedro to the count of Foix. It contained a map and passwords for provisioning stations in Iberia, where fodder and food had been stockpiled for Pedro's forces. The other letter described who Durán should trust and who he should watch among the count's men, matching what Chrétien had already explained. Plus, a puzzling footnote.

"What does this mean?" He attempted to hand it Chrétien, who was too absorbed in his own letter.

"It's a note from our mother." Numa graciously claimed Durán as one of her sons when she came from Cyprus. She'd done a better job than Chrétien at teaching Durán *mathematica*. "She reminds us to pray, to avoid the midday sun, and to not—"

"Drink too much wine," Durán said. Numa's usual counsel was more like a song than a warning.

"She sent a packet of saffron for our feast at Pentecost." Chrétien seemed his most beautiful after any word from his mother, causing Durán to miss his own mother, remembering her at work, distaff and spindle in hand, telling him to be cautious of strangers whenever he departed for another adventure on the streets of Toulouse.

While Chrétien studied the second letter, his bright joy from reading Numa's missive faded to grey.

"What is it?" Durán saw the letter's seal. Pedro *El Rei*.

"Tomás is dead." He handed the letter to Durán. Written by a scribe, it commanded Chrétien to action:

'Tomás of Morella is dead in Barcelona. You are commanded by Pedro d'Aragón to assume care of your brother's chattel, both family and worldly goods.'

"Is this true?" Durán immediately felt the fool for saying it.

From the slow bob of his Adam's apple, Chrétien seemed to swallow grief. "I should have gone to him the moment we heard about Isabella."

"Your mother needed you."

"She damn sure needs two sons, not just me. I should have gone to him. I could have saved him."

"You don't even know how he died."

"I know it in my bones. Tomás would be alive if he hadn't lost Isabella. I should have gone to him."

"He was with Pedro." Durán, choking on grief once more for Isabella and now for Tomás, too, couldn't stop the argument they seemed to be having. "Tomás wrote us at Twelfth Night that he'd made Pedro a bonfraire. He had a friend with him."

"This must be what Ramón-roger's note meant. That Tomás is dead." Durán forced his letter onto Chrétien, who read it aloud.

'Your Montcava cousins have again appealed to the bishops because of Tomás of Morella. Beware Crux Lunata, bonfraires. *Sodalitas, fidelitas, virtus.*'

Chrétien chanted expletives, as if to calm himself. "They still want to roast us both on a heretic's pyre. Unless you're ready to say a damned creed and give up on sniveling ideas of heaven. Oh wait, it isn't even heaven you seek. Just another round of this life till you get it right."

"Are you blaming me?" This wasn't any fight they'd ever had.

"Never." Chrétien calmed himself. "I blame the devil. I blame Simon and Arnau Amalric. I blame Pedro. He was with Tomás. He should have taken care of him, as a brother."

Durán half listened to Chrétien's grief while he again read the letter from Pedro's scribe. "Pedro wants you to do all of this? You'll have to go to Barcelona. How can you also do what the count of Foix asked?" Durán had a hundred questions. How to find Tomás's steward in Aragón? How to find Sebastián and Yusuf in Pedro's army? What did Pedro mean about taking care of Tomás's chattel?

"I don't know. I don't know. I don't know." Chrétien pounded his fists, enraged again. "I know we can't risk a Church court questioning you again about whatever lies your Montcava cousins dream up. We need to join Pedro as soon as possible."

"Should we discard the wagons so we can travel faster? Rely on the provisioning stations?"

Chrétien crooked his arm around Durán's neck, jerking him close. "I need to keep you alive, *cor dolç*. Whatever Pedro asks, our own needs come first. We need to find Sebastián and Yusuf."

Before Durán could ask more, Chrétien stalked off into the night, cursing God and all the golden angels in heaven. Durán read the letter from Pedro's scribe again. It didn't include the bonfraires' salutation. No *brotherhood, fidelity, courage.* He covered the fire and went in search of Chrétien, hoping to offer comfort.

And promising himself that he'd never say it aloud, that this is what comes of mercenary life, when one's work is dedicated to killing.

17
Paradise

YEARS AGO IN ZARA, BEFORE Tomás and Chrétien quit that ill-fated crusade to Constantinople, the wife of a French lord slipped into Tomás's bed, hot and damp from the Mediterranean summer. Her husband was a knight from the Pays de France with whom Chrétien had been embroiled in a love affair since Sicily. The knight broke Chrétien's heart with a petty act of faithlessness (that story no longer bore retelling). Out of solidarity with Chrétien, Tomás insisted the woman leave his bed. She claimed that Tomás broke her heart (which he didn't believe existed) and caused enough commotion that the landlord evicted him.

In Famagusta, two summers before his father Miquel died, the aging wife of the regent of Cyprus demanded Tomás's performance when he wasn't in a position to refuse.

After Tomás found Isabella in the stony foothills of the Pyrenees, he never had another woman for pleasure or love (neither of which happened that one drunken night in Barcelona when Pedro forced him to marry Dolç).

Tomás lay on the perfumed herb-and-lamb's wool pallet in the little cell that Abu Jossep's steward gave him. He'd enjoyed better food and company than any mercenary might expect in a new town. Yet when a hot, bare body slipped into his bed in Baeza, Tomás faced the greatest jeopardy since those *franj* bandits destroyed his life. His woke to find his hands pinioned by the woman, her beautiful face a hand's breadth from his.

"I don't want to die with a woman's hand where you have yours. The guards pass near here often."

She laughed. "All guards but my own are far away. What's the use of being the consort of the greatest general in Al-Andalus if I cannot come and go as I like?

"What do you want?" he asked, certain that his head would be separated from his body in the next few heartbeats.

"To be the consort of the new king, the inheritor of Rodrigo *El Rei*. The liberator destined to free us for greatness."

"You'll get us both killed."

"The stars say you are mine," she purred, nuzzling his bare torso. "Whatever your lips say, the rest of you wants me."

She murmured words, like a prayer in a language he'd never heard. She was taller than he was, longer limbed. Her thighs were as firm as any horseman's. Her breath was scented with cinnamon and jasmine tea. The soft skin around her mouth tasted sweet and salty.

He pushed her off him.

"Come here," she whispered. "We must consummate the divine if we're to rule Andalusia."

"You are my cousin. I'm here to serve your husband. And my heart belongs—"

"To me," she breathed. "It's written in the stars. Testing fate is like rousing an angry woman. You know what an angry woman can do."

"What is that?" Tomás wanted to change the subject.

"The general's old cow of a wife beat me." She moved toward him; he scooted away. "Like that old bastard my aunts first made me marry. I had to do something about it. You don't want life here to be like that."

It took a moment to comprehend.

"You killed her? Abu Jossep's wife?"

She was gone, as silently as she'd come in.

Through the arched slit high up the plaster wall of his alcove, Tomás watched the dark sky grow grey. Taking inventory like a man who'd been robbed. How to lock things up for safety in a place with hardly any doors? He meticulously searched his bed and clothes, tossing objects into a pile.

A rusty red horseshoe nail, once bent, now straightened, which he tasted. Blood.

Two iron rings, linked together, polished so that only tiny flecks of rust appeared, and stuffed into his herb-filled mattress.

Three stalks of yarrow bound with a hank of black thread that trailed a long, thin braid, slipped under the woven mat where he left his boots.

Four petals from what had been a red, red rose, but now black at the edges.

Tying it all up in a strip of linen, he tossed the bundle onto Qasim's bedroll. He'd ask Qasim later to make sure the laundry women burned it in their fire.

.

In the sun-dappled shade of the orange grove, dried leaves crackled where Tomás stepped through exercises. He concentrated on the fire in his muscles, the arc of his short sword, where he placed each foot. What he owed Pedro and what he owed Yusuf warred with each swing of his sword.

And what Pedro would say? *Perhaps if you believed in prayer. Or if you trusted your friends.*

Or what his father or brother Chrétien would say: *You learned as a boy how to be a warrior. Pack your kit and go.*

The drums of Abu Jossep's army beat without pause. Tomás chased off all thought with each swing and thrust against the phantoms he battled, which spoke with the voices of his old masters in Cairo, drunken sometimes, cruel at moments, caustic always.

You sweat like an infidel's pet pig in a muddy pond.

You move like a whore, inviting that sword into her secret places.

Your own prick is stuck too far up your dark side.

You have the grace of a camel in heat who'd couple with a donkey.

Harder. Higher. Think. Don't think, move.

"Ibn Mikhail, may I join you?"

It took a moment for Tomás to hear his own name and reply.

"It's hot. Most prefer to slumber in this part of the day."

"I prefer to work, if you'll have me." Rashid stripped as Tomás had, to only his white cotton *sarawil*, though the vizier's thin trousers were immaculate while Tomás's were coated in dust, sodden with sweat, clinging to his thighs.

"I am delighted you came," Tomás said.

The vizier glanced around the grove. Qasim dozed under a tree. "I'm without my servants. Yours appears to sleep."

"That's what boys do. As often as they can," Tomás said. "He might as well sleep, since the army isn't moving soon."

"That's unfortunate, but true." Rashid folded his tunic and laid it atop his cuirass.

"It might be equally true that the infidels will merely bake under the sun and then go home."

"You lived with those *franj* devils. Do you believe they will?" Rashid pulled his sword from its sheath. Tomás envied that sheath's clean iron-and-leather lines.

"No swords today. Only daggers." Tomás sheathed his own sword and answered Rashid's question with half-truths. "The infidel invaders heard about the riches of Al-Andalus. Perhaps their covetous hearts will lead them into the embrace of the caliph's mercenaries."

"Our riches?" Rashid said. "Perhaps this land was rich, back when our great-great-grandfather met these grandees. The caliph complains that men here have grown soft with easy comforts."

"Do you believe that?"

"Look at our general, who was once the hero. Now he plays with his djinni instead of marching out to expand the frontier."

"Perhaps you're too harsh. Show me your dagger." He took the blade from Rashid to examine it. Locally made. Better than most he could buy in Barcelona or Toulouse. But not as good as the Damascene dagger that he'd purchased in Valencia. Or his father's sword, forged in Damascus.

"We should find that blasted boy when he reads the stars tonight. Wring his neck and throw him into the courtyard."

"You aren't often one to indulge fantasies." Tomás handed Rashid back his dagger. "He's only a child."

"Indeed," Rashid said. He stretched, his long fingers grazing the branches of the grove's canopy. "It's not your bastard nephew that irritates. I'm disappointed to be consigned here instead of with the caliph."

A note in Rashid's voice asked more than Tomás could answer. "Do we practice or talk?"

"A lesson, please." Rashid bowed, following the form Tomás had taught him.

"First, I warn you. Training or real fight, you will bleed."

Tomás motioned for Rashid to copy his stance. They were closely matched in height, though Rashid, a better horseman, had stronger thighs and Tomás had broader shoulders. Rashid had a smaller, fine-featured skull, but was no more handsome than Tomás had once been.

"Your footing matters. That's the only way that a knife fight resembles sword work."

While Tomás called out instructions, they moved together in the dappled light of the grove, first with Rashid mirroring Tomás's actions.

"Choose where you want to be cut."

Rashid glanced at Tomás, who stepped close from an unexpected side to demonstrate.

"Your adversary is looking at your knife. That's where he will attack."

The vizier nodded and made his move. Tomás deflected it, but allowed a slice across his forearm, which surprised his student.

Tomás stepped away. "When you must take a cut, do not allow a cut under your arm. It would destroy you."

"You're wounded!"

"Stings like I've been whipped by a fire djinni." Tomás shook off modest crimson drops. He raised his dagger. "Try again. Disarm me. Don't try to kill me."

"We're only practicing." Rashid scanned for an opening.

"In a real fight with knives, seek to disarm, not kill." Tomás kept distracting Rashid with words. "It's not a sword fight. Use more than your dagger. Your other hand. Your foot."

He kicked, sending Rashid to the dusty floor of the grove. And then stood over him. "Strike where he isn't looking."

"*Aiieee!*"

Tomás held out a hand, helping Rashid back to his feet. "Dagger up! Disarm me."

He sliced the vizier's forearm before his student even raised his dagger to fight.

"Where are your feet? You plod like an ox. I know you can't fight." Tomás took another slice, only enough to sting, while he continued to talk, flustering his student.

"Stop me. Strike."

But he was already two arm lengths away, so Rashid sliced nothing but air.

"I said deflect or disappear. That's what I meant."

Tomás switched his dagger to the other hand. Rashid recognized that sign. Tomás was going easy on him. He advanced in a fury.

"Where are you?" Once more, Tomás wasn't there to make contact. "What are your feet doing?"

Rashid copied one of Tomás's attack moves.

Tomás again flew out of the vizier's reach. "You like order. You can't have it here."

Rashid's face darkened with each failed attempt to come close to Tomás, while Tomás sacrificed opportunities to cut him.

"Come, old man. Look at your flat feet."

Tomás allowed him to advance. He kicked Tomás's dagger from his hand, then toppled Tomás and gripped him so close neither of them could move.

The two bare bodies lay beside each other, slick with sweat and blood, shining in the dappled light, both men breathing hard, like exhausted lovers.

"No quarter?" Tomás panted. The scar on his lip twitched. "Or will you take me as prisoner?"

Just as breathless as Tomás, Rashid sighed. "You're free, if you can escape." He let his dagger slip from his hand. His teeth flashed white at the challenge. Still holding Tomás in a prisoner's grip, Rashid's hands were strong, though Tomás's fingers were longer.

"I made you angry." Tomás relaxed under Rashid's grip. His heart pounded, so those cuts ached.

"I never plod," Rashid growled.

"No. You lose focus if you allow anger in a fight. You must work hard to have all the control you wish for yourself."

Tomás wriggled from Rashid's grasp and motioned a hand-to-hand challenge. They wrestled then, the leaves and grass sticking to their sweat-slicked bodies, each smeared with the other's blood from knife cuts. Rashid knew moves Tomás had never seen, but Tomás had the advantage of greater hand-to-hand experience than his cousin, who'd learned to fight as a cavalry leader.

"What's this here?" Rashid held Tomás in a lock, pointing to the slash across Tomás's belly.

"Once I wasn't so lucky with a knife."

"So," Rashid breathed in his ear, "you aren't invincible."

Instead of taunting, Tomás demonstrated in rapid order the five classic moves his masters taught. In the final move, he pinned Rashid, just as a breeze came up from the canyon to stir the leaves of the orange grove, drying their sweat in the sudden gust.

Tomás shivered.

Locked in Tomás's defeating grip, Rashid gazed up at him with an expression Tomás last saw a dozen years before, when he wrestled with Chrétien in Cairo.

A man in love.

■

"Rashid? Is it you? Ibn Abd al-Aziz?"

The shadow of a very wide man blocked the sun.

Tomás, who was on top, scrambled upright and stepped out of the way to let Rashid rise and greet his visitor.

That angry man from the caliph's delegation in Barcelona craned his neck like an aggressive bull straining through a fence hole for green grass.

"Marzuq al-Jayyani! You honor me." Rashid still panted from their fight, a last trickle of sweat wending from his forehead down his cheek. He bowed in a way that, Tomás assumed, indicated the guest held high status. "You've come all this way from Jaén? In this heat? Let me take you to my house, where it's cool."

"I've just come from there." Al-Jayyani fished a silk cloth from a hidden pocket, wiped his brow. "It's a long winding way up to where you're perched in this little town."

He accepted Rashid's invitation and huffed his way out of the grove, leading Rashid when he should more logically be following. The man wore a sword too long for his wide body and short arms; it swung wildly at his side, bashing into Rashid's calf as they walked.

Tomás remained behind, gathering knives and swords, but Rashid called for him to follow and join them. By the time Tomás slipped into the portico's shade at Rashid's house, the servants were already bearing trays of spiced nuts, dried figs, and cold squashed orange where Rashid reclined with his guest.

The delegate from Jaén finally took notice of Rashid's companion. "You!" His plump moist lips quivered. "You're that unbelieving *batini* from the infidel's court in Barcelona."

"No," Rashid said, "he's my cousin. I freed Tuma al-Makkzan from bondage to that king. Now he works for Abu Jossep."

Al-Jayyani laughed, a deep blast that again put Tomás to mind of a fighting bull, the kind put to pasture yet still seeking a quarrel. "More of your clan sent to help with the recalcitrant general?"

Rashid offered the man another plate of refreshments, indicating that the cheese was fresh and local, that the membrillo as fine as any cook in Jaén might prepare. After a decent amount of empty chat, Rashid said, "Sent by the caliph to scold me, Marzuq?" He glanced over at Tomás, who'd stayed out of the small talk. "Marzuq and I first came to the caliph's court together. How many years ago was that, my friend?"

Al-Jayyani ignored the second question. "Only to help you, Rashid. And to bring the caliph's best wishes that the one true God will guide you in all things."

"As I pray every day." Rashid pushed another plate of sweetmeats toward Al-Jayyani.

"Have you convinced the great general that his men need to fight for their own land?" Al-Jayyani asked, his tone as sticky as his fingers had become. Rashid offered a finger bowl. While Al-Jayyani wiped his hands, he pretended to drag Tomás into the conversation. "You see, Ibn Mikhail, all the insipid sons of old taifa generals want to stay home, tucked into their little citadels and rancheros, happy to let mercenaries do the hard work."

"Abu Jossep's men are well trained, the best in the countryside." Rashid sipped at a tiny cup of mint tea. "Other taifa generals can only dream they might accomplish as much for Al-Andalus."

Tomás dawdled with his tea, interested to hear Rashid defend the general against the same complaints he himself had made.

"Why does the caliph need Abu Jossep and his army? With two hundred thousand mercenaries in the caliph's camp?" Tomás pretended innocent curiosity.

Al-Jayyani glared at Tomás over the brim of his tea cup.

Hoping he appeared innocent, Tomás continued. "Have the soldiers recruited from Al-Andalus ever seen more than mere border raids? This is a land of peace. Is that why the caliph, with so many mercenaries, still calls on Abu Jossep for help?"

"Now is the most important time of our lives." Al-Jayyani smacked his moist, sticky lips. "The best time under heaven for great men to show that they, like our caliph, serve God above all things."

Rashid poured more mint tea. "Please excuse me for asking, my dear friend. Why did the caliph choose you to help me?"

"I volunteered. Every man wants to be close to the caliph for battle, but I know he needs help elsewhere. And you need special help here."

"So, it's me alone you came here for?" Rashid asked.

"Yes, all other troubles are in the past. I'm here to help you."

"You could have remained in Jaén, at great comfort, and convinced the caliph that I'm able to manage my duties."

"The caliph is a hard man to convince otherwise when he's made up his mind."

"Indeed."

"The caliph is convinced spies are interfering on the frontier. You know I'm especially good at uprooting spies and conjurors. Like a cat sent to trap mice in the granary. And, of course, the situation with the caliph is what you've always known." Marzuq dropped his voice, speaking as if an intimate friend. "If you can't bring Baeza to battle, Rashid al-Rashid, you'll serve as a backcountry vizier for the rest of your life on earth. Counting sheep instead of infantry." Al-Jayyani sipped tea. A thin stream escaped his thick lips and dribbled, undetected, down his exquisite green silk *jubba*. "Out of friendship, I volunteered to help you."

Rashid acknowledged a servant who'd stood in the shade waiting for attention.

"Ah, your rooms await, Marzuq. My servants will guide you to the bath. You must be exhausted from your journey. Shall I see you at dinner with the general, after all the harms of your journey have been repaired?"

With several overly formal salutations and mutual offers of gratitude exchanged, Al-Jayyani tottered off, that too-long sword repeatedly interfering with his walk and his passage through doorways.

"What was that about?" Tomás said when Al-Jayyani had gone.

"What didn't I understand?"

"He's our cousin Ríma's former husband."

"The one who beat her and had to be forced to divorce her?" Tomás dreaded having to rescue the disquieting Ríma after all.

"Yes. He may have come to help the caliph, but he isn't here to help me. He has the kindness of a common viper. By the time I warn Abu Jossep about him, Marzuq will already have spit his venom into the general's heart. Venom for both Ríma and me."

"Therefore, now it's even more important that you move this army? Why does the caliph require these farmers?"

"In truth, the caliph's numbers aren't that great," Rashid said. He seemed abstract, lost in thought. "And Baeza is much closer to the infidel army than Jaén. If we move the army now, we place trained men in the infidels' path." He stared off into the grove canopy. "As for me, I can't rise higher, as the caliph always promised me, unless I succeed here."

"You'll be stuck in the backcountry?"

"Marzuq understated the case. By sending him here, the caliph sends a far worse message. The caliph will see me as a traitor if I fail. If I can't move the army, it means my head."

"Surely our clan can find other options for you."

Rashid shook his head, laughing. "If I fail the caliph, I fail our clan. I'd become a nothing, a man with no name. Failing is not a choice for me."

"We'll think of something." Tomás masked his alarm. The safety Pedro promised, that he could always find shelter with the Rodriguez clan, proved illusory. "Shall we try to subvert the djinni? That child might convince Abu Jossep to join the caliph's army."

"Do you think so?"

"We'll do what we can." Tomás intended nothing of the sort, though it became harder each day to do what he must for Pedro. He put off calculating how many people he had to rescue in Baeza now that a spy-catcher had arrived. "But, my friend, you can always travel with me, a mercenary without a master."

Rashid studied Tomás, his eyes warm and soft. "God has never before sent me a friend like you."

·

Yet another night, the same as the night before. After the drums ceased, after prayers, Tomás shed Rashid's company and ate millet bread and cheese with Zaheid. Then he fought to the death for Pedro d'Aragón, applying his best skills and using superior weapons.

Ivory.

The white gold that the caliphs brought to Al-Andalus. So superior to the bone dice Tomás had to settle for in Christendom.

Backgammon stones.

Markers for a complicated war strategy game called *al-shatranj*.

Dice. In several shapes, tossed with a thousand variations.

He found friends, balancing how much silver he won against how much he lost. He asked questions and listened, to learn about life under the best of the frontier emirs (Abu Jossep), and to hear complaints about interloping caliphs who made themselves rich, but shared the wealth only with their tribes in Tunis, then expected farmers to get up on a spring day to fight invaders. Invaders who'd stay out of Al-Andalus if boastful caliphs left the emirs to protect the frontier. Hadn't they all lived in peace for five hundred years? It was foreigners who brought chaos to Paradise. The Almohads were just trumped-up mercenaries, making themselves lords over peaceful farmers.

Complaints grew greater each night, the longer that farmers-turned-soldiers baked in this camp. They needed to be home tending their orchards. Tomás tossed dice far from the prying eyes of captains while he asked questions and spent each night losing silver and gaining trust and suggesting that good men needed to do what was right for their families.

As if he knew how to do that. He could toss dice by rote, while in a daydream he listened to Isabella speaking in backcountry Catalan. Not words of comfort, just common-sense advice.

'Time to rest the horses.'

'The best camp is over there.'
'You don't care about sleeping on rocks, but I prefer not.'
'Qui s'ho creu? Us together by this stream.'
A rousing call: "Hey, dog! Take your turn."
One of the Mozarab mercenaries he'd been gaming with for the past three nights called on Tomás to play. Tomás prepared to lose one last time. The men in this circle of the camp especially didn't want to be here. Word was getting around that only those closest to the caliph had any chance of being paid. These men were ready to depart for Jaén. Tomás intended to leave enough silver behind that night to ensure they deserted soon.

He didn't like these men. Not that Tomás made friends everywhere; that was always Chrétien's job. But no one liked these men. Thieving mountain bandits, that's what Zaheid said, though he said the same about all country people.

True, in this case. This band had been forced to move camp three times because of other soldiers' complaints. And because the army hadn't yet joined the caliph, these men were among the scant handful who had little good to say about Abu Jossep, even jeering when others cited the general's heroic past.

That night, Tomás let two of them win, expecting they'd be gone by dawn. He marked them, should he find them later when he joined the caliph's two hundred thousand mercenaries in Jaén.

Ali, a wizened fellow, the color of toasted almonds, his nose broken twice, from cheating at dice, if Tomás was any judge.

Umar, with thighs as thick as tree stumps, dressed in dusty, un-mended linen beneath the ancient cuirass and kazaghand he always wore, even at night, poorly mended chainmail clinking whenever he tossed the dice.

After losing all he intended to lose, and mildly cursing in false despair, Tomás said good night and slipped inside the city gates just before curfew. He walked the dark streets, headed for his alcove and a night's sleep, lost again in lonely, lucid dreams with Isabella.

The jagged cooing of *tórtora turca* broke into his thoughts.

Dove is best, Isabella once said, when roasted on a stick, not cooing on the rooftops.

The moon shone. It was just past midnight. The air lay hot on his skin and the smell of lemons in a nearby courtyard filled his head. No breeze now. He hadn't lived this far from the sea since...forever. Landlocked.

He again refigured every element of escape. The gate to take out of Baeza. The path to take across the plateau and into the mountains. How to collect his horse and two boys, his armor, and sufficient food and water. They needed another burro, but Abu Jossep's army commandeered all spare animals and provender from every casa up every arroyo from here to the La Mancha frontier.

That cursed cooing. No, a hoopoe called from down the street. Which wasn't probable. It's a wild breed, not domesticated and running among the chickens, peacocks, and guinea hens in the barracks or courtyards.

Tomás followed that false hoopoe call through the alleys of Baeza. He'd learned how to stalk quietly before he learned to read, practicing in the streets of Famagusta with Chrétien. He recalled those skills while shadowing two boys who seemed to have mastered the streets of Baeza.

And to have made friends among other boys in the city.

Near each market square, Yusuf and Qasim conferred, illuminated by the moon. Youths muttered in low voices. Fingers shot overhead to count. Coins jangled (copper, from the sound) amid muffled exclamations and hissed pleas for silence.

The two boys journeyed through the alleys, dodging the patrol, and stopped at the city gates.

"What for?" Yusuf's beautiful voice rose above a whisper.

"A traitor to Islam," one voice said in the Baeza dialect. "He spied for the infidel invaders."

The boys gazed up at a body hung near the wall, stripped naked, the flesh whipped before death to bare bones. A small man, not anyone Tomás knew in Baeza.

"Let's go." Yusuf's voice.

"Not tonight, master. It's not safe."

"Flying djinn might get you? A hungry ifrit?"

"I have a bad feeling."

"We already paid the porter."

Which was when Tomás learned that his son had a talent for subverting others' good sense. He watched the porter let the boys escape the city through his portal. Then he had to threaten the porter's life to be let through the door. Yusuf, it seems, got what he wanted by reading the man's stars.

To follow them, Tomás retraced the dark path he'd just come up from the camps. But instead of descending into gamblers' dens, Yusuf visited three of Abu Jossep's captains, slipping into their tents while Qasim stood outside. Yusuf emerged, a familiar jingle ringing between the two boys, the sound of square silver dirham coins dropping into a bag with their cousins.

At the edge of camp, the sentry nodded to Yusuf as if well-acquainted. Tomás stepped closer.

"Can I buy some of whatever you're selling?"

Of course, Qasim wasn't surprised; he'd called Tomás to follow them. Yusuf said, "The market-cart is empty."

A hot summer night's breeze came up, infusing the air with the scent of too-ripe lemons. And dust.

"Do you sell the general's favors?"

"I'm not a traitor like you." Yusuf sped up, just enough that Qasim was between them on the trail up toward town.

"What's he selling, Qasim?"

"Don't make him a traitor, too." Yusuf stopped on the trail, so that Qasim stepped back onto Tomás, who pushed his servant behind him. "I sell hope. Though some might call them fortunes. I don't know the future. Only what the stars say."

"What do your stars say?"

"That I'm descended from a goatherd and destined to—"

"Master!" Qasim, so close by, jumped past Tomás, grabbing for his dagger.

"Your silver, lads."

Like the tale of the donkey and two wise men, they were set upon. Only Tomás was the donkey. The bandits?

Ali and Umar.

Their daggers out, threatening Yusuf. Qasim pushed his way to confront them.

Because Qasim was so intent, Tomás stepped back to let him do his best. In a move that could have been learned only by watching Tomás at practice, Qasim disarmed one and kicked him into the dust. The other, Umar of the thick thighs, stumbled over his friend, then charged for Qasim.

Who shoved Yusuf out of the way.

Tomás caught Yusuf, wrapping his arms around his son to keep him out of the fray. Yusuf quivered, so thin that Tomás felt the angles of his bones, like the first time Tomás ever held him. Why did he ever let go?

"Help Qasim." Yusuf jerked away.

Qasim had his dagger in Umar's thick thigh, and only needed Tomás to shout the battle-cry that roused fear in a thousand Ayyubid infantrymen. Or so Miquel always said.

"Both of you. Back to town. Now."

18
Xirgú

GRATEFUL FOR PONÇ'S HELP IN bearing Matheus's bleeding body into the house and up the stairs, Isabella took more of the weight when Ponç knocked on Constanza's door and quietly asked for her help, as if the seigneur's half-dead presence were just another chore.

Felip came to open the door but stood in shock while Constanza rose from her bed and took command.

"Put him here," Constanza said. "Ponç, call Guillema from the kitchen to help."

She directed Felip to peel the blood-soaked clothes from his brother. Isabella retreated to stand by the window, staring at the night sky and wishing she'd made it to the army camp, while explaining what had happened. Fortunately, the servant woman, Guillema, appeared with clean linen and hot water from the kitchen fires, and ready to work without expressing either alarm or dismay at the condition of her seigneur.

Not happy to gaze on Matheus's gore and torn flesh, Isabella stared at the door, considering every step needed to leave Narbonne and be back on the road to Barcelona. Near the door, Ponç had dropped Matheus's pack. Isabella knelt beside it, examining what Matheus kept close to him. A parchment packet, which she slipped into her jerkin. A scarlet silk scarf that must be a woman's token. A small round of cheese, its rind unbroken. One of those tiny books of prayer that had become a fashion among rich seigneurs. The kind that St-Pere produced for money.

Gently turning the pages of the gilded versal, she recognized her own hand. Another monk had carved and stitched her work into a book and then bound it in tooled leather.

Not one of Lorenç's treasures. Matheus may have stopped at St-Pere and learned of the abbot's death, but he didn't have that chalice with him, either to sell it or to carry out the magic Lorenç described, or to accuse her of murder. Unless Matheus had found Lorenç's goods and left them elsewhere.

"Cranesbill powder." Constanza gave Ponç a list of what else was needed. She and Guillema worked with few words. Guillema did the sewing while Constanza worried whether Matheus was warm enough, rubbing his feet and hands.

"We don't want him slipping into delirium," Constanza said.

"We can't get beef-tea into him yet." Guillema stuffed the smeared orange silks into a basin to carry away. "Call me when he wakes. I'll have a potion for him."

The door closed, leaving Isabella, Felip, and Constanza alone with the lord of Xirgú, whose breathing scarcely moved the coverlet that Constanza tugged over him.

"You k–killed m–my brother." Felip finally got words out.

"He's not dead." Isabella turned back from the window. "Matheus attacked a young woman. When I protected her, he turned on me."

"Òc, a Jewess." Felip's jaw jutted, obstinate, angry.

"Does that matter one jot of lamp-black ink in the eyes of God?" Isabella sat, uninvited, at the foot of Constanza's great bed. "I stabbed a man who tried to kill me."

"He's my b–brother. You killed him."

"Mercy!" Isabella, head in hands, begged for mercy. He was just a sadly untutored lad, but sometimes his ignorance was like a bottomless well. "Do you imagine that this is a moment of joy? Allow me peace to pray."

"First my uncle. Now m–my brother."

"One stole your birthright. Like Esau. The other tried to steal your soul. Both tried to kill me." Isabella leaped from the bed, standing with hands on hips over Felip, as if she were a sister scolding him. "Thank me for saving that young woman. And prepare yourself to serve as seigneur of Xirgú."

"What? I c–can't—"

"Sancta Maria!" Isabella turned to Constanza, who sat on the other edge of the bed, unhappily wrenching her hands, as if washing them, though she'd already cleaned them in the basin Guillema carried away. "Ma dòmna, speak now, please. Even if Matheus lives, Felip needs to serve as lord of Xirgú now. Tell him it's his birthright. He's suffered enough from Xirgú secrets."

"S–secrets?"

Constanza said, "*Fadrin*, I love you. As much as a mother loves her best child."

"*Òc*, Grandmother, I have always felt it."

"Look at him." Constanza pointed at the ashen, inert figure in the bed. "He doesn't resemble his mother, God grant peace to her restless soul. Nor a whit like my Justí, who carried away the spirit of Xirgú when he left on crusade."

"Yet here's Felip," Isabella said. "He's Xirgú."

Constanza no longer wrenched her hands. "The old count of Barcelona insisted Justí marry again before going to Jerusalem. He and Sibilia had only a fortnight before Justí sailed to Jerusalem."

"Joining Xirgú and Montcava one more time." Isabella whispered, keeping the bitterness to herself.

Constanza grew sadder. "The old count did not choose well for my Justí. He died before he saw Jerusalem, not knowing he had a new son. Who looks just like him."

"And whose mother abandoned Felip to you, and then to the Church. It's rude to scold you, ma dòmna. But think what that so-called brother and his mother have done to Felip."

"It's n–not your p–place." Felip rose in a heat, but Constanza tugged him to sit by her, apparently agreeing with Isabella now.

Constanza had firm hold of Felip's forearm. "Did you never wonder why Justí sent Matheus to his mother's uncles when he was barely out of swaddling clothes? Look at that creature." Her voice crackled with cold when she again pointed at the pale form in the bed. She stroked Felip's face. "And behold this man."

"Th–that's b–blasphemy!" Felip spluttered. His grandmother released his arm and laid her finger on his lips to quiet him.

"The man lying here is nothing like my Justí. He resembles most his mother's cousin."

"Renoud or Nicolau?" Isabella interrupted. It was now so obvious, and the injustice to Felip. "Which Montcava cousin visited Justí's first bride?"

Constanza held her arms out to Felip, trembling. "You, *fadrin*, you are the image of Justí. No one can doubt who your father is."

Felip, obviously wretched when he finally understood, fell to his knees beside Constanza. "I'm a fool, like Matheus always said."

"No, *fadrin*. I kept the truth from you."

"And you sent me away." It hurt to watch Felip's pain while these truths washed over him.

His grandmother stroked the coverlet she'd laid over Matheus. "I wanted you to live, Felip. Sibilia and Matheus have no inclination to share. It's a wonder those two aren't at each other's throats."

"W–w–w…" Speech once more betrayed Felip.

Isabella said, "Senhóra, here in the south, we don't live in the foolish way that Franks and Angevines do, leaving all but the oldest son with no land. Felip has his own place, as a donzel of Xirgú."

Constanza was still unloading the burden of secrets she'd carried. "They are ruthless, those two. From the beginning, Matheus saw his infant brother as a threat. I believed Felip would be safer in a monastery than in this house.

"Not in a monastery where Sibilia's brother ruled."

"I never would dream that Churchmen might break God's laws," Constanza said.

Isabella had struggled years before with that misperception, punished and condemned by her own confessor. "It takes living in a hard world, ma dòmna, to learn otherwise."

Felip sat back, his face wet, his eyes dark. "F–for years I prayed that Matheus would die, so I'd have Sibilia to myself. Then I prayed for forgiveness." Constanza lifted a hand in protest, but Felip continued. "N–no, *Àvia*. She never loved me. I've been s–stupid and blind."

Forgetting all caution, Isabella embraced Felip, holding him tight. "*Ai, mon amic.* Your world's torn to shreds. Nothing hurts worse. I'm so sorry."

He shuddered in her arms, so she had to say more, whispering, "May God's light shine on you soon. You are good, and your domus needs you to be strong."

After a few heartbeats, his trembling stopped. "Thank you."

"It's nothing." Isabella let loose of Felip. "I have to go, now that it's dark. Farewell!"

"Òc, you must f–flee. I'll fetch the horses with Ponç."

"You must go too, *fadrin*." Constanza stood.

"I need to stay with you, *Àvia*." He didn't stutter now.

"Ponç is all I need until you return. You must do what your father would. Travel to save your king. And your brave friend Vidal can't travel alone."

"Don't send me away again!" Felip cried.

Isabella opened the bedchamber door.

"Stop!" Constanza called. "Take Felip with you."

"Why? You need him here, and I can travel faster on my own."

Constanza dragged Felip up from his knees.

"Felip owes Xirgú service to Pedro. It's what Justí would do."

After one embrace, Constanza sent Felip out for the horses, with a command to return to her when the king of Aragón was safe. "Do as Justí would. Revive Xirgú honor."

■

Isabella quashed her impatience to be gone. Felip sent Ponç to the city's guard post, proclaiming that the seigneur of Xirgú had been attacked in the streets. When he returned, Ponç repeated the story he'd spread through the city.

"A Jew from the quarter saw the attack. Several ultramontanos fled past the Jew."

Constanza, a black silk veil draped over her head, came down to greet the captain of the guard and solemnly reported that Matheus was at death's door. A huddle of Matheus's men had been roused from the taverns and listened to Constanza's report with dismay. "Have you found these heinous attackers?"

The captain bowed. "Most all ultramontanos returned to their camps at sunset."

Constanza regarded the captain sternly. "*Francimand* soldiers come to our town and murder our seigneurs. And you do nothing?"

"Tomorrow, ma dòmna. In the morning we will ask the leaders in the camps."

"Ask? You'll ask?" Constanza stiffened. "In times past, the Girona seigneurs and captains commanded."

She stared stone-faced while the captain claimed no ability to find the attackers. In a thin voice, Constanza commanded Felip to take the place of his brother.

"Our king asks our service, *fadrin*. You must lead the Xirgú men. And people will expect you to seek your brother's murderer among the ultramontanos."

"*Àvia*, I…" Felip had pulled himself together. "*Òc, Àvia.* I shall go now."

Constanza persisted, next addressing the Xirgú knights who stood leaderless. "You are camped with the crusaders?"

While they fumbled, guessing who should speak as the leader, she commanded them to accompany Felip to join Matheus's knights.

"Don Felip is Xirgú now," Constanza commanded, imperious.

It was, Isabella thought, a magnificent performance.

●

Felip had never seen his grandmother Constanza in that way, as cold and bold as a great queen.

The Xirgú knights believed the story Constanza told, including her insistence that Felip and Vidal had been with her for the past fortnight. Under her spell, Jaufrés, the Xirgú captain who'd been to the Outremer, swore to search among the men traveling to Toledo to find Matheus's would-be assassin.

With her formal goodbye, Constanza gave Felip an old silk surcoat that had been his father's, preserved only Gold knows how. Vidal gave him Matheus's dagger and sword. Felip listened to the men—his men—explain the camp location. He tried to remember each man's name in spite of all the commotion, and his thoughts about Matheus sleeping upstairs. Sleeping, or dying.

The Xirgú men had been busy buying and loading provisions all afternoon, and now both Felip and Vidal had fresh Xirgú horses.

Bells rang for curfew moments before the Xirgú band reached the city gates. The gatekeepers called a warning, that once outside the gates, there was no returning that night.

Riding alongside Vidal, Felip asked the first of the many questions on his mind.

"Who will truly believe I can lead these men?"

"You're the seigneur, Felip. People will do what you say."

"How can this work?"

"We're safer than when we traveled alone. We have to worry about whether anyone besides Matheus is pursuing us from St-Pere. But let's just get on with it. I need sleep."

When they joined the army camp in the valley outside of town, Jaufrés spread the story of Matheus's dire injuries and Felip's new place as their leader. In Matheus's tent (now Felip's), Vidal quickly prepared to sleep, piling chainmail and arms in one corner, and then stripping to a linen shirt and hose.

"I'm not sure you should trust those men," Vidal said. "Except for your captain Jaufrés, they are mostly *francimand* mercenaries."

In the dark, only the outline of his friend's form appeared, darker than their surroundings. *How did I ever think that's a man?* "I don't recognize any of them. Except Jaufrés."

What was her real name?

The narrow tent forced them to bed down more closely than Vidal ever allowed when they slept rough on the road to Girona.

"What next?" Felip whispered.

"We have to discover who to trust. Like when I found you at the monastery. Before then, there was no one I trusted."

Her soft breath became even and gentle. She'd fallen asleep. Then she startled him.

"Felip, when we left St-Pere, I was cruel."

"*Òc.*" He didn't want to answer, but had to. "I was such a fool."

"No. You're not fit for life in a monastery. I should have known our friendship would mean a great deal to you."

"I lusted after w–women before." Felip stopped, then tried again. "You made it so confusing."

"There isn't room in my heart for anyone. I still mourn a lost husband and son."

"No, I thought you w–were a man. I didn't know you were a woman until you jumped out the window today." His bitterness flowed like a spring flood.

"*Ai*, my poor boy."

"Don't call me a b–boy. You all lied. My mother, sending me to the monks. My brother, who isn't my brother. You, pretending to care about me."

More silence. Then she whispered, "My name is Isabella of Valerós. At St-Pere I selfishly tended only my own wounds. I am grievously sorry that I hurt you."

"Why were you there? Why didn't you find a women's house? Or return to your home."

"I was too ill to travel farther. And I can't return to my old life now, because of the evil my family and my villages have endured. I've been falsely condemned as a heretic three times. I'm a danger to Valerós and Montcava villages."

"You are indeed a goodman?"

"No. This new crusade just makes it convenient for people to lie about their enemies. I say my creed like any good Catholic." Her voice, always raspy, dropped lower. "But I have burns on my legs to prove I know what it's like to be cast on the heretics' pyre. The smell of burning human flesh is in my nose. It never goes away, night or day. I will do anything to protect the villages of my domus from Simon de Montfort's evil. And from any more Crux Lunata lies and plots."

"My brother hurt you."

"He's not your brother. Yes, Matheus and his men killed my family. But he's only one among others who intend harm to my people."

"I want to compensate for his sins."

"Let's just find Pedro. He's the only man in Christendom who can convince the pope to stop Simon de Montfort's terror."

"Xirgú owes you protection. I promise you that. For all time…" He paused. "Ma dòmna. Is that how you're called in your home?"

"Just Vidal, still. You are kind, Felip, a better man than this new world deserves."

After a while she slept. Felip lay awake, wondering what miracles had lifted him in only a few days from his wood chopping, cold life at St-Pere to a crusader camp outside Girona. Thirty men now believed he was their seigneur, while his brother, who was not truly his brother, lay swaddled and bleeding in his grandmother's bed. Unless angels had already taken the man.

Felip counted each of the soft breaths beside him, ticking off numbers into the thousands before he too slept.

∎

"Off, *fadrin!*"

Felip woke to massive pain in his shoulder and then, worse, his groin. He'd been pushed into the heap of arms and armor. She stood over him in the tent.

"Keep your hands off me."

"I n–n–never…"

"Your hands roam in your sleep? Whispering *eu vos amor?*"

"It must have been a dream."

"Dress. You need to command your knights."

Vidal…no, Isabella pulled on the doublet and boots she'd cast aside the night before, all the while haranguing him. "You will observe new rules, *fadrin*, more than any Rule at St-Pere. Do not talk to me of love. Keep your body covered in my presence."

"I can't help how I feel."

"In my experience, a Montcava man says 'I love you' just before I'm attacked. But never again."

"I'm Xirgú. Not Montcava." Not one slip of stutter.

His shoulder still numb, his groin aching, Felip dressed. He buckled his cuirass at the sides, settling it over the packet of letters and that chalice inside his shirt. He wandered into the camp, seeking water and then the latrine while assaulted by the noise and stench of a hundred men rousing to greet the day. A marine fog had engulfed the camp, but not so thick that it hid the Xirgú colors marking the tents and beds of thirty men.

Around that group, now rousing from their night's sleep, other groups belonged to lords from Narbonne and the surrounding lands. The camp smelled worse than the fetid cells of the oldest monks at St-Pere. The mucked-out stalls of the monastery barns smelled better than this encampment of soldiers. Horse. Sweat. An unbathed, flatulent community of would-be crusaders tugging on leggings and socks that begged to be laundered. And it was weeks of travel until they reached Toledo.

Yet as the early fog lifted while he toured the camp, immense satisfaction settled. Felip was on crusade.

He had, at this moment, almost everything he'd dreamed of.

No longer bound body and soul in that monastic prison. No longer dreaming of glory. Truly on the road, reasserting Xirgú honor. In one way, he'd woken that day to having the greatest possible portion of everything he'd dreamed of as a child. Though no one warned him a crusade smelled this bad.

He spied Isabella across an alleyway between camps, busy with the horses, brushing one and talking into its ear, the beast receiving more kindness than Felip had ever known. For the first days on the road, before they came to Girona, they talked together as friends. Now, all he had was hope. Whatever she was in the world, "Brother Vidal" had been his only friend.

He headed for the corral, intending to make amends before the long road ahead. Voices from the waking camp rose around him while he walked to join her.

Isabella combed that horse's mane with deep concentration, the same way Vidal concentrated over parchment and ink in the scriptorium. She blinked when Felip approached, and then smiled at him with more joy than he'd ever believed might happen.

Pure delight. Like he felt, waking up on crusade.

Rather than whining ultramontanos, an odd accent called out, "*Vivètz* Valerós!"

Her comb dropped to the ground, stamped on by the horse. She ran toward him, arms open. Joyous.

Past Felip.

To leap into the arms of a tall Celt, the kind of soldier who'd slice you open at breakfast and sing about it at supper.

Then she kissed the Toulousain seigneur. Who wore Montcava colors, like Felip's mother's knights in Narbonne.

Isabella held the seigneur in an embrace, laughing, like one would greet a long-lost brother. Behind her, though, the Celt was signaling the Montcava seigneur to be silent, a finger pressed against his lips. Then the Celt embraced her once again.

She might have new friends, but Felip still needed to protect her on the long journey ahead. Like a good and meritorious knight does in the troubadours' songs.

.

The camp was laid out in a neat crusaders' grid, similar to how Pèire Leteric and Marshall Guillem arrayed their camps. The little army had camped in such a narrow valley, however, that the smell of latrine and horse and campfire and sweating men roused buried memories, nothing masked by the dawn's marine fog.

Men's voices called minor profanities from the cooking fires, cursing a Narbonnese cook for burning the porridge, complaining that the provisioners bought sheep's rather than goats' milk.

"Fine if we wanted to make cheese. But we want breakfast. Without a tongue coated in mutton tang."

"No bacon? We only just left home. Hiding it already, you peccador?"

This felt more like home than anywhere Isabella had been since… the world fell apart.

And now Isabella ran through the camp, her heart bursting, feeling that God had delivered an unasked-for gift.

She blinked away tears, though it didn't matter; no need to worry here about giving into weeping. Chrétien laughed when he crushed her in his arms, then shouting as if she were a long-lost comrade-at-arms.

"Hola, bon amic!"

When Durán braced her forearms, she felt him trembling. As handsome as ever, even though his hair was short and his eyes more serious than before, as if he carried a burden. "We thought you were dead. Why didn't you come to us?"

"A Good Christian woman rescued me. But then crusader-bandits condemned us as heretics and killed my friends." She had to catch her breath, crushed again by Chrétien. "I'm a danger to you and to Valerós."

"Then what are you doing here, ma dòmna?" Chrétien wiped at his nose savagely, but not at his wet cheeks. He'd tied up his long hair, which meant he was prepared to fight at any moment.

"I'm not called 'your lady,' please. I'm Vidal of Valerós, traveling with the master of Xirgú. We need to find Pedro, because the Crux Lunata—"

Chrétien stopped her. "Hush. This camp has Crux Lunata knights. Or did until this morning. A dozen rode off to join the archbishop of Narbonne when they heard Matheus of Xirgú is at death's door."

"To return in the next life. In a different form," Durán said.

"Perhaps he'll come back as a dog, instead of the wolf he was in this life?" Chrétien said. "We're happy to no longer live at close arms with men who wish us dead."

"You can thank me for stopping Matheus. I caught him attacking a woman in Girona. We fought and…I suppose you'd say that I won." Isabella didn't repeat the details, remembering how it felt when her blade plunged into living flesh. "I'm not proud of what I had to do."

"You saved Durán a great deal of trouble, if that consoles you." Matheus's catastrophe seemed to give Chrétien certain satisfaction.

Durán scanned the campground. "We came to find the new seigneur of Xirgú. I'm the master of this little army."

"*Adouçar enfant Jhezu!*"

Isabella swore a man's oath—a new bad habit—at seeing Felip thirty paces way, being badgered by Colomb de Beaurain, who tapped Felip's cuirass as if scolding him.

"That's the new head of the Xirgú domus." She pointed across the way. Felip stood taller, pushed Colomb's hand off his chest, and answered. Seeing Felip assert himself added to her happiness. "We're traveling together to warn Pedro that the Crux Lunata—"

"Happy chance! I never throw the dice so well." A grin distorted Chrétien face. Then he finally wiped at his wet cheek. "The count of Foix sent us on the same mission. Oh, and to keep Durán from being burned as the devil's adulterous heretic. That's why our Durán chose to lead a hundred knights across the God-forsaken desert to war against the Saracens."

"Except I'm not going to kill anyone," Durán said. "I just count beans and fodder. Look, here's Thierry come to report whether the latrines were dug properly."

Thierry, wearing Montcava house colors, jogged through the camp to greet them. Isabella knew the Norman mercenary as Tomás's old companion. He rushed through his message.

"Those moon-cross knights stole ten of the Foix pack-mules, loaded with our provisions. And three of the nicest Arab palfreys in our string. Give me fifteen men, and we'll hunt those goat-legged weasels. *Aiieee!*"

Recognition washed over Thierry's face like water doused on a heated man. He begged God, in Norman-inflected French, to bless his hairy balls.

"A ghost, ma dòmna!"

"It's Vidal of Valerós." Chrétien clapped a hand on Thierry's shoulder. "And I'll shave your balls with a dull dagger if you ever say otherwise."

Durán and Thierry discussed what to do, concluding with the little Norman unhappy about the decision not to pursue the thieves. While the two talked, sounds carried over from the nearby corral of curry-combs jangling and men preparing the horses for the day.

"*Òc, you're a beauty, you are. Let no man ever say otherwise.*"

"*You like that carrot, my dear girl? Now you hold still while...*"

"*Ai, my love, I stole this wizened apple for you.*"

"*Sweeting, sweeting, calm, calm. Don't I always love you?*"

Loving words in the common tongue. Soothing the horses, soothing her soul. Safe. At last.

Thierry spit in vehement French, rousing Isabella from reverie. He finished with, "Let a race of leper-knights go free and the whole country will rot for it!"

"We're already pushing our horses hard," Durán said. "We'll find the thieves later. Get our men ready to ride."

Thierry, just barely stopping himself from addressing Isabella improperly, said adieu and bounded off. Across the way, Felip and the Xirgú knights were packing up, nearly prepared to ride. Colomb still lingered nearby, but no longer haranguing Felip, who seemed to stand tall. Felip pointed to the Xirgú camp and then tapped his chest, seeming to be asserting himself as master.

Isabella asked, "Why is Colomb de Beaurain traveling with Foix and Montcava? Is he one of the Crux Lunata?"

"At the very least, he's a mercenary for Maria de Montpelhièr, who hired assassins to help make her son king sooner rather than later." Chrétien also watched the exchange between Felip and Colomb. "But Colomb stayed here with twenty of Maria's knights when the Crux Lunata men left this morning."

"He's here because that ugly toad paid him to spy on us." Durán seemed more furious than Isabella thought possible. "That, and he thinks God wants him up my backside every single day with one sermon after another about honor. The Dark God of creation prompts my great-uncle Colomb to harass me daily, while I'd rather be home, minding our business"

"What toad?" Isabella asked.

"The archbishop of Narbonne. Who'd love to burn me for being a heretic."

"Our old friend among the crusader-priests. Arnau Amalric," Chrétien said.

"Who carries the Crux Lunata tattoo on his arm." Durán shook like a damp puppy, discarding his sulk. "He made Colomb my nurse-maid, to keep my soul from drifting into heresy."

"We have to ride with Crux Lunata among us?" That newborn sense of safety died within her before it breathed.

"You, Vidal, already carved a significant hole in their plans," Chrétien said. "You put Matheus in his grave. Or at least put him to bed. Was it your dagger that did it?"

"Tomás's short-sword."

They stopped talking when she said Tomás's name.

For a moment, no one could speak. Isabella, relieved to have found her friends, glanced between the two men. Chrétien tried to speak first, but his lower lip twitched. He blinked and glanced away. Durán watched Chrétien, then caught Isabella's gaze, his brown eyes moist with tears.

"I'm sorry we…" Durán faltered.

She grasped his elbow. "I'm happy you two were together when you learned of it. It was hard to weep alone. But this many months later, I…"

"Tell me you remembered all our lessons." Chrétien interrupted. "When you fought Matheus. Tell me it wasn't mere chance that defeated him."

"It was as if I heard your voice."

"*Vivètz* Vidal!" Chrétien twitched again, trying to smile, but then he looked past her, into the distance.

"I'm against bloodshed," Durán said. He'd reached for Chrétien, then folded his arms, as if to stop himself. "But I'm happy you stopped the plot that Crux Lunata hoped to ignite. Matheus went to fetch a magic cup and sword. You'll never guess where."

"The monastery at St-Pere," Isabella said. "That's where I've been since All Saints. The abbot at St-Pere believed he had the chalice from the Savior's last Supper. That sham magic cup is still there."

Chrétien sang a colorless nursery ditty:

'When the Grail and the sword are enchained,
One man dies so the best can reign.
Iberia passes to the anointed son.
What was divided becomes one.'

Durán said, "You spoiled Maria's spell. She needs that cup and a magical sword to claim Aragón for her son."

"Then that cup's best left tucked on a high shelf in the monastery." Isabella decided to save the story of the dead abbot for another time. "The abbot also believed Tomás's sword was magical."

Durán said, "The magic is that you found his sword."

"You in a monastery, Vidal? Delightful! How did it work in the baths and latrines?" Chrétien fingered the buckle of her baldric and flicked the strings of her jerkin. "Tell me, do the monks wear small-clothes under those robes? Or go fresh?"

"Welcome to the joy of life with Chrétien," Durán said.

Isabella described what she'd learned reading enigmatic letters in the scriptorium. "Crux Lunata plots to destroy Pedro while he's in Andalusia. They've been grabbing land all over the Languedoc and donating it to the Church, including land like Valerós that's supposed to be under Pedro's protection. And a Beaurain brother and yet another Beaurain bastard both serve Crux Lunata."

"Yet another?" Durán puzzled over her words.

273

"Colomb is Matheus's uncle," Isabella said. "The same as you. My friend Felip didn't know until yesterday, but Matheus de Xirgú is the bastard son of Nicolau of Montcava."

"Blessed Mary and all the perpetual virgins." Chrétien cursed softly. "He's Durán's brother. Why didn't we see it before?"

"Who knew?" Durán murmured. His tongue probed his cheek while he mulled the idea. "So why did Matheus try to kill me?"

"O you blessed innocent!" Chrétien tapped Durán's nose.

Isabella said, "For the same reason he tried to kill me, twice. For the same reason he attacked us and killed Sebastián. He wants Montcava and Valerós for himself."

Chrétien grasped her shoulders, shaking her, no longer teasing. "Sebastián isn't dead."

Fire pumped through her veins, as if the old, cold fluid hadn't been life's blood at all. The ever-present mist evaporated. She felt the same relief as when she woke after birthing her son. He lived!

"I thought…"

"He and Yusuf survived. They're with Pedro in Castile, on their way to Andalusia."

"How? I barely lived through that massacre. How did they manage to survive?"

Chrétien lifted empty hands. "We don't know. We only have letters from them."

Tears streaked her cheeks. Her heart grew larger, filling the void that had been empty so long. "I thought all I had left to do in life was warn Pedro. So, he could free Valerós from interdiction and any more Crux Lunata evil."

"We have a heroic task ahead." Durán squeezed her elbow. "We need to make sure Pedro survives the Crux Lunata, so that he can save the Languedoc from Simon de Montfort."

Chrétien coughed, again swiping at his cheek with his gloved hand. "I'm happy to simply protect Valerós and Durán's hide from the heretic hunters. But it seems we need Pedro's help for that."

Thierry appeared again, dressed to ride, weighed down with several leather botas, which he passed around. "Senhórs, we're ready to ride. Ma dòmna…I mean, Master Vidal, I took the liberty of saddling your horse and loading your pack. Though I know you prefer to care for your horse yourself. Isn't this a special day?"

"Let's go find Sebastián and Yusuf," Chrétien said. "This enterprise of peace and faith among the Saracens is now far more delightful than I expected. We can't let Sebastián have all the fun."

The stone that protected her heart rolled away. She, too, wasn't dead any more. Sebastián, alive!

Thierry offered Isabella a bota filled with water for traveling. "If only Tomás were here. He did so love a good lark. Pray God he's happy in Paradise."

19

Paradise Redux

Tomás in Baeza
Late April

WHY HADN'T HE INSISTED YUSUF learn to fight? Or forced him, using a rod the way Tomás's masters taught? He should have made Qasim attend all those lessons with Rashid. Miquel hadn't failed his sons that way. Tomás, failing as a teacher and a master, had opened the way to catastrophe.

After disarming Ali and Umar and kicking them senseless, and then paying a small fortune to keep the porter quiet, Tomás again stalked the dark streets of Baeza, searching for boys, who can always hide better than anyone else.

Qasim and Yusuf had gone, not home, but to the stable, a safe enough place since Qasim was due at daybreak to tend to al-Malik and his own burro. By the time Tomás found them, they were chatting casually with the sleepy stable boy. A copper coin bounced toward Tomás on the hard-packed alleyway. The lad chased it while the other two boys crept into the stable.

In the local tongue, Qasim greeted al-Malik. "O my King! You should be worshipped for your goodness."

The horse neighed like a beggar and then fell silent, likely rewarded with food.

The stable lad approached Tomás, who hung back in the shadows. "This place is forbidden. Only guests of our great general are allowed."

When Tomás stood in the moonlight and motioned for silence, the lad recognized him. Tomás entered the stable, which was surely the cleanest of all stables in Al-Andalus. Qasim spoke to Yusuf, "Here, give my King this sugar so he knows you're a friend. You mustn't be afraid. You have to trust each other."

Yusuf, intent on watching al-Malik nibble the sugar in his hand, missed seeing Tomás. His magnificent servant Qasim shifted into his most stubborn stance.

"I do my duty, as you commanded," Qasim said.

"I'd never think otherwise. You are indeed magnificent."

Yusuf attended only to al-Malik. "I suppose it isn't good to give him more sugar."

"Let him have one of the dried peaches." Qasim passed fruit from the cloth bag slung over his shoulder. Then he kicked at a pile of hay at the back of the stall, unearthing one of their leather travel packs, where he deposited the contents of his cloth bag.

Qasim the Magnificent, working on the knot of problems for leaving Baeza that Tomás had yet to resolve.

"I best do my chores now." Qasim fetched an iron curry comb, its bells jingling. The sound soothed the horse, who seemed as happy as Qasim was with his chore. "There's no chance of sleep before dawn."

"I honor your hard work." Tomás pointed to a bench at the end of the stable and motioned for Yusuf to follow him.

"Your magnificent Qasim won't betray me to you." Yusuf settled on the bench four hands' breadth away from Tomás. As usual, Yusuf spoke with his perpetual hostility. "I've made him my friend."

"I didn't send him to spy on you. He's supposed to protect you."

"Night is always safer than day."

"Can you claim that after the fracas on the trail, *fadrin?*"

"At night, our cousin Ríma pursues you and leaves me alone. You need to be careful, Ibn Mikhail. She's a snub-nosed viper who betrayed her husbands. She'll betray you, too. Why do you let her near you?"

"What do you know about women?"

"In my home in Cairo, I lived with them. And I chose knowledge as a way to survive."

"So wise." Tomás chose to ignore Yusuf's anger, since he couldn't quell it without sharing secrets that would endanger his son. "What have you learned about this city at night?"

"Because Abu Jossep's night guards are thorough, no one but ambitious market boys dare leave their houses. That's why we have to slip outside the city walls to learn anything. For that, will you now seek to punish me?"

"On the contrary. I applaud you." A bubble of joy. Tomás had a brave, adventurous son.

"Do you want to know what we learned?" Yusuf whispered. "The men from the Baeza countryside all want to go home."

"Men who aren't professional soldiers always want to go home." Also, Tomás had been working diligently to encourage them.

"Several leave every night. The caliph has two hundred thousand men, and the infidels have only fifty thousand. Abu Jossep's men know there will be no booty. They want to go tend their fields and kiss their wives."

Tomás, happy to hear about his success, hated to hear once again the caliph's numbers. "Farm boys don't belong in any army. Can the stars tell Abu Jossep to keep his men safely in Baeza?"

"The stars say what they say." Yusuf had forgotten for a moment to be angry with Tomás, while discussing his adventures. But now he returned to his usual aloof, scholarly self. "Astrology does not provide a wishing well."

"I've come to know the men here," Tomás said. "They don't belong at war. The caliph has all those mercenaries. These farmers don't need to risk their lives fighting infidels. It would be a good deed under heaven if the general let them go home."

Yusuf changed the subject without answering. "When the Christian army goes home, we'll go with them, won't we, Father? We can just cross the mountains. I know where there's a path over."

"Warriors go where they are sent."

"Warriors don't betray their lords by joining the enemy."

A clang rang from the stall. Qasim returned the curry comb to its peg and took up a horse-hair brush, and then began wiping al-Malik with straw in one hand and a brush in the other.

"Father, if you'd gone with Sebastián and Pedro's army, Dolç wouldn't cry her heart out. She's humiliated that you deserted us."

"That isn't how it was."

"In what philosophy is it otherwise, *Walidi*? In Cairo when you came to fetch me, you said we'd all stay together. We'd be a family. You cannot desert those children like you deserted me. Not those little girls. But especially not my brother."

"Sebastián is fine. He's riding with Pedro."

"But you have to take care of your new son, even if you never cared for me."

"I do care for you, *fadrin*. That boy we rescued in Barcelona is just an orphan from my father's village."

"I mean the new one. Dolç is sure it's a boy. She'll name him Miquel. For your father."

Tomás's heart raced. He rested his hand on Yusuf's shoulder. "What do you mean, *fadrin*?"

"You deserted Dolç even though she carries your child. Please come home. Beg Pedro to forgive you."

"Now hell is on earth." That poor woman, alone, left to…

"How can you say hell is on earth? You don't believe in heaven." Yusuf grabbed Tomás's hand and held it to his breast. "I beg you. Please, let's go home, Father."

"I wish we could. I can't leave yet." How would he ever make this turn out well for that sweet woman? For Yusuf?

"You can do anything. That's what Sebastián says."

"The men in Pedro's army left their wives and children to get on as best they can. It's what I must do, *fadrin*."

"Don't call me a boy." Yusuf's voice broke. "If you're afraid of Pedro, then send for Dolç. We can all go to Valencia."

"Stop, Yusuf." To ease the boy's pain, Tomás had to tell the truth. "Pedro sent me here. I have a job to do for him. Do you understand?"

"Father!"

"Shh, *fadrin*. That quarrel Doménec told you about was a sham. But you must act as if it's God's own truth. Or Allah's. Or whatever you believe. Do not speak a word about this. Not to Qasim or any other friend you have here."

"A sham?" Yusuf repeated.

"We feigned a quarrel. In case anyone in Al-Andalus might know me from Barcelona. Please understand. Pedro promised to take care of Dolç and her children. And you."

The quick churring of a nightjar carried up from outside the city walls. The cricket's stridulating creaks meant summer had settled on the land. Leather boots tramped the walls along the edge of the city, though no invaders camped within a hundred leagues of Baeza. Yusuf wheezed, a single gasp.

"*Ai*, my son." Tomás whispered in the wrong tongue. Yusuf raised the flood-tide of his loneliness. "I need to keep you safe while I do Pedro's work."

"You're supposed to halt this army, aren't you?" Yusuf's eager whisper would have broken Tomás's heart if its shell weren't already smashed to pieces.

"That's a grand way of saying it."

"Let me help."

"How, *kalila*?" Tomás used his mother's word for *beloved*.

"I'm the djinni. It's my job to name the propitious day to join the caliph. I'll help hold the army back."

"Can you indeed give the general excuses to delay?" Tomás lowered his voice further. "I must leave soon. To join the caliph, where I can do more for Pedro."

"Take me with you!" Yusuf's form in the stable shadows lost all its arrogant erectness. He hunched, a child lost in a strange country. "Don't leave."

"I will never leave you again, *fadrin*."

Yusuf sniffed, the first indication in the dim light that he'd been crying. "When we finish Pedro's business, we can return to Dolç and my new brother. *Òc*, Father?"

·

Qasim again collapsed on his pallet. Tomás longed for sleep, too, but there wasn't time for either of them. He wished for enough night breeze to dry his cotton shirt, which he'd drenched while fighting.

"*Sst*. Qasim. We need to leave today."

"I know, master."

"There's only al-Malik and your burro for the three of us. Get Yusuf and meet me after midday prayers, when everyone is indoors out of the heat."

"In the north arroyo, there's a trail that leads up into the hills."

"Good lad. Lend Yusuf clothes. Find what water you can."

They whispered more, but then Tomás lost the exhausted Qasim to sleep. He listened to the boy breathe, wishing he could afford deep, thought-free escape in sleep. He had a son that he had to rescue, and a new one coming, whose safety he had to ensure.

"You can't leave me here." Ríma slipped in beside him, her fingers over his lips so that he couldn't answer. She smelled of sandalwood and bergamot. "Not with two husbands to threaten me. I'm in greater danger than ever."

"I don't think so," Tomás whispered. She might be a danger, but he didn't think she was a victim.

"Your king promised my family that you'd rescue me. If you won't do that, they won't help your king's army."

"You'll be safe here for the summer. I'll come back later."

"O my love, do you think Marzuq will let either of us live? He's here only to stop fate. He was born to serve a false god that's in battle with the real God, the one you and I were created to serve."

"He's here to help Rashid, or ruin him. Neither Rashid nor the general will let Marzuq come near you."

"Rashid will never help me. He only cares about being a grand vizier." She raked her nails over Tomás's chest. "Are you falling in love with him, Tomás? They say you're everywhere with Rashid, every day. His servants say he calls you brother instead of cousin."

He removed her hand from his chest. "You'll be perfectly safe here. Worry instead about what Marzuq might do to Rashid. You should warn the general about him."

"It's your job to stop both Marzuq and Abu Jossep from destroying our clan's dreams. Ask the general to send me to our family in Jaén, so I'll be safe when the army moves. You can be my guardian and ride there with me, in comfort. Our clan will know you kept your king's promise. Then you can join the caliph. To kill him."

Tomás imagined asking Abu Jossep for permission to take his djinni and wife to Jaén. It would never happen.

A voice echoed through the city, calling men to dawn prayers.

And she was gone, of course.

He dressed and quickly rolled his gear and Qasim's into travel packs. Then he prodded Qasim awake to go to prayers.

.

By the time the drums began their daily pounding, two more bodies hung from the gibbets at the city's wall. Two Mozarab mercenaries, each half-clad in a tattered kazaghand. The chainmail had raked deep wounds in their flesh before they'd been hung to bake black in the summer sun.

"Qasim."

Tomás jerked on the boy's shirt to pull his attention away.

"Master, are we going?"

"Ibn Mikhail!"

Al-Jayyani hailed Tomás from across the street, his scrawny scribe Ibn Jafar trailing behind like a stray dog. That over-long sword bashed his scribe's knees when Al-Jayyani whipped around to beg Tomás to accompany him.

"I'm on my way to Abu Jossep's court."

At the arched entryway, a pair of guards stood at the doorway. Al-Jayyani raised a hand to greet Rashid and then crossed the court to stand by him. Rashid flashed a glance, his eyes begging Tomás to join him. But Qasim had a grip on Tomás's *jubba*, so he paused with the boy at the archway.

Abu Jossep sat alone, his head in his massive, gnarled hands. Yusuf slipped into his usual place by the general, greeting him warmly and calling down a blessing.

"Shall I tell you what the stars said last night, *Walidi*?"

Abu Jossep raised a hand, motioning to his guards.

Who seized Qasim.

"Your servant placed my son in jeopardy, Ibn Mikhail."

"Qasim protects your djinni every moment they're together."

"Your slave led my djinni on a lark through the city. They were seen outside the city walls, where he had no protection."

"It was my idea, *Walidi*," Yusuf said. "I forced Qasim to come."

Qasim, held firmly by the two guards, appeared as stoic as any good soldier. Likely only Tomás caught the flare of fright in Qasim's dark eyes.

"He will be flogged," Abu Jossep said.

"No, you mustn't." Yusuf laid his hand on top of Abu Jossep's. Which no one else dared do. "Qasim tried to stop me, but I made him go with me."

"Why? Why so much danger, my son? My good son."

"I wanted to hear what people in this city think of you, *Walidi*. What your army thinks. One cannot learn that by divination."

Abu Jossep shook his big head. "And what did you learn?"

"The men in your army thank God every day that you are their leader and always do right by them." Yusuf called down blessings and paused. "People think they're blessed that you protect them and preserve the peace."

"This is too much flattery." The general folded his arms, still stern. "You promised me the truth. In life. In heaven."

"Yes, I did." Yusuf wiped his eyes, as if brushing away tears. "I'm a poor master. But my servant shouldn't suffer for my feeble judgment. Please do for him the same as you do for your own people. Show mercy to loyal men who err."

Abu Jossep leaned back against a cushion, tears streaming down his face. However great a leader he'd once been, he now had no check on his emotions. "It is how my father taught me to judge men. With mercy. Therefore, you, my son, must promise not to lead your servant into evil. Can you do this?"

"I promise, *Walidi*. You are a wise and generous teacher."

"Let him go." The general pointed to his guards, who stepped away from Qasim. Tomás stood close by, wishing he could put his arm around the boy.

"Thank you, *Walidi*." Yusuf held the previous night's horoscope. "Shall we study what I learned from the stars last night?"

The general was immediately intent on what Yusuf wanted to show him, his shaggy head bent in concentration over the map of last night's stars.

Rashid asked a question, and the general mumbled that he'd attend to matters later, dismissing all of them. Al-Jayyani, close as a shadow, followed Rashid out to review the army.

Tomás cupped Qasim's head while they backed out of the general's court, guiding the frightened boy away from the guards. The general's voice drifted through the archway. "You know, lad, that you must accept punishment for that lark. I can't let my son run wild in the streets."

"I know, *Walidi*. I am prepared. But please let it come from your own hand."

"And I will double your guard. My men must work harder, to ensure you are safe. No more roaming in the city, my dear boy. I must keep you even closer by my side."

·

On the street outside, Qasim shivered, then shook like a dog that's come in from the cold. The drum beat echoed up from the valley.

Tomás spoke close to Qasim's ear, wanting to calm him. "Yusuf is a grand liar. In a heartbeat, he made the general believe he loves him. He can make Abu Jossep do whatever he wants."

"Will the general hurt him?"

"I think not." Tomás swallowed the bitter fear coating his tongue. "Yusuf did a masterful job of lying."

"It's my fault. I wasn't careful, like you asked me. Now we can't leave today. How will we get Yusuf free now?" After those words, Qasim hurried across the square to his favorite *mutawwama* seller, dragging Tomás after him. "I need breakfast."

"Hold up. I don't have any coins with me."

"We can use Yusuf's silver." Qasim dug in his *sarawil* for a leather purse. He held up four fingers to the vendor and traded a silver-copper penny for hot chicken wrapped in thin, folded bread. He handed one to Tomás and ate his first roll in three bites, talking while he chewed.

"Say it again, slowly, my magnificent friend and companion."

Qasim swallowed a bite, pausing before attacking his second roll. "Yusuf can't tell lies. He's not capable. He loves the general."

Tomás cradled the warm roll in his hand, smelling spices and warm bread. Scents of home. Like the home Dolç made for his sons, which Tomás discarded when he let Pedro persuade him to leave his sons. To change worlds, to spy instead of fighting like a soldier. Where he was a stranger in someone else's camp. Where he spent nights encouraging men to go home, to hold their children. To leave it to mercenaries to risk their lives for the caliph's grand scheme. Where he'd dragged Yusuf into jeopardy.

Tomás whistled briefly, discarding the worry that sharing his secret with Yusuf might endanger the boy even more. They were stuck here until he found a way to leave Paradise safely. Which seemed a more urgent need than helping to incite a victory for Pedro.

What would Miquel do? Well, what Miquel did not do was appear here on earth again to goad and advise Tomás. In case at least one prayer might ever be answered, Tomás prayed that Miquel and Isabella enjoyed heaven together. And that they weren't seeing what a mess Tomás had made for his family.

"Master? If you aren't going to eat that roll, may I have it? Oh no, they're back."

The bright sun blinded him when Tomás glanced around.

Rashid, as immaculate and erect as a vizier should be, came down the street, Marzuq al-Jayyani at his side. That wispy scribe trailed behind as if lost in a daydream.

"Tomás! Well met. Join us? Abu Jossep summoned us back. My friend Marzuq insists that this is the day we convince the general to move his army."

Tomás passed his roll to Qasim. "I'm willing to do whatever God wills."

"God, who is merciful," Qasim whispered at his side.

"Whatever it takes." Tomás sent Qasim to bed and followed his cousin and Al-Jayyani back into the general's court, where he sat on a cushion, listening as they worked to convince the general, who'd glance at Yusuf and then shake his head in refusal.

Al-Jayyani grew dour and demanding. Rashid turned glum.

Tomás, exhausted body and soul, longed for sleep and just a single dream where Miquel and Isabella might appear to tell him how to go home. The parade drums stopped; it must be midday. New sounds rose when the drums ceased. Bees in the courtyard; merchants in the square; iron-straked wheels over cobbles; donkeys and dogs in debate.

"I know how best to care for my son." The timbre of Abu Jossep's voice roused Tomás.

"Please accept my help," Al-Jayyani said. "Last night your son was attacked by spies. They hang in the gibbet now, but what happens next, if he continues to keep company with that Valencian ruffian?"

"My son is perfectly safe." The general sounded more vehement, less jolly than his usual self. "He won't play more tricks with servant boys. He'll sleep near me at night. And he'll spend his days with my wife, who begged to help me with the lad. Because she is the best kind of woman."

Rashid coughed, drawing the general's attention from Al-Jayyani, while Tomás pondered the catastrophic idea of Yusuf locked up every day with moon-witted Ríma.

"Can we turn our attention from boys to the army?" Rashid said. "The caliph has called us to action. We must answer that call."

Feeling Yusuf's eyes on him, Tomás said, "I agree with Rashid. Your men are prepared. It's time to join the caliph." How else to let Yusuf know their plans had changed, except to say so, right here?

Glancing from Rashid to the general, barely catching Tomás's gaze, Yusuf said, "*Walidi*, perhaps this is the meaning of the alignment with Al-Tair the Eagle. We should listen to their counsel."

"I would say," Al-Jayyani intoned, "that any man disputing this decision is not Abu Jossep's friend. Making him either a spy, a fool, or a conjuror." He smacked his moist lips, as if pondering a tasty meal. "Men who love God long to be at the caliph's side at this moment under heaven."

The general scratched at his eye. No, he wiped away a tear. "This is what you say also?" He was asking Rashid.

As upright as ever, Rashid said, "No, I know that you love God, whatever you decide to do. Every man can see what's in your heart, as you see into others."

Abu Jossep stared in Tomás's direction, as if considering what to do. Like Tomás had done for so many nights. The answer was clear. Tomás said, "Your djinni can determine the best day to set forth."

"While Rashid is preparing your men," Al-Jayyani licked his lips, again relishing an idea, "I'll find every spy who might hinder your plans. The gibbet serves as both punishment and warning."

"You are that good at finding evil men?" Abu Jossep seemed to be baiting the spy-catcher, who didn't notice. "I believe I've fared well in my time."

"By seeing into men's hearts?" Al-Jayyani repeated the phrase. He shook his head in a way Tomás had seen recently: a stalking cat breaking a mouse's neck. "It requires more than that. With my methods, even if a spy lived in your own household, I'd find him. The same as I'll find anyone who practices apostasy and witchcraft, sins that also merit death."

"Let me help," Tomás said. He'd been trapped like a rat once on Cyprus and had his face carved. He'd vowed never to be trapped again. The chaos of moving the army created the only opportunity for escape. "While Rashid prepares the army to move."

Rashid suppressed a smile, though Tomás caught his effort.

"Excellent!" Abu Jossep clapped his hands, his spirits higher than they'd been that day. "You two shall share a house, Ibn Mikhail. I now have too many honored guests and heroes to entertain you both in the way that honor requires."

.

On the way out of the general's court, Tomás followed the wide, silk-clad figure of his new housemate and adversary.

"Shall we meet at dinner?" Marzuq licked his lips. "I'll have my servants arrange the house and prepare a meal."

"I always dine with my cousin." Tomás had to strive not to flinch when the man touched him.

"Rashid can join us."

Behind Marzuq, Rashid shook his head, eyes wide. Perhaps preferring the gibbet.

"Another cousin," Tomás said. "Many of the Rodriguez clan serve here. This cousin is a station below what you should ever enjoy as company. I maintain the connection only for the sake of family."

Marzuq nodded, accepting Tomás's advice. Swinging that ridiculously long sword when he turned, grazing Tomás's shin, he tramped down the street, with his wisp of a scribe following behind.

"Thank you, my dear friend." Rashid whispered. "My brother."

"What for?"

"How you persuaded the general. Any more delays and Marzuq will carry tales of my failure to the caliph. With just your few words, you've kept this head attached to this body. I thank you." He touched Tomás's shoulder, the way men did here when they swore truths. "I'm more grateful than if you were a brother of my blood."

Unbearable shame rushed through Tomás's veins. The scar across his lips twitched as he endeavored to return Rashid's genuine smile. Rashid, the man who he'd tried to betray for months, who wanted to call him brother. The mirror of Miquel. Rashid laughed, a sudden bark of joy.

"And you're doing the entire Rodriguez clan a kindness. Living with Marzuq, you'll keep him from plaguing our cousin Ríma. It's as if you've been sent by God to save us all."

"You're just happy not to have Marzuq at your house."

Elated, clapping Tomás's arm, Rashid laughing looked more like Miquel—and Yusuf—than ever. He said, "Shall we spar in the orange grove while ordinary men rest at midday?" Rashid dropped his voice to a whisper again. "Marzuq hates the heat of the day."

In the bare place where they practiced under the sun-splashed canopy of the orange grove, they stripped their tunics. Rashid bowed and raised his sword into the first position that Tomás called to him. The vizier Rashid—Tomás's cousin, friend, would-be brother—perspired in the midday heat, his greyhound body glistening.

Tomás bowed. He lifted his sword, Miquel's sword from Antioch. A son to rescue. A brother to save. A servant to protect. Dinner with Zaheid, to warn him about Marzuq. Even that moon-mad Ríma to preserve from Marzuq's witch- and spy-catching depredation. It seemed that he had to forego what Pedro sent him here to do. In order to save his family, this new family.

"Show me the way!" Rashid called. "I long to be as good as you, my brother."

An unexpected wind rushed through the grove, shaking the leaves, releasing the scent of oranges and dust, the kind of wind that made Tomás turn, looking for angel wings or the kindly ghost of Isabella, calling to him.

Life would be so much easier if he were just riding with Sebastián in Pedro's army, the way they'd always planned.

20

Malagón

FOR WEEKS AFTER THE Easter riots in Toledo, the guards kept men (and women) from wandering into the valley's woods at night. Sebastián went out at nightfall to trade Taresa his sweat-drenched shirt for the fresh one she'd washed. His shirts had been clean all through April and half of June, but he'd seldom found Taresa free to talk, like in the days before they'd kissed.

"Come where we can talk alone." Her invitation thrilled him.

The last two times he'd talked alone with Taresa, in a huddle of boulders near the river, they used their tongues to exchange more than words, and only stopped at curfew when several women whistled to rouse their friends to return to camp.

"My tent is over there." She pointed into a maze.

To follow her, Sebastián ducked rope lines strung between tents and wagons, tripping twice over small dogs and once over a toddler that scampered in front of him and then disappeared in the jumble of tents. Voices in other tents were muffled amidst camp noises. A woman called out when they passed.

"Take care, *xiqueta!*" A Catalan caution for a girl.

"Always!" Taresa called back.

Sebastián bent to enter her tent. She pulled him down beside her on a bedroll, near three more stacked in the low shelter.

"Will the others return soon?" he asked.

"They're out until curfew. The army will move any day now. We want to see our friends before you march."

When he leaned forward to hear what she said, she tugged his undershirt ties free. Then she kissed him. Because they'd practiced in the boulders, he knew how to return the kiss, holding her head in his hands, trapping her hands between them against her bosom, then dropping his hand to where her back curved, bringing her closer while he knelt before her.

Taresa scratched at his chest to free her hands. When he let her free, she had hold of the edges of his doublet and pulled it down, so that he was trapped in his own clothes. She laughed, watching him struggle free.

"Take this off." She twirled the tie-strings of his undershirt. At her command, he pulled it over his head, then got stuck in the shirt, knocking a knuckle against one of the tent's brass rings. While he wriggled to get his arms out of the long sleeves, she untied her robe, letting the top fall to her waist. She pulled off her own under-tunic.

She glowed in the scant twilight and flickering campfires.

"You are beautiful." He whispered in Catalan.

Of course, she laughed.

"Touch them." She didn't wait for him to find courage; she made him touch her breasts, her hands over his, guiding him to hold and knead them. One finger forced his to circle the hard point.

"Hah!"

"Stop laughing at me."

"It's not a laugh, senhór knight."

She drew him down onto her until he lay with his face cupped between her breasts. He kissed those wondrous, soft orbs, smothered in her flesh. She licked a finger and wet his nipple, rubbing and making it hard while she writhed under him. When he took her *mugró* into his mouth, she moaned, a sound that only angels make. He kissed her until his face and her breasts were drenched in his spit. Taresa, her hands at his shoulders, coaxed him up further, until he lay beside her and they kissed in the way they'd practiced on the boulders.

"Take this off, too." She tugged at his breeches. "And your boots, for the love of all the saints in heaven."

He sat at the edge of the bedroll to do what she commanded, kicking his boots to the edge of the tent and leaving his breeches and leggings in a pile with his doublet and shirt. He knelt again, leaning toward her for more wet kisses.

"No, stop." She rose on her elbow. "I want to look at you."

"It's dark. I can only see your face. It's so white against your dark hair."

"And you are so white. I can tell that you take your shirt off in the sun." Taresa traced with a finger where his sword belt girdled his hips when they practiced. "Oh, I made you hard."

She made him throb harder than he'd ever known before.

"I've never done this."

"Shh!" She touched him there, running a finger down it in the same way she'd fingered his nipple. "Neither have I."

"Hold it tighter," he whispered. "No, tighter than that. Don't tickle me." He closed his hand over hers to show her how.

After a moment, she fell back on her bedroll, lifting both arms to bring him to her. He smothered her with kisses, and again pressed against the mound where her legs joined, her rumpled robe still between them.

"I think I love you."

"Like a troubadour in a song?" Taresa kissed his eyes, sending a shiver down his spine. He pressed harder against her, wanting this thing that he'd only seen other men do. "Then I must love you, too."

She pulled her robe down over her hips, then embraced him again, so that his *punxor* was buried in the hair she had down there. "I think it's supposed to go like this." She slipped a hand between them, guiding him to where she was hot and wet.

A dog barked. A child called.

"This way, senhór. I believe your friend is here."

It was the woman who'd called out for Taresa to take care.

"Valerós?" A Norman inflected voice. Father Anselm. "Pedro has called for us."

Taresa squirmed out from under him. "Goodbye, Senhór Sebastián. Good travels."

"Òc, off to lead a herd of mercenaries on a flea-infested, monkey-loving crusade."

She giggled, too loudly. He pulled on his breeches and tumbled out of the tent with leggings, shirt, and boots in his hands, covering the hardness that hadn't gone away at the interruption.

And greeted a torch-bearing Diego Lopez standing alongside Father Anselm.

"What do you need?" Sebastián pulled on his boots, pretending nonchalance about his future wife's guardian finding him in the laundry-women's camp. Diego Lopez remained maddeningly impassive. There was no reading that man.

"The kings want us to ride out at dawn," Father Anselm said. "Pedro has orders for you. Right now."

.

Sebastián on the Castile frontier
June 21

"A Saracen general in Seville could follow the progress of this army," Sebastián said.

He twisted in his saddle and pointed to the wide, tall cloud of dust behind them. Though of course the caliph knew they were coming; it'd take a miracle to surprise the Moors.

"Praise God that you ride in front." Diego Lopez, his doggedly close companion, returned to his sermons on how a man leads other men. "You must learn to control what men say about you. Consider this rumor, that men of Valerós are wild savages. What will you do to stop it?"

"I shall follow your advice, señor. My captains are strict. There'll be no trophies. No excesses with sword or ax."

Diego replied in brief Castilian, most of which Sebastián didn't understand.

Sebastián offered a neutral reply. "We teach our men what Pedro insists. The people we conquer in Andalusia must prefer their new masters. We must appear to these people as good Christians."

"How do you think your men appear, Señor Valerós? You must consider that."

Sebastián knew his men appeared as if they'd been eating dirt; as if the sons of Adam had never discovered baths; as if black flies and lice ruled Iberia. He called to the water captain to make sure every-one had water rations now, instead of waiting until *migdiada*. Midday was too far away.

That brief interruption sent Diego in another direction, with a new sermon topic. His father-in-law was drier than powdered bones, yet he never finished all his water ration. Drinking must get in the way of his preaching. Sebastián finished his water ration and returned to eating dust.

"In Toledo, Don Carlos introduced me to an order of knights who begged me to join them," Diego said.

"Congratulations." Sebastián had seen the Order of the Knights of Calatrava in action in Toledo. It was fact, not rumor, that Alfonso *El Rei* promised the Calatrava knights first pickings at every siege. The order had already absorbed lesser bands of priest-knights. But the Calatrava knights rode with Alfonso, while Diego preferred the vanguard. "My grandfather belonged to a confraternity of knights. He insisted that a band of brothers can—"

Diego continued, ignoring Sebastián. "But to join would be to betray my men. I cannot put aside loyalty to them or the promise I made to serve Alfonso. And I have farms and children to tend when we go home."

"Still, the Knights of Calatrava aren't like the Templars or Hos-pitallers. They aren't all monk-priests. You could—"

"Templars?" Diego shook his head so hard that his horse danced to the side for a moment. "No, it was the Knights of the Lunate Cross who invited me. From your part of the world, aren't they?"

"Knights of—"

"Crux Lunata. They speak the same tongue as your wild band. But no one here calls them savages. You should study that. Their simple white gambesons are so handsome."

Crux Lunata. A pretend order invented in the Outremer; now recruiting knights in Castile. Sebastián lost the thread of what Diego was preaching.

"All the same, I approve of your modest armor." Diego rode so erect you'd think that he kept his lance up his skinny rear end. "You don't want experienced men to think you're profligate. Though perhaps younger men might claim you're too modest. Younger men like to see wealth glimmering around their leader."

"Not my men. Not Valerós."

"Your ultramontanos certainly do. For those men, you need to put on more of a show. It's part of knowing how to do right. To know what right action is, you must follow the lessons taught by your own father, for he traveled the path before you. What did you learn from that great man?"

"I never knew my father," Sebastián said. Crux Lunata. "From what they say, he had nothing good to teach."

"Then you were coddled by women." Diego stated it, rather than asking a question. "Real knights know the right path and don't behave like savages."

For the first time in a fortnight, Sebastián thought of his mother, and hated Diego for raising her ghost, hated the idea of this man being his father-in-law, stuck with him for the rest of his life. "No. My grandfather Pèire, who was not a savage, taught paratge. And my stepfather Don Tomás taught—"

"What is this paratge?"

"That which is right and in harmony with God. The honor and justice of our domus and our forefathers. How to be worthy of the land and home you earn from your fathers. How to endure."

"Those are gifts that come from loving God. When you are guided by the Church."

"No, that's different. Paratge is what men build together as sons and brothers and soldiers. How they bring justice to the world."

Diego shook his head, as if he were arguing with a child. "A good soldier must cleave to the Word of God, using prayer to keep God in your heart and to hate evil. Then when God sends adversity…"

"That's for religion, which belongs to priests." Sebastián knew he should stop answering and just let Diego say whatever he wanted. Tomás wouldn't argue. His grandfather Pèire…well, no one dared argue with him. Best to treat Diego as if he were Pèire Leteric.

Even though Diego was wrong.

"To do what is right for the men God gave you to lead, you must be upright in your behavior. Avoid the wicked. All must trust that you are a just man. Confer with your men often so they know God guides your heart and…"

Sebastián might as well have ridden alone, since riding beside Diego left him so lonely. He missed Marshal Guillem's avuncular scolding. Father Anselm shifted positions in the column every quarter day, riding with this and that contingent, since he was the only priest in the band of men the kings had sent in the vanguard.

On the plain of La Mancha, the eagles and kites that circled over them at dawn surrendered when the sun moved high overhead. This army left nothing to scavenge. The early-morning lizards and vipers scurried off the trail when the horses advanced, finding shelter in the stones to keep their blood from boiling in the midday heat. The army reached a cairn left by Valerós outriders to indicate that this was the best place for a midday pause. Just in time. The men needed rest, having ridden since before the sun broke over the horizon. Diego nodded to Sebastián, who called commands to their captains.

Horses watered, men watered, a latrine dug in haste. In the heat, no one cared to eat more than another ration of dry bread and dried sausage. They used javelins to stake blankets for shade, since the willows along the narrow stream didn't cast sufficient shadows for so many men to rest in the heat of the day. Near where his own hobbled horses grazed, Sebastián laid his head on his saddle, two javelins holding up his blanket. Diego Lopez camped with his own Castilian band. Valerós took first watch, as usual.

The noise gradually died away, while men found respite. There was no cooling breeze, which was just as well; the one time the wind came up, flecks of sand cut their faces and hands like pottery shards.

Sun, dirt, an endless road. Hardly land worth quarreling with Saracens to control if it were not for Pedro's greater purpose. If only Tomás were here, like they planned. Just to have someone to talk to. He wondered if it was this hot and dirty deep in Andalusia.

■

Sebastián outside Malagón
June 23

"We just celebrated the feast day of St-Novatus." Diego Lopez sought to stir their souls for the first siege. "Good Novatus carried the Cross to Rome for St-Peter, the first Christian to enter that city. You will be the first to carry the Cross into this den of Saracens."

The men cheered.

Sebastián knew that wasn't correct, yet he stayed silent at Diego's side. The Moors let Christians worship, and this frontier citadel had been traded between Moors and Christians for centuries.

A contingent of ultramontanos had arrived at midday, *francimand* knights riding under Alfonso's banner, doubling the size of the army outside Malagón. The dust from another of Alfonso's contingents hung on the distant horizon. The Valerós men, including Catalan Mozarabs and ultramontanos, shuffled in their places, deployed exactly the way Diego prescribed, though at odds with how Marshal Guillem would have done. Yet it didn't seem worth quarrelling over. The men stood outside the walls of Malagón, presenting greater numbers than would fit inside this citadel. Formation didn't matter, because they'd just sit outside until the town surrendered.

At a motion from Diego, the archers sent burning arrows over the city walls. Sebastián, knowing they'd camp here for a few days to wait for Pedro and Alfonso before launching any significant action, had his men beat their shields and sing a round of battle songs that emphasized blood, valor, and death, all in crusaders' rough Latin, which the defenders of Malagón were unlikely to understand.

Late afternoon, with the sun three fingers above the horizon, the men on the walls of Malagón signaled surrender.

"Not good for the men," Diego Lopez muttered beside Sebastián. "Four days on a dusty road. They want to taste blood."

Diego motioned for Sebastián to follow him into the citadel. From the gates of Malagón, Sebastián saw that the men on the walls had bowed to a seething sea of men encircling the city walls, their banners and beasts and dust stretching out to the horizon.

"It shall be as it pleases Allah," the Saracen captain on the walls was saying. This was what Pedro wanted; not war, but a peaceful transfer of each city to a Christian king. *"We must be better masters if we want to lead them to Christ."* Exactly how Pedro had instructed all his captains.

Diego Lopez accepted the surrender. "This is an enterprise of peace and faith. You will leave in the morning, with what goods you can carry."

The captains of the citadel murmured comments, amazed.

"God shows mercy, and begs us to do the same," Diego said.

With Diego and the other captains, Sebastián passed through the market square of the citadel, just like any other armed city in La Mancha or Aragón. Women with blue or gold or green veils over their heads clutched their infants. Small children huddled against their skirts. Little boys held onto shaggy-coated dogs that panted in the late afternoon heat. Young boys in no better armor than heavy leather vests stood with their fathers and captains, holding spears and short swords. Fires around the square smelled of roasting goat, beans, burning sugar.

At the gate, the sun hung on the horizon, a blood-red ball in the dusty veil raised by the marching army. Men stamped again, some beat their shields the way they had when first circling the city. Marching away from the gates, Diego traveled to the heart of his army, then climbed a wagon to stand above the men. Sebastián and the others stood below. After three shouted lines of prayer in praise to God and His Son, the baking, reeking mass of men quieted.

"Today, with God on our side, we have won!" Diego shouted. Voices among the captains echoed the words back through the ranks of men, who cheered and again beat their shields.

"In this Holy War," Diego paused while the captains shouted his words back through the ranks of infantry and knights, "the first citadel now passes from Saracens to Christendom."

He waited for the shouts and cheers to die down. "To show that we bring the Peace of God to Andalusia..." He paused, the audience silent with anticipation. "We shall allow the Moors to pass freely from Malagón tomorrow with their goods, and then—"

Whatever Diego Lopez intended to say, his words were lost in the surge of shouting, blaspheming ultramontanos who stormed the open gates of Malagón.

.

Malagón was not like Toledo with its warrens of alleys. Once the rioting ultramontanos entered the gates, no force inside the city— even the hands of angels—could divert them.

Sebastián ran among Valerós ranks, commanding them to stand down. His own men from the Pyrenees and Narbonne hills remained in the orderly ranks set that afternoon, standing with their backs to the city, braced to push back the onslaught of ultramontanos. Sebastián again shouted until he was hoarse, calling on the names of God and several kings for Valerós to hold.

For Valerós to keep its honor.

A sliver of moon hung overhead when the screams and shrieks ended, replaced with laughter and shouts while men hauled booty out of the citadel. The sickly smell of burning flesh mixed with the dust one sucked in with each breath.

Valerós went silent in the night. Sebastián and his captains had succeeded. Their wild savages from the Pyrenees remained outside the city, resisting chaos.

"Our captains have accounted for all our men." Father Anselm walked with Sebastián through the quiet camp to confer with Diego Lopez about the catastrophe.

"It's like Toledo," Sebastián said. "We fought each other instead of battling enemies. I feel like hot slag-iron replaced my soul. This isn't what I thought we'd be doing."

Father Anselm clenched Sebastián's shoulder, bracing him the way Chrétien used to when demanding attention. "*Ai*, the Master of Valerós has proved to be a leader of men. You've succeeded in the middle of chaos. Twice. Pèire Leteric didn't do so well till he was twice your age."

The weariness of the night's work wafted away, rising up to the sky with the first of the day's heat shimmer.

"You won't let it go to your head." Anselm frowned sternly, but the rest of his face told another story. Praise. A man who'd survived the Horns of Hattin and Jaffa and forty years crusading in the Outre-mer called Sebastián a leader of men. What better blessing could he ask from a soldier-priest?

"*Hola!*" Sebastián called to a clutch of Diego Lopez's captains and asked in his best Castilian whether they'd accounted for all of their men.

"*Si.*" The men agreed, but each with a mask of deep concern. They'd huddled together in conference.

Everyone was accounted for except Diego Lopez.

By mid-morning, when the sun already baked soldiers in their leather-and-steel shells, Sebastián and Anselm had searched through a thousand men in the camp, seeking Diego. With nowhere else to search, they entered the citadel.

Where formerly veiled women still clutched infants. Most had been stripped naked.

No weapons had been left behind. No earthly goods.

Just naked human corpses and dead dogs. And flies settling among the gore congealing in the cracks of cobbles and the dust outside the emptied stables.

"Let's see if anyone is lost here," Anselm said.

"They're all lost, Monsenyor." Sebastián blinked. The stench of roasted flesh and blood and dust burned in his nose.

"Maybe a child hiding…" Anselm's thoughts trailed off.

"Or embraced in the arms of the angels."

This wasn't what Sebastián had dreamed of. Years of training to fight, to lead Valerós. Yearning for the honor Pèire Leteric gained in the Outremer.

We're going to be heroes. That's what he'd said to Tomás, instead of goodbye.

Shocked, and as lonely as he'd ever been, Sebastián walked through the citadel with Father Anselm and a few Valerós men, hoping to find Diego, opening doors, peering into houses that held only empty cupboards, plastered walls charred inside and out. Shanties near the market square had been torched. Nothing could live under those embers.

In the mosque at the end of the square, where Sebastián knew they shouldn't tread in their filthy boots, bodies were piled, though not defiled in any way worse than the others. On the other side of the market square, in the shadows of stables and barracks, bodies had fallen outside the heavy doors of a cave-like Roman church.

Moor and Mozarab alike lay naked, speared, and burned, all darkened in death. Sebastián and three Valerós men shifted the bodies and heaved open the church doors.

Where a solitary figure fervently prayed in the low-arched cavern of the church. Diego Lopez wept and beat his chest, promising St-Martín and Our Lord's sanctified mother that he would fight no more forever.

"*Mi padre.*" Sebastián spoke in bad Castilian. He touched Diego's shoulder. "Let's go home, amigo. This isn't our place under heaven."

Home is our stinking army camp. The place Sebastián had always longed to live. But not side-by-side with the *francimand* scum who'd burned this town.

Yet he was now the captain who must order Castilian and Aragónese fighters to pack up and move to the next mud-and-stone cow town that Pedro and Alfonso wanted to conquer.

One of his men called out when Sebastián and Father Anselm emerged from the citadel's gate with their arms around Diego.

"*Vivètz* Valerós!"

An Angel and a Djinni Discuss Good and Evil

AHRIMAN THE DJINNI SAID, "We might at times find ourselves in a trap like fish in a net, but it's never forever. Sands shift, captors lose their will or interest. And so, we are free again."

"What you describe is why we need Salvation through our Father." Grigor the angel spoke softly, the way one does with willful children who cannot sit still. "When the Dark Angel rebelled, cracks appeared in the uncreated world. Through one crack the *lapis exillis* fell to earth. The angels who fell to earth, neither saved nor unsaved, fashioned the Grail from that stone and took refuge within it."

"Thousands of angels making themselves comfortable inside a chalice, because they couldn't choose sides."

Grigor agreed with a graceful nod, not knowing what the djinni found humorous about a truth.

"Then when the Mother of the Savior of Men—"

"—the Prophet Jesus." Ahriman spoke like a pedant.

"—caught His blood in the stone chalice, those Angels were freed. And they all turned toward the Light and chose that side against the Dark Angel."

"If you persist, my dear brother Grigor, in believing that it's all a battle between Good and Evil, then you'll find yourself always teetering on the brink of what you most fear. Other, greater tensions than Good and Evil cause the sun to rise and the stars to shine."

"What is it you claim that I fear? I am prepared for battle."

"Heresy." The djinni shifted lazily. "Whenever you say 'battle,' I think, 'futile entertainment for the impure of heart.'"

> — *Ibn Jafar, The Poet*
> *From Tales of the Angel and the Djinni*

END BOOK 3 • ACCIDENTAL HERETICS

Next in this series:
BOOK 4: SONG OF VALERÓS

The Mad Woman of La Catalane

AN ACCIDENTAL HERETICS TALE

1

The Market Town

The Narbonne–Girona road
September 1211

"AI, DONZEL. IF YOU DRESSED better, you'd get more respect."

A southern seigneur pushed his way inside the market booth to purchase a painted leather baldric, shoving past Isabella, who held the modest cuirass she intended to buy, forcing her to stumble and knock over the vendor's stand of freshly tanned belts and baldrics, the smell of hot leather filling her nose, cows-foot oil smearing her hands. The seigneur's dog, more wolf than Great Pyr and big as a vintner's pony, buried its nose in her breeches. After regaining her balance, she scratched that place near its ears. The beautiful beast looked up at her as if in love, slobbering over her hand and sleeve.

"Leave my dog alone, boy. If you don't want to lose your hand and half your *punxor*."

Being mistaken for a man was good. The disguise had kept her safe while travelling with Tomás and Sebastián in Cairo and on Cyprus. Now they were traveling from the Languedoc to Barcelona, but even on this peaceful road between Narbonne and Girona, she preferred having all the benefit of unadorned squire's leathers and light chainmail.

Being shoved aside: not so good. Isabella glanced back at Tomás, who was dickering for woolen stockings at the stall next door. She waved off Tomás's concern about the man who brushed against her. It was her duty to assert the honor of the inheritors of Castell-de-Valerós. In this part of the Pyrenees, even these lower hills, household honor was a newborn's first breath.

"Girona, isn't it?" She guessed from the man's accent that he hailed from a Catalan city further south. "The town that's never under siege? High walls? That's why your fathers don't have to teach their sons honor?" She called it paratge: the honor as practiced everywhere between the Rhone and Dordogne and Tyr rivers. People in this southern part of Christendom held paratge as an ancient tradition, the honor one owed to forefathers and to every person in one's household. She addressed the big dark dog in an elegant Narbonne accent, while scratching its head: "Who's a good dog? Who's so pretty? Yes, God made you good and pretty, didn't He?"

The dog loved her.

Behind Isabella, Tomás sighed, likely thinking he'd have to rescue her, though he surely knew better. She'd married him, yes, but when dressed as Vidal of Valerós, she invited only problems she could solve without his help.

"I'm the seigneur of Xirgú." The arrogant knight dropped silver in the shopkeeper's hand, not bothering to look her way. "My father died carrying the Cross to Jerusalem. I know paratge."

"Your father knew honor, but died before he could teach it." She didn't remember Xirgú in any crusader stories told by her grandfather, Pèire Leteric. "I am Vidal of Valerós. The seigneur who raised me saw Jerusalem. And Jaffa. And Damascus. And carried home more honor than you've pissed into the gutters of Girona."

Grabbing his fancy baldric from the shopkeeper's hands, the man confronted her, a sneer distorting his too-handsome face.

A leonine mane, like the yellow-haired crusader Simon de Montfort, only in the ruddy shade you find in the south. A bold chin, never challenged when jutted into others' business. Dark, southern eyes under heavy brows. A familiar stare, like in a forgotten dream. Growling, while his dog panted amiably.

"Did your honorable seigneur warn you that undersized donzels must defer to their betters?"

"My seigneur was Pèire Leteric of Valerós. He didn't have betters. Anywhere in the south."

Tomás again stirred behind her, likely ready for a brawl.

The man's brows twitched, his eyes flashed, as if trying to remember a forgotten message. He shoved her aside again and strode past Tomás, intending to bump him in the same way as he did Vidal of Valerós. Tomás stepped back, so the seigneur missed and stumbled. The tall seigneur righted himself and stared down at Tomás. Then he sneered.

"How our blood has weakened. Paratge is sunk in heresy. Our race of men dirtied by blackamoors and Saracen filth."

"It's Kurd and Berber and a landed Castilian grandmother." Tomás quietly repeated his heritage after the rude man had passed out of hearing.

Isabella entered the narrow stall, which smelled of sun-warmed leather tanned just enough for road- and battle-wear. The leatherworker glanced up, more intent on the lunch he'd spread on his workbench than the altercations between seigneurs. He quoted an unjust price, and Isabella considered how badly she wanted this particular cuirass.

"Seven silver morabatins? How about four?" She agreed to five, since the tattered cuirass she'd worn over the past year's travel wouldn't hold up to any more repair. When she pulled off her old vest, that wolf-dog prodded at the gap of her breeches again, wanting another scratch.

"*Hola, gos!*" the rude seigneur called, then whistled for his dog, scowling when he found his pet, its big, beautiful head being scratched by the irascible donzel of Valerós. The dog followed its master, one last look back at Isabella.

"You are a mad woman." Tomás's burned-honey voice in her ear. "Was that really necessary?"

"It was amusing." She tugged on her new cuirass and left the old one to the leatherworker, to do with it what he might. "Your brother Chrétien would have—"

"Been able to protect himself if his challenge came to blows."

"And what would you have done if he insulted your honor and your family?"

"Punched him in the *punxor*."

.

Yusuf's and Sebastián's perpetual banter pulled Isabella back into the world, to the scents and sounds of the market.

"This is the best market town since Toulouse." Yusuf insisted on his claim, likely so that Sebastián might argue against it.

"I can't agree, Yusuf. Narbonne has a better market than Toulouse. Anywhere is better."

"You're prejudiced. You hate Toulouse. Admit it."

"It's no secret. The gutters of Toulouse are full of false crusaders wanting to burn heretics. Even if you call them heretics, it's a point of honor for people in this land to protect their own. We don't need French invaders telling us what's moral and right to do."

"Perhaps you can buy a charm here, to scare away the French." Yusuf pointed at the red bag of salt tied to Sebastián's belt. "Like you paid to ward off toothache. *Renrén*."

At being called a fool, Sebastián punched Yusuf's arm. Yusuf rubbed where it hurt, but still hadn't learned to punch back. "Come on. There's more to see."

Sebastian and Yusuf twisted their way through crowd and the aisles of vendors, two paces ahead of Isabella and Tomás. When they'd gone to Cairo the year before to fetch Yusuf (Tomás's son;

now hers), Sebastián (her son; now Tomás's) had bonded immediately as a brother with Yusuf. Though they couldn't be more different in appearance or temperament. Sebastián promised to be tall,
and at thirteen already had broad shoulders as magnificent as any
Valerós knight. Yusuf's beautiful face was just like his father's—or
like Tomás's had been before enemies slashed it to ribbons—but he
was lighter skinned, slim as a Persian greyhound, and walked like
a scholar from the universities of Cairo. Which he was. An exotic
creature compared to the Catalan backwoods heritage that Isabella
and Sebastián carried into the world.

Yusuf and Sebastián stopped dead still, each chewing on a stick
of sugar cane (alleged to have come straight from Cairo), to watch
a prize-fight that was beginning in the market square. Men crowded
against each other, closing the circle around the fighters, until the
four travelers were close enough to be doused by flecks of the
fighters' sweat.

One, dressed as a crusader knight, wore a much-mended Templars tunic, stealing glory from Jerusalem's heroes. The other man,
bare chested, wore a stained turban and loose cotton trousers like
Arab mercenaries. He was darker than Tomás, and many in the
crowd were shouting, "Kill the Moor!"

A shill wriggled through the crowd, taking bets. Tomás, the
perpetual gambler, waved him off.

"I thought you liked betting!" she shouted in his ear, most words
lost in the noise of the crowd.

"Not when the winner is chosen before the fight."

Sebastián called to Yusuf. "Our uncle Chrétien is better than that
crusader. Too bad you didn't get to see him fight when we were in
Toulouse."

"And yet, our father is better than both of them." Yusuf glanced
at Isabella, seeking confirmation.

"You don't know that." Sebastián punched Yusuf's arm. "You
haven't seen Chrétien—"

Tomás grasped both boys by the elbow, steering them free of
the crowd. "Our Vidal is better than the fellow in the kerchief."

Isabella barely heard his words, busy instead staring across the
ring of shouting men at the rude seigneur, who held his dog by its

studded collar, either spurring the dog to bark at the fight or hold-ing it back. The intention was hard to interpret, since the seigneur seemed to attend only to Vidal of Valerós, tossing daggers of hatred with his eyes while jutting that proud, too-handsome jaw.

■

When Isabella caught up again, the boys were still arguing about that fight.

"No one fights better than our father. I saw him in Cairo." Yusuf defended Tomás as best in the known world.

"He was being kind to that old man who used to be his teacher. If you saw Chrétien in a dagger fight, like that one in the market between a Saracen and a crusader—"

"The Saracen loses." Tomás interrupted them. "Every time."

"Why?" Yusuf asked, always eager to learn from Tomás.

"He's too dark."

"He's not as dark as you."

Tomás waved away Yusuf's claim before Isabella could say it: *But just as dark as you, dolç Yusuf.*

"This isn't for scholars to debate. The purpose of that fight— and every mummers' show in the south—is to make everyone believe that Christians will beat the Saracens when Pedro goes crusading in Andalusia."

Sebastián continued to argue. "The Saracen was a decent enough fighter. As good as the other fellow."

"The dark one with no shirt? He's no more Saracen than I am. But if he wins, the crowd will rip him to pieces. His job in every marketplace is to beg the fake-crusader for mercy."

"His job?" Sebastián remained puzzled.

"They split the winnings. Then ride to the next town and play at daggers-and-infidels again."

"And riding to the next town is what we should be doing," Isabella said, since it was her job to be the most practical.

■

After they reclaimed their horses and joined the small train of merchants they traveled with, Isabella recounted the hostile stares from the rude seigneur.

"What were you doing staring at a man?" Tomás said. "Don't look at men. You're supposed to be a grown boy. At your age, you should be watching skirts."

"Is that what you teach our sons?"

"Never in this life."

This good life, where they were all four together, on the road to Barcelona, to prepare for battle and to ride with Pedro, the king of Aragón, to recapture Andalusia.

Sebastián rode jittery with anticipation, eager to join a real army and fight a real war.

Yusuf, curious, wanted to see the king's court and his scholars, and longed to see whether Andalusia was truly the fabled place he'd learned about in school.

Tomás admitted he longed to be in action again, after a year away from the mercenary work he'd been trained to do since leaving his cradle.

Only Isabella rode relaxed, content with the moment, a good horse to ride, a peaceful journey, and to have all she loved with her. In just weeks, they'd join the Valerós knights who'd been hired by Pedro d'Aragón to teach battle tactics. Drowsing on the sunny trail, she couldn't imagine what a better life might be. The sound of the boys' mild squabbles drifted on the breeze. Tomás half rose and turned in his saddle to share that lovely twisted, ruined grin: he, too, couldn't be happier.

Sebastián was tutoring Yusuf on kings and counts in Christendom. "Count Raymond of Toulouse is supposed to be a vassal of Philippe Augustus, but that doesn't amount to much. Raymond's entire strategy was to just wait until the French knights got too hot and went home."

"That didn't turn out to be true," Yusuf said. "There are French knights everywhere we've been."

"That's because Philippe lets his Pays de France knights go crusading in the south. He's not worried anymore about disruptions from John, the king of the Angevines, or from the count of Burgundy or his other counts."

"He *lets* them go on crusade?" Yusuf murmured.

"Keeps them from fighting at home." Tomás interrupted Sebastián's lesson. "The best place for an army of trained knights is in someone else's countryside. Cheaper that way."

Ignoring the interruption, Sebastián resumed teaching. "Alfonso, the king of Castile, took Gascony from the Angevine king John because his wife is a daughter of Eleanor of Aquitaine. John's brother was Ricart Còr de Leon, whom we despise."

"He's dead now," Isabella said. "And whether that king is in heaven or hell—"

"Hell," Tomás said. "Definitely. If there is such as place."

Sebastián again disregarded his parents' intrusion on the lesson. "That leaves Pedro, the king of Aragon, who also holds Barcelona, Catalunya, and Provence. He's a Catholic, so he has to do what the pope says to put down heresy, but he respects paratge and doesn't want to fight his own people. Our Valerós knights are his mercenaries, and our father is his friend. He's the only king to whom we pay tribute."

"Happily." Tomás interrupted again.

"How can you be happy to pay tribute?" Yusuf asked. "Men in Cairo shout in grief when they have to send tribute to the Ayyubid sultan."

"It's what you pay so you have an army great enough to do good in the world. My *àvi* Pèire said that merchants and seigneurs who don't pay their taxes don't understand how big the world is. They think their little personal armies can defend against a king's army. Of course, nobody wants to pay a shaved brass barcelones if they owe tribute to a fool like King John in the Angleterre."

Isabella felt the thunder of horses vibrating in her breastbone, before she could trace the direction of the sound or warn the others. Mounted bandits galloped into the midst of gentle, armor-free merchants. Out of the thunder of riders, someone hurled a javelin, striking Tomás, who toppled from his horse.

Yusuf lost control of his horse and fell near Tomás. The merchants were screaming for mercy, but the attackers slashed at neck and shoulder, butchering them.

The last that Isabella saw, Sebastián stood alone, unhorsed, in the middle of the massacre, his dagger in one hand, sword in the other, screaming a Valerós battle-cry: *"Desperta, ferro!"*

Awake, steel!

■

END PREVIEW ▪ THE MAD WOMAN OF LA CATALANE

Available as an ebook
and in the print edition of *The Blue Door*

Learn more at
http://eastewartauthor.com/books/madwoman

Heretics' Glossary

The non-English phrases in *Accidental Heretics* stories are for fun and color, not linguistic purity. The characters in these stories speak or read several languages.

A

adouçar enfant Jhezu: Sweet baby Jesus.

affinity (canon law): Kinship by marriage; at this time, affinity and consanguinity restricted marriage to fourth degree relationships.

ahl al-dhimmi: Abrahamic believers who are not Muslim.

Ai Dèu: O God.

alcade: A local judge.

Almòinas: Merciful.

Almohad: The Muslim dynasty in Iberia at the time of this story. In Arabic: *Al-Muwahhidun*.

al-shatranj: Chess.

amiga: A female friend.

Angevines: The Plantagenet dynasty that ruled from Ireland to the Pyrenees. The Angevine empire grew through the marriage of Henry II and Eleanor of Aquitaine.

aventail: A chainmail curtain to cover the neck and shoulders.

àvi, àvia: Grandfather, grandmother.

B

baquelar: Villainous rogue.

barcelonese: A silver coin under the Count of Barcelona.

batini: An unbeliever.

bazasa: bastard.

benvingut: Welcome.

bon amic: Good friend, or boyfriend.

bon Dèu: Good God.

bon día: Good day.

bon nuoit, bona nuèch, bon vèspre: Good night.

bonfraires: A brotherhood.

booty: Treasure; during the crusades, the primary way crusaders financed their armies or paid their mercenaries. Rather than "looting," these cultures considered booty as legitimate plunder.

bordonier: A freeholder who arms and fights, freely, for a baron.

botifarres fresques: Fresh sausage.

brioix: Bread.

bruixa; bruja: Witch.

C

calamarson: Baby squid.

cançó d'amor: Love song.

Candlemas: Feast of the Purification, February 2.

Catalan: In the Middle Ages, a language, not a political entity.

cavaller: Cavalier, knight.

Cistercian Order: The White Monks, a reformist Benedictine order, who stressed manual labor and a return to the Rule of St Benedict.

conill: Rabbit.

consanguinity: Laws governing the degree of relationship that will prohibit marriage among people with a shared ancestor. A convenient reason for marriage annulment among European ruling classes.

converso: A Jew or Muslim who converted to Christianity.

convivencia: "The Coexistence," the period of relative peaceful coexistence among Muslims, Jews, and Christians in Iberia under Muslim rulers.

cor dolç: Sweetheart, an endearment.

cortezia: The southern value of grace and courtly honor.

crux lunata: Lunate cross, featuring lunar crescents at each terminus; a pagan symbol; war tokenism imported to Europe by returning crusaders, adding the Islamic crescent in heraldic and other symbols.

cuirass: A rigid armor covering the torso. At this period, it was still made of leather.

D

deniers: A French coin.

Desperta, Ferro: Awake, steel!

Deus noluit: God didn't will it.

Deus vult: God wills it! (A crusader cry.)

domus: The economic household of a titled landholder.

don: A courtesy title for a gentleman from the landed classes.

donzel: A young gentleman, in training for knighthood.

Doutz Jhezu: Sweet Jesus.

E–F

escudella i carn d'olla: A Catalan stew.

eu vos amor: I love you.

fada: Fairy.

fadrin: A lad, a term of endearment.

faitdits knights: Southern knights who have no lord, who have foresworn their previous oaths.

francimand, francimandalha: Frenchman.

Franks: At the time of this story, a reference used by Muslims and others for western European people.

fustian: A heavy cotton fabric.

G–I

gambeson: A padded jacket worn under armor or alone as a defensive covering.

goodmen, goodwomen: A reference to the people whom the Church called heretics; now commonly called Cathars.

gos: Dog.

hauberk: A chainmail shirt.

hereticated: Having decided to adopt a heresy.

hola: Hello.

Hospitallers of Jerusalem: A Christian military order, originally founded in Jerusalem to care for sick pilgrims.

imama: A turban cloth.

J–K

Jhezu adouçar: Sweet Jesus.

Jhezu del tron: Jesus in heaven.

jizya: A tax in Al-Andalus on non-Muslims.

jongleurs: Medieval minstrels who sang the songs of the troubadours.

jubba: An ankle-length robe.

kalila: Sweetheart, an endearment.

Knights Templar: A monastic crusader military order, the most elite of the crusader armies.

khuf: Boots.

L

lapis exillis: The Stone that is the Grail.

Latins: How Muslims referred to the invading western Christian armies.

lenga romana: The common tongue of the Languedoc in the Middle Ages, now called Old Occitan.

litham: A cloth that's would around the head, revealing only the eyes, worn in the Saharan desert.

M

ma dòmna: My lady.

maledicta: Crude and blasphemous words.

marquis, marquesa: A lord (and his wife) whose land is on a frontier border, and so must be a capable defender.

mestitz: A person of mixed heritage.

migdiada: Midday rest.

mon amics: My friends.

mon fil, mon frère, mon fraire: My brother.

Monsenyor: An honorific, such as for a king or archbishop.

mongetas gigantescas: Large white beans.

Moors: People from northern Africa who settled on the Iberian peninsula under Muslim leadership. Colloquially at this time, a person of mixed heritage with a dark complexion.

morabatin: Gold coins in Aragón, where a horse cost about one hundred morabatins.

N–Q

na maliciosa: Malicious woman.

Normans: Descendants of the Viking Northmen who settled Normandy, and later invaded Britain and conquered the Muslims on Sicily in the eleventh century.

òc: Yes.

Outremer: The lands across the Great Sea, where the Crusader States were founded and other territory seized by Christian invaders.

peccador: Sinner.

per l'amor de Dèu: For the love of God.

punxor: Prick.

qandura: A tunic-like shift.

Qui s'ho creu: Who'd believe it?

qutn: Cotton.

R–S

renrén: Fool.

salsiccia fresca: Fresh sausages.

Sancta Maria: A woman's oath, calling on Saint Mary.

Saracen: Colloquial term used in Europe for Muslims.

sarawil: Trousers.

scrofula: Tuberculosis of the neck; colloquially, part of an insult.

seigneur: A man of rank who rules lands and a household.

senhór, senhóra, senhóreta: Titles of respect; equivalent to señor, señora, señorita.

Sodalitas, fidelitas, virtus: Latin motto of the bonfraires: fraternity, fidelity, virtue.

squire: In the southern lands, a fighter of rank between knights and foot soldiers, for his lifetime. In the southern world, squires did not rise to become knights.

surcoat: A long coat worn over other clothes or armor.

T – Z

taifa: An independent principality in Muslim Al-Andalus.

viscount: A European noble rank, above a baron, below a marquis.

vivètz: Live!

Walidi: Father.

woad: A plant used to create a blue dye, grown as a cash crop around Toulouse.

Place Names

Valerós, Fontcours, Montcava, St-Félíu, St-Joachim, and Monasterio de St-Pere de Selva exist within the Accidental Heretics world, but nowhere else.

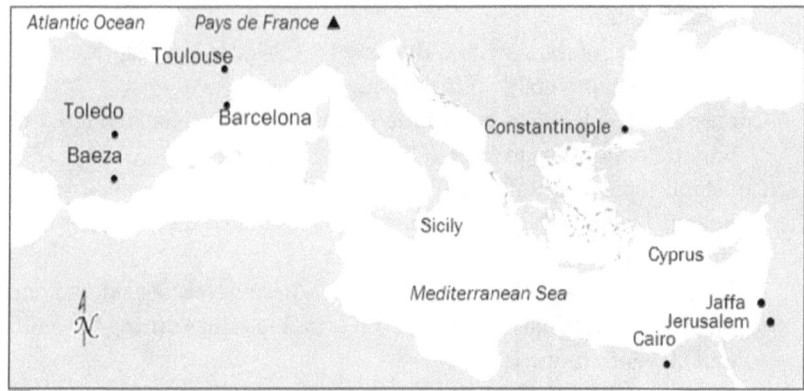

The Crusaders' World

A–C

Acre: A city on Haifa Bay in the Outremer, now part of Israel. At the time of this story, it served as the capital of what was left of the Kingdom of Jerusalem.

Al-Andalus (in country; Andalusia in Christendom): The land of the Moorish caliphates on the Iberian Peninsula.

Alcazaba: A Muslim fortification at Málaga in Al-Andalus.

Aleppo: One of the oldest continuously inhabited cities. In Syria, at the end of the Silk Road, and now undergoing new travails, Aleppo was besieged twice by Crusaders but never conquered.

Al-Mansha: La Mancha.

Almería: A port and fortress city on the southeastern coast of the Iberian Peninsula.

Antioch: A city in what is now eastern Turkey that was conquered in the First Crusade, and then endured centuries of political quarrels and sieges by Christian lords until it fell to the Mongols later in the thirteenth century.

Aquitaine: A duchy in what is now southwest France that was a key portion of the Angevine empire under Henry II and Eleanor of Aquitaine.

Aragón: In the mid-thirteenth century, a union of the Kingdom of Aragón and the County of Barcelona established the dynastic Crown of Aragón, with tributaries across the Languedoc at the time of this story.

Baeza: A cliff-side city in the province of Jaén in Al-Andalus, at the edge of the mountains separating La Mancha from Granada.

Barcelona: A territory on the Mediterranean, now approximately the political entity of Catalonia, for which Pedro II held the title Count of Barcelona.

Cairo: The seat of the Ayyubid dynasty that Saladin founded, with the third oldest university in the world.

Carcassonne: A fortified city in the Languedoc, which surrendered to Simon de Montfort in 1209.

Constantinople: Capital of the Eastern Roman Empire, sacked in the Fourth Crusade, becoming the seat of Norman rulers for the next fifty years.

Cordoba: A southern city and province in Al-Andalus, considered one of the most culturally advanced and populous cities during the tenth and eleventh centuries.

Cyprus: An island in the Mediterranean, south of Turkey and north of Cairo. During the Third Crusade, its Muslim rulers were conquered by Richard Lionheart who sold it to the Knights Templar, who in turn sold it to Guy de Lusignan.

D–L

Dordogne: A region of Aquitaine between the Loire Valley and the Pyrenees, known for a series of caves along the Dordogne River.

Edessa: An Armenian city, ruled by Crusader lords and under frequent attacks by Turks. First of the Crusader States to be lost.

Espanya: Catalan and Romance language word for Hispania, as it had been called by the Romans.

Famagusta: A city on Cyprus; formerly Tomás's home.

Girona: An ancient city in the northeast corner of Catalunya; part of the countship of Barcelona at the time of this story.

Holy Roman Empire: The successor in central Europe to Charlemagne's empire. During the high Middle Ages, this included parts of Germany, Burgundy, Italy, and Bohemia.

Iberia: The old Roman name for the peninsula now called Spain.

Jaén: A city and province in south-central Spain, geographically strategic between Castile and Al-Andalus.

Jaffa: The southern part of what is now Tel Aviv, captured after the First Crusade, conquered by Saladin, and then reclaimed by Richard Lionheart. After again fighting off Saladin, the crusaders held the city until 1268.

Jerusalem: Captured by the crusaders in 1099, recaptured by Saladin in 1187, traded back and forth for several decades until finally captured by the Mamluks and lost forever by the crusaders.

Lérida: Now Lleida in western Catalunya, this city was the traditional royal residence of the kings of Aragón.

M–Q

Minerve: A town in the Languedoc that sheltered refugees from the massacre of Béziers and was subsequently defeated by Simon de Montfort and its own heretics burned by the conquerors.

Montpelhièr: A walled city in the Languedoc, near the Mediterranean, with the second oldest university in Europe.

Morella: A town near Valencia, taken from the Moors by El Cid, lost again later before finally becoming part of Aragón in the Reconquista.

Morocco: At the time of this story, a region in northern Africa, including Marrakesh, that was part of the Almohad caliphate.

Narbonne: A rich Mediterranean port in the Languedoc that was the seat of the archbishop and home to a significant Jewish community.

Naxos: A Greek island in the Aegean Sea, alternately under Byzantine and Venetian rule.

Outremer: The Crusader States, the land overseas.

Pays de France: The historic personal domain of the king of France; most of this area became the province Ile de France.

Provence: A county on the Mediterranean, ruled by the counts of Barcelona; governed by Pedro's brother Alfonso at this time.

R–Z

Rhône: A major river running from the Alps to the Mediterranean.

Roussillon: A region in the southeastern Pyrenees and foothills.

Seville: The capital in Al-Andalus for a series of Moorish caliphates from the eighth through the thirteenth centuries.

Sicily: A Norman kingdom during much of the Crusades era, after Normans conquered the Arab rulers of Sicily and southern Italy.

St-Sernin: A Romanesque basilica in Toulouse.

Toulouse: A county in the Languedoc, whose count owed allegiance to the king of France at the time of this story. The city, on a major trade route between the Mediterranean and central France, was a bishop's seat.

Urgell: A county in Catalan-speaking lands between the Pyrenees and Lérida. Pedro d'Aragón and the count of Foix defended the rights of the countess of Urgell to inherit.

Valencia: A region and ancient Roman port city on the Mediterranean peninsula. Seized from the Moors by El Cid in the eleventh century, then retaken a hundred years later and still held by the Moors in Pedro's time.

Zara: Now Zadar in Croatia, this Dalmatian city on the Adriatic Sea was a stopping place for crusaders waiting for transports from the Venetian doge in 1204.

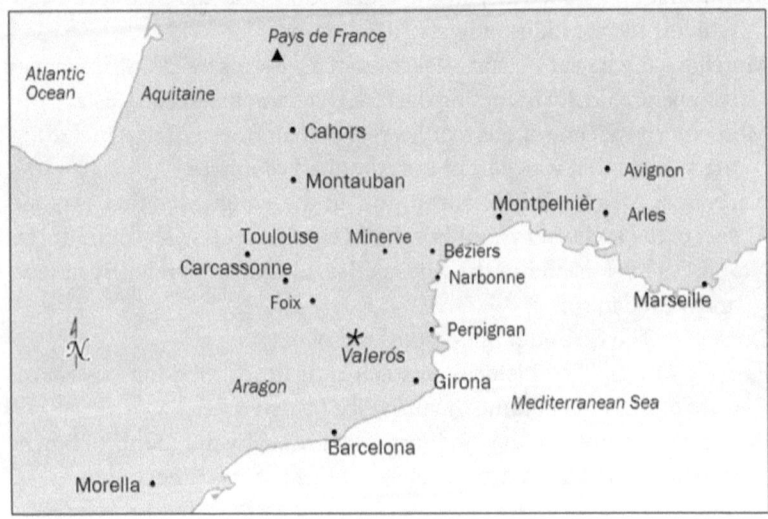

The Languedoc, 1212

About the Author

E.A. STEWART is an American writer whose *Accidental Heretics* series explores intrigues in France and Spain in the thirteenth century. Annie Stewart worked for many years as a technical writer and project manager in Pacific Northwest software companies.

Ms. Stewart lives and writes in Seattle.

www.eastewartauthor.com

Acknowledgments

THANKS TO: Ajax Bell, Elizabeth Bjorkman, Laurie Cropp, Jacyn Stewart, Susan Urban, Martin Fossum.

About the Accidental Heretics Series

Lost in the Languedoc Crusade

Find this series in your favorite online store
or ask your independent local bookseller.

ACCIDENTAL HERETICS SERIES
Book 1: *Bone-mend and Salt*
Book 2: *Trebuchets in the Garden*
Book 3: *Crux Lunata*
Book 4: *Song of Valerós*
The Mad Woman of La Catalane: A Novella
The Blue Door… and More Accidental Heretics Tales

LEGENDS OF VALERÓS SERIES
Wheel and Serpent: 1
Traitor: 2
Hero: 3

To learn more about
the Accidental Heretics series, visit:
www.eastewartauthor.com

From Jugum Press

HISTORICAL AND CONTEMPORARY FICTION

Nzinga, African Warrior Queen by Moses L. Howard

Nzinga is a brilliant leader during a time of violent upheaval. This fictional biography brings to life the 17th century flourishing African kingdom, now lost, where early explorers' maps of West Africa call out: "Here reigned the celebrated Queen Nzinga!"

Nine Volt Heart by Annie Pearson

He said, "I love you." She said, "You don't even know the real me." He said, "Great song lyrics. Key of G? Can we try close harmony?" Jason and Susi meet by accident in Seattle. Secrets, songs, and stalkers quickly entwine their lives in unpredictable ways.

This Charming Man by Ajax Bell

A chance encounter with an intriguing older man inspires Steven Frazier with visions of a more rewarding life. A vibrant snapshot of Seattle in the early 1990s, this story captures the drama of coming into one's own as an adult.

A Summer in Peach Creek by Michele Malo

Teenaged Faith travels to Peach Creek, West Virginia for a visit with relatives in 1932. When a scandalous murder occurs, Faith discovers the corrupt underbelly of Logan County. As summer progresses and peaches grow, Faith finds her own moral center.

PERSONAL VOICES IN HISTORY SERIES

Journey into Gold Country: Memories of a Forty-Niner
by Ralph Buckingham; foreword by Charles Barker

The California Gold Rush, remembered sixty years later by a New England younger son who went to seek his fortune.

We Were Walimu Once and Young, edited by Brooks E. Goddard

True stories from the Teachers for East Africa and Teacher Education for East Africa experience in the 1960s.

Find print and ebook editions:
www.jugumpress.net